FUTURES IMPERFECT

FUTURES IMPERFECT

- Uncharted Territory
- Remake
- Bellwether

Connie Willis

GUILDAMERICA BOOKS®

UNCHARTED TERRITORY
Copyright © 1994 by Connie Willis
map design by GDS/Jeffrey L. Ward

REMAKE
Copyright © 1995 by Connie Willis

BELLWETHER
Copyright © 1996 by Connie Willis

Published by arrangement with Bantam Books
A Division of Bantam Doubleday Dell Publishing Group, Inc.
1540 Broadway
New York, New York 10036

ISBN 1-56865-186-4

Printed in the United States of America

Uncharted Territory

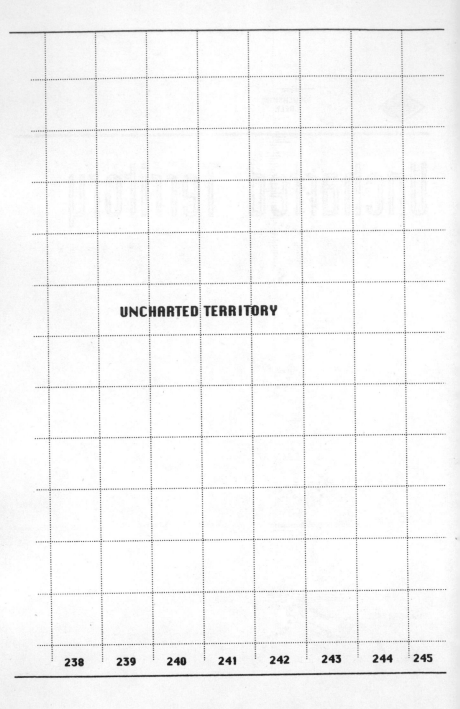

UNCHARTED TERRITORY

238	239	240	241	242	243	244	245

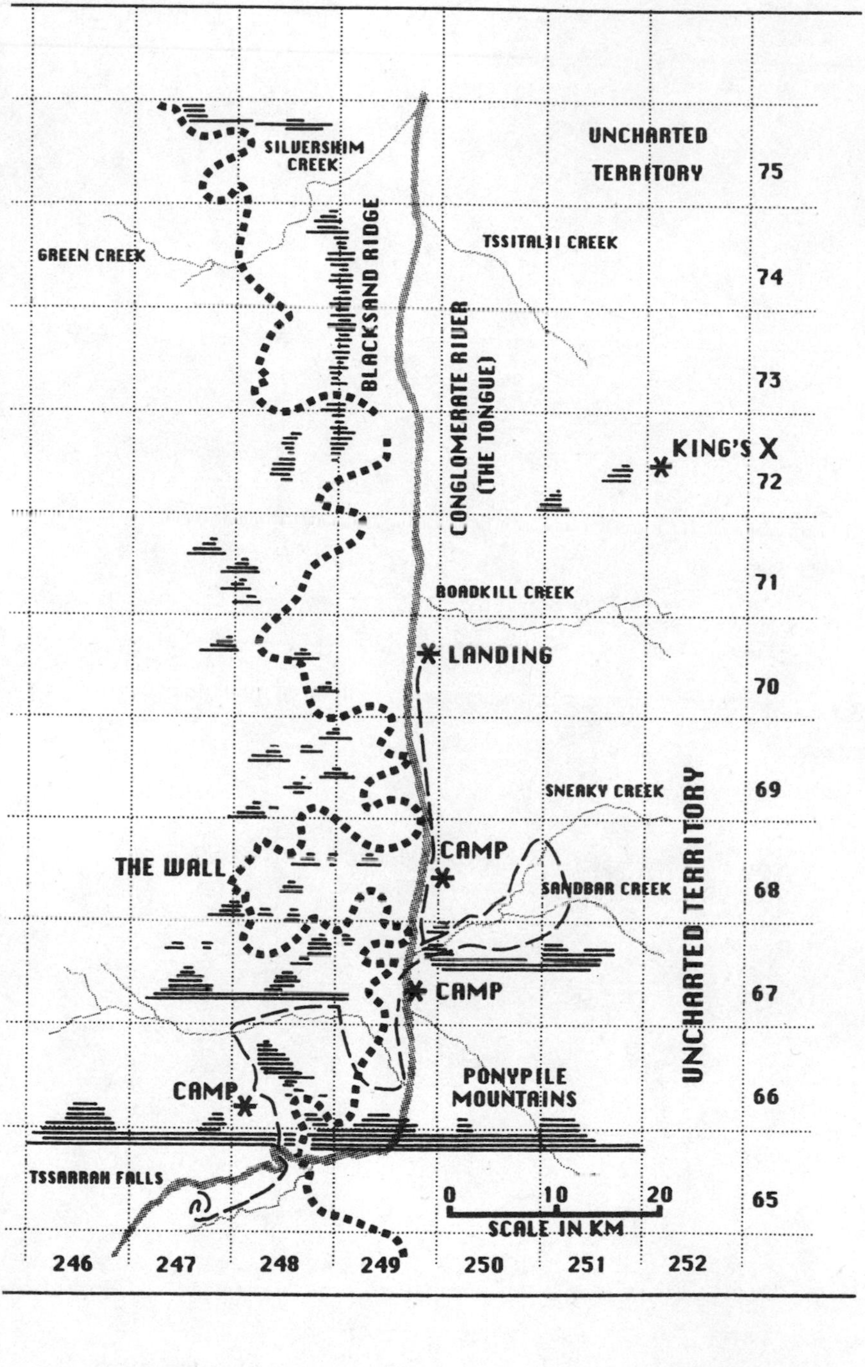
UNCHARTED TERRITORY
SILVERSHIM CREEK
GREEN CREEK
BLACKSAND RIDGE
TSSITALJI CREEK
CONGLOMERATE RIVER (THE TONGUE)
KING'S X
BOADKILL CREEK
LANDING
SNEAKY CREEK
CAMP
THE WALL
SANDBAR CREEK
UNCHARTED TERRITORY
CAMP
PONYPILE MOUNTAINS
CAMP
TSSARRAH FALLS
0 10 20
SCALE IN KM
75
74
73
72
71
70
69
68
67
66
65
246
247
248
249
250
251
252

expedition 183: day 19

We were still three kloms from King's X when Carson spotted the dust. "What on hell's that?" he said, leaning forward over his pony's pommelbone and pointing at nothing that I could see.

"Where?" I said.

"Over there. All that dust."

I still couldn't see anything except the pinkish ridge that hid King's X, and a couple of luggage grazing on the scourbrush, and I told him so.

"My shit, Fin, what do you mean you can't—" he said, disgusted. "Hand me the binocs."

"You've got 'em," I said. "I gave 'em to you yesterday. Hey, Bult!" I called up to our scout.

He was hunched over the log on his pony's saddlebone, punching in numbers. *"Bult!"* I shouted. "Do you see any dust up ahead?"

He still didn't look up, which didn't surprise me. He was busy doing his favorite thing, tallying up fines.

"I gave the binocs back to you," Carson said. "This morning when we packed up."

"This morning?" I said. "This morning you were in such an all-fired hurry to get back to King's X and meet the new loaner you probably went off and left 'em lying in camp. What's her name again? Evangeline?"

"Evelyn Parker," he said. "I was not in a hurry."

"How come you ran up two-fifty in fines breaking camp, then?"

"Because Bult's on some kind of fining *spree* the last few days," he said. "And the only hurry I've been in is to finish up this expedition before every dime of our wages goes for fines, which looks like a lost cause now that you lost the binocs."

"You weren't in a hurry yesterday," I said. "Yesterday you were all ready to ride fifty kloms north on the off-chance of running into Wulfmeier, and then C.J. calls and tells you the new loaner's in and her name's Eleanor, and all of a sudden you can't get home fast enough."

"Evelyn," Carson said, getting red in the face, "and I still say Wulfmeier's surveying that sector. You just don't like loaners."

"You're right about that," I said. "They're more trouble than they're worth." I've never met a loaner yet that was worth taking along, and the females are the worst.

They come in one variety: whiners. They spend every minute of the expedition complaining—about the outdoor plumbing and the dust and Bult and having to ride ponies and everything else they can think of. The last one spent the whole expedition yowling about "terrocentric enslaving imperialists," meaning Carson and me, and how we'd corrupted the "simple, noble indigenous sentients," meaning Bult, which was bad enough, but then she latched onto Bult and told him our presence "defiled the very atmosphere of the planet," and Bult started trying to fine us for breathing.

"I laid the binocs right next to your bedroll, Fin," Carson said, reaching behind him to rummage in his pack.

"Well, I never saw 'em."

"That's because you're half-blind," he said. "You can't even see a cloud of dust when it's coming right at you."

Well, as a matter of fact, we'd been arguing long enough that now I could, a kicked-up line of pinkish cloud close to the ridge.

"What do you think it is? A dust tantrum?" I said, even though a tantrum would've been meandering all over the place, not keeping to a line.

"I don't know," he said, putting his hand up to shade his eyes. "A stampede maybe."

The only fauna around here were luggage, and they didn't stampede in dry weather like this, and anyway the cloud wasn't wide enough for a stampede. It looked like the dust churned up by a rover, or a gate opening.

I kicked my terminal on and asked for whereabouts on the gatecrashers. I'd shown Wulfmeier on Dazil yesterday when Carson'd been so set on going after him, and now the whereabouts showed him on Starting Gate, which meant he probably wasn't either place. But he'd have to be crazy to open a gate this close to King's X, even if there was anything underneath here—which there wasn't, I'd already run terrains and subsurfaces—especially knowing we were on our way home.

I squinted at the dust, wondering if I should ask for a verify. I could see now it was moving fast, which meant it wasn't a gate, or a pony, and the dust was too low for the heli. "Looks like the rover," I said. "Maybe the new loaner—what was her name? Ernestine?—is as jumped for you as you are for her, and she's coming out here to meet you. You better comb your mustache."

He wasn't paying any attention. He was still rummaging in his pack, looking for the binocs. "I laid 'em right next to your bedroll when you were loading the ponies."

"Well, I didn't see 'em," I said, watching the dust. It was a good thing it wasn't a stampede, it would have run us over while we stood there arguing about the binocs. "Maybe Bult took 'em."

"Why on hell would Bult take 'em?" Carson bellowed. "His are a hell of a lot fancier than ours."

They were, with selective scans and programmed polarizers, and Bult had hung them around the second joint of his neck and was peering through them at the dust. I rode up next to him. "Can you see what's making the dust?" I asked.

He didn't take the binocs down from his eyes. "Disturbance of land surface," he said severely. "Fine of one hundred."

I should've known it. Bult could've cared less about what was making the dust so long as he could get a fine out of it. "You can't fine us for dust unless we make it," I said. "Give me the binocs."

He bent his neck double, took the binocs off, and handed them to me, and then hunched over his log again. "Forcible confiscation of property," he said into his log. "Twenty-five."

"Confiscation!" I said. "You're not going to fine me with confiscating anything. I *asked* if I could borrow them."

"Inappropriate tone and manner in speaking to an indigenous person," he said into the log. "Fifty."

I gave up and put the binocs up to my eyes. The cloud of dust looked like it was right on top of me, but no clearer. I upped the resolution and took another look. "It's the rover," I called to Carson, who'd gotten off his pony and was taking everything out of his pack.

"Who's driving?" he said. "C.J.?"

I hit the polarizers to screen out the dust and took another look. "What'd you say this loaner's name was, Carson?"

"Evelyn. Did C.J. bring her out with her?"

"It's not C.J. driving," I said.

"Well, who on hell is it? Don't tell me one of the indidges stole the rover again."

"Unfair accusation of indigenous person," Bult said. "Seventy-five."

"You know how you always get mad over the indidges giving things the wrong names?" I said.

"What on hell does that have to do with who's driving the rover?" Carson said.

"Because it looks like the indidges aren't the only ones doing it," I said. "It looks like now Big Brother's doing it, too."

"Give me those binocs," he said, grabbing for 'em.

"Forcible confiscation of property," I said, holding them away from him. "Looks like you could've taken your time this morning and not gone off in such a hurry you forgot ours."

I handed the binocs back to Bult, and just to be contrary, he handed them to Carson, but the rover was close enough now we didn't need them.

It roared up in a cloud of dust, skidded to a halt right on top of a roadkill, and the driver jumped out and strode over to us without even waiting for the dust to clear.

"Carson and Findriddy, I presume," he said, grinning.

Now usually when we meet a loaner, they don't have eyes for anybody but Bult (or C.J., if she's there and the loaner's a male), especially if Bult's unfolding himself off his pony the way he was now, straightening out his back joints one after the other till he looks like a big pink Erector set. Then, while the loaners are still picking their jaws up out of the dirt, one of the ponies keels over or else drops a pile the size of the rover. It's tough to compete with. So we usually get noticed last or else have to say something like, "Bult's only dangerous when he senses your fear," to get their attention.

But this loaner didn't so much as glance at Bult. He came straight over to me and shook hands. "How do you do," he said eagerly, pumping my hand. "I'm Dr. Parker, the new member of your survey team."

"I'm Fin—" I started.

"Oh, I know who *you* are, and I can't *tell* you what an *honor* it is to meet you, Dr. Findriddy!"

He let go of my hand and started in on Carson's. "When C.J. told me you weren't back yet, I couldn't wait till you arrived to meet you," he said, jerking Carson's hand up and down. "Findriddy and Carson! The famous planetary surveyors! I can't believe I'm shaking hands with you, Dr. Carson!"

"It's kind of hard for me to believe, too," Carson said.

"What'd you say your name was, again?" I asked.

"Dr. Parker," he said, grabbing my hand to shake it again. "Dr. Findriddy, I've read all your—"

"Fin," I said, "and this is Carson. There's only four of us on the planet, counting you, so there's not much call for fancy titles. What do you want us to call you?" but he'd already left off pumping my hand and was staring past Carson.

"Is that the Wall?" he said, pointing at a bump on the horizon.

"Nope," I said. "That's Three Moon Mesa. The Wall's twenty kloms the other side of the Tongue."

"Are we going to see it on the expedition?"

"Yeah. We have to cross it to get into uncharted territory," I said.

"Great. I can't wait to see the Wall and the silvershim trees," he said, looking down at Carson's boots, "and the cliff where Carson lost his foot."

"How do you know about all this stuff?" I asked.

He looked back and forth at us in amazement. "Are you kidding? Everybody knows about Carson and Findriddy! You're famous! Dr. Findriddy, you're—"

"Fin," I said. "What do you want us to call you?"

"Evelyn," he said. He looked from one to the other of us. "It's a British name. My mother was from England. Only they pronounce it with a long *e."*

"And you're an exozoologist?" I said.

"Socioexozoologist. My speciality's sex."

"C.J.'s the one you want then," I said. "She's our resident expert."

He blushed a nice pink. "I've already met her."

"She told you her name yet?" I said.

"Her name?" he said blankly.

"What C.J. stands for," I said. "She must be slipping," I said to Carson.

Carson ignored me. "If you're an expert on sex," Carson said, looking over at Bult, who was heading for the rover, "you can help us tell which one Bult is."

"I thought the Boohteri were a simple two-sex species," Evelyn said.

"They are," Carson said, "only we can't tell which one's which."

"All their equipment's on the inside," I said, "not like C.J.'s. It—"

"Speaking of which, did she have supper ready?" Carson said. "Not that it makes any difference to us. At this rate we'll still be out here tomorrow morning."

"Oh. Of course," Evelyn said, looking dismayed, "you're eager to get back to headquarters. I didn't mean to keep you. I was just so excited to actually meet you!" He started off for the rover. Bult was hunched over the front tire. He unfolded three leg joints when Evelyn came up. "Damage to indigenous fauna," he said. "Seventy-five."

Evelyn said to me, "Have I done something wrong?"

"Hard not to in these parts," I said. "Bult, you can't fine Evelyn for running over a roadkill."

"Running over—" Evelyn said. He leapt in the rover and roared it back off the roadkill, and then jumped out again. "I didn't see it!" he said, peering at its flattened brown body. "I didn't mean to kill it! Honestly, I—"

"You can't kill a roadkill just by parking a rover on it," I said, poking it with my toe. "You can't even wake it up."

Bult pointed at the tire tracks Evelyn'd just made. "Disruption of land surface. Twenty-five."

"Bult, you can't fine Evelyn," I said. "He's not a member of the expedition."

"Disruption of land surface," Bult said, pointing at the tire tracks.

"Shouldn't I have come out here in the rover?" Evelyn said worriedly.

"Sure you should," I said, clapping him on the shoulder, " 'cause now you can give me a ride home. Carson, bring in my pony for me." I opened the door of the rover.

"I'm not getting stuck out here with the ponies while you ride back in style," Carson said. *"I'll* ride in with Evelyn, and *you* bring the ponies."

"Can't we all go back in the rover?" Evelyn said, looking upset. "We could tie the ponies to the back."

"The rover can't go that slow," Carson muttered.

"You've got no reason to get back early, Carson," I said. "I've got to check the purchase orders, and the pursuants, *and* fill out the report on the binocs you lost." I got in the rover and sat down.

"I lost?" Carson said, getting red in the face again. "I laid 'em—"

"Expedition member riding in wheeled vehicle," Bult said.

We turned around to look at him. He was standing beside his pony, talking into his log. "Disruption of land surface."

I got out of the rover and stalked over to him. "I told you, you can't fine somebody who's not a member of the expedition."

Bult looked at me. "Inappropriate tone and manner." He straightened some finger joints at me. "You member. Cahsson member. Yahhs?" he said in the maddening pidgin he uses when he's not tallying fines.

But his message was clear enough. If either of us rode back with Evelyn, he could fine us for using a rover, which would take the next six expeditions' wages, not to mention the trouble we'd get into with Big Brother.

"You expedition, yahhs?" Bult said. He held out his pony's reins to me.

"Yeah," I said. I took the reins.

Bult grabbed his log off his pony's saddlebone, jumped in the rover, and folded himself into a sitting position. "We go," he said to Evelyn.

Evelyn looked questioningly at me.

"Bult here'll ride in with you," I said. "We'll bring the ponies in."

"How on hell are we supposed to bring three ponies in when they'll only walk two abreast?" Carson said.

I ignored him. "See you back at King's X." I slapped the side of the rover.

"Go fahhst," Bult said. Ev started the rover up and waved and left us eating a cloud of dust.

"I'm beginning to think you're right about loaners, Fin," Carson said, coughing and smacking his hat against his leg. "They're nothing but trouble. And the males are the worst, especially after C.J. gets to 'em. We'll spend half the expedition listening to him talk about her, and the other half keeping him from labeling every gully in sight Crissa Canyon."

"Maybe," I said, squinting at the rover's dust, which seemed to be veering off to the right. "C.J. said Evelyn got in this morning."

"Which means she's had almost a whole day to give him her pitch," he said, taking hold of Bult's pony's reins. It balked and dug in its paws. "And she'll have at least another two hours to work her wiles before we get these ponies in."

"Maybe," I said, still watching the dust. "But I figure a presentable-looking male like Ev can jump just about any female he wants without having to do anything for it, and you notice he didn't stay at King's X with C.J. He came tearing out here to meet *us.* I think he might be smarter than he looks."

"That's what you said the first time you saw Bult," Carson said, yanking on Bult's pony's reins. The pony yanked back.

"And I was right, wasn't I?" I said, going over to help. "If he wasn't, he'd be here with these ponies, and *we'd* be halfway to King's X." I took over the reins, and he went around behind the pony to push.

"Maybe," he said. "Why wouldn't he want to meet us? After all, we're planetary surveyors. We're famous!"

I pulled and he pushed. The pony stayed put. "Get moving, you rock-headed nag!" Carson said, shoving on its back end. "Don't you know who we are?"

The pony lifted its tail and dumped a pile.

"My *shit!*" Carson said.

"Too bad Evelyn can't see us now," I said, holding the reins over my shoulder and hauling on the pony. "Findriddy and Carson, the famous explorers!"

Off in the distance, to the right of the ridge, the dust disappeared.

interim: at King's X

It took us four hours to make it into King's X. Bult's pony keeled over twice and wouldn't get up, and when we got there, Ev was waiting out at the stable to ask us when we were going to start on the expedition. Carson gave him an inappropriate-in-tone-and-manner answer.

"I know you just got back and have to file your reports and everything," Ev said.

"And eat," Carson muttered, limping around his pony, "and sleep. And kill me a scout."

"It's just that I'm so excited to see Boohte," Ev said. "I still can't believe I'm really *here,* talking to—"

"I know, I know," I said, unloading the computer. "Findriddy and Carson, the famous surveyors."

"Where's Bult?" Carson asked, unstrapping his camera from his pony's saddlebone. "And why isn't he out here to unload his pony?"

Evelyn handed Carson Bult's log. "He said to tell you these are the fines from the trip in."

"He wasn't *on* the trip in," Carson said, glaring at the log. "What on hell are these? 'Destruction of indigenous flora.' 'Damage to sand formations.' 'Pollution of atmosphere.' "

I grabbed the log away from Carson. "Did Bult give you directions back to King's X?"

"Yes," Ev said. "Did I do something wrong?"

"Wrong?!" Carson spluttered. *"Wrong?!"*

"Don't get in a sweat," I said. "Bult can't fine Ev til he's a member of the expedition."

"But I don't understand," Ev said. "What did I do wrong? All I did was drive the rover—"

"Stir up dust, make tire tracks," Carson said, "emit exhaust—"

"Wheeled vehicles aren't allowed off government property," I explained to Ev, who was looking amazed.

"Then how do you get around?" he asked.

"We don't," Carson said, glaring at Bult's pony, which looked like it was getting ready to keel over again. "Explain it to him, Fin."

I was too tired to explain anything, least of all Big Brother's notion of how to survey a planet. "You tell him about the fines while I go get this straightened out with Bult," I said, and went across the compound to the gate area.

In my log, there's nothing worse than working for a government with the guilts. All we were doing on Boohte was surveying the planet, but Big Brother didn't want anybody accusing them of "ruthless imperialist expansion" and riding roughshod over the indidges the way they did when they colonized America.

So they set up all these rules to "preserve planetary ecosystems" (which was supposed to mean we weren't allowed to build dams or kill the local fauna) and "protect indigenous cultures from technological contamination" (which was supposed to mean we couldn't give 'em firewater and guns), and stiff fines for breaking the rules.

Which is where they made their first mistake, because they paid the fines to the indidges, and Bult and his tribe knew a good thing when they saw it, and before you know it we're being fined for making footprints, and Bult's buying technological contamination right and left with the proceeds.

I figured he'd be in the gate area, up to his second knee joint in stuff he'd bought, and I was right. When I opened the door, he was prying open a crate of umbrellas.

"Bult, you can't charge us with fines the rover incurred," I said.

He pulled out an umbrella and examined it. It was the collapsible kind. He held the umbrella out in front of him and pushed a button. Lights came on around the rim. "Destruction of land surface," he said.

I held out his log to him. "You know the regs. 'The expedition is not responsible for violations committed by any person not an official member of the expedition.' "

He was still messing with the buttons. The lights went off. "Bult member," he said, and the umbrella shot out and open, barely missing my stomach.

"Watch it!" I jumped back. "You can't incur fines, Bult."

Bult put down the umbrella and opened a big box of dice, which would make Carson happy. His favorite occupation, next to blaming me, is shooting craps.

"Indidges can't incur fines!" I said.

"Inappropriate tone and manner," he said.

I was too tired for this, too, and I still had the reports and the whereabouts to do. I left him unpacking a box of shower curtains and went across to the mess.

I opened the door. "Honey, I'm home," I called.

"Hello!" C.J. sang out cheerfully from the kitchen, which was a switch. "How was your expedition?"

She appeared in the doorway, smiling and wiping her hands on a towel. She was all done up, clean face and fixed-up hair and a shirt that was open down to thirty degrees north. "Dinner's almost ready," she said brightly, and then stopped and looked around. "Where's Evelyn?"

"Out in the stable," I said, dumping my stuff on a chair, "talking to Carson, the planetary surveyor. Did you know we're famous?"

"You're filthy,"she said. "And you're late. What on hell took you so long? Dinner's cold. I had it ready two hours ago." She jabbed a finger at my stuff. "Get that dirty pack off the furniture. It's bad enough putting up with dust tantrums without you two dragging in dirt."

I sat down and propped my legs up on the table. "And how was your day, sweetheart?" I said. "Get a mud puddle named after you? Jump any loners?"

"Very funny. Evelyn happens to be a very nice young man who understands what it's like to be all alone on a planet for weeks at a time with nobody for hundreds of kloms and who knows what dangers lurking out there—"

"Like losing that shirt," I said.

"You're not exactly in a position to criticize my clothes," she said. "When's the last time you changed *yours?* What have you been doing, rolling in the mud? And get those boots off the furniture. They're disgusting!" She smacked my legs with the dish towel.

This was as much fun as talking to Bult. If I was going to be raked over the coals, it might as well be by the experts. I heaved myself out of the chair. "Any pursuants?"

"If you mean official reprimands, there are sixteen. They're on the computer." She went back to the kitchen, her shirt flapping. "And get cleaned up. You're not coming to the table looking like that."

"Yes, dear," I said and went over to the console. I fed in the expedition report and took a look at the subsurfaces I'd run in Sector 247-72, and then called up the pursuants.

There were the usual loving messages from Big Brother: we weren't covering enough sectors, we weren't giving enough f-and-f indigenous names, we were incurring too many fines.

"Pursuant to language used by members of survey expeditions, such members will refrain from using derogatory terms in reference to the government, in particular, abbreviations and slang terms such as 'Big Brother' and 'morons back home.' Such references imply lack of respect, thereby undermining relations with the indigenous sentients and obstructing the government's goals. Members of survey expeditions will henceforth refer to the government by its proper title in full."

Evelyn and Carson came in. "Anything interesting?" Carson asked, leaning over me.

"We're wearing our mikes turned up too high," I said.

He clapped me on the shoulder. "I'm gonna go check the weather and then take a bath," he said.

I nodded, looking at the screen. He left, and I started through the pursuants again and then looked back behind me. Ev was leaning over me, his chin practically on my shoulder.

"Do you mind if I watch?" he said. "It's so exc—"

"I know, I know," I said. "There's nothing more exciting than reading a bunch of memos from Big Brother. Oh. Sorry," I said, pointing at the screen, "we're not supposed to call them that. We're supposed to use appropriate titles. There's nothing more exciting than reading memos from the Third Reich."

Ev grinned, and I thought, Yep, smarter than he looks.

"Fin," C.J. called from the door of the mess. She'd unstripped her blouse another ten degrees. "Can I borrow Evelyn for a minute?"

"You bet, Crissa Jane," I said.

She glared at me.

"That's what C.J. stands for, you know," I said to Ev. "Crissa Jane Tull. You'll need to remember that for when we go on expedition."

"Fin!" she snapped. "Ev," she said sweetly, "can you come help me with dinner?"

"Sure," Ev said and was after her like a shot. All right, not that much smarter.

I went back to the pursuants. We weren't showing "proper respect for indigenous cultural integrity," which meant who knows what, we hadn't filled out Subsection 12-2 of the minerals report for Expedition 158, we had left two gaps of uncharted territory on Expedition 162, one in Sector 248-76 and the other in Sector 246-73.

I knew what the 246-73 gap was but not the other one, and I doubted if it was still a gap. We'd been over a lot of the same territory the next-to-last expedition.

I called up the topographicals and asked for a chart overlay. Big Bro—Hizzoner was right for once. There were two holes in the chart.

Carson came in, carrying a towel and a clean pair of socks. "We fired yet?"

"Just about," I said. "How's the weather look?"

"Rain down in the Ponypiles start of next week. Otherwise, nothing. Not even a dust tantrum. Looks like we can go anywhere we want."

"What about in charted territory? Up along 76?"

"Same thing. Clear and dry. Why?" he said, coming over to look at the screen. "What've you got?"

"I don't know yet," I said. "Probably nothing. Go get cleaned up."

He went off toward the latrine. Sector 248-76. That was over on the other side of the Tongue and, if I remembered right, close to Silvershim Creek. I frowned at the screen a minute and then asked for Expedition 181's log and started fast-forwarding it.

"Is that the expedition you were just on?" Ev said, and I jerked around to find him hanging over me again.

"I thought you were helping C.J. in the kitchen," I said, cutting the log off.

He grinned. "It's too hot in there. Were you sending the log of the expedition to NASA?"

I shook my head. "The log goes out live. It transmits straight to C.J. and she sends it on through the gate. I was just finishing up the expedition summary."

"Do you send all the reports?"

"Nope. Carson sends the topographicals and the f-and-f; I send the geologicals and the accountings." I asked for the tally of Bult's fines.

Ev looked uneasy. "I wanted to apologize to you for driving the rover. I didn't know it was against regs to use nonindigenous transportation. The last thing I wanted to do on my first day was to get you and Dr. Carson in trouble."

"Don't worry about it. We still had wages left over this expedition, which is better than we've made out the last two. The only things that really get you in trouble are killing fauna and naming something after somebody," I said, staring at him, but he didn't look especially guilty. C.J. must not have gotten around to her sales pitch yet.

"Anyway," I said, "we're used to trouble."

"I know," he said earnestly. "Like the time you got caught in the stampede and nearly got trampled, and Dr. Carson rescued you."

"How'd you know about that?" I asked.

"Are you kidding? You're—"

"Famous. Right," I said. "But how—"

"Evelyn," C.J. called, dripping honey with every syllable, "can you help me set the table?" and he was off again.

I got 181's log again and then changed my mind and asked for the whereabouts. I checked them for the two times we'd been in Sector 248-76. Wulfmeier'd been on Starting Gate both times, which didn't prove anything. I asked for a verify on him.

"Nahhd khompt," Bult said.

I looked up. He was standing next to the computer, pointing his umbrella at me.

"I need the computer, too," I said, and he reached for his log. "Besides, it's almost dinnertime."

"Nahhd tchopp," he said, moving around behind me so he could see the screen. "Forcible confiscation of property."

"That's what it is, all right," I said, wondering which was worse, being stuck with his bayonet of an umbrella or another fine. Besides, I couldn't find out what I needed to know with all these people hanging over my shoulder. And dinner was ready. Evelyn pushed the kitchen door open with his shoulder and brought out a platter of meat. I asked for the catalog.

"Here you go," I said, standing up. "Nieman Marcus at your disposal. Go at it. Tchopp."

Bult sat down, shot his umbrella open, and started talking to the computer. "One dozen pair digiscan polarized field glasses," he said, "with telemetry and object enhancement functions."

Ev stared.

"One 'High Rollers Special' slot machine," Bult said.

Ev came over with the platter. "Bult can speak English?" he said.

I grabbed a chunk of meat. "Depends. When he's ordering stuff, yeah. When you're talking to him, not much. When you're trying to negotiate satellite surveys or permission to set up a gate, *no hablo inglais.*" I grabbed another hunk of meat.

"*Stop* that!" C.J. said, bringing in the vegetables. "Honestly, Fin, you've got the manners of a gatecrasher! You could at least wait till we get to the table!" She set the vegetables down. "Carson! Dinner's ready!" she called and went back into the kitchen.

He came in, wiping his hands on a towel. He'd washed up and shaved around his mustache. He came over close to me. "Find anything?" he muttered.

"Maybe."

Ev, still holding the meat platter, was looking at me inquiringly.

I said, "I found out those binocs you lost are gonna cost us three hundred."

"*I* lost?" Carson said. "You're the one who lost 'em. I laid 'em right next to your pack. Why on hell's it three hundred?"

"Possible technological contamination," I said. "If they turn up on an indidge it'll be five hundred you lost us."

"*I* lost us!" he said.

C.J. came in, carrying a bowl of rice. She'd switched her shirt for one with even lower coordinates, and lights around the edges like the ones on Bult's umbrella.

"You were the one in a hurry to get back here and meet *Evelyn,"* I said. I pulled a chair out from the table, stepped over it, and sat down.

He grabbed the platter out of Ev's hands. "Five hundred. My *shit!"* He set the platter on the table. "How much were the rest of the fines?"

"I don't know," I said. "I haven't tallied 'em yet."

"Well, what on hell were you doing all this time?" He sat down. "It's plain to see you weren't taking a bath."

"C.J.'s cleaned up enough for both of us," I said. "What're the lights for?" I asked her.

Carson grinned. "They're like those landing strip beacons, so you can find your way down."

C.J. ignored him. "You sit here by me, Evelyn."

He pulled out her chair, and she sat down, managing to lean over so we could all see the runway.

Ev sat down next to her. "I can't believe I'm actually eating dinner with Carson and Findriddy! Tell me about your expedition. I'll bet you had a lot of adventures."

"Well," Carson said, "Fin lost the binocs."

"Have you decided when we leave on the next expedition yet?" Ev asked.

Carson gave me a look. "Not yet," I said. "A few days, probably."

"Oh, good," C.J. crooned, leaning in Ev's direction. "That'll give us more time to get to know each other." She latched onto his arm.

"Is there anything I can do to help so we can leave sooner?" Ev said. "Loading the ponies or something? I'm just so eager to get started."

C.J. dropped his arm in disgust. "So you can spend three weeks sleeping on the ground and listening to these two?"

"Are you kidding?" he said. "I put in four years ago for the chance to go on an expedition with Carson and Findriddy! What's it like, being on the survey team with them?"

"What's it like?" She glared at us. "They're rude, they're dirty, they break every rule in the book, and don't let all their bickering fool you—they're just like *that.*" She crossed one finger over another. "Nobody has a chance against the two of them."

"I know," Ev said. "On the pop-ups they—"

"What are these pop-ups?" I said. "Some kind of holo?"

"They're DHVs," Ev said, as if that explained everything. "There's a whole series of them about you and Carson and Bult." He stopped and looked around at Bult hunched over the computer under his umbrella. "Doesn't Bult eat with you?"

"He's not allowed to," Carson said, helping himself to the meat.

"Regs," I said. "Cultural contamination. Asking him to eat at a table and use silverware is imperialistic. We might corrupt him with Earth foods and table manners."

"Small chance of that," C.J. said, taking the meat platter away from Carson. "You two don't *have* any table manners."

"So while we eat," Carson said, plopping potatoes on his plate, "he sits there ordering demitasse cups and place settings for twelve. Nobody ever said Big Brother was big on logic."

"Not Big Brother," I said, shaking my finger at Carson. "Pursuant to our latest reprimand, members of the expedition will henceforth refer to the government by its appropriate title."

"What, Idiots Incorporated?" Carson said. "What other brilliant orders did they come up with?"

"They want us to cover more territory. And they disallowed one of our names. Green Creek."

Carson looked up from his plate. "What on hell's wrong with Green Creek?"

"There's a senator named Green on the Ways and Means Committee. They couldn't prove any connection, though, so they just fined us the minimum."

"There're people named Hill and River, too," Carson said. "If one of them gets on the committee, what on hell do we do then?"

"I think it's ridiculous that you can't name things after people," C.J. said. "Don't you, Evelyn?"

"Why can't you?" Ev asked.

"Regs," I said. " 'Pursuant to the practice of naming geological formations, waterways, etc., after surveyors, government officials, historical personages, etc., said practice is indicative of oppressive colonialist attitudes and lack of respect for indigenous cultural traditions, etc., etc.' Hand the meat over."

C.J.'d picked up the platter, but she didn't pass it. "Oppressive! It is not. Why shouldn't we have something named after us? We're the ones stuck on this horrible planet all alone in uncharted territory for months at a time and with who knows what dangers lurking. We should get something."

Carson and I have heard this pitch a hundred or so times. She used to try it on us before she decided the loaners were more susceptible.

"There are hundreds of mountains and streams on Boohte. You can't tell me there isn't some way you could name *one* of them after somebody. I mean, the government wouldn't even notice."

Well, she's wrong there. Their Imperial Majesties check every single name, and even if all we tried to sneak past them was a bug named C.J., we could get tossed off Boohte.

"There's a way you can get something named after you, C.J.," Carson said. "Why didn't you say you were interested?"

C.J. narrowed her eyes. "How?"

"Remember Stewart? He was one of the first pair of scouts on Boohte," he explained to Ev. "Got caught in a flash flood and swept smack into a hill. Stewart's Hill, they named it. *In memoriam.* All you've got to do is take the heli out tomorrow and point it at whatever you want named after you, and—"

"Very funny," C.J. said. "I'm serious about this," she said to Ev. "Don't you think it's natural to want to have some sign that you've *been* here, so after you're gone you won't be forgotten, some monument to what you've done?"

"My *shit,*" Carson said, "if you're talking about doing stuff, Fin and I are the ones who should have something named after us! How about it, Fin? You want me to name something after you?"

"What would I do with it? What I *want* is the meat!" I held out my hands for it, but nobody paid any attention.

"Findriddy Lake," Carson said. "Fin Mesa."

"Findriddy Swamp," C.J. said.

It was time to change the subject, or I was never going to get any meat. "So, Ev," I said. "You're a sexozoologist."

"Socioexozoologist," he said. "I study instinctive mating behaviors in extraterrestrial species. Courtship rituals and sexual behaviors."

"Well, you've come to the right place," Carson said. "C.J.—"

C.J. cut in, "Tell me about some of the interesting species you've studied."

"Well, they're all interesting, really. Most animal behaviors are instinctive, they're hardwired in, but reproductive behavior is really complicated. It's part hardwiring, part survival strategies, and the combination produces all these variables. The charlizards on Ottiyal mate inside the crater of an active volcano, and there's a Terran species, the bowerbird, which constructs an elaborate bower fifty times his size and then decorates it with orchids and berries to attract the female."

"Some nest," I said.

"Oh, but it's not the nest," Ev said. "The nest is built in front of the bower, and it's quite ordinary. The bower is just for courtship. Sentients are even more interesting. The Inkicce males cut off their toes to impress the female. And the Opantis' courtship ritual—they're the indigenous sentients on Jevo—takes six months. The Opanti female sets a series of difficult tasks the male must perform before she allows him to mate with her."

"Just like C.J.," I said. "What kind of tasks do these Opantis have to do for the females? Name rivers after them?"

"The tasks vary, but they're usually the giving of tokens of esteem, proofs of valor, feats of strength."

"How come the male's always the one who has to do all the courting?" Carson said. "Giving 'em candy and flowers, proving they're tough, building bowers while the female just sits there making up her mind."

"Because the male is concerned only with mating," Ev said. "The female is concerned with ensuring the optimum survival of her offspring, which means she needs a strong mate or a smart one. The male doesn't do all the courting, though. The females send out response signals to encourage and attract the males."

"Like landing lights?" I said.

C.J. glared at me.

"Without those signals, the courtship ritual breaks down and can't be completed," Ev said.

"I'll keep that in mind," Carson said. He pushed back from the table. "Fin, if we're gonna start in two days, we'd better take a look at the map. I'll go get the new topographicals." He went out.

C.J. cleared off the table, and I threw Bult off the computer and set up the map, filling in the two holes with extrapolated topographics before I went back over to the table.

Ev was bending over the map. "Is that the Wall?" he said, pointing at the Tongue.

"Nope. That's the Tongue. *That's* the Wall," I said, sticking my hand in the middle of the holo to show him its course.

"I hadn't realized it was so long," he said wonderingly, tracing its meandering course along the Tongue and into the Ponypiles. "Which part is uncharted territory?"

"The blank part," I said, looking at the huge western expanse of the map. The charted area looked like a drop in the bucket.

Carson came back in and called Bult and his umbrella over, and we discussed routes.

"We haven't mapped any of the northern tributaries of the Tongue," Carson said, circling an area in light marker. "Where can we cross the Wall, Bult?"

Bult leaned over the table and pointed stiffly at two different places, making sure his finger didn't go into the holo.

"If we cross down here," I said, taking the marker away from Carson, "we can cut across here and follow Blacksand Ridge up." I lit a line up to Sector 248-76 and through the hole. "What do you think?"

Bult pointed at the other break in the Wall, holding his hinged finger well above the table. "Fahtsser wye."

I looked across at Carson. "What do you think?"

He looked steadily back at me.

"Will we get to see the trees that have the silver leaves?" Ev said.

"Maybe," Carson said, still looking at me. "Either way looks good to me," he said to Bult. "I'll have to check on the weather and see which one'll work. It looks like there's a lot of rain down here." He poked his finger at the route Bult'd marked. "And we'll have to run terrains. Fin, you want to do that?"

"You bet," I said.

"I'll check the weather, and see if we can work a route through some silvershims for Evie here."

He went out. "Can I watch you run the terrains?" Ev asked me.

"You bet," I said. I went over to the computer.

Bult was on it again, hunched under his umbrella, buying a roulette wheel.

"I've got to figure the easiest route," I said. "You can come back to the mall when I'm done."

He got out his log. "Discriminatory practices," he said.

That was a new one. "Why all these fines, Bult?" I said. "You saving up to buy a—" I was about to say "casino" but the last thing I wanted to do was give him any ideas. "To buy something big?" I ended up.

He reached for his log again.

"I need the computer if you want me to enter those fines you ran up with the rover today," I said.

He hesitated, wondering whether fining me for "attempt to bribe indigenous scout" would be worth more than the rover's fines, and then unfolded himself joint by joint and let me sit down.

I stared at the screen. There was no point in running terrains when I already knew the route I wanted, and I couldn't look at the log with Bult and Ev there either. I started tallying the fines.

After a few minutes C.J. came in and dragged Ev off to convince him Big Brother wouldn't catch him if he named one of the hills Mount C.J., but Bult was still hovering behind me, his umbrella aimed at my back.

"Don't you need to go unpack all those umbrellas and shower curtains you bought?" I said, but he didn't budge.

I had to wait till everybody was bedded down, including C.J., who'd flounced into her bunk in a hide-nothing nightie and then leaned out to say good night to Ev and give him one last eyeful, before I could take a look at that log.

I figured Bult would be in the gate area, unpacking his purchases, but he wasn't. Which meant he was still "tchopping," and I'd never get time alone on the computer. But he wasn't in the mess either.

I checked the kitchen and then started over to the stables. Halfway there I caught sight of a half circle of lights out by the ridge. I didn't have any notion of what he was doing clear out there—probably trying to collect fines from the luggage, but at least he wasn't hogging the computer.

I walked out far enough to make sure it was him and not just his umbrella and then went back into the mess and asked Starting Gate for a verify on Wulfmeier. I got it, which didn't mean anything either. Bult could make more selling fake verifies than he makes off us.

I asked for a trace, then checked on the rest of the gatecrashers. We had beacons on Miller and Abeyta, and Shoudamire was in the brig on the *Powell,* which left Karadjk and Redfox. They were out on the Arm.

The trace showed Wulfmeier on Dazil until yesterday afternoon. I thought about it, and then asked for the log and frame-by-frame coordinates and leaned back to watch it.

I'd been right. Sector 248-76 was next to the Wall, about twenty kloms down from where we'd crossed, an area of grayish igneous hills covered with knee-high scourbrush, which was probably the reason we'd skirted it.

I asked for an aerial. C.J.'d sideswiped 248-76 on one of her trips home. I put privacies on and asked for visuals. It looked the way I remembered it—hills and scourbrush, a few roadkill. The visual said fine-grained schist with phyllosilicates all the way down. I asked for the earlier log. That expedition we were south of it. It was hills and scourbrush on that end, too.

The schist we'd found on Boohte wasn't gold-bearing, and there were no signs of salt or drainage anomalies, so it wasn't an anticline. And we'd had good reasons for missing it both times—the first time we'd been following the Wall, looking for a break, and the second time we were trying to avoid 246-73. I couldn't see any indications either time that Bult was avoiding it. Even if he was, it was probably because the ponies would balk at the steepness of the hills.

On the other hand, we'd gone right by it twice, and you could hide almost anything in those hills. Including a gate.

I erased my transactions, took the privacies off, and walked back to the bunkhouse to talk to Carson.

Ev was leaning against the door. He looked so sappy-eyed and relaxed I wondered if C.J.'d broken down and given him a jump. She used to and then tried to get the loaners to name something for her afterward, but half the time they forgot, and she decided it worked better the other way around. But I figured the way she was looking at him at dinner it was just possible.

"What are you doing out here?" I asked him.

"I couldn't sleep," he said, looking out in the direction of the ridge. "I still can't convince myself I'm really here. It's beautiful."

He had that right. All three of Boohte's moons were up, strung out in a row like an expedition and turning the ridge a purplish-blue. I leaned against the other side of the door.

"What's it like, out in uncharted territory?" he said.

"It's like those mating customs of yours," I said. "Part instinct, part survival strategies, way too many variables. Mostly, it's a lot of dust and triangulations," I said, even though I knew he wouldn't believe me. "And ponypiles."

"I can't wait," he said.

"Then you'd better be getting to bed," I said, but he didn't move.

"Did you know a lot of species perform their courtship rituals by moonlight?" he said. "Like the whippoorwill and the Antarrean cowfrog."

"And teenagers," I said, and yawned. "We'd better be getting to bed. We've got a lot to do in the morning."

"I don't think I could sleep," he said, still with that dopey look. I began to wonder if I'd been wrong about him being all that smart.

"I saw the vids, but they don't do it justice," he said, looking at me. "I had no idea everything would be so beautiful."

"You should be using that line on C.J. and her nightie," Carson said, poking his head around the door. He was wearing his liner and his boots. "What on hell's going on out here?"

"I was telling Ev how he'd better get to bed so we can start in the morning," I said, looking at Carson.

"Really?" Ev said. The sappy-eyed look disappeared. *"Tomorrow?"*

"Sunup," I said, "so you'd better get back to your bunk. It's the last chance you'll have at a mattress for two weeks," but he didn't show any signs of leaving, and I couldn't talk to Carson with him hanging over me.

"Where are we going?"

"Uncharted territory," I said. "But you'll be asleep in the saddlebone and miss it if you don't get to bed."

"Oh, I couldn't possibly sleep now!" he said, gazing out at the ridge. "I'm too excited!"

"You'd better pack your gear then," Carson said.

"I'm all packed."

C.J. came out, pulling a hide-nothing robe on over her nightie.

"We're leaving at sunup," I told her.

"Oh, but you can't go *yet,"* she said and yanked Ev inside.

Carson motioned me out halfway between the bunkhouse and the stable. "What did you find?"

"A hole in Sector 248-76. We've missed it twice, and Bult was leading both times."

"Fossil strata?"

"No. Metamorphic. It's probably nothing, but Wulfmeier was on Dazil yesterday afternoon, *and* verified on Starting Gate. I don't think he's either place."

"What do you think he's doing? Mining?"

"Maybe. Or using it as headquarters while he looks around."

"Where'd you say it was?"

"Sector 248-76."

"My shit," he said softly. "That's awfully close to 246-73. If it is Wulfmeier, he's bound to find it. You're right. We'd better get out there." He shook his head. "I wish we weren't stuck taking this loaner with us. What was he doing out here? Resting between rounds with C.J.?"

"We were discussing mating customs," I said.

"Sexozoologist!" he said. "Sex can mess up an expedition quicker than anything."

"Ev can handle C.J. Besides, she's not going on the expedition."

"It's not C.J. I'm worried about."

"What *are* you worried about, then? Him trying to name one of the tributaries Crissa Creek? Him building a nest fifty times his size? What?"

"Never mind," he said and stomped off toward the gate area. "I'll tell Bult," he said. "You load the ponies."

expedition 184: day 1

We ended having C.J. fly us as far as the Tongue. Carson and I tallied up how long it would take to get to uncharted territory and how many fines we'd run up on the way and decided it was cheaper to go by heli, even with the airborne vehicle fines. And C.J. was overjoyed to have a few last chances at Ev. She kept him up front with her the whole way.

"Quit lollygagging with Evie and send him back here," Carson called to C.J. when the Tongue came in sight. "We've got to check his gear."

He came back into the bay immediately, looking as excited as a kid. "Are we in uncharted territory yet?" he asked, squatting down and looking out through the open hatch.

"We charted all this side of the river last time," I said. "The regs are no alcohol, no tobacco, no rec drugs, no caffeine. You carrying any of those?"

"No," he said.

I handed him his mike, and he stuck it on his throat. "No advanced technology except for scientific equipment, no cameras, no lasers or firearms."

"I've got a knife. Can I take that?"

"Only if you don't kill anything indigenous with it," I said.

"If you get the urge to kill something, kill Fin," Carson said. "There's no fine on us."

The heli swooped down to the Tongue and hovered above the near shore. "You're the first out," I said, pushing him over to the door. "It's too big a fine to land," I shouted. "C.J.'s going to hover it. We'll throw down the gear to you."

He nodded and got ready to jump. Bult elbowed him aside, shot his umbrella open, and floated down like Mary Poppins.

"Second out," I shouted. "Don't land on any flora if you can help it."

He nodded again, looking down at Bult, who already had his log out.

"Wait!" C.J. said and came shooting out of her pilot's seat and past Ev and me. "I couldn't let you go without saying good-bye, Ev," she said, and flung her arms around his neck.

"What on hell are you doing, C.J.?" Carson said. "Do you know how big the fine is for crashing a heli?"

"It's on automatic," she said, and planted a wet one on Ev. "I'll be waiting," she said breathily. "Good luck, I hope you find lots of things to name."

"We're all waiting," I said. "All right, you told her good-bye, Ev. Now, jump."

"Don't forget," C.J. whispered, and leaned forward to kiss him again.

"Now," I said, and gave him a push. He jumped, and C.J. latched onto the edge of the bay and glared at me. I ignored her and started handing the bedrolls and the surveying equipment down to him.

"Don't set the terminal on any flora," I shouted down to him, too late. He'd already laid it in a patch of scourbrush.

I glanced at Bult, but he'd gone down to the river's edge and was looking at the other side with his binocs.

"Sorry," Ev shouted to me. He jerked the terminal back up and looked around for a bare spot.

"Stop gossiping and jump," Carson said behind me, "so I can get the ponies unloaded."

I grabbed the supply packs and handed them down to Ev. "Stand back," I shouted to him, scanning the ground for a clear patch.

"What on hell's keeping you?" Carson shouted. "They're going to unload before I unload them."

I picked a bare spot and jumped, but before I'd so much as hit, Carson yelled, "Lower, C.J.," and I nearly cracked my head on the heli when I straightened up.

"Lower!" Carson bellowed over his shoulder, and C.J. dipped the heli down. "Fin, take the reins, dammit. What on hell are you waiting for? Lead 'em off."

I grabbed for the dangling reins, which did about as much good as it always does, but Carson always thinks the ponies are gonna suddenly turn rational and jump off. They reared and shied and backed Carson against the side of the heli's bay, like always, and Carson said, like always, "You rock-headed morons, get off me!" which Bult entered in his log.

"Verbal abuse of indigenous fauna."

"You're gonna have to push 'em off," I said, like always, and climbed back on.

"Ev," I shouted down, "we're bringing this down as far as it'll go. Signal C.J. when it touches the tops of the scourbrush."

C.J. circled the heli and came in lower. "Up a little," Evelyn said, gesturing with his hand. "Okay."

We were half a meter from the ground. "Let's try it one more time," Carson said, like always. "Take the reins."

I did. This time they squashed him against the back of C.J.'s seat.

"Goddammit, you shit-brained sonsabitches," he shouted, swatting at their hind ends. They backed against him some more.

I maneuvered around to Carson's side, and picked up a hind paw of the one that was standing on his bad foot. The pony went over like it'd been doped, and we dragged it to the edge of the bay and pushed it out. It landed with an "oof" and laid there.

Evelyn hurried over. "I think it's hurt," he said.

"Nope," I said. "Just sulking. Stand back."

We upended the other three and dumped them on top of the first one and jumped down.

"Shouldn't we do something?" Evelyn said, looking anxiously at the heap.

"Not till we're ready to go," Carson said, picking up his gear. "They can't shit in that position. Come on, Bult. Let's get packed."

Bult was still over by the Tongue, but he'd dropped his binocs and was squatting on the bank, peering into the centimeter-deep water.

"Bult!" I shouted, walking over to him.

He stood up and got out his log. "Disturbance of water surface," he said, pointing up at the hovering heli. "Generation of waves."

"There's not enough water for a wave," I said, sticking my hand in it. "There's hardly enough to wet your finger."

"Introduction of foreign body into waterway," Bult said.

"Foreign—" I started and was drowned out by the heli. It flew over the Tongue, rippling the centimeter's worth of water, and came back around, skimming the bushes. C.J. swooped past us, blowing kisses.

"I know, I know," I said to Bult, "disturbance of waterway."

He stalked over to a clump of scourbrush, unfolded an arm under it, and came up with two wiry leaves and a shriveled berry. He held them out to me. "Destruction of crop," he said.

C.J. banked and turned, waving, and headed off northeast. I'd told her to swing over Sector 248-76 on her way home and try to get an aerial. I hoped she wasn't so busy flirting with Ev that she'd forget.

Ev was looking south at the mountains. "Is that the Wall?" he said.

"Nope. The Wall's off that direction," I said, pointing across the Tongue. "Those are the Ponypiles."

"Are we going there?" Ev said, looking sappy-eyed again.

"Not this trip. We'll follow the Tongue south a few kloms and then head northwest."

"Will you two stop sight-seeing and get over here and load these ponies?" Carson shouted. He had the ponies up and was strapping the wide-angle to Speedy's pommelbone.

"Yes, ma'am," I said. Ev and I picked our way over to him between grass clumps. "Don't worry about the Wall," I told Ev. "We'll see plenty of it. We have to cross it to get to where we're going, and after we do we'll follow it all the way north to Silvershim Creek."

"Not unless we get these ponies loaded," Carson said. "Here," he said, handing the reins of one of the ponies to Ev. "Get Cyclone loaded."

"Cyclone?" Ev said, looking warily at the pony, which looked to me like it was getting ready to fall over again.

"There's nothing to it," I said. "Ponies—"

"Fin's right," Carson said. "Just don't make any sudden movements. And if he tries to throw you, hang on for dear life, no matter what. Cyclone doesn't get violent except when he senses fear."

"Violent?" Ev said, looking nervous. "I haven't had much experience riding."

"You can ride mine," I said.

"Diablo?" Carson said. "You think that's a good idea after what happened before? No, I think you'd better ride Cyclone." He held out the stirrup. "You just put your foot in here and take hold of the pommelbone nice and slow," he said.

Ev took hold of the pommel like it was a hand grenade. "There, there, Cyclone," he murmured, bringing his foot up in slow motion to the stirrup. "Nice Cyclone."

Carson looked across at me, the edges of his mustache quaking. "Isn't he doing good, Fin?"

I ignored him and went on attaching the wide-angles to Useless's chest.

"Now swing your other leg up and over, real slow. I'll hold him till you're on," Carson said, holding on tight to the bridle. Evelyn did it and got a death grip on the reins.

"Giddyap!" Carson shouted and smacked the pony on the flank. The pony took a step forward, and Ev dropped the reins and grabbed for the pommelbone. The pony took two more steps toward Carson, lifted its tail, and dumped a pile the size of Everest.

Carson came over to me, laughing fit to kill.

"What are you picking on Ev for?" I said.

He laughed awhile before he answered. "You said he was smarter than he looks. I was just checking it out."

"You should be checking out your scout," I said, pointing at Bult, who had his binocs up to his eyes again, "if you want to depart any time today."

He laughed some more and went over to talk to Bult. I finished attaching the surveying equipment. Bult had his log out, and from the looks of it Carson was yelling at him again.

I swung up onto Useless and rode over to where Ev was sitting on his pony. "Looks like we'll be here awhile," I said. "Sorry about Carson. It's his idea of a joke."

"I figured that out," he said. "Finally. What's his real name?" he said, gesturing at the pony. It took a step forward and stopped.

"Speedy," I said.

"And this is as fast as it goes."

"Sometimes it doesn't go this fast," I said.

Useless lifted its tail and unloaded.

"Tell me they don't do this all the time," Ev said.

"Not like this," I said. "Sometimes after we have 'em in the heli they get the runs."

"Great," he said. "I suppose sudden movements don't spook them?"

"Nothing spooks them," I said, "not even nibblers chewing on their toes. If they're scared or they don't want to do something, they just stand there and won't budge."

"What don't they like?"

"People riding them," I said. "Hills. They won't go up more than a two percent grade. Backtrailing over their own pawprints. Going more than two abreast. Going more than a klom an hour."

Ev was looking at me warily, like I was putting him on, too.

I held up my hand. "Scout's honor," I said.

"But you can walk faster than that," he said.

"Not when there's a fine for footprints."

He leaned sideways to look at Useless's paws. "But they leave footprints, don't they?"

"They're indigenous," I said.

"But how do you cover any territory?"

"We don't, and Big Bro yells at us," I said, looking over at the

Tongue. Carson had given up yelling and was watching Bult talk into his log. "Speaking of which, I'd better fill you in on the rest of the regs. No personal holo or picture-taking, no souvenirs, no picking wildflowers, no killing of fauna."

"What if you're attacked?"

"Depends. If you think you can survive the heart attack you'll have when you see the fine and all the reports you'll have to fill out, go ahead. Letting it kill you might be easier."

He looked suspicious again.

"We probably won't run into anything dangerous where we're going," I said.

"What about nibblers?"

"They're farther north. Hardly any of the f-and-f are dangerous, and the indidges are peaceful. They'll rob you blind, but they won't hurt you. You wear your mike all the time." I reached over and took it off and stuck it back on lower down on his chest. "If you get separated, wait where you are. Don't go trying to find anybody. That's the surest way to get yourself killed."

"I thought you said the f-and-f weren't dangerous?"

"They're not. But we're going to be in uncharted territory. That means landslides, lightning, roadkill holes, flash floods. You can cut your hand on scourbrush and get blood poisoning, or get too far north and freeze to death."

"Or get caught in a luggage stampede."

I wondered how he knew about that. The pop-ups, whatever they were. "Or wander off and never be found again, which is what happened to Stewart's partner, Segura," I said. "And you won't even get a hill named after you. So you stay where you are, and after twenty-four hours you call C.J. and she'll come and get you."

He nodded. "I know."

I was going to have to find out what these pop-ups are. "You call C.J.," I said, "and you let her worry about finding the rest of us. If you're injured and can't call, she'll know where you are by your mike."

I paused, trying to remember what else I should tell him. Carson was yelling at Bult again. I could hear him clear over by the ponies.

"No giving the indidges gifts," I said, "no teaching them how to make a wheel or build a cotton gin. If you figure out what sex Bult is, no fraternizing. No yelling at the indidges," I said, looking over at Carson.

He was coming this way, his mustache quivering again, but he didn't look like he was laughing this time.

"Bult says we can't cross here," he said. "He says there's no break in the Wall here."

"When we looked at the map, he said there was," I said.

"He says it's been repaired. He says we'll have to ride south to the other one. How far is it?"

"Ten kloms," I said.

"My shit, that'll take us all morning," he said, squinting off in the direction of the Wall. "He didn't say anything about it being repaired when we did the map. Call C.J. Maybe she got an aerial of it on her way home."

"She didn't," I said. Swinging north to Sector 248-76, she wouldn't have gotten any pictures of where we were going.

"Dammit," he said, taking his hat off, looking like he was going to throw it on the ground and then thinking the better of it. He looked at me and then stomped back toward the Tongue.

"You stay here," I said to Ev. I dismounted and caught up to Carson. "You think Bult's got it figured out?" I asked him as soon as we were out of Ev's earshot.

"Maybe," he said. "So what do we do?"

I shrugged. "Go south to the next break. It's no farther from the northern tributaries, and by that time we'll know if we have to check 248-76. I sent C.J. up there to do an aerial." I looked at Bult, who was still talking into his log. "Maybe he doesn't have it figured out. Maybe there are just more fines this way."

"Which is just what we need," he said glumly.

He was right. Our departure fines came to nine hundred, and it took a half hour to tally them up. Then it took Bult another half hour to get his pony loaded, decide he wanted his umbrella, unload everything to find it and load it again, and by that time Carson had used inappropriate manner and tone and thrown his hat on the ground, and we had to wait while Bult added those on.

It was ten o'clock before we finally got started, Bult leading off under his lighted umbrella, which he'd tied to his pony's pommelbone, Ev and I side by side, and Carson in the rear where he couldn't swear at Bult.

C.J.'d landed us at the top end of a little valley, and we followed it south, keeping close to the Tongue.

"You can't see much from here," I told Ev. "This really only goes another klom or so, and then you should get a better view of the Wall. And five kloms down it comes right up next to the Tongue."

"Why is it called the Tongue? Is that a translation of the Boohteri name for it?"

"The indidges don't have a name for it. Or half the stuff on this planet." I pointed at the mountains ahead of us. "Take the Ponypiles. Biggest natural formation on the whole continent, and they don't have a name for it, or most of the f-and-f. And when they do give stuff names, they don't make any sense. Their name for the luggage is *tssuhlkahttses.* It means Dead Soup. And Big Brother won't let us give things sensible names."

"Like the Tongue?" he said, grinning.

"It's long, it's pink, and it's hanging out like it's going 'aah' for a doctor. What else would you call it? That's not its name anyway. The Tongue's just what we call it. The name on the map's Conglomerate River, after the rocks it was flowing between up where we named it."

"An unofficial name," Ev said, half to himself.

"Won't work," I said. "We already named Tight-ass Canyon after C.J. She wants something named after her officially. Passed, approved, and on the topographicals."

"Oh," he said, and looked disappointed.

"What about that?" I said. "Any species besides homo sap have to carve a female's name on a tree to get a jump?"

"No," he said. "There's a species of water bird on Choom where the males build plaster dikes around the females that look a lot like the Wall."

Speaking of which, there it was. The valley had been climbing and opening out as we rode, and all of a sudden we were at the top of a rise and looking out across what looked like one of C.J.'s aerials.

It was flat all the way to the feet of the Ponypiles, with the Tongue slicing through it like a map boundary. Boohte's got as many oxides as Mars, and lots of cinnabar, so the plains are pink. There were mesas here and there off to the west, and a couple of cinder pyramids, and the blue of the distance turned them a nice lavender. And meandering around them and over the mesas, down to the Tongue and then away again, arched white and shining in the sun, was the Wall. At least Bult hadn't been lying about the break. The Wall marched unbrokenly as far as I could see.

"There she is," I said. I turned and looked at Ev.

His mouth was hanging open.

"Hard to believe the Boohteri built it, isn't it?"

Ev nodded without closing his mouth.

"Carson and I have this theory that they didn't," I said. "We think some poor species of indidges who lived here before built it, and then Bult and his pals fined them out of it."

"It's beautiful," Ev, who hadn't heard me, said. "I had no idea it was so long."

"Six hundred kloms," I said. "And getting longer. An average of two new chambers a year, according to C.J.'s aerials, not counting repaired breaks."

Which meant our theory didn't wash at all, but neither did the idea of the indidges doing all the work.

"It's even more beautiful than the pop-ups," Ev said, and I was going to ask him what exactly they were, but I didn't think he'd hear that either.

I remembered the first time I'd seen the Wall. I'd only been on Boohte a week. We'd spent the whole time struggling up a draw in pouring rain and *I'd* spent the whole time wondering how I'd let Carson talk me into this, and we came out on top of a mesa a lot higher than what we were now, and Carson said, "There she is. All yours."

Which got us a pursuant on incorrect imperialistic attitudes and how "Pursuant to proprietorship, planets are *not* owned."

I looked over at Ev. "You're right. It is presentable-looking."

Bult finished writing up his fines, and we started out across it. He was still keeping close to the Tongue, and after half a klom he got out his binocs, looked through them at the water, and shook his head, and we plodded on.

It was already after noon, and I thought about getting lunch out of my pack, but the ponies were starting to drag and Ev was intent on the Wall, which was close to the Tongue here, so I waited.

The Wall disappeared behind a low step-mesa for a hundred meters and then curved down almost to the Tongue, and Carson's pony apparently decided he'd gone far enough and stopped, swaying.

"Uh-oh," I said.

"What is it?" Ev said, dragging his eyes away from the Wall.

"Rest stop. Remember how I told you they're not dangerous?" I said, watching Carson, who'd gotten down off his pony and was standing clear. "Well, that's if they don't fall over with your legs under 'em. Think you can get down off him faster than you got on?"

"Yes," Ev said, jumping down and away like he expected Speedy to explode.

I tightened the straps on the computer, dismounted, and stepped back. Up ahead, Carson's pony had stopped swaying, and Carson had gone back up to it and was trying to untie the food packs.

Ev and I walked up and watched him struggle with the line. The pony dumped a pile practically on Carson's foot and started swaying again.

"Tim-berr," I said, and Carson jumped back. The pony took a couple of tottering steps forward and fell over, its legs out stiff at its side.

The pack was half under it, and Carson started yanking it out from under the motionless carcass. Bult unfolded himself and stepped decorously off his pony holding his umbrella, and the rest of the ponies went over like dominoes.

Ev went over to Carson and stood looking down on him. "Don't make any sudden movements," he said.

Carson stomped past me. "What are *you* laughing at?" he said.

We had lunch and incurred a few fines, but I didn't get a chance to talk to Carson alone. Bult stuck like glue to us, talking into his log, and Ev kept asking questions about the Wall.

"So they make the chambers one at a time," he said, looking across at it. We were on the wrong side of the Wall here, so all you could see were the back walls of the chambers, looking like they'd been plastered and painted a whitish-pink. "How do they build them?"

"We don't know. Nobody's ever seen them doing it," Carson said. "Or seen them doing anything worthwhile," he added darkly, watching Bult tallying up, "like finding us a way across it so we can get on with this expedition."

He went over to Bult and started talking to him in an inappropriate manner.

"And what *are* they?" Ev asked. "Dwellings?"

"And storerooms for all the stuff Bult buys, and landfills. Some of them are decorated, with flowers hanging in the opening and nibbler bones laid out in a design in front of the door. Most of them stand empty."

Carson stomped back, his mustache quaking. "He says we can't cross here either."

"The other break's been repaired, too?" I said.

"No. Now he says there's something in the water. *Tssi mitss.*"

I looked over at the Tongue. It was flowing over quartzite sand here and was clear as glass. "What's that?"

"Your guess is as good as mine. It translates as 'not there.' I asked him how much farther we have to go, and all he'll say is 'sahhth.' "

Sahhth apparently meant halfway to the Ponypiles because he didn't even glance at the Tongue again once we had the ponies up and moving, and he didn't even bother to lead. He motioned Ev and me ahead, and went back to ride with Carson.

Not that we could get lost. We'd charted all this territory before, and all we had to do was keep close to the Tongue. The Wall dipped away from the water and off toward a line of mesas, and we went up a hill through a herd of luggage, grazing on dirt, and came out at another Scenic Point.

The thing about these long vistas is that you're not going to see anything else for a while, and we'd already catalogued the f-and-f along here. There weren't any, anyway—a lot of luggage, some tinder grass, an occasional roadkill. I ran geological contours and double-checked the topographicals, and then, since Ev was busy gawking at the scenery, ran the whereabouts.

Wulfmeier was on Starting Gate after all. He'd been picked up by Big Brother for removing ore samples. So he wasn't in Sector 248-76, and we could've spent another day at King's X, eating C.J.'s cooking and catching up on reports.

Speaking of which, I figured I might as well finish them up now. I asked for Bult's purchase orders.

He must've worked fast while we were at King's X. He'd spent all his fines and then some. I wondered if that was why we were heading south, because he'd *tchopped* himself into a hole.

I went through the list, weeding out weapons and artificial building materials and trying to figure out what he was going to do with three dozen dictionaries and a chandelier.

"What are you doing?" Ev said, leaning across to look at the log.

"Screening out contraband," I said. "Bult's not allowed to order anything with weapon potential, which in his case should have included umbrellas. It's hard to catch everything."

He leaned farther across. "You're marking them 'out of stock.' "

"Yeah. If we tell him he can't order them, he fines us for discrimination, and he hasn't figured out yet that he doesn't have to pay for out-of-stock items, which keeps him from ordering even more stuff."

He looked like he was going to keep asking questions, so I called up the topographical instead and said, "Tell me some more about these mating customs you're an expert on. Are there any species who give their girlfriends dictionaries?"

He grinned. "Not that I've run across so far. Gift-giving is a major part of a majority of species' courtship rituals, though, including *Homo sapiens.* Engagement rings, and the traditional candy and flowers."

"Mink coats. Condos. Islands in the Tobo Sea."

"There are several theories about its significance," Ev said. "Most zoologists think the bestowing of a gift proves the male's ability to obtain and defend territory. Some socioexozoologists believe gift-giving is a symbolic enactment of the sex act itself."

"Romantic," I said.

"One study found gift-giving triggered pheromones in the female, which in turn produced chemical changes in the male that led to the next phase of the courtship ritual. It's hardwired into the brain. Sexual instincts pretty much override rational thought."

Which is why females'll run off with the first male who smiles at them, I thought, and why C.J. had been acting like an idiot at the landing. Speaking of which, here she was calling on the transmitter. "Home Base to Findriddy. Come in, Fin."

"What is it?" I said, taking off my mike and moving it up so she could hear me.

"You got a reprimand," she said. " 'Pursuant to relations between members of the survey expedition and native planet dwellers. All members of the expedition will show respect for the ancient and noble cultures of indigenous sentients and will refrain from making terrocentric value judgments.' "

Which could have waited till we got back from the expedition. "What did you really call for, C.J.?" I asked. As if I didn't know.

"Is Evelyn there? Can I talk to him?"

"In a minute. Did you get a picture of that northwest section?"

There was a long pause before her answer came back. "I forgot."

"What do you mean, you forgot?"

"I had other things on my mind. The heli prop sounded funny."

"On hell it did. The only thing on your mind was jumping Ev."

"I don't know what you're so upset about," she said. "That whole area's charted, isn't it?"

"Here's Ev," I said. I patched her through and showed Ev the transmit button, and then looked back at Carson.

He'd want to know what I'd found out or hadn't found out, but he and Bult were too far back to shout at, and besides, I didn't want Bult figuring out why we'd picked the route we had.

If he hadn't already. We'd long since passed the second break in the Wall, and he didn't show any signs of crossing the Tongue.

"I'll try," Ev said earnestly into his mike. "I promise."

It's about time for a dust storm, I thought, looking at the sky. Carson usually likes to have one on the first day anyway, just in case something comes up where we need one, but he was deep in conversation with Bult, probably trying to talk him into crossing the Tongue.

"I miss you, too, C.J.," Ev said.

Nothing was stopping me from pointing the camera at a likely suspect and doing one myself, but there wasn't so much as a haze on the horizon. The Wall was only half a klom off along this stretch, and sometimes there are little kick-up breezes along it, but not today. The air was as still as a roadkill.

"Look!" Ev said, and I thought he was talking to C.J., but he said, "Fin, what's that?" and pointed at a shuttlewren that was flying toward us.

"Tssillirah," I said. "We call them shuttlewrens."

"Why?" he said, watching the little bird fly over my head and back toward the other two ponies.

I didn't waste breath answering. The shuttlewren circled Carson's head and started back for us, flapping its stubby pinkish wings like it was about to wear out. It made two trips around Ev's hat and started back for Carson again.

"Oh," Ev said, turning around to see it making the circuit again, flapping for dear life. "How long can it keep that up?"

"A long time. We had one follow us for fifty kloms like that one time up by Turquoise Lake. Carson figured up it flew almost seven hundred kloms."

Ev started asking for stuff on his log. "What does the Boohteri name for them mean?" he asked me.

"Wide mud," I said, "and don't ask what that's supposed to mean. Maybe they build their nests out of mud. But there's no mud around here."

Or dust, I thought. I went back to thinking about dust storms. If Bult and Carson had been up ahead of us, I'd've taken my foot out of the stirrup and dragged it in the dirt to stir up some dust, but the way it was, Bult would catch me, and Ev would stop talking about shuttlewrens and ask what I was doing.

I looked back at Carson and waved, thinking maybe that would signal him to do something, but he was so busy talking to Bult I couldn't get his attention. The shuttlewren, on its tenth lap, skimmed the top of his hat, but that didn't get his attention either.

"Oh, look!" Ev said.

I turned back around. He was half up in the saddle, pointing off toward the Wall. I couldn't see what at, which meant neither could the scans.

"Where?" I said.

"Over there," he said, pointing.

I finally saw what he was looking at—a couch potato lying down behind a roundleaf bush and looking like a ponypile with fur.

I didn't think the scan had enough res to pick it up, but I said, "I don't see anything," to stall while I set the camera on a narrow focus to the far left of it, just in case.

"Over *there,*" Ev said. "Is that—"

I cut him off before he could get more specific. "My shit!" I shouted. "Put the shield on. That's a . . ." and hit the disconnect.

"What is it?" Ev said, reaching for his knife. "Is it dangerous?"

"What?" I said, locking the disconnect in for twelve minutes.

"That!" Ev said, waving his hand in the direction of the couch potato. "That brown thing over there."

"Oh, *that,"* I said. "That's a couch potato. It's not dangerous. Herbivore. Lies down most of the time, except to eat. I didn't notice it lying there." I set my watch alarm for ten minutes.

"Then what were you looking at?" he said, staring worriedly at the horizon.

"The weather," I said. "We get dust tantrums close to the Wall, and they play hob with the transmitter." I punched the transmitter's send three or four times and then held it down. "C.J., you there? Calling Home Base. Come in, Home Base." I shook my head. "It's out. I was afraid of that."

"I didn't see any dust," Ev said.

"They're only a meter or so wide," I said, "and nearly invisible unless they're in your line of sight." I hit a few more keys at random. "I better go tell Carson."

I yanked hard on the pony's reins and prodded it in the sides. "Carson," I called. "We got a problem."

Carson was still deep in conversation with Bult. I gave the pony another prod, and it gave me an evil look and started backing. At this rate, the dust storm'd be over before I even made it back there. I should've made it twenty minutes. "C.J., you there?" I said into the transmitter, just to make sure it was off, and got down off the pony.

"Hey, Carson," I yelled, "the transmitter's down." I walked back to his pony. "Wind's picking up," I said. "Looks like we're in for a dust tantrum."

"When?" he said, with a glance at Bult, who was busy digging for his log to fine me for being off Useless.

"Now," I said.

"How long do you think it'll last?"

"Awhile," I said, looking speculatively at the sky. "Twelve minutes, maybe twelve and a half."

"Rest stop," Carson called, and Bult leapt off his pony and stalked over to look at my footprints.

Carson walked off in the direction of the couch potato. I looked back at Ev. He was standing with his head up and his mouth open, watching the shuttlewren. I caught up with Carson, and we squatted so we wouldn't attract the attention of the shuttlewren.

"What's wrong?" he said.

"Nothing," I said. "I just thought we should have one dust storm before we crossed into uncharted territory."

"You could have waited, then," Carson said. "We're not crossing anytime soon."

"Why not? Is this break fixed, too?"

He shook his head. *"Tssi mitsse,* which means big *tssi mitss,* which I figure translates as he's going to see to it we don't get anywhere near Sector 248-76. What did you find out from C.J.? Did the aerial show anything?"

"She didn't get it. She was too busy batting her eyes at Ev and forgot."

"Forgot?!" he said. He stood up. "I told you he was going to louse up this expedition. I suppose you were too busy pointing out the sights to run whereabouts either."

I stood up and faced him. "What on hell's that supposed to mean?"

"It means you two've been so busy talking I figured you'd forgotten all about a little detail like what's going on in 248-76. What on hell's interesting enough to talk about all day long anyway?"

"Mating customs," I said.

"Mating customs," he said disgustedly. "That's why you didn't run whereabouts?"

"I did run them. Whatever's in that sector, it's not Wulfmeier. He's on Starting Gate, and he's under arrest. I got a verify."

Carson stared south at the Ponypiles. "Then what on hell's Bult up to?"

The shuttlewren changed course in midflap and started toward us. "I don't know," I said, taking off my hat and waving with it to keep it away. "Maybe the indidges have got a gold mine up there. Maybe they're secretly building Las Vegas with all the stuff Bult's ordered." The wren circled my head and made a pass at Carson. "Maybe Bult's just trying to run up our fines by taking us the long way around. Did he say how much farther we'd have to go before we could cross the Tongue?"

"Sahhth," Carson said, mimicking Bult holding his umbrella and pointing. "If we go much farther south, we'll be in the Ponypiles. Maybe he's going to lead us into the mountains and drown us in a flash flood."

"And then fine us for being foreign bodies in a waterway." My watch beeped. "Looks like it's starting to clear up," I said. I picked up a handful of dirt, and we started back for the ponies.

Bult met us halfway. "Taking of souvenirs," he said, pointing sternly at the dirt in my hand. "Disturbances of land surface. Destruction of indigenous flora."

"Better transmit all those right away," I said, "before you forget."

I went over to Ev's and my ponies, the shuttlewren tailing me. While

Ev was watching it circle his head, I blew dirt off my hand onto the camera lens and then swung up and looked at my watch. A minute to go.

I messed with the transmitter a little and called to Carson, "I think I've got it fixed. Come on, Ev."

I messed some more for Ev's benefit, taking off a chip and snapping it back into place, but I didn't need to have bothered. He was still gawking at the shuttlewren.

"Is that shuttlewren a male?" he asked.

"Beats me. You're the expert on sex." I released the disconnect, counted to three, hit it again, and counted to five. "Calling Ki—" I said, and kicked it on again. "—ng's X, come in C.J."

"C.J. here," she said. "Where on hell did you go?"

"Nothing serious, C.J. Just a dust tantrum. We're too close to the Wall," I said. "Is the camera back on?"

"Yes. I don't see any dust."

"We just caught the edge of it. It lasted about a minute. I've been spending the rest of the time trying to get the transmitter up and running."

"It's funny," she said slowly, "how a minute's worth of dust could do so much damage."

"It's one of the chips. You know how sensitive they are."

"If they're so sensitive, how come all that dust from the rover didn't jam them?"

"The rover?" I said, looking around blankly like one might drive up.

"When Evelyn drove out to meet you yesterday. How come the transmitter didn't cut out then?"

Because I'd been too busy worrying about Wulfmeier and wrestling the binocs away from Bult to even think of it, I thought. I'd stood there coughing and choking in the rover's dust and it hadn't even crossed my mind. My shit, that was all we needed, for C.J. to catch on to our dust storms. "No accounting for technology," I said, knowing she was never going to buy it. "Transmitter's got a mind of its own."

Carson came up. "You talking to C.J.? Ask her if she's got an aerial of the Wall along here. I want to know where the breaks are."

"Sure," I said, and hit disconnect again. "We got a problem. C.J.'s asking questions about the dust storm. She wants to know why the transmitter didn't go out with all that dust from the rover."

"The rover?" he said, and I could see it dawn on him like it had on me. "What did you tell her?"

"That the transmitter's temperamental."

"She'll never buy that," he said, glaring at Ev, who was watching the shuttlewren start another lap. "I told you he'd cause trouble."

"It's not Ev's fault. We're the ones who didn't have sense enough to recognize a dust storm when we saw it. I'm going back on. What do I tell her?"

"That it's dust getting in the chip that does it," he said, stomping back to his pony, "not just dust in the air."

Which maybe would have worked, except two expeditions ago I'd told her it was dust in the air that did it.

"Come on, Ev," I said. He came over and got on his pony, still watching the shuttlewren. I took my finger off the disconnect. "—ase, come in, Home Base."

"Another dust storm?" C.J. said sarcastically.

"There must still be some dust in the chip," I said. "It keeps cutting out."

"How come the sound cuts out at the same time?" she said.

Because we're still wearing our mikes too high, I thought.

"It's funny," she went on. "While you were out, I took a look at the meteorologicals Carson ran before you left. They don't show any wind for that sector."

"No accounting for the weather either, especially this close to the Wall," I said. "Ev's right here. You want to talk to him?"

I patched him in before she could answer, thinking sex wasn't always such a bad thing on an expedition. It would take her mind off the dust anyway.

Bult and Carson rode in a wide circle around us to get in the lead again, and we followed, Ev still talking to C.J., which mostly consisted of listening and saying "yes" every once in a while, and "I promise." The shuttlewren followed us, too, making the circuit back and forth like a sheep dog.

"What kind of nests do the shuttlewrens have?" Ev asked.

"We've never seen them," I said. "What did C.J. have to say?"

"Not much. Their nests are probably in this area," he said, looking across the Tongue. The Wall was almost up next to the bank, and there were a few scourbrush in the narrow space between, but nothing that looked big enough to hide a nest. "The behavior they're exhibiting is either protective, in which case it's a female, or territorial, in which case it's a male. You say they've followed you for long distances. Have you ever been followed by more than one at a time?"

"No," I said. "Sometimes one'll fall away and another one'll take over, like they're working in shifts."

"That sounds like territorial behavior," he said, watching the shuttlewren make the turn past Bult. It was flying so low it brushed Bult's umbrella, and he looked up and then hunched over his fines again. "I don't suppose there's any way to get a specimen?"

"Not unless it has a coronary," I said, ducking as it skimmed my hat. "We've got holos. You can ask the memory."

He did, and spent the next ten minutes poring over them while I worried about C.J. We'd talked her into believing the transmitter could be taken out by a gust of dust that wouldn't even show on the log, and then I'd stood there yesterday and let the transmitter get totally smothered with it and hadn't even had the sense to disconnect.

And now that she was suspicious, she wouldn't let it go. She was probably checking all the logs for dust storms right now and comparing them to the meteorologicals.

Bult and Carson were looking in the water again. Bult shook his head.

"The staking out of territory is a courtship ritual," Ev said.

"Like gangs," I said.

"The male butterfish sweeps an area of ocean bottom clear of pebbles and shells for the female and then circles it constantly."

I looked at the shuttlewren, which was rounding Bult's umbrella again. Bult put down his log and collapsed the umbrella.

"The Mirgasazi on Yoan stake out a block of airspace. They're an interesting species. Some of the females have bright feathers, but they're not the ones the males are interested in."

The shuttlewren flapped past us and up to Bult and Carson again. It rounded the bend, and Bult shot his umbrella open. The shuttlewren fell in midflap, and Bult stabbed it with the tip of the umbrella a couple of times.

"I knew I should have put umbrellas on the weapons list," I said.

"Can I have it?" Ev said. "To see if it's a male?"

Bult unfolded his arm, picked up the shuttlewren, and rode on, plucking the feathers off it. When he had half of them off, he stuck the shuttlewren in his mouth and bit it in half. He offered Carson half. Carson shook his head, and Bult crammed the whole thing in.

"Guess not," I said. I leaned down and got a feather and handed it to him.

He was watching Bult chew. "Shouldn't there be a fine for that?" he said.

" 'All members of the expedition shall refrain from making value judgments regarding the indigenous sentients' ancient and noble culture,' " I said.

I picked up the pieces Bult spit out, which didn't amount to much, and gave 'em to Ev. And looked off at the horizon.

The Wall curved back away from the Tongue and out across the plain in a straight line. Beyond it there was a scattering of scourbrush and trees. There wasn't any wind, the leaves were hanging limp. What we needed was a good dust storm to throw C.J. off, but there wasn't so much as a breeze.

It wasn't C.J.'s figuring the dust storms out that worried me. She'd try to blackmail us into naming something after her, but she'd been doing that for years. But I didn't want her talking about it over the transmitter for Big Brother to hear. If they started looking at the log, they'd be able to see for themselves. There was no way there'd been a dust tantrum in this weather. There wasn't even any air. The feathers Bult was spitting out up ahead fell straight down.

Half a klom later we ran into a dust tantrum that was more like a full-blown rage. It got in the transmitter (but not before we'd gotten a full five minutes of it on the log), and up our noses and down our throats, and made it so dark we had to navigate by following the lights on Bult's umbrella.

By the time we got clear of it, it was getting dark for real, and Bult started looking for a good place to camp, which meant someplace knee-deep in flora so he could get the maximum in fines out of us. Carson wanted to get across the Tongue first, but Bult peered solemnly into the water and pronounced *tssi mitsse,* and while Carson was yelling, "Where? I don't see a damn thing!" the ponies started to sway, so we camped where we were.

We set up camp in a hurry, first because we didn't want to have to unload the ponies after they were down, and then because we didn't want to be stumbling around in the dark, but all three of Boohte's moons were up before we got the transmitter unloaded.

Carson went off to tie the ponies up downwind, and Ev helped me spread out the bedrolls.

"Are we in uncharted territory?" he asked.

"Nope," I said, shaking the dust out of my bedroll. "Unless you count what's on us." I spread the bedroll out, making sure it wasn't on any flora. "Speaking of which, I'd better go call C.J. and tell her where we are." I handed Carson's bedroll to him and started over to the transmitter.

"Wait," he said.

I stopped and turned back to look at him.

"When I talked to C.J., she wanted to know why the dust tantrum hadn't shown up on the log."

"And what did you tell her?"

"I said it came in at an angle and blindsided us. I said it blew up so fast I didn't even see it till you shouted, and by that time we were in the middle of it."

I *told* Carson he was smarter than he looked, I thought.

"How come you did that?" I said. "C.J.'d probably give you a free jump for telling her we blew up that storm ourselves."

"Are you kidding?" he said, looking so surprised I was sorry I'd said it. Of course he wouldn't betray us. We were Findriddy and Carson, the famous explorers who could do no wrong, even if he'd just caught us red-handed.

"Well, thanks," I said and wondered exactly how smart he was and what explanation I could get away with. "Carson and I had things we needed to discuss, and we didn't want Big Brother listening."

"It's a gatecrasher, isn't it? That's why the expedition left in such a hurry and why you keep running whereabouts when there isn't supposed to be anybody but us on the planet. You think somebody's illegally opened a gate. Is that why Bult's leading us south, to try to keep us from catching him?"

"I don't know what Bult's doing," I said. "He could have kept us away from a gatecrasher by crossing where we were this morning and leading us up along the Wall past Silvershim Creek. He didn't have to drag us clear down here. Besides," I said, looking at Bult, who was down by the Tongue with Carson and the ponies, "he doesn't like Wulfmeier. Why would he try to protect him?"

"Wulfmeier?" Ev said, sounding excited. "Is that who it is?"

"You know Wulfmeier?"

"Of course. From the pop-ups," he said.

Well, I should have known.

"What do you think he's doing?" Ev said. "Trading with the indigenous sentients? Mining?"

"I don't think he's doing anything. I got a verify this morning that he's on Starting Gate."

"Oh," he said, disappointed. In the pop-ups we must have gone after gatecrashers with lasers blasting. "But you want to go there just to make sure?"

"If Bult ever lets us cross the Tongue," I said.

Carson came stomping up. "I ask Bult if it's safe to water the ponies, and he pretends to look in the water and says, *'tssi mitss* nah,' so I say, 'Well, fine, since there aren't any *tssi mitss,* we can cross first thing in the morning,' and he hands me a pair of dice and says, 'Sahthh. Brik lilla fahr.' " He squatted down and rummaged in his pack. "My shit, 'lilla fahr' is practically in the Ponypiles." He glared at the mountains. "What on hell is he up to? And don't give me that stuff about fines." He pulled out the water analysis kit and straightened up. "He's got enough already to buy himself a different planet. Fin, did you get that aerial of the Wall from C.J. yet?"

"I was just calling her," I said. He stomped off, and I went over to the transmitter.

"What can I do?" Ev said, tagging after me like a shuttlewren. "Should I gather some wood for a fire?"

I looked at him.

"Don't tell me," he said, catching my expression. "There's a fine for gathering wood."

"And starting a fire with advanced technology, and burning indigenous flora," I said. "We usually try to wait till Bult gets cold and builds one."

Bult didn't show any signs of getting cold, even though the wind over the Ponypiles that had sent that dust tantrum into us had a chill to it, and after supper he gave Carson some more dice and then went off and sat under his umbrella out by the ponies.

"What on hell's he doing now?" Carson said.

"He probably went to get the battery-powered heater he bought last expedition," I said, rubbing my hands together. "Tell us some more about mating customs, Ev. Maybe a little sex'll warm us up."

"Speaking of which, Evie, have you figured out which brand Bult is yet?" Carson said.

As near as I could tell, Ev hadn't so much as looked at Bult since we started, except when Bult was snacking on the shuttlewren, but he spoke right up.

"Malc," he said.

"How do you figure that?" Carson said, and I was wondering, too. If it was table manners he was going by, that wasn't any sign. Every indidge I'd seen ate like that, and most of them didn't bother about taking the feathers off first.

"His acquisitive behavior," Ev said. "Collecting and hoarding property is a typical male courtship behavior."

"I thought collecting stuff was a female behavior," I said. "What about all those diamonds and monograms?"

"Gifts the male gives to the female are symbols of the male's ability to amass and defend wealth or territory," Ev said. "By collecting fines and purchasing manufactured goods, Bult is demonstrating his ability to gain access to the resources necessary for survival."

"Shower curtains?" I said.

"Utility isn't the issue. The male burin fish collects large quantities of black rock clams, which are of no practical value, since the burin fish only eats flora, and piles them into towers as part of the courtship ritual."

"And that impresses the female?" I said.

"Ability to amass wealth is indicative of the genetic superiority of the male, and therefore the increased chance of survival for her offspring. Of course she's impressed. There are other qualities that impress her, too. Size, strength, the ability to defend territory, like that shuttlewren we saw this afternoon—"

Which the female shuttlewrens probably hadn't been very impressed with, I thought.

"—virility, youth—"

Carson said, "You mean we're here freezing our hind ends off because Bult's trying to impress some *female?"* He stood up. "I told you sex can louse up an expedition faster than anything else." He grabbed up the lantern. "I'm not gonna end up with frostbite just because Bult wants to show his genes to some damn female."

He went stomping off into the dark, and I watched the bobbing lantern, wondering what had gotten into him all of a sudden and why Bult wasn't following him with his log if what Ev said was true. Bult was still sitting out by the ponies—I could see the lights on his umbrella.

"The indigenous sentients on Prii built bonfires as part of their courtship ritual," Ev said, rubbing his hands together to warm them. "They're extinct. They burned down every forest on Prii in less than five hundred years time." He tipped his head back and looked at the sky. "I still can't believe how beautiful everything is."

It was presentable-looking. There were a bunch of stars, and the three moons were jostling for position in the middle of the sky. But my teeth were chattering, and there was a strong whiff of ponypile from downwind.

"What are the names of the moons?" he said.

"Larry, Curly, and Moe," I said.

"No, really. What are the Boohteri names?"

"They don't have names for them. Don't get any idea of naming one after C.J., though. They're Satellite One, Two, and Three until Big Brother surveys them, which it won't anytime soon since the 'Boohteri won't agree to satellite surveys."

"C.J.?" he said, like he'd forgotten who she was. "They don't look anything like they did on the pop-ups. Nothing on Boohte has, except you. You look exactly like I thought you would."

"These pop-ups you're always talking about? What are they? Holo books?"

"DHVs." He got up, went over to his bedroll, and squatted down to get something out from under it. He came back, holding a flat square the size of a playing card, and sat down beside me.

"See?" he said and opened the flat card up like a book. "Episode Six," he said.

Pop-ups was a good name for them. The picture seemed to jump out of the middle of the card and into the space between us, like the map back at King's X, only this was full-size and the people were moving and talking.

There was a presentable-looking female standing next to a horse made up to be a pony and a squatty pink thing like a cross between an accordion and a fireplug. They were having an argument.

"He's been gone too long," the female said. She had on tight pants and a low-slung shirt, and her hair was long and shiny. "I'm going to go find him."

"It's been nearly twenty hours," the accordion said. "We must report in to Home Base."

"I'm not leaving here without him," the female said, and swung up on the horse and galloped away.

"Wait!" the accordion shouted. "You can't! It's too dangerous!"

"Who's that supposed to be?" I said, sticking my finger into the accordion.

"Stop," Ev said, and the scene froze. "That's Bult."

"Where's his log?" I said.

"I told you things were different from what I'd expected," he said, sounding embarrassed. "Go back."

There was a flicker, and we were back at the beginning of the scene.

"He's been gone too long!" Tight Pants said.

"If that's Bult, then who's that supposed to be?" I said.

"You," he said, sounding surprised.

"Where's Carson?" I said.

"In the next scene."

There was another flicker, and we were at the foot of a cliff, with big, fake-looking boulders all around. Carson was sitting at the bottom of the cliff, sprawled out against one of the boulders with a big gash in the side of his head and a fancy mustache that curled at the ends. Carson's mustache had never looked that good, not even the first time I saw him, and they had the nibblers all wrong, too—they looked like guinea pigs with false teeth—but what they were doing to Carson's foot was pretty realistic. I hoped they got to the part where I found him pretty soon.

"Next scene," I said, and it flickered to me coming straight down the cliff in those tight pants, blasting at the nibblers with a laser.

Which wasn't the way it happened at all. Unless I'd wanted to go down the same way Carson did, there was no way off the cliff. The nibblers had run off when I yelled, but I'd had to go back along the cliff till I came to a chimney and work my way down and back around, and it took three hours. The nibblers had run off again when they heard me coming, but they hadn't been gone long.

Tight Pants jumped the last ten feet and knelt down beside Carson, and started tearing strips she couldn't afford to lose off her shirt and tying them around Carson's foot, which only looked a little bloody around the toes, sobbing her eyes out.

"I didn't cry," I said. "You got any others?"

"Episode Eleven," Ev said, and the cliff flicked into a silvershim grove. Tight Pants and Fancy Mustache were surveying the grove with an old-fashioned transit and sextant, and the accordion was writing down the measurements.

It looked like somebody'd cut up pieces of aluminum foil and hung them on a dead branch, and Carson was wearing a blue fuzzy vest that I had a feeling was supposed to be luggage fur.

"Findriddy!" the accordion said, looking up sharply. "I hear someone coming!"

"What are you two doing?" Carson said and walked right into a silvershim. He looked around, his arms full of sticks. "What on *hell* is this?"

"You and me," I said.

"A pop-up," Ev said.

"Turn it off!" Carson said, and the other Carson and Tight Pants and the silvershims compressed into a black nothing. "What on hell's the matter with you, bringing advanced technology on an expedition? Fin, you were supposed to see to it he followed the regs!" He dumped the sticks with a clatter onto where the accordion'd been standing. "Do you know how big a fine Bult could slap us with for that?"

"I . . . I didn't know . . ." Ev was stammering, stooping down to pick up the pop-up before Carson stepped on it. "It never occurred to me . . ."

"It's no more advanced than Bult's binocs," I said, "or half the stuff he's ordered. And even if it was, he doesn't know anything about it. He's over there tallying up his fines." I pointed off toward the lights of his umbrella.

"How do you know he doesn't know? You can see it for kloms!"

"And you can hear you twice as far!" I said. "The only way he's going to find out about it is if he comes over to see what all the hollering's about!"

Carson snatched the pop-up away from Ev. "What else did you bring?" he shouted, but softer. "A nuclear reactor? A gate?"

"Just another disk," Ev said. "For the pop-up." He pulled a black coin out of his pocket and handed it to Carson.

"What on hell's this?" he said, turning it over.

"It's us," I said. "Findriddy and Carson, Planetary Explorers, and Our Faithful Scout, Bult. Thirteen episodes."

"Eighty," Ev said. "There are forty on each disk, but I only brought my favorites."

"You gotta see 'em, Carson," I said. "Especially your mustache. Ev, is there some way you can tone down the production so we can watch without letting the rest of the neighborhood in on it?"

"Yeah," Ev said. "You just—"

"Nobody's watching anything till we get a fire built and I make sure Bult's out there under that umbrella," he said, and stomped off for about the fourth time.

I got the sticks made into a passable fire by the time he got back, looking mad, which meant Bult *was* there.

"All right," he said, handing the pop-up back to Ev. "Let's see these famous explorers. But keep it down."

"Episode Two," Ev said, laying it on the ground in front of us. "Reduce fifty percent and cloak," and the scene came up, smaller and in a little box this time. Fancy Mustache and Tight Pants were clambering over a break in the Wall. Carson was wearing his blue fuzzy vest.

"You're the one with the fancy mustache," I said, pointing.

"Do you have any idea what kind of fine we'd get for killing a suitcase?" he said. He pointed at Tight Pants. "Who's the female?"

"That's Fin," Ev said.

"Fin?!" Carson said, and let out a whoop. "Fin?! Can't be. Look at her. She's way too clean. And she looks too much like a female. Half the time with Fin you can't even tell!" He whooped again and slapped his leg. "And look at that chest. You sure that's not C.J.?"

I reached out and slapped the pop-up shut.

"What'd you do that for?" Carson said, holding his middle.

"Time to turn in," I said. I turned to Ev. "I'm gonna keep this in my boot tonight so Bult can't get hold of it," I said and went over to my bedroll.

Bult was standing next to Carson's bedroll. I glanced out toward the Tongue. The umbrella was still there, burning brightly.

Bult picked up my bedroll to look under it. "Damage to flora," he said, pointing at the dirt underneath.

"Oh, shut up," I said and crawled in.

"Inappropriate tone and manner," he said, and went back out toward his umbrella.

Carson laughed himself sick for another hour, and I lay there after that an hour or so waiting for them to go to sleep and watching the moons jostling for positions in the sky. Then I got the pop-up out of my boot and opened it on the ground beside me.

"Episode Eight. Reduce eighty percent and cloak," I whispered and lay there and watched Carson and me sitting on horses in a pouring rain and tried to figure out which expedition this was supposed to be. There was a blue buffalo standing up the hill from where we were, and the accordion was pointing at it. "It is called *soolkases* in the Boohteri tongue," he said, and I knew which one this was, only that wasn't the way it happened.

It had taken us four hours to figure out what Bult was saying. *"Tssilkrothes?"* I remembered Carson shouting.

"Tssuhhtkhahckes!" Bult had shouted back.

"Suitcases?!" Carson said, so mad his mustache looked like it'd shake off. "We can't name them suitcases!" and right then a couple thousand suitcases had come roaring up over the hill at us. My pony stood there like an idiot and nearly got both of us trampled.

In the pop-up version my pony ran off, and I was the one who stood there looking dumb till Carson galloped up and swung me up behind him. I was wearing high-heeled boots and pants so tight it was no wonder I couldn't run, and Carson was right, she was way too clean, but he hadn't had to fall in the fire laughing about it.

Carson swung me up, and we rode off, my tight pants hugging the horse and my hair streaming out behind me.

"Nothing here's what I expected," Ev had said back at King's X, "except you." Tonight he'd said, "You looked exactly the way I pictured you." Which, I thought, trying to figure out how to make the pop-up run it again, was pretty damn good.

expedition 184: day 2

By noon the next day we were still on this side of the Tongue and still heading south, and Carson was in such a foul mood I steered clear of him.

"Is he always this irritable?" Ev asked me.

"Only when he's worried," I said.

Speaking of which, I was getting a little worried myself.

Carson's water analysis hadn't showed up anything but the usual f-and-f, but Bult had insisted there were *tssi mitss* and led us south to a tributary. There were *tssi mitss* in the tributary, too, and he led us east along it till we came to one of its tributaries. This onc didn't have any *tssi mitss,* but it zigzagged down through a draw too steep for the ponies, so Bult led us north along it, looking for a placc to cross. At this rate we'd be back at King's X by suppertimc.

But that wasn't what was worrying me. What was worrying me was Bult. He hadn't fined us for anything all morning, not even when we broke camp, and he kept looking off to the south through his binocs. Not only that, but Carson's binocs had turned up. He found them in his bedroll after breakfast.

"Fin!" he'd shouted, dangling them by the strap. "I knew you had 'em. Where'd you find 'em, in your pack?"

"I haven't seen 'em since the morning we left for King's X when you borrowed 'em," I said. "Bult must've had 'em."

"Bult? Why would he've taken 'em?" he said and gestured at Bult, who was peering through his own binocs at the Ponypiles.

I didn't know, which was what was worrying me. The indidges don't steal, at least that's what Big Brother tells us in the pursuants, and in all the expeditions we'd gone on, Bult hadn't ever taken anything away from us but our hard-earned wages. I wondered what else he might start doing—like take us deep into uncharted territory and then steal our packs and the ponies. Or lead us into an ambush.

I wanted to talk about it with Carson, but I couldn't get close to him, and I didn't want to risk another dust storm. I tried riding up alongside him, but Bult kept his pony dead even with Carson's and glared at me when I tried to move up.

Ev stuck almost as close to me, asking questions about the shuttlewren and telling me about appetizing mating customs, like the male hanging fly, which spins a big balloon of spit and slobber for the female to mess with while he jumps her.

We finally found a place to cross the creek as it zagged sideways across a momentarily flat space, and headed southwest through a series of low hills, and I did a triangulation and then started running terrains.

"Well, we're in uncharted territory now," I told Ev. "You can start looking around for stuff to name after C.J. so you can get your jump."

"If I wanted a jump, I could get it without that," he said, and I thought, I bet you could.

"I know how C.J. feels, though," he said, looking out across the plain. "Wanting to leave some mark. You go through that gate, and you realize how big a planet is, and how insignificant you are. You could be here your whole life and never even leave a footprint."

"Try telling that to Bult," I said.

He grinned. "Okay, maybe footprints. But nothing lasting. That's why I wanted to come on this expedition. I wanted to do something that would make me famous, like you and Carson. I wanted to discover something that would get me on the pop-ups."

"Speaking of which," I said, leaning down to pick up a rock, "how did we get on them?" I stuck the rock in my pack. "How'd they find out about the suitcases? And Carson's foot?"

"I don't know," Ev said slowly, as if the question hadn't ever occurred to him. "Your logs, I guess."

It hadn't been in the logs about my finding Carson right when the twenty-four hours were up, though. We'd told some of the stories to loaners, and one of the female ones had kept a diary. But Carson wouldn't have told her about my crying over him.

The hills through here were covered with scraggly plants. I took a holo of them and then halted Useless, which didn't take much, and dismounted.

"What are you doing?" Ev asked.

"Collecting pieces of the planet for you to leave C.J.'s mark on," I said, digging around the roots of a couple of the plants and sticking them in a plastic bag. I picked up two more rocks and handed them to him. "Either of these look like a C.J. to you?"

I got back on, watching Bult. He hadn't even noticed I was off my pony, let alone reached for his log. He was peering through his binocs at the hills beyond the tributary.

"Don't you ever wish you could have something named after you, Fin?" Ev was asking.

"Me? Why on hell would I want that? Who the hell remembers who Bryce Canyon or Harper's Ferry are named after even when they've got their names on them? Besides, you can't name a thing just by putting it on a topographical map. That's not the way it works." I gestured at the Ponypiles. "When people get here, they won't call those the Findriddy Mountains. They'll call 'em the Ponypiles. People name things after what they look like, or what happened there, or what the indidge name sounds like, not according to regs."

"People?" Ev said. "You mean gatecrashers?"

"Gatecrashers," I said, "and miners and settlers and shopping mall owners."

"But what about the regs?" Ev said, looking shocked. "They're supposed to protect the natural ecology and the sovereignty of the indigenous culture."

I nodded my head at Bult. "And you think the indigenous culture wouldn't sell them the whole place for some pop-ups and a couple of dozen shower curtains? You think Big Brother's paying us to survey all this for his health? You think as soon as we find something they want, they won't be down here, regs or no regs?"

Ev looked unhappy. "Like tourists," he said. "Everybody's seen the silvershims and the Wall on the pop-ups, and they all want to come see them."

"And take holos of themselves being fined," I said, even though I hadn't really thought of Boohte as a tourist attraction. "And Bult can sell them dried ponypiles for souvenirs."

"I'm glad I came before the rush," he said, looking at the water ahead. The hills parted on either side of the tributary, and it wouldn't matter whether there were *tssi mitss* or not. A wide sandbar stretched almost the full width of the water.

The ponies picked their way across it like it was quicksand, and Ev just about fell off, trying to lean down to look at it. "The female willowback needs to lay her eggs in still water, so the courtship ritual involves the male doing a swimming dance that dams up sand across the stream."

"And that's what this is?" I said.

"I don't think so. It looks like it's just a sandbar." He sat up in the saddlebone. "The female shale-dwelling lizard scratches a design in the dirt, and then the male scratches the same design on the shale."

I wasn't paying any attention. Bult was peering through the binocs at the hills between us and the Tongue, and Carson's pony was starting to sway. "Here's your big chance, Ev," I said. "Rest stop!"

After Carson and I did the topographicals and we had lunch, I hauled out my rocks and plastic bags and Carson emptied his bug-catcher, and we settled down to naming.

Carson started with the bugs. "Do you have a name for it?" he asked Bult, holding it away from Bult so he couldn't stuff it in his mouth, but Bult didn't even look interested.

He looked at Carson for a minute like he was thinking of something else, and then said what sounded to me like steam hissing and then metal being dragged over granite.

"Tssimrrah?" Carson said.

"Thssahggih," Bult said.

"This'll take a while," I said to Ev.

Figuring out the indidge name for a thing isn't so much about understanding what Bult says as trying to keep it from all sounding the same. f-and-f all sounds like steam escaping in a blizzard, lakes and rivers sound like a gate opening, and rocks all begin with a belching "B," which makes you wonder about the indidges' opinion of Bult. All of them sound more or less the same, and none of them sound like English letters, which is a good thing, or everything would have the same name.

"Thssahggah?" Carson said.

"Shhoomrrrah," Bult said.

I glanced at Ev, who was looking at the rocks and the bagged plants. It was fairly slim pickings—the only rock that didn't look like mud warmed over was horneblende, and the only flower had five ragged-looking petals, but I didn't think Ev would try what the loaners usually did, anyway, which was try to name the first flower we found a chrysanthemum, no matter what it looked like. Chrysa, for short.

Carson and Bult finally agreed on *tssahggah* for the bug, and I took holos of it and of the piece of horneblende and transmitted them and their names.

Bult had the flower, and was shaking his head.

"The indidges don't have a name for it," Carson said, looking at Ev. "How about it, Evie? What do you want to call it?"

Ev looked at it. "I don't know. What kind of things can you name them after?"

Carson looked irritated. It was obvious he'd expected "chrysanthemum." "No proper names, no technological references, no Earth landmarks with 'new' in front of them, no value judgments."

"What's left?" Ev said.

"Adjectives," I said, "shapes, colors—except for Green—natural references."

Ev was still examining the plant. "It was growing out by the sandbar. How about sandpink?"

Carson looked like he was trying to figure out if there was any way to make sandpink into Crissa. "A pink's an Earth genus, isn't it, Fin?" he growled at me.

"Yeah," I said. "It'll have to be sandblossom. Next?"

Bult had names for the rocks, which took forever, and even he started to look impatient, picking his binocs up and then putting them down without looking through them, and nodding at whatever Carson said.

"Biln," Carson said, and I entered it. "Is that everything?"

"We need to name the tributary," I said, pointing at it. "Bult, do the Boohteri have a name for this river?"

He already had his pony up and was climbing on it. I had to ask him again.

He shook his head and got down off the pony and picked up his binocs.

Carson came up beside me. "There's something wrong," I said.

"I know," he said, frowning. "He's been jittery all morning."

Bult was looking through his binocs. He took them down from his eyes and then held them up to his ear.

"Let's go," I said, and went to gather up the specimens. "Wagons ho, Ev!"

"What about the tributary?" Ev said.

"Sandbar Creek," I said. "Come on."

Bult was already going. Carson and I grabbed up the specimens and Carson's binocs, but Bult was already up the bank and heading west between the hills.

"What about the other one?" Ev said.

"Other what?" I said, jamming the specimens in my pack. I slung Carson's binocs around the pommelbone.

"The other tributary. Do the Boohteri have a name for it?"

"I doubt it," I said, swinging up onto Useless. Carson was having trouble with his pony. If we waited for him, we were going to lose Bult. "Come on," I said to Ev and started after Bult.

"Accordion Creek," Ev said.

"What?" I said, trying to decide which way Bult had gone. I caught a flash of light from his binocs off to the left and urged the pony that way.

"As a name for the other tributary," Ev said. "Accordion Creek, because of the way it folds back and forth."

"No technological references," I said, looking back at Carson. His pony had stopped and was unloading a pile.

"Oh, right," Ev said. "Then how about Zigzag Creek?"

I caught sight of Bult again. He was on top of the next rise, off his pony, looking through his binocs.

"We've already got a Zigzag Creek," I said, waving to Carson to come ahead. "Up north in Sector 250-81."

"Oh," he said, sounding disappointed. "What else means back and forth? Crooked? Tortuous?"

We caught up to Bult, and I unhooked Carson's binocs from the pommelbone and put them up to my eyes, but I couldn't see anything through them but hills and sandblossoms. I upped the resolution.

"Ladder," Ev was muttering beside me. "No, that's technological . . . crisscross . . . how about Crisscross Creek?"

Well, it was a good try. It wasn't "chrysanthemum," and he'd waited till Carson wasn't there and I was worrying about something else. He was definitely smarter than he looked. But not smart enough.

"Nice try," I said, still scanning the hills with the binocs. "How about Sneaky Creek?" I said as Carson caught up to us. "For the way it tries to slip past you when you're not looking?"

Either Bult had seen what he was looking for through his binocs, or he'd given up. He didn't try to ride ahead for the rest of the afternoon, and after our second rest stop, he put his binocs in his pack and got out his umbrella again. When I asked him the name of a bush during the rest stop, he wouldn't answer me.

Ev wasn't talking either, which was fine because I had a lot to think about. Bult might have calmed down, but he still wasn't levying fines, even though the rest stop had been on a hillside covered with sandblossoms, and two or three times I caught him glaring at me from under his umbrella. When his pony wouldn't get up, he kicked it.

I wondered if irritability was a sign of mating behavior, too, or if he was just nervous. Maybe he wasn't just trying to impress some female. Maybe he was taking us home to meet her.

I called C.J. "I need a whereabout on the indidges," I told her.

"And I need a whereabout on you. What are you doing down in 249-68?"

"Trying to cross the Tongue," I said. "Are there any indidges in our sector?"

"Not a one. They're all up by the Wall in 248-85."

Well, at least they weren't in 248-76.

"Any unusual movements?"

"No. Let me talk to Ev."

"Sure thing. Ask him about the creek we named this morning," I said.

I patched him through and thought about Bult some more, and then asked for another whereabout on the gatecrashers. Wulfmeier still showed on Starting Gate, probably trying to come up with the money to pay his fines.

We got back to the Tongue by late afternoon, but it was still hilly, and the Tongue was too narrow and deep for us to cross. We were close to the Wall—it wound up and down over the hills on the other side—and apparently in a shuttlwren's territory again. Ev alternated between watching it make its rounds and trying to shoo it away so Bult couldn't harpoon it.

Bult headed south, winding up over the tops of hills about like the Wall. I shouted ahead to Carson that it was too steep for the ponies, and he nodded and said something to Bult. Bult plodded on, and ten minutes later his pony keeled over in a dead faint.

Ours followed suit, and we sat down and waited for them to recover. Bult took his umbrella halfway up the hill and sat down under it. Carson lay back and put his hat over his eyes, and I got out Bult's purchase orders and went over them again, looking for clues.

"Do you always see shuttlewrens close to the Wall like this?" Ev asked. He was apparently recovered from the tongue-lashing C.J.'d given him.

"I don't know," I said, trying to remember. "Carson, do we always see shuttlewrens when we're close to the Wall?"

"Mmph," Carson said from under his hat.

"These species that give gifts to their mates," I said to Ev, "what other kinds of courting do they do?"

"Fighting," he said, "mating dances, displays of sexual characteristics."

"Migration?" I said, looking up the hill at Bult. The umbrella was sitting propped against the hill, its lights on. Bult wasn't under it. "Where's Bult?"

Carson sat up, putting his hat on. "Which way?"

I stood up. "Over there. Ev, tie up the ponies."

"They're still out cold," he said. "What's going on?"

Carson was already halfway up the hill. I scrambled after him.

"Up this gully," he said, and we clambered up it. It led up between two hills, a trickle of water at the bottom, and then opened out. Carson signaled me to wait and went up a hundred meters.

"What is it?" Ev said, coming up behind me, panting. "Has something happened to Bult?"

"Yeah," I said. "Only he doesn't know it yet."

Carson was back. "Just like we thought," he said. "Dead end. What say you go up there"—he pointed—"and I go around that way?"

"And we meet in the middle," I said, nodding. I headed up the side of the gully with Ev behind me. I ran along the crest of the hill in a half crouch, and then dropped to all fours and crawled the rest of the way.

"What is it?" Ev whispered. "A nibbler?" He looked excited.

"Yeah," I whispered back. "A nibbler."

He pulled his knife out.

"Put that away," I hissed at him. "You're liable to fall on it and kill yourself." He put it away. "Don't worry. It's not dangerous unless it's doing something it shouldn't."

He looked confused.

"Down," I said, and we crawled out onto a ledge looking down on the space where the gully widened out. Below us, I could see the flattened area of a gate and a lean-to made of a tarp on sticks. In front of it was Bult.

A man was standing half under the tarp, holding out a handful of rocks to Bult. "Quartz," the man said. "It's found in igneous outcroppings, like this." He reached forward to show Bult a holo, and Bult stepped back.

"You ever seen anything like this around here?" the man said, holding up the holo.

Bult took another step backward.

"It's only a holo, you moron," the man said, holding it out to Bult. "Did you ever see anything like this around here?" and Carson came strolling into the clearing, carrying his pack.

He stopped short. "Wulfmeier!" he said, sounding surprised and amused. "What on hell are you doing on Boohte?"

"Wulfmeier," Ev breathed beside me. I put my finger to my lips to shush him.

"What's that?" Carson said, pointing at the holo. "A postcard?" He walked up next to Bult. "My pony wandered off, and I came looking for him. Same as Bult. How about you, Wulfmeier?"

I wished I could see Wulfmeier's face from where we were. "Something went wrong with my gate," he said, taking a step back under the tarp and looking behind him. "Where's Fin?" he said, and lowered his hand to his side.

"Right here," I said, and jumped down. "Wulfmeier," I said, holding out my hand. "Fancy meeting you here. Ev," I called up, "come on down here and meet Wulfmeier."

Wulfmeier didn't look up. He looked at Carson, who'd moved off to the side. Ev landed on all fours and stood up quickly.

"Ev," I said, "this is Wulfmeier. We go way back. What are you doing on Boohte? It's restricted."

"I told Carson," he said, looking warily from one to the other of us, "something must have gone wrong with my gate. I was trying to get to Menniwot."

"Really?" I said. "We had a verify that you were on Starting Gate." I walked over to Bult. "What you got there, Bult?"

"I was emptying out my boot, and Bult wanted to see it," Wulfmeier said, still watching Carson.

Bult handed me the chunks of quartz. I examined them. "Tch, tch, taking of souvenirs. Bult, looks like you're going to have to fine him for that."

"I told you, I got them in my shoe. I was walking around, trying to figure out where I was."

"Tch, tch, tch, leaving footprints. Disturbance of land surface." I went over to the gate and peered underneath it. "Destruction of flora." I leaned inside the gate. "What's wrong with it?"

"I got it fixed," Wulfmeier said.

I stepped inside, and came back out again. "Looks like dust, Carson," I said. "We have a lot of trouble with dust. Does it get in the chips? He better check it while we're here, just in case."

Wulfmeier glanced back at the lean-to and over at Ev, and then back at Carson. He moved his hand away from his side.

"Good idea," he said. "I'll get my stuff."

"Better not," I said. "You wouldn't want to overload the gate. We'll send it along afterward." I went up to the gate controls. "Where'd you say you were trying to go? Menniwot?"

He opened his mouth to say something and then closed it. I asked for coordinates and fed the data into the gate. "That should do it," I said. "You shouldn't end up here again."

Carson walked him over to the gate, and he stepped inside. His hand dropped to his side again, and I hit activate and got out of the way.

Carson was already back at the lean-to, rummaging through Wulfmeier's stuff.

"What'd he have?" I said.

"Ore samples. Gold-bearing quartz, argentite, platinum ore." He leafed through the holos. "Where'd you send him?"

"Starting Gate," I said. "Speaking of which, I better go tell them he's coming. And that somebody's been messing with Big Brother's arrest records. Bult, figure up the fines on this stuff, and we'll send 'em special delivery. Come on," I said to Ev, who was standing there looking at the place where the gate had been like he wished there'd been a fight. "We've gotta call C.J."

We started down the gully. "You were great!" Ev said, scrambling over rocks. "I couldn't believe you faced him down like that! It was just like in the pop-ups!"

We came out of the gully and down the hill to where he'd tied the ponies. They were still lying down.

"What'll happen to Wulfmeier on Starting Gate?" he asked while I wrestled the transmitter off Useless.

"He'll get fined for faking his location and disturbing land surface."

"But he was gatecrashing!"

"He says he wasn't. You heard him. There was something wrong with his gate. He'd have to have been drilling, trading, prospecting, or shooting luggage for Big Brother to confiscate his gate."

"What about those rocks he was giving Bult? That's trading, isn't it?"

I shook my head. "He wasn't giving them to Bult. He was asking if he'd ever seen anything like them. At least he wasn't pouring oil on the ground and lighting it like the last time we caught him with Bult."

"But that's prospecting!"

"We can't prove that either."

"So he gets fined, and then what?" Ev said.

"He'll scrounge up the money to pay the fines, probably from some other gatecrasher who wants to know where to look, and then he'll try again. Up north, probably, now that he knows where we are." Up in Sector 248-76, I thought.

"And you can't stop him?"

"There are four people on this whole planet, and we're supposed to be surveying it, not chasing after gatecrashers."

"But—"

"Yeah. Sooner or later, there'll be one we won't catch. I'm not worried about Wulfmeier—the indidges don't like him, and anything he gets he'll have to find himself. But not all of the gatecrashers are scum. Most of them are people looking for a better place to starve, and sooner or later they'll figure out where a silver mine is from our terrains, or they'll talk the indidges into showing them an oil field. And it'll be all over."

"But the government—what about the regs? What about—"

"Preserving the indigenous culture and the natural ecology? Depends. Big Brother can't stop a mining or drilling operation without sending forces, which means gates and buildings and people taking excursion trips to see the Wall, and forces to protect *them,* and pretty soon you've got Los Angeles."

"You said it depends," Ev said. "On what?"

"On what they find. If it's big enough, Big Brother'll come to get it himself."

"What'll happen to the Boohteri?"

"The same thing that always happens. Bult's a smart operator, but not as smart as Big Brother. Which is why we're putting the money from those out-of-stocks in the bank for him. So he'll have a fighting chance."

I punched send. "Expedition calling King's X. Come in, King's X." I grinned at Ev. "You know, there *was* something wrong with Wulfmeier's gate."

C.J. came on, and I told her to send a message through the gate to Starting Gate and handed her over to Ev so he could fill her in on the details. "Fin was great!" he said. "You should have seen her!"

Bult and Carson were back. Bult had his log out and was talking into it.

"You find anything?" I said.

"Holos of anticlines and diamond pipes. Couple cans of oil. A laser."

"What about the ore samples? Were they indigenous?"

He shook his head. "Standard Earth samples." He looked at Bult, who'd stopped tallying fines and was going up the hill to get his umbrella. "At least now we know why Bult was leading us down here."

"Maybe." I frowned. "I got the idea he was just as surprised to see Wulfmeier as we were. And Wulfmeier was definitely surprised to see us."

"He'd probably told Bult to sneak off and meet him after dark," he said. "Speaking of which, we'd better get going. I don't want Wulfmeier to come back and find us still here."

"He's not coming back for a while," I said. "He's got a loose T-cable. It'll fall off by the time he gets to Starting Gate."

He smiled. "I still want to make it to the other side of the Wall by tonight."

"If Bult'll let us cross the Tongue," I said.

"Why wouldn't he? He's already had his conference with Wulfmeier."

"Maybe," I said, but Bult didn't go half a klom before he led the ponies across, and not a word about *tssi mitss, e* or otherwise, which shot my theory to pieces.

"You know the best part about that scene back there with Wulfmeier?" Ev said as we splashed across and headed south again. "The way you and Carson worked together. It's even better than on the pop-ups."

I'd watched that pop-up last night. We'd caught Wulfmeier threatening the accordion and come out punching and kicking, lasers blazing.

"You don't even have to say anything. You both know what the other one's thinking." Ev gestured expansively. "On the pop-ups they show you working together, but this was like you were reading each other's minds. You do what the other one wants you to do without even being told. It must be great to have a partner like that."

"Fin, where on hell do you think you're going?" Carson said. He was off his pony and untying the cameras. "Stop jabbering about mating customs and come help me. We're camping here."

It wasn't a bad place to camp, and Bult was back to fining us, or at least me, for every step I took, but I was still worried. Carson's binocs disappeared again, and Bult paced back and forth between the three of us while we were setting up camp and eating supper, giving me murderous looks. After supper he disappeared.

"Where's Bult?" I asked Carson, looking out into the darkness for Bult's umbrella.

"Probably looking for diamond pipes," Carson said, huddling next to the lantern. It was chilly again, and there were big clouds over the Ponypiles.

I was still thinking about Bult. "Ev," I asked, "do any of these species of yours get violent as part of their courtship rituals?"

"Violent?" Ev said. "You mean, toward their mate? Bull zoes sometimes accidently kill their mates during the mating dance, and spiders and praying mantis females eat the male alive."

"Like C.J.," Carson said.

"I was thinking more of violence against something else, to impress the female," I said.

"Predators sometimes kill prey to present to the female as a gift," Ev said, "if you'd call that violence."

I would, especially if it meant Bult was leading us into a nibbler's nest or over a cliff so he could dump our carcasses at his girlfriend's feet.

"Fahrrr," Bult said, looming out of the darkness. He dumped a big pile of sticks in front of us. "Fahrrr," he said to Carson, and squatted to light it with a chemical igniter. As soon as it was going, he disappeared again.

"Rivalry among males is common in almost all mammals," Ev said, "elephant seals, primates—"

"Homo sap," Carson said.

"Homo sapiens," Ev said, unruffled, "elk, woodcats. In a few cases they actually fight to the death, but in most it's symbolic combat, designed to show the female who's stronger, more virile, younger—"

Carson stood up.

"Where are you going?"

"To run meteorologicals. I don't like the looks of those clouds over the Ponypiles." You couldn't see the clouds over the Ponypiles, it was so dark, and he'd already run meteorologicals. I'd watched him while we were setting up camp. I wondered if he was worried about Bult and had gone to check on him, but Bult was right here, with another armful of sticks.

"Thanks, Bult," I said. He glared at Ev and then at me again and walked off, still carrying the sticks.

I stood up.

"Where are you going?" Ev said.

"To run a whereabout on Wulfmeier. I want to make sure he made it to Starting Gate." I pulled his pop-up out of my boot and tossed it to him. "Here. Tight Pants and Fancy Mustache'll keep you company."

I went over to the equipment. Carson was nowhere to be seen. I got the log and called up Bult's fines. "Breakdown by day," I said. "Secondary breakdown by person," and watched it for a while, thinking about Bult and the binocs and Ev's mating customs.

When I got back to the fire, Ev was sitting in front of an officeful of terminals, which didn't look much like a Findriddy and Carson adventure.

"What's that?" I said, sitting down beside him.

"Episode One. That's you," he said, pointing at one of the females.

I wasn't wearing tight pants in this one. I was wearing a skimpy little skirt and one of C.J.'s shirts, landing lights and all, and talking into a screen with a geological on it.

Carson strolled into the office in his luggage vest, fringed pants, and a pair of boots the nibblers wouldn't have even had to bite through. His mustache was slicked down and curled up, and all the females simpered at him like he was a buck with big horns.

"I'm looking for someone to go with me to a new planet," he said, his eyes sweeping the room and coming to rest on Skimpy Skirt. Music from somewhere under the terminals started to play, and everything went pinkish. Carson walked over to her desk and stood over her, looking down her blouse.

After a while he said, "I'm looking for someone who longs for adventure, who's not afraid of danger." He held out his hand, and the music got louder. "Come with me," he said.

"Is that how it was?" Ev said.

Well, my shit, of course it wasn't like that. He'd swaggered in, sat down at my desk, and propped his muddy boots up on it.

"What are you doing here?" I'd said. "You run up too many fines again?"

"Nope," he said, grabbing for my hand. "I wouldn't mind running up a few more fraternizing with the sentients, though. How about it?"

I yanked my hand free. "What are you really doing here?"

"I'm looking for a partner. New planet. Surface survey and naming. Any takers?" He grinned at me. "Lots of perks."

"I'll bet," I said. "Dust, snakes, dehyde food, and no bathrooms."

"And me," he said with that smug grin. "Garden of Eden. Wanta come?"

"Yeah," I said, watching the pop-up go pinker. "That's how it was."

"Come with me," Carson said again to Skimpy Skirt, and she stood up and gave him her hand. A draft from somewhere started blowing her hair and her skimpy skirt.

"It'll be uncharted territory," he said, looking in her eyes.

"I'm not afraid," she said, "as long as I'm with you."

"What on hell's *that* supposed to be?" Carson said limping up.

"The way you and Fin met," Ev said.

"And I suppose those landing lights are supposed to be Fin's?"

"You finish your meteorologicals?" I cut in before he could say anything about not being able to tell I was a female half the time.

"Yeah," he said, warming his hands over the fire. "Supposed to rain in the Ponypiles. I'm glad we're heading north tomorrow." He looked back at Carson and Skimpy Skirt, who were still holding hands and looking sappy-eyed at each other. "Evie, which adventure did you say this was supposed to be?"

"It's when you first met," Ev said. "When you asked Fin to be your partner."

"*Asked* her?" Carson said. "My shit, I didn't ask her. Big Brother said my partner had to be a female, for gender balance, whatever on hell that is, and she was the only female in the department who knew how to run terrains and geologicals."

"Fahrrr," Bult said and dumped his load of sticks on Carson's bad foot.

expedition 184: day 3

I hauled my bedroll out by the ponies so I didn't have to listen to Carson, and in the morning I said, "Come on, Ev, you're riding with me. I want to hear all about mating customs from you."

"Chilly around here this morning," Carson said.

I strapped the camera on Useless and cinched it tight.

"I don't like the look of those clouds," Carson said, looking at the Ponypiles. They were covered with low clouds that were spreading out. Half the sky was overcast. "It's a good thing we're heading north."

"Sahhth," Bult said, pointing south. "Brik."

"I thought you said there was a break north of here," Carson said.

"Sahtth," Bult said, glaring at me.

I glared back.

"I don't like the way he's acting," Carson said. "He was gone half the night, and this morning he left a bunch of dice in my bedroll. And Evie says his pop-up's missing."

"Good," I said, climbing up on Useless. "Ev, tell me again about what males do to impress their females."

Bult led us south most of the morning, keeping close to the Tongue, even though the Wall was at least two kloms to the west and there was nothing between us and it but one sandblossom and a lot of pink dirt.

Bult kept sending murderous glances back at me, and kicking his pony to make it go faster. Not only did it, our ponies keeping up with it, but they didn't keel over once all morning. I wondered if Bult had been faking rest stops the way we did dust storms. And what else he'd been faking.

Around noon, I gave up waiting for a rest stop and hauled dehydes out of my pack for lunch, and right after we ate, we came to a creek, which Bult crossed without even looking in, and a handful of silvershims. The whole sky was gray by then, so they didn't look like much.

"Sorry the sun's not out," I told Ev. I looked at their grayish leaves, hanging limp and dusty. "They don't look much like the pop-ups, do they?"

"I'm sorry I lost the pop-up," Ev said. "I put it under my bedroll instead of in my boot." He hesitated. "You didn't know that was how you got chosen to be Carson's partner, did you?"

"Are you kidding?" I said. "That's how Big Brother always does things. C.J. got picked because she was one-sixteenth Navajo." I looked ahead at Carson.

"Why did you come to Boohte?" Ev said.

"You heard the man," I said. "I wanted adventure, I wasn't afraid of danger, I wanted to be famous."

We rode on a ways. "Is that really why?" Ev said.

"Let's change the subject," I said. "Tell me about mating customs. Did you know there's a fish on Starsi that's so dumb it thinks it's being courted when it's not?"

A half a klom after the silvershims, Bult turned west toward the Wall. It bulged out to meet us, and where it did, a whole section was down, a heap of shiny white rubble with high-water marks on it. A flood must've taken it out, even though it was an awfully long way from the Tongue.

Bult led us over the break and, finally, north, keeping next to the Wall all the way back up to the creek we'd crossed. Ev was excited about seeing the front side of the Wall, even though only a few of the chambers looked like they'd been lived in lately, and even more excited about a shuttlewren that tried to divebomb us riding through the break.

"Their territory obviously involves the Wall in some way," he said, leaning sideways to get a look inside. "Have you ever seen one of their nests in the chambers?"

If he leaned over any farther he was going to fall off his pony. "Rest stop!" I called up to Carson and Bult, and pulled back on the reins. "Come on, Ev," I said, and dismounted. "It's against regs to go inside the chambers, but you can peek in."

He looked up ahead at Bult, who had his log out and was glaring back at us. "What about the fine for leaving footprints?"

"Carson can pay it," I said. "Bult hasn't fined him in two days." I went over to a chamber and looked inside the door.

They're not real doors, more like a hole poked in the middle of the side, and there's no floor either. The sides curve up like an egg. There was a bunch of sandblossoms laid out on the bottom of this one, and in the middle of it one of the American flags Bult had bought two expeditions ago.

"Courtship ritual," I said, but Ev was looking up at the curved ceiling, trying to see if there was a nest. "There are several species of birds that nest in the homes of other species. The panakeet on Yotata, the cuckoo."

We started back to the ponies. It was starting to sprinkle. Up ahead, Bult was getting his umbrella out of his pack and putting it up. Carson was off his pony stomping back to us. "Fin, what on hell do you think you're doing?" he said when he got up to us.

"Taking a rest stop," I said. "We haven't had one all day."

"And we're not going to. We're finally heading north." He took hold of Useless's reins and yanked him forward. "Ev, you stay back here and bring up the rear. Fin's coming up to ride with me."

"I like it back here," I said.

"Too bad," he said, and dragged my pony forward. "You're riding with me. Bult, you lead. Fin and I are riding together."

Bult gave me a murderous glance and lit up his umbrella. He crossed the creek and then rode up along it, going west.

"Now, get on," Carson said and mounted his pony. "I want to be away from the mountains by nightfall."

"And that's why I have to ride with you," I said, swinging my leg up, "so I can tell you which way's north? It's that way."

I pointed north. There was a high bluff in that direction, and between it and the Ponypiles a strip of flat grayish-pink plain, splotched here and there with whitish and dark patches. Bult was heading catty-corner across the flat, still following the stream, his pony leaving deep pawprints in the soft ground.

"Thanks," Carson said. "The way you been acting, I didn't figure you knew which end was up, let alone north."

"What on hell's that supposed to mean?"

"It means you haven't been paying attention to anything since Evelyn showed up and started talking about mating customs. I'd've thought you'd've run out of species by now."

"Well, we haven't," I snapped.

"You're supposed to be surveying, not listening to the loaners. In case you haven't noticed, we're in uncharted territory, we don't have any aerials, Bult's half a klom ahead of us—" He pointed up ahead.

Bult's pony was drinking out of the stream. It was still sprinkling, but Bult turned off his umbrella and collapsed it.

"—and who knows where he's going. He could be leading us into a trap. Or around in circles till the food runs out."

I looked ahead at Bult. He'd crossed the creek and ridden a little way up the other side. His pony was taking another drink.

"Maybe Wulfmeier's back and Bult's leading us straight to him. And you haven't looked at a screen all morning. You're supposed to be running subsurfaces, not listening to Evie Darling talk about sex."

"Listening to him is one hell of a lot more fun than listening to you tell me how to do my job!" I kicked the log on and asked for a subsurface. Up ahead, Bult's pony was stopped and drinking again. I looked down at the stream. Where it cut the low banks, the rock looked like mudstone. "Cancel subsurface," I said.

"You haven't been paying attention to anything," Carson said. "You lose the binocs, you lose the pop-up—"

"Shut up," I said, looking at the bluff, backing the full length of the plain. The plain tilted slightly to its base. "Terrain," I said. "No. Terrain cancel." I looked out at the closest whitish patch. Where the drops of rain were sticking to it, it was pocked with pink.

"You were supposed to keep the pop-up in your boot. If Bult gets hold of it—"

"Shut up," I said. Where Bult's pony had walked there were fifteen-centimeter-deep pawprints in the grayish-brown dirt. The ones up ahead were dark on the bottom.

"If you'd have been paying attention, you'd have realized Wulfmeier—" Carson was saying.

"My shit!" I said, "Dust storm!" and jammed the disconnect. "Shit."

Carson jerked around in the saddlebone as if he expected to see a dust tantrum roaring down on him, and then jerked back and stared at me.

"Subsurface," I said to the terminal. I pointed at the pony's pawprints. "Off-line, and no trace."

Carson stared at the pawprints. "Is everything off?" he said.

"Yes," I said, checking the cameras to make sure.

"Are you running a subsurface?"

"I don't have to," I said, waving at the plain. "It's right there on top. Shit, shit, shit."

Evelyn rode up. "What is it?" he asked.

"I knew he was up to something," Carson said, looking ahead at

Bult. He was off his pony and squatting down at the edge of a dark patch. "I *told* you I thought he was leading us into a trap."

"What *is* it?" Ev said, pulling his knife out. "Nibblers?"

"No, it's a couple of royal saps," Carson said. "Was the log on?"

"Of course it was on," I snapped. "This is uncharted. Terrain, off-line and no trace," I said, but I already knew what it was going to show. A bluff backing a tilted plain. Mudstone. Salt. Seepage. A classic anticline, just like in Wulfmeier's holos. Shit, shit, shit.

"What *is* it?" Evelyn said.

The terrain came up on the screen. "Subsurface overlay," I said.

"Nahtth," Bult called.

I looked up. He had his umbrella up and was pointing with it at the bluff.

"The sneak," Carson said. "Where's he leading us now?"

"We've got to get out of here," I said, scanning the subsurface. It was worse than I thought. The field was fifteen kloms square, and we were right in the middle of it.

"He wants us to follow him," Carson said. "He probably wants to show us a gusher. We've got to get out of here."

"I know," I said, scanning the subsurface. The salt dome went the whole length of the bluff and all the way to the foot of the Ponypiles.

"What do we do?" Carson said. "Go back to the Wall?"

I shook my head. The only sure way out of this was the way we'd come, but the ponies wouldn't backtrail, and the subsurface showed a secondary fault south of the creek. If we went off at an angle we were liable to run into seep, and we obviously couldn't go north.

"Distance overlay," I said. "Off-line and no trace."

"We can't stay off-line all day," Carson said. "C.J.'s already suspicious."

"I *know,*" I said, looking desperately at the map. We couldn't go west. It was too far, and the subsurface showed seepage that way. "We've got to go south," I said, pointing at the foothills of the Ponypiles. "We need to get up on that spur so we'll be up above the natural table."

"Are you sure?" Carson said, coming around to look at the screen.

"I'm sure. The rocks are gypsum." Which is frequently associated with an anticline. Shit, shit, shit.

"And then what? Go up into the Ponypiles in that weather?" He pointed at the low clouds.

"We've got to go somewhere. We can't stay here. And any other way's liable to lead us straight into Oklahoma."

"All right," he said, getting up on his pony. "Come on, Ev. We're going."

"Shouldn't we wait for Bult?" Ev said.

"My shit, no. He's already gotten us in enough trouble. Let him find his own way out. That goddamn Wulfmeier. You lead," he said to me, "and we'll follow you."

"You stay right behind me," I said, "and holler if you see something I don't."

Like an anticline. Like an oil field.

I looked at the screen, wishing it would show a path for us to follow, and started slowly across the plain, watching for seep and hoping the ponies wouldn't suddenly go in knee-deep. Or decide to keel over.

It started to drizzle, and then rain, and I had to wipe the screen off with my hand. "Bult's following us," Carson said when we were halfway to the spur.

I looked back. He had his umbrella down and was kicking his pony to catch up.

"What are we going to tell him?" I said.

"I don't know," he said. "Damn Wulfmeier. This is all his fault."

And mine, I thought. I should have recognized the signs in the terrain. I should have recognized the signs in Bult.

The ground turned paler, and I ran a geological and got a mix of gypsum and sulfur in with the mudstone. I wondered if I could risk turning the transmitter back on, and about that time Useless stepped in seep over his paw. It started to drizzle again.

It took us an hour and a half to get out of the oil field and the rain and up into the first hills of the spur. They were gypsum, too, eroded by the wind into flattened and whorled mounds that looked exactly like ponyshit. It apparently hadn't rained as much up here. The gypsum was dry and powdery, and before we'd climbed fifty meters we were coated in pinkish dust and spitting plaster.

I found a stream, and we waded the ponies up it to get the oil off their paws. They balked at the cold water and the incline, and I finally got off and walked Useless, yanking on its reins and cursing it every step of the way up.

Bult had caught up. He was right behind Ev, dragging on his pony's reins and watching Carson thoughtfully. Ev was looking thoughtful, too, and I hoped that didn't mean he'd figured things out, but it didn't look like it. He craned his neck to look at a shuttlewren flying reconnaissance above us.

I needed to get the transmitter back on, but I wanted to make sure we were out of camera range of the anticline first. I dragged Useless up above a clear pool and into a little hollow with rocks on all sides, and unloaded the transmitter.

Ev came up. “I’ve got to ask you something,” he said urgently, and I thought, Shit, I knew he was smarter than he looked, but all he said was “Is the Wall close to here?”

I said I didn’t know, and he climbed up the rocks to look for himself. Well, I thought, at least he hadn’t said anything about how well Carson and I worked together in a crisis.

I erased the subsurfaces and geologicals and reran the log to see how bad the damage was and then reconnected the transmitter.

“Now what happened?” C.J. said. “And don’t tell me it was another dust storm. Not when it was raining.”

“It wasn’t a dust storm,” I said. “I thought it was, but it was a wall of rain. It hit us before I could get the equipment covered.”

“Oh,” she said, as if I’d stolen her thunder. “I didn’t think you could have a dust storm in that mud you were going through.”

“We didn’t,” I said. I told her where we were.

“What are you doing up there?”

“We got worried about a flash flood,” I said. “Did you get the subsurface and terrain?” I asked. “I was working on them when the rain hit.”

There was a pause while she checked and I wiped my hand across my mouth. It tasted like gypsum. “No,” she said. “There’s an order for a subsurface and then a cancel.”

“A cancel?” I said. “I didn’t cancel anything. That must have happened when the transmitter went down. What about aerials? Have you got anything on the Ponypiles?” I gave her our coordinates.

There was another pause. “I’ve got one east of the Tongue, but nothing close to where you are.” She put it on the screen. “Can I talk to Evelyn?”

“He’s drying off the ponies. And, no, he hasn’t named anything for you yet. But he’s been trying.”

“He has?” she said, sounding pleased, and signed off without asking anything else.

Ev came back. “The Wall is just the other side of those rocks,” he said, wiping dust off his pants. “It goes over the top of the ridge up there.”

I told him to go dry off the ponies and reran the log again. The footprints did look like mud, especially with the rain pocking the gray-brown dirt, and it was cloudy, so there wasn’t any iridescence. And there wasn’t a subsurface. Or an aerial.

But there was me, saying to cancel the subsurface. And the terrain was right there on the log for them to see—the sandstone bluff and the grayish-brown dirt and the patches of evaporated salt.

I looked at the ponies' pawprints. They looked a little like mud, maybe, but they wouldn't when they did the enhances. Which there was no way they wouldn't. Not with C.J. talking about phony dust storms, not when we'd had the transmitter down for over two hours.

I should go tell Carson. I looked down toward the pool, but I didn't see him, and I didn't feel like going to look for him. I knew what he was going to say—that I should have realized it was an anticline, that I wasn't paying attention, that it was my fault and I was a crummy partner. Well, what did he expect? He'd only picked me because of my gender.

Carson came clambering up the rocks. "I got a look at Bult's log," he said. "He didn't write up any fines down there."

"I know," I said. "I already checked. What'd he say?"

"Nothing. He's sitting up in one of those Wall chambers with his back to the door."

I thought about that.

"His feelings are probably hurt that we didn't pay him for leading us there. Wulfmeier obviously offered him money to show him where there was an oil field." He took off his hat. There was a line of gypsum dust where the brim had been. "I told him we got worried about the rain, that we thought that plain might flood, so we decided to come up here."

"That won't keep him from leading us straight back down there now that it's stopped," I said.

"I told him you wanted to run geologicals on the Ponypiles." He put his hat back on. "I'm gonna go look for a way past the field." He squatted down beside me. "How bad is it?"

"Bad," I said. "You can see the tilt and the mudstone on the log, and I'm on, canceling the subsurface."

"Can you fix any of it?"

I shook my head. "We had the transmitter off too long. It's already through the gate."

"What about C.J.?"

"I told her we ran into rain. She thinks the pawprints are mud. But Big Brother won't."

He came around to look at the screen. "It's that bad?"

"It's that bad," I said bitterly. "Any fool can see it's an anticline."

"Meaning I should've noticed it," he said, bristling. "I wasn't the one dawdling behind talking about sex." He threw his hat down on the ground. "I told you he was going to louse up this expedition."

"Don't you dare blame this on Ev!" I said. "He wasn't the one yelling at me for half an hour while the scans got the whole damned anticline on film!"

"No, he was the one busy noticing birds! And watching pop-ups! Oh, he's been a lot of use! The only thing he's done this whole expedition is try to get a jump out of you!"

I slammed the erase button, and the screen went black. "How do you know he hasn't already gotten one?" I stomped past him. "At least Ev can tell I'm a female!"

I stormed down the rocks, so mad I could have killed him, fine or no fine, and ended up sitting on a gypsum ponypile next to the pool, waiting for him to go off and look for a way down.

After a few minutes he did, clambering up beside the stream without a glance in my direction. I saw Ev come down from the Wall and say something to him. Carson barged past him, and went out along the spur, and Ev stood there staring after him, looking bewildered, and then looked down at me.

He was right about one thing, in all his talk about mating customs. When the hardwiring kicks in, it overrides rational thought, all right. And common sense. I was mad at myself for not seeing the anticline and madder at Carson, and half-sick about what was going to happen when Big Brother saw that log. And I was covered with dried-on gypsum dust and oil and reeking of ponypiles. And, on the pop-ups, my face was always washed.

But that was no reason to do what I did, which was to strip off my pants and shirt and wade into that pool. If Bult saw me I'd be fined for polluting a waterway and Carson would have killed me for not running an f-and-f check first, but Bult was sulking up in the Wall, and the water was so clear you could see every rock on the bottom. It spilled down over rounded boulders into the pool and poured out through a carved-out spout below.

I waded out to the middle, where it was chest-deep, and ducked under.

I stood up, scrubbed gypsum plaster off my arms, and ducked under again. When I came up, Ev was leaning against my gypsum ponypat.

"I thought you were up at the Wall watching shuttlewrens," I said, smoothing back my hair with both hands.

"I was," he said. "I thought you were with Carson."

"I was," I said, looking at him. I sank into the water, my arms out. "Have you figured out the shuttlewrens' courtship ritual?"

"Not yet," he said. He sat down on the rock and took his boots off. "Did you know the mer-apes on Chichch mate in the water?"

"You sure know a hell of a lot of species," I said, treading water. "Or do you just make them up?"

"Sometimes," he said, unbuttoning his shirt. "When I'm trying to impress a female."

I paddled out to where the water came up to my shoulders and stood up. The current was faster here. It rippled past my legs. "It won't work on C.J. The only thing that'll impress her is Mount Crissa Jane."

He peeled off his shirt. "It's not C.J. I'm trying to impress." He pulled off his socks.

"It's not a good idea to take your boots off in uncharted territory," I said, swimming toward him through the deep water. The current rippled past my legs again.

"The female mer-ape invites the male into the water by swimming toward him," he said. He stripped off his pants and stepped into the water.

I stood up. "Don't come in," I said.

"The male enters the water," he said, wading in, "and the female retreats."

I stood still, peering into the water. I felt the zag, wider this time, and looked where it should be. All I could see was a ripple over the rocks, like air above hot ground.

"Step back," I said, putting my hand up. I walked carefully toward him, trying not to disturb the water.

"Look, I didn't mean to—"

"Slowly," I said, bending down to get the knife out of my boot. "One step at a time."

He looked wildly down at the water. "What is it?" he said.

"Don't make any sudden movements," I said.

"What is it?" he said. "Is there something in the water?" and splashed wildly out of the water and up onto the ponypile.

What looked like a blurring of the current zagged toward me, and I plunged the knife down with a huge splash, hoping I was aiming at the right place.

"What is it?" Ev said.

Now that its blood was spreading in the water, I could see it, and it was definitely *e.* Its body was longer than Bult's umbrella, and it had a wide mouth. "It's a *tssi mitsse,"* I said.

It was also indigenous fauna, and I'd killed it, which meant I was in big trouble. But blood in the water and a fish you couldn't see weren't exactly small trouble. I got away from the blood and out of the water.

Ev was still crouching bare-beamed on the rock. "Is it dead?" he said.

"Yeah," I said, drying off my hair with my shirt and then putting it on. "And so am I." I started pulling the rest of my clothes on.

He got down off the gypsum, looking anxious. "You're not hurt, are you?"

"No," I said, looking in the water and wishing I had been. At least then I could have claimed "self-defense" on the reports.

The blood had spread over the lower half of the pool and was spilling over the spout into the stream. The *tssi mitsse* was drifting toward the spout, too, and I didn't see any activity around it, but I wasn't going back in the water to get it.

I left Ev getting his clothes on and went up to the ponies, which were all lying squeezed in among the rocks. Their paws were still wet, and I thought about us walking them up the stream, and Bult not saying a word. Nobody on this expedition was doing their job.

I took a grappling hook and Bult's umbrella and went down to get the *tssi mitsse* out of the water. Ev was buttoning his shirt and looking embarrassedly at Bult, who was over by the spout, hunched over and looking at the bloody water. I sent Ev to get the holo camera. Bult unfolded himself. He had his log, and he looked pointedly at the umbrella in my hand.

"I know, I know. Forcible confiscation of property," I said. It didn't much matter. Bult's fines were nothing compared to the penalty for killing an indigenous life-form.

The *tssi mitsse* had floated in close to the bank. I hooked it with the umbrella handle and pulled it to the edge and onto the bank, stepping away from it in a hurry, in case it wasn't dead, but Bult went right over to it, unfolded an arm, and started poking his hand into its side.

"Tssi mitss," he said.

"You're kidding," I said. "How big are the big ones?"

It was over a meter long and was perfectly visible now that it was out of the water, with transparent jellylike flesh that must have the same refraction index as water.

"Tith," Bult said, pulling the mouth back. "Keel bait."

They looked like they could kill bite, all right, or at least take off a foot. There were two long, sharp teeth on either side of its mouth and little serrated ones in between, and that was good. At least it wasn't a harmless algae-eater.

Ev came back with the camera. He handed it to me, looking at the *tssi mitss.* "It's huge," he said.

"That's what you think," I said. "You'd better go find Carson."

"Yeah," he said, and stood there, hesitating. "I'm sorry I jumped out of the water like that."

"No harm done," I said.

I took holos and measurements and brought down the scale to weigh it. When I started to pick it up by the head, Bult said, "Keel bait," and I dropped it with a thud and then took a closer look at its teeth.

Definitely not an algae-eater. The long teeth on either side weren't teeth. They were fangs, and when I ran an analysis of the venom, it ate right through the vial.

I hauled the *tssi mitss* by the tail up the rocks to camp and started in on the reports. "Accidental killing of indigenous fauna," I told the log. "Circumstances—" and then sat and stared at the screen.

Carson came back, scrambling up the rocks from the direction of the pool and stopping short when he saw the *tssi mitss.* "Are you all right?"

"Yeah," I said, looking at the screen. "Don't touch the teeth. They're full of acid."

"My shit," he said softly. "Is this what was in the Tongue when Bult wouldn't let us cross?"

"Nope. This is the small version," I said, wishing he'd get on with it.

"It didn't bite you? You're sure you're all right?"

"I'm sure," I said, even though I wasn't.

He squatted down and looked at it. "My shit," he said again. He looked up at me. "Evie says you were in the pool when you killed it. What on hell were you doing in there?"

"I was taking a bath," I said, looking at the screen.

"Since when do you take baths in uncharted territory?"

"Since I ride all afternoon through gypsum dust," I said. "Since I get covered with oil, trying to wash it off the ponies. Since I find out you can't even tell half the time whether I'm female or not."

He stood up. "So you take off all your clothes and go in swimming with Evie?"

"I didn't take off all my clothes. I had my boots on." I glared at him. "And I don't have to have my clothes off for Ev to be able to tell I'm a female."

"Oh, right, I forgot, he's the expert on sex. Is that what that was down at the pool, some kind of mating dance?" He kicked at the carcass with his bad foot.

"Don't do that," I said. "I've got enough to worry about without having to fill out a form for desecrating remains."

"Worry about!" he said, his mustache quivering. *"You've* got enough to worry about? You know what *I've* got to worry about? What on hell you're going to do next." He kicked the *tssi mitss* again. "You let Wulfmeier open a gate right under our noses, you lead us into an oil field, you take a bath and nearly get yourself killed."

I slammed the terminal off and stood up. "And I lost the binocs! Don't forget that! You want a new partner, is that what you're saying?"

"A new—?"

"A new partner," I said. "I'm sure there are plenty of females to choose from who'd traipse off with you to Boohte the way I did."

"That's what all this is about, isn't it?" Carson said, frowning at me. "It's not about Evie at all. It's about what I said the other night about picking you as a partner."

"You *didn't* pick me, remember?" I said furiously. *"Big Brother* picked me. For gender balance. Only it obviously didn't work because half the time you can't tell which gender I am."

"Well, I sure can right now. You're acting worse than C.J. We been partners for a hundred and eighty expeditions—"

"Eighty-four," I said.

"We've been eating dehydes and putting up with C.J. and getting fined by Bult for eight years. What on hell difference does it make how I picked you?"

"You *didn't* pick me. You sat there with your feet up on my desk and said, 'Wanta come?' and I came, just like that. And now I find out all you cared about is that I could do topographicals."

"All I cared about—?" He kicked the *tssi mitss* again, and a big piece of clear jelly flew off. "I rode into that luggage stampede and got you. I never even looked at any of those female loaners. What do you want me to do? Send you flowers? Bring you a dead fish? No, wait, I forgot, you got one of those for yourself. Lock horns with Evie so that you can tell which one of us is younger and's got both feet? What?"

"I want you to leave me alone. I have to finish these reports," I said, and looked at the screen. "I want you to go away."

Nobody said a word during supper, except Bult, who fined me for dusting off a lump of gypsum before I sat down. It started to rain and all evening Carson kept going out to the edge of the overhang and looking at the sky.

Ev sat in a corner, looking miserable, and I worked on the reports. Bult didn't show any inclination to build any more fires. He sat in the opposite corner watching pop-ups until Carson took it away from him and snapped it shut, and then he opened his umbrella, nearly poking me in the eye with it, and went off up to the Wall.

I wrapped up in my bedroll and worked on the reports some more, but it was too cold. I went to bed. Ev was still sitting in the corner, and Carson was still watching the rain.

I woke up in the middle of the night with water dripping on my neck. Ev was still asleep in his bedroll, snoring, and Carson was sitting in the corner, with the pop-up spread out in front of him. He was watching the scene in Big Brother's offices, the scene where he asked me to go with him.

expedition 184: day 4

In the morning he was gone. It was raining really hard, and the wind had started to blow. There was a stream running through the middle of the overhang and pooling at the back. The foot of Ev's bedroll was already wet.

It was a lot colder, and I figured Carson had gone after firewood, but when I went outside his pony was gone.

I climbed up to the Wall to look for Bult. He wasn't in any of the chambers. I went back down to the pool.

He wasn't there, and the pool wasn't either. Water was pouring everywhere over the rocks, white with gypsum. The ponypile Ev had crouched on was completely covered.

I climbed back up to the Wall and followed it over the ridge. Bult was at the top, looking south toward what you could see of the Ponypiles, which wasn't much, the clouds were so low.

"Where's Carson?" I shouted over the rain.

He looked west and then down at the oil field we'd crossed yesterday. "Dan nah," he said.

"He took one of the ponies," I shouted. "Which way did he go?"

"Nah see liv," he said. "Nah gootbye."

"He didn't say good-bye to anybody," I said. "We've got to find him. You go up along the ridge, and I'll check the way we came up."

But the way we came up was flowing with water, too, and too slick for a pony to have gotten down, and when I went up to the overhang to get Ev, the whole back half was underwater and Ev was piling everything on a damp ledge.

"We've got to move the equipment," he said when he saw me. "Where's Carson?"

"I don't know," I said. I found another overhang higher up, not as deep and tilted up toward the back, and we carried the transmitter and the cameras up. When I went down for the rest of the equipment, I found Carson's log. And his mike.

Bult came back, sopping wet. "Nah fine," he said.

And apparently he doesn't want to be found, I thought, turning the mike over in my hands.

"That overhang isn't going to work," Ev said. "There's water spilling down the side."

We moved the equipment again, into a carved-out hollow away from the stream. It was deep, and the bottom was dry, but by afternoon there was a river running past it, spilling down catty-corner from the ridge, and by morning we'd be cut off from the ponies. And any way out if the water rose.

I went looking again. Water was pouring from both overhangs we'd been in, and there was no way we could get to the other side of the stream, even without *tssi mitss.* I climbed up onto the ridge. It was high enough, but we'd never last out here in the open. I tried not to think about Carson, out in this somewhere with nothing but his bedroll. And no mike.

A shuttlewren dived at my head and around to the Wall again. "Better get in out of this," I said.

I went back down to the hollow and got Ev and Bult. "Come on," I said, picking up the transmitter. "We're moving." I led them up to the ridge and over to the Wall. "In here," I said.

"I thought this was against the regs," Ev said, stepping over the rounded bottom of the door.

"So's everything else," I said. "Including drowning and polluting the waterways with our bodies."

Bult stepped over the door and set his equipment down, and got out his log. "Trespassing on Boohteri property," he said into it.

It took us four trips to get everything up, and then we still had the ponies, which were all lying in a waterlogged pile and wouldn't get up. We had to push them up through the rocks, protesting all the way. It was dark before we got them to the Wall.

"We aren't going to put them in the same chamber with us, are we?" Ev said hopefully, but Bult was already lifting them over the door, paw by paw.

"Maybe we could knock out a door between this passage and the next one," Ev said.

"Destruction of Boohteri property," Bult said, and got out his log.

"At least with the ponies we'll have something to eat," I said.

"Destruction of alien life-form," Bult said into his log.

Destruction of alien life-form. I should get busy on those reports.

"Where was Carson going?" Ev said, as if he'd just remembered he was missing.

"I don't know," I said, looking out at the rain.

"Carson would've waded right in when he saw that thing and killed it," Ev said.

Yeah, I thought, he would have. And then yelled at me for not running an f-and-f check.

"They would have done a pop-up about it," he said, and I thought, Yeah, and I know what that would have looked like. Old Tight Pants without her pants yelling, "Help, help!" and a fish with false teeth lunging up out of the water, and Carson splashing in with a laser and blasting it to hell.

"I told you to get out of the water, and you did," I said. "I would've jumped out myself if I hadn't been so far out."

"Carson wouldn't have," he said. "He would have come to get you."

I looked out at the darkness and the rain. "Yeah," I said. He would have. If he'd known where I was.

expedition 184: day 5

It took me all the next day to fill out the reports on the *tssi mitss,* which was probably a good thing. It kept me from standing in the door of the Wall like Ev, staring out at the rain and the rising water.

And it kept me from thinking about Stewart, and how he'd drowned in a flash flood, and about his partner Annie Segura, who'd gone off looking for him and never been found. It kept me from thinking about Carson, washed up somewhere along the Tongue. Or sitting at the bottom of a cliff.

The chamber wasn't much of an improvement on the overhang. The ponies got the runs, and the shuttlewren flew frantically back and forth around our heads. With the rounded floor, there was no place to sit, and the wind kept blowing rain in. Ev and I could've used one of Bult's shower curtains.

Bult didn't need one. He sat under his umbrella watching pop-ups all day. Carson had left it behind, too. I tried to take it away from him, which got me a fine, and then made Ev show him how to make it not take up the whole chamber, but as soon as Ev went back to watching out the door, Bult put it back to full size.

"He's been gone too long," Tight Pants said, swinging up onto her horse, which was in the middle of the ponies. "I'm going to find him."

"It's been nearly twenty hours," the accordion said. "We must report in to Home Base."

"It's been more than twenty-four hours," Ev said, coming back in from the door. "Aren't we supposed to call C.J.?"

"Yeah," I said, and started filling in Form R-28-X, Proper Disposal of Indigenous Fauna Remains. In all those trips up the ridge in the pouring rain, I hadn't thought to bring the *tssi mitss,* which meant I was going to get slapped with another fine.

"Are you going to call her?" Ev said.

I kept filling out the report.

Toward evening C.J. called. "The scans have been showing the same thing all day," she said.

"It's raining. We're waiting it out in a cave."

"But you're all all right?"

"We're fine," I said.

"Do you want me to come pull you out?"

"No."

"Can I talk to Ev?"

"No," I said, looking at him. "He's out with Carson seeing how bad the flooding is." I signed off.

"I wouldn't have told her," Ev said.

"I know," I said, looking at Bult.

Carson and Fin were standing in front of him. "It'll be uncharted territory," Carson said, holding out his hand.

"I'm not afraid," Fin said, "as long as I'm with you."

"What are you going to do?" Ev said.

"Wait," I said.

expedition 184: day 6

The next morning the rain let up a little and then started again. The roof of the chamber developed a leak, right over where we had the equipment piled, and we had to move it over next to the ponies.

It was getting a little crowded. During the night four roadkill had dragged themselves over the door, and the shuttlewren went crazy, wheeling and circling at the top of the chamber, making passes at Ev and me, and at Tight Pants climbing down the cliff.

Bult wasn't watching. He'd gotten up for the hundredth time and gone outside to stand on the ridge.

"What's he doing?" Ev said, watching the shuttlewrens.

"Looking for Carson," I said. "Or a way out of here."

There wasn't any way out. Water was flowing off of every mound, carrying what looked like half the Ponypiles with it, and a raging stream cut across the end of the ridge.

"Where do you think Carson is?" Ev said.

"I don't know," I said. During the night it had occurred to me that Wulfmeier might have gotten his gate fixed and come back to get even. And Carson was alone, no pony, no mike, nothing.

I couldn't tell Ev that, and while I was trying to think of something I could, Ev said, "Fin, come look at this."

He was peering up at the leak in the ceiling. The shuttlewren was making little dives at it.

"It's trying to repair it," Ev said thoughtfully. "Fin, do you still have those parts of the one Bult ate?"

"There wasn't much left," I said, but I dug in my pack and got them out.

"Oh, good," he said, examining the fragments. "I was afraid he'd eaten the beak." He settled down against the wall with them.

The pop-up was still on. Fin was binding up the stub of Carson's foot and bawling. "It's all right," Carson was saying. "Don't cry."

The pop-up went dark and words appeared in the middle of the chamber. The credits. "Written by Captain Jake Trailblazer."

"Look at this," Ev said, bringing over one of the shuttlewren pieces. "See how the beak is flat, like a trowel? Can I run an analysis?"

"Sure." I went over to the door and looked out. Bult was standing on the ridge, where the stream cut across, in the rain.

"I should have figured it out before," Ev said, looking at the screen. "Look at how high the door is. And why would the Boohteri make a curved floor like that?" He stood up and looked at the leak again. "You said you've never seen the Boohteri building one of the chambers?" he said. "Is that right?"

"Yeah."

"Do you remember me telling you about the bowerbird?" he said.

"The one that builds a nest fifty times its size?"

"It's not a nest. It's a courtship chamber."

I couldn't see where this was going. We already knew the indidges used the Wall for courting.

"The male Adelie penguin gives a round stone to the female as a courting gift. But the stone doesn't belong to him. He stole it from another nest." He looked expectantly at me. "Who does that sound like?"

Well, Carson and I'd always said we thought somebody else built the Wall. I looked up at the shuttlewren. "But it's too small to build something like this, isn't it?" I said.

"The bowerbird's bower is fifty times its size. And you said the Wall was only growing by two new chambers a year. Some species only mate every three years, or five. Maybe they work on it several years."

I looked at the curved walls. Three to five years work, and then the imperialistic indidges move in and take it over, knock the door out to make it bigger, put up flags. I wondered what Big Brother was going to say when he heard about this.

"It's just a theory," Ev said. "I need to run probabilities on size and strength and take samples of the Wall's composition."

"It sounds like a pretty good theory," I said. "I've never seen Bult use a tool. Or order one either." The Boohteri word for the wall was "ours," but so was the word for most of Carson's and my wages. And that was Ev's pop-up he'd been watching.

"I'll need a specimen," Ev said, looking speculatively at the shuttlewren making frantic circles around us.

"Go ahead," I said, ducking. "Wring its neck. I'll write up the reports."

"First I want to get this on holo," he said, and spent the next hour filming the shuttlewren poking at the leak. It didn't do anything to it that I could see, but by midmorning the ceiling had stopped leaking, and there was a tiny patch of new-looking white shiny stuff on the ceiling.

Bult came in, with his umbrella and two dead shuttlewrens.

"Give that to me," I said, and snatched one away from him.

He glared at me. "Forcible confiscation of property."

"Exactly." I handed it to Ev. " 'Ours.' You'd better stick it in your boot."

Ev did, and Bult watched him, glaring, and then stuffed the other one in his mouth and went outside. Ev got out his knife and started chipping flakes off of the Wall.

The rain was letting up, and I went out and took a look around. Bult was standing where the stream cut across the ridge, staring up into the Ponypiles. While I watched, he splashed across and went on along the ridge.

The stream must be down, and the pool definitely was. Milky water was still spilling off every surface, but you could see Ev's ponypat rock and the spout at the bottom of the pool. Off to the west the clouds were starting to thin.

I went back up to the ridge. Bult had disappeared. I went into the chamber and started stuffing things in my pack.

"Where are you going?" Ev said. He'd looked around to make sure it wasn't Bult and then started scraping again.

"To find Carson," I said, fixing the straps so I could put the pack on my back.

"You can't," he said, holding the knife. "It's against the regs. You're supposed to stay where you are."

"That's right." I took off my mike and handed it and Carson's to him. "You wait here till afternoon and then call C.J. to come get you. We're only sixty kloms from King's X. She'll be here in a flash." I stepped over the door.

"But you don't know where he is," Ev said.

"I'll find him," I said, but I didn't have to. He and Bult were coming across the stream talking, their heads bent together. Carson was limping.

I ducked back in the chamber, dumped my pack on the floor, and asked for R-28-X, Proper Disposal of Indigenous Fauna Remains.

"What are you doing?" Ev said. "I want you to take me with you. It's uncharted territory. I don't think you should go look for Carson by yourself," and Carson appeared in the door. "Oh," Ev said, surprised.

Carson stepped over the door and into the middle of the pop-up Bult had been watching. It was raining, and Fin was standing watching two thousand luggage bear down on her. Carson swung into the saddle and galloped toward her.

Carson snapped the pop-up shut. "How wide do you think the field is?" he said to me.

"Eight kloms. Maybe ten. That's how long the bluff is," I said. I handed him his mike. "You lost this."

He put it on. "Are you sure eight is as far as it goes?"

"No, but after that there's caprock, so there won't be any seepage. If we don't run a subsurface, we'll be okay," I said. "Is that where you were, finding a way past it?"

"I want to leave by noon," he said and walked over to Bult. "Come on, we've got work to do."

They squatted in a corner, and Carson emptied out his pockets. Wherever he'd been, he'd collected lots of f-and-f. He had three plants in plastic bags, a holo of some kind of ungulate, and a whole pocketful of rocks.

He ignored us, which didn't bother Ev, who was busy dissecting his specimen. I packed up everything and got the wide-angles on the ponies.

Carson picked up one of the rocks and handed it to Bult. It was a crystal of some kind, transparent with triangular faces. By rights, I should be running a mineralogical to see if it already had a name, but I wasn't about to say anything to Carson, not when he was so pointedly not looking at me.

"Do the Boohteri have a name for this?" Carson asked Bult.

Bult hesitated, as if looking for some cue from Carson, and then said, *"Thitsserrah."*

"Tchahtssillah?" Carson said.

Books are supposed to begin with a belching "b," but Bult nodded. *"Tchatssarrah."*

"Tssirroh?" Carson said.

They went on like that for fifteen minutes while I strapped the terminal on my pony and rolled up the bedrolls.

"Tssarrah?" Carson said, sounding irritated.

"Yahss," Bult said. *"Tssarrah."*

"Tssarrah," Carson said. He stood up, went over to my pony, and entered the name. Then he went back to where Bult was squatting and started picking up the plastic bags. "We'll do the rest of these later. I don't want to spend another night in the Ponypiles."

And what was that all about? I thought, watching him put the plants in his pack.

Ev was still working on his specimen. "Come on," I said. "We're leaving."

"Just a couple more holos," he said, grabbing up the camera.

"What's he doing?" Carson said.

"Gathering data," I said.

Ev had to take holos of the outside, too, and scrape a sample of the outside surface.

It was another half hour before he was finished, and Carson acted fidgety the whole time, swearing at the ponies and looking at the clouds. "It looks like it's going to rain," he kept saying, which it didn't. The rain was obviously over. The clouds were breaking up and the puddles were already drying up.

We finally set off a little past midday, Bult and Carson in the lead and Ev bringing up the rear, taking holos of the Wall and the shuttlewren who was supervising our departure.

The stream that had cut across the ridge was already down to a trickle. We followed it down to where it connected with the Tongue, and began following it east.

It made a wide canyon here with room on the far side for ponies. Bult knelt down on the bank and inspected it, though I didn't see how he'd be able to see a *tssi mitss* in the muddy pink water. But they must all have been washed downriver in the flood because he gave the go-ahead and we waded the ponies across and started up the canyon.

After the first klom or so the bank got too rocky to be muddy and the clouds started to drift off. The sun even came out for a few minutes. Ev messed with his specimen, Carson and Bult talked and gestured, deciding which way to go, and I fumed. I was so mad I could've killed Carson. I'd been picturing him washed up in some gulch, half-eaten by a nibbler, for the last three days. And not so much as a word when he came back about how on hell he'd made it through the flood or where on hell he'd been.

We began to climb, and I could hear a faint roar up ahead.

"Do you hear that?" I asked Ev.

He had his head in his screen, working on his shuttlewren theory, and I had to ask him again.

"Yeah," he said, looking up blankly. "It sounds like a waterfall," and a couple of minutes later there was one. It was just a cascade, and not very high, but right above it the river twisted out of sight, so it was a real waterfall and not just a rough section of river, and we'd gotten above where the rain started, so the water ran a nice clear brownish color.

The gypsum piles made a whole series of bubbling zigzag rushes, and it was presentable-looking enough I figured Ev would at least make a try at naming it after C.J., but he didn't even look up from his screen and Carson rode right past it.

"Aren't we gonna name it?" I hollered ahead to him.

"Name what?" he said, as blank as Ev when I'd asked him about the roar.

"The waterfall."

"The water—?" he said, turning fast to look not at the waterfall, which was right in front of him, but up ahead.

"The *water*fall," I said, pointing at it with my thumb. "You know. Water. Falling. Don't we need to name it?"

"Of course," he said. "I just wanted to see what was up ahead first," which I didn't believe for a minute. Naming it hadn't so much as crossed his mind till I said it, and when I'd pointed at it he'd had an expression on his face I couldn't make out. Mad? Relieved?

I frowned. "Carson—" I started, but he'd already twisted around to look at Bult.

"Bult, do the indidges have a name for this?" he said.

Bult looked, not at the waterfall, but at Carson, with a questioning expression, which was peculiar, and Carson said, "He hasn't been this far up the Tongue. Ev, you got any ideas?"

Ev looked up from his screen. "According to my calculations, a shuttlebird could construct a Wall chamber in six years," he said happily, "which matches the mating period of the blackgull."

"What about Crisscross Falls?" I said.

Carson didn't even look annoyed, which was even more peculiar. "What about Gypsum Falls? We haven't used that yet, have we?"

"They'd have to begin building before maturation," Ev said, "which means the mating instinct would have to be activated at birth."

I checked the log. "No Gypsum Falls."

"Good," Carson said and set off again before I even had it entered.

We'd never named a weed that fast, let alone a waterfall, and Ev had apparently forgotten all about C.J. and sex, unless he thought there'd be plenty of other waterfalls to pick from. He might be right. I could still hear the roar of water, even when we went around the curve in the canyon, and around the next curve it got even louder.

Bult and Carson had stopped up above the waterfall and were consulting. "Bult says this isn't the Tongue," Carson said when we came up. "He says it's a tributary, and the Tongue's farther south."

He hadn't said that. Carson had just told me the Boohteri hadn't been up this far, and besides, Bult hadn't opened his mouth. And Carson looked preoccupied, the way Bult had right before the oil field episode.

But Carson was already splashing us back across the river and up the side of the canyon, not even looking at Bult to see which way he was going. He stopped at the top. "This way?" he asked Bult, and Bult gave him that same questioning look and then pointed off up a hill. And what was he leading us into now? *If* he was the one leading us.

We were above the gypsum now, the soapy slopes giving way to a brownish-rose igneous. Bult led us up a break in another, steeper hill, and toward a clump of silvershim trees. They were old ones, as tall as pines and in full leaf. They would have been blinding if the sun had been out, which it looked like it might be again in a minute.

"Here're the silvershims you were so anxious to see," I said to Ev, and after talking to his screen he raised his head and looked at them.

"They'd look a lot better if we were out in the sun," I said, and right then it put in an appearance and lit them up.

"I told you," I said, putting up my hand to shade my eyes.

Ev looked dazed, and no wonder. They glittered like one of C.J.'s shirts, the leaves shimmering and reflecting in the breeze.

"Not much like the pop-ups, is it?" I said.

"That's what gives the Wall its shiny texture!" he said, and slapped his forehead with the flat of his hand. "That was the only part I couldn't figure out, what gave it that shine." He started taking holos. "The shuttlewrens must chew the leaves up."

Well, so much for the silvershims he'd come all the way to Boohte to see. Was C.J. going to be mad when she found out Ev had forgotten her and taken up with some leaf-chewing, plaster-spitting bird!

The ponies had slowed to a crawl, and I would have been happy to take a rest stop and sit and look at the trees for a few minutes, but Bult and Carson rode on through the middle of them. When Bult wasn't looking, I picked a handful of the leaves and handed them to Ev, but I doubted if Bult would have fined me if he'd seen me. He was too busy looking ahead at a stream we were coming to.

It wasn't much bigger than the trickle up on top of the ridge, and it was coming from the wrong direction, but Bult claimed it was the Tongue. We started up it, winding in and out between the trees till the igneous on either side began to shut them out. It stacked up in squarish piles like old red bricks, and I grabbed a loose piece and ran an analysis. Basalt with cinnabar and gypsum crystals mixed in. I hoped Carson knew where he was going, because there was no room to backtrail here.

The canyon was getting steeper, too, and the ponies started to complain. The stream climbed up in a little series of cascades that chortled instead of roaring, and the banks turned into reddish-brown blocks, as steep as stairs.

The ponies'll never make it, I thought, and wondered if that was what Carson was up to—leading us into some defile so steep we'd have to carry the ponies through it on our shoulders just for spite. Carson'd have to carry his, too, though, and the way he was kicking his and swearing at it I didn't think he was playacting.

Carson's pony stopped and leaned back so far on his rear legs I thought he was going to pitch back onto me. Carson got off and pulled on the reins. "Come on, you beam-headed, rock-brained hind end," he shouted, leaning right in his pony's face, which must have scared him because he dumped a huge pile and started to topple over, but the rock wall stopped him.

"Don't you *dare* try that," Carson bellowed, "or I'll dump you in this stream for the *tssi mitss* to eat. Now, come *on!*" He gave a mighty yank on the reins, and the pony stepped back, dislodged a rock, which went clattering down into the stream, and took off up the steps like he was being chased.

I hoped my pony would get the hint, and he did. He lifted his tail and plopped a big pile. I got off and took hold of his reins. Bult took out his log and looked at Ev expectantly.

"Come on, Ev," I said.

Ev looked up from his screens, blinking in surprise. "Where are we going?" he said, like he hadn't so much as noticed we weren't still meandering through the silvershims.

"Up a cliff," I said. "It's a mating custom."

"Oh," he said, and dismounted. "The shuttlewren's flight range puts the silvershims well within range. I need to run tests on the plaster's composition to make sure, but I can't do that till I get back to King's X."

I knotted the reins tight under Useless's mouth, and whispered, "You lazy, broken-down copy of a horse, I'm going to do everything Carson's ever threatened you with and some he hasn't even thought of, and if you shit one more time before we're out of this canyon, I'll pull that pommelbone right out of your neck."

"What on hell's keeping you?" Carson said, coming back down the steps. He didn't have his pony.

"I'm not carrying this pony," I said.

He sidestepped the piles and got behind Useless and pushed for a while.

"Turn her around," he said.

"It's too narrow," I said. "You know ponies won't backtrail."

"Yeah," he said and took the reins and yanked her around till she was nose to nose with Ev's pony. "Come on, you poor imitation of a cow, let alone a horse," he said, and pulled, and she backed right up the canyon.

"You're smarter than you look," I called after him as he went back for Ev's.

"You ain't seen nothin' yet," he said.

We didn't have any more trouble with the ponies—they hung their heads like they'd been outsmarted and plodded steadily upward, but it still took us the better part of an hour to climb half a klom, and we were going nowhere. The stream shrank to a trickle and half disappeared between the rocks. It obviously wasn't the Tongue, and Carson must have had the same idea, because the next side canyon we came to he led us into it back the direction we'd come.

It was just as steep and twice as narrow. I didn't have to stop and take mineral samples, I just scraped them off with my legs as we rode past. The basalt blocks got smaller and began to look like a brick wall, and between them there were zigzag veins of the triangle-faceted crystals Carson had brought home. They acted like prisms, flashing pieces of the spectrum across the narrow canyon when the sun hit them.

Just about when I'd decided the canyon was going to run into a bricked-up dead end, we climbed up and onto the flat and back into silvershims.

We were on a wide overhang with trees growing right up to the edge, and I could see, off to the right, the Tongue far below and hear the roar of its waterfalls. Carson ignored it and rode off through the middle of the trees, heading straight for the far edge, not even bothering now to pretend Bult was leading.

I was right, I thought, he is leading us over a cliff, and came out of the trees. He'd tied his pony to a trunk and was standing close to the edge, looking out across the canyon. Ev rode up, and then Bult, and we just sat there on our ponies, gawking.

"Well, what do you know?" Carson said, trying to sound astonished. "Will you look at that? It's a waterfall."

That cascade with the gypsum piles was a waterfall. There was no word for what this was, except that it was obviously the Tongue, meandering through the silvershim forests on the far side and then plunging a good thousand meters into the canyon below us.

"My shit!" Ev said and dropped his shuttlewren. "My *shit!*"

My sentiments exactly. I'd seen holos of Niagara and Yosemite Falls when I was a kid, and they were pretty impressive, but they were only water. This—

"My *shit!*" Ev said again.

We were standing a good five hundred meters above the canyon floor and opposite a rose brick cliff that rose up another two hundred meters. The Tongue leapt out of a narrow V in the top of it and flung itself like a suicide down into the canyon with a roar I should never have mistaken for a cascade, throwing up a billow of mist and spray I could almost feel, and crashing into the swirling green-white water below.

The sun ducked under a cloud and then came out again, and the waterfall exploded like fireworks. There was a double rainbow across the top of the spray, and that one was probably from the water's refracting the sunlight, but the rest of them were from the cliff. It was crisscrossed with veins of the prismatic crystal, and they sparkled and glittered like diamonds, flashing chunks of rainbow onto the cliff, onto the falls, into the air, across the whole canyon.

"My *shit!"* Ev said again, hanging on to his pony's reins like they could hold him up. "That's the most beautiful thing I've ever seen!"

"Lucky us stumbling onto it this way," Carson said, and I turned to look at him. He had his thumbs in his belt loops and was looking smug. "If we'd kept on up that canyon," he said, "we'd have missed it altogether."

Lucky, my boots, I thought. All that dragging us through silvershims and up steps and consulting with Bult like you didn't know where you were going. This is what you were doing while I was waiting for you in the Wall, worried sick. Off chasing rainbows.

He must have found it by following the Tongue, looking for a way around the anticline, and then gone off wandering up cliffs and in and out of side canyons, searching for the best vantage point to show it to us from. If we'd stayed on the Tongue, the way he probably had when he found it, we'd have caught a half glimpse of it around some bend, or heard the roar get louder and guessed what was coming, instead of having it burst on us all at once like some view of rainbow heaven.

"Really lucky!" Carson said, his mustache quivering. "So, what do you want to name it?"

"Name it?" Ev's head jerked around to look at Carson, and I thought, Well, so much for birds and scenery, we're back to sex.

"Yeah," Carson said. "It's a natural landmark. It's gotta have a name. How about Rainbow Falls?"

"Rainbow Falls?" I snorted. "It's gotta have a better name than that," I said. "Something big, something that'll give some idea of what it looks like. Aladdin's Cave."

"Can't name it after a person."

"Prism Falls, Diamond Falls."

"Crystal Falls," Ev said, still staring at it.

He'd never get it past them. Chances were Big Brother, ever vigilant, would spot it and send us a pursuant that said Crissa Jane Tull worked on the survey team and the name was ineligible, and this time they'd be able to prove a connection, and we'd get fined to within an inch of our lives.

It was too bad, because Crystal Falls was the perfect name for it. And until Big Brother caught it, Ev would get a lot of jumps out of C.J.

"Crystal Falls," I said. "You're right. It's perfect."

I looked at Carson, wondering if he was thinking the same thing, but he wasn't even listening. He was looking at Bult, who had his head bent over his log.

"What's the Boohteri name for the waterfall, Bult?" Carson asked, and Bult glanced up, said something I couldn't hear, and looked down at his log again.

I left Ev drooling into the canyon and went over by them, thinking, Great, it's going to end up being called Dead Soup Falls or, worse, "Ours." "What'd he say?" I shouted to Carson.

"Damage to rock surface," Bult said. He was catching up his fines. "Damage to indigenous flora."

I figured he was going to have to add, "Inappropriate tone and manner," but Carson didn't look so much as annoyed. "Bult," he shouted, but only because of the roar, "what do you call it?"

He looked up again and stared vaguely off to the left of the waterfall. I took the opportunity to snatch the log out of his hands.

"The waterfall, you pony-brained nonsentient!" I said, pointing, and he shifted his gaze in the right direction, though who on hell knows what he was really looking at—a cloud maybe, or some rock slung halfway down the cliff.

"Do the Boohteri have a name for the waterfall?" Carson said patiently.

"Vwarrr," Bult said.

"That's the word for water," Carson said. "Do you have a name for this waterfall?" and Bult looked at Carson with that peculiar questioning look, and I thought, amazed, he's trying to figure out what Carson wants him to say.

"You said your people had never been in the mountains," Carson said, prompting him, and Bult looked like he'd just remembered his line.

"Nah nahm."

"You can't call it Nah Nahm," Ev said from behind us. "You've got to name it something beautiful. Something grand!"

"Grand Canyon!" I said.

"Something like Heart's Desire," Ev said. "Or Rainbow's End."

"Heart's Desire," Carson said thoughtfully. "That's not bad. Bult, what about the canyon? Do the Boohteri have a name for that?"

Bult knew his line this time. "Nah nahm."

"Crown Jewels Canyon," Ev said. "Starshine Falls."

"It should really be an indidge name," Carson said piously. "Remember what Big Brother said, 'Every effort should be made to discover the indigenous name of all flora, fauna, and natural landmarks.' "

"Bult just told you," I said. "They don't have a name for it."

"What about the cliff, Bult?" Carson said, looking hard at Bult. "Or the rocks? Do the indidges have a name for those?"

Bult looked like he needed a prompter, but Carson didn't seem mad. "What about the crystals?" he said, digging in his pocket. "What did you name that crystal?"

The roaring of the falls seemed to get louder.

"Thitsserrrah," Bult said.

"Yeah," Carson said. *"Tssarrrah.* You said Crystal Falls, Ev. We'll name it *Tssarrrah* after the crystals."

The roar got so loud it made me go dizzy, and I grabbed on to the pony.

"Tssarrrah Falls," Carson said. "What do you think, Bult?"

"Tssarrrah," Bult said. "Nahm."

"How about you?" Carson said, looking at me.

Ev said, "I think it's a beautiful name."

I walked over to the edge of the overhang, still feeling dizzy, and sat down.

"That settles it," Carson said. "Fin, you can send it in. Tssarrrah Falls."

I sat there listening to the roar and watching the glittering spray. The sun went in behind a cloud and burst out again, and rainbows darted across and above the cliff like shuttlewrens, sparkling like glass.

Carson sat down beside me. "Tssarrrah Falls," he said. "It was lucky the indidges had a word for those crystals. Big Brother's been wanting us to give more stuff indigenous names."

"Yeah," I said. "Lucky. What does *tssarrrah* mean, did Bult say?"

" 'Crazy female,' probably," he said. "Or maybe 'heart's desire.' "

"How much did you have to bribe him with? Next year's wages?"

"That was what was funny," he said, frowning. "I was going to give him the pop-up since he likes it so much. I figured I might have to give him a lot more than that after the oil field, but I asked him if he'd help, and he said yes, just like that. No fines, nothing."

I wasn't surprised.

"Did you get the name sent?" he said.

I looked at the falls for a long minute. The water roared down, dancing with rainbows. "I'll do in on the way down. Hadn't we better get going?" I said, and stood up.

"Yeah," he said, looking south at where the clouds were accumulating again. "Looks like it's going to rain again."

He held out his hand, and I yanked him to his feet. "You didn't have any business going off like that," I said.

He still had hold of my hand. "You didn't have any business nearly getting yourself killed." He let go of my hand. "Bult, come on, you've got to lead us back down."

"How on hell are we supposed to do that when the ponies won't backtrail?" I said, but Bult's pony walked right through the silvershims and down into the narrow canyon, and ours followed single file without so much as a balk.

"Dust storms aren't the only things being faked around here," I muttered.

Nobody heard me. Carson was up behind Bult, still doing the leading, down the side canyon, back through the one where the ponies had given us so much trouble, and then into another side canyon. I let them get ahead and looked back at Ev. He was bent over his terminal, probably looking at shuttlewren stats. I called C.J.

After I talked to her, I looked ahead and caught a glimpse of the side of the falls. The rainbows were lighting up the sky. Ev caught up to me. "They'll never get it on the pop-ups like it really was," he said.

"No," I said. "They won't."

The canyon widened, and we could see the falls from an angle, the water leaping sideways off the crystal-studded cliff and straight down.

"Speaking of which," Ev said, "what's Carson's first name?"

I'd told Carson he was smart. "What?"

"His first name. I got to thinking that I don't know it. On the pop-ups you never call each other anything but Findriddy and Carson."

"It's Aloysius," I said. "Aloysius Byron. His initials are A.B.C. Don't tell him I told you."

"*His* first name's Aloysius," he said thoughtfully. "And yours is Sarah."

As smart as they come.

"Did you know that in some species the males all compete for the most desirable female?" he said, smiling wryly. "Most of them don't stand a chance, though. She always picks the one who's the bravest. Or the smartest."

"Speaking of which, you were pretty smart to figure out the shuttlewrens built the Wall."

He brightened. "I still have to prove it," he said. "I'm going to have to run content analyses and work/size probabilities when I get back to King's X. And write it up."

"It'll be on the pop-ups, too," I said. "You'll be famous. Ev Parker, Socioexozoologist."

"You think so?" he said, as if it hadn't occurred to him before.

"I know so. A whole episode."

He looked hard at me. "It's you, isn't it? You're the one writing the episodes. You're Captain Jake Trailblazer."

"Nope," I said, "but I know who is." And her initials are C.J.T., I thought. "My shit, you may get a whole series."

The canyon opened out, and we were on another overlook, as big as a field this time, and lower down. Off to one side there was a way down, a slope leading back along the canyon to its floor. Beyond the canyon you could see the plains, pink and lavender. I could see the bluff that backed the anticline off to the east, too far off the scans to notice anything.

"Rest stop," Bult said and got off his pony. He sat down under a silvershim and opened out the pop-up.

"Do you hear that?" Carson said, looking up in the sky.

"It's C.J.," I said. "I told her to come get Ev so he can work on his theory. He's gotta run some tests."

"Is she doing aerials?" he said, looking anxiously back in the direction of the bluff.

"I told her to go south and come in over the Ponypiles, that we needed an aerial of them," I said.

"What about on the way back?"

"Are you kidding? She's going to have Ev with her. She won't be running any aerials with him in the heli. My shit, she probably forgot to do the aerials on the way down, she was so excited."

Carson looked at me questioningly. The heli swooped in and hovered above the field. C.J. jumped down from the bay, ran across to Ev, and practically knocked him down, kissing him.

"What's all that about?" Carson said, watching them.

"Courtship ritual," I said. "I told her Ev named the falls after her. I told her he named it Crystal Falls." I looked at Carson. "It was the only way he was ever going to get a jump. On this planet, anyway."

They were still in a clinch.

"When she finds out what we really named it," Carson said, grinning, "she's gonna be really mad. When are you gonna tell her?"

"I'm not," I said. "That's the name I sent."

He quit grinning. "What on hell did you do that for?"

"The other day Ev almost got a name past me. Crisscross Creek. You were worrying about what Bult was up to, and I was busy trying to load everything on the ponies, and when he asked me what we were going to name that little stream we crossed, I wasn't paying any attention. It wouldn't have gotten past Big Brother, but it got past me. Because I was busy worrying about something else."

Ev and C.J. had come out of their clinch and were looking at the waterfall. C.J. was making squealing noises that practically drowned out the falls.

"Crystal Falls won't get past Big Brother either," Carson said. "And *Tssarrrah* Falls would have."

"I know," I said, "but maybe they'll be so busy yelling at us over naming it that and killing the *tssi mitss* that they'll forget about the oil field."

He stared at Ev. C.J. was kissing him again. "What about Evie?"

"He won't tell," I said.

"What about Bult? How do we know he won't lead us out of these mountains and straight into another anticline? Or a diamond deposit?"

"That's not a problem either. All you've got to do is tell him."

He turned and looked at me. "Tell him what?"

"Can't you tell when somebody's got a crush on you? Making you fires, watching your scenes on the pop-ups over and over, giving you presents—"

"What presents?"

"All those dice. The binocs."

"They were *our* binocs."

"Yeah, well, the indidges seem to have a little trouble with that word. He gave you half a shuttlewren, too. And an oil field."

"That's why he said he'd help me with the waterfall." He stopped. "I thought Ev said he was a male."

"He is," I said, grinning. "And apparently he's got as much trouble telling what sex we are as we did with him."

"He thinks I'm a *female?"*

"It's an easy enough mistake," I said, grinning. I started to walk away.

He grabbed my arm and swung me around to face him. "You're sure you want to do this? We could get fired."

"No, we won't. We're Findriddy and Carson. We're too famous to get fired." I smiled at him. "Besides, they can't. After this expedition, we're going to owe them our wages for the next twenty."

We went over to C.J. and Ev, who were glued together again. "Ev, you and your pony go back with C.J. to King's X," I said. "You've gotta get that theory on the Wall written up."

"Evelyn told me about his theory," C.J. said. I wondered when he'd had the time. "And how he saved you from the *tssi mitss.*"

"We're gonna go ahead and finish out the expedition," Carson said, dragging Ev's pony over. "I thought we'd survey the Ponypiles as long as we're here."

We heaved the pony into the bay, and told C.J. to swing west over the Ponypiles and then north on the way home and try to get an aerial.

She wasn't paying any attention. "Take all the time you need surveying," she said, climbing on. "And don't worry about us. We'll be fine." She went forward.

Carson handed Ev his pack. "If you could take holos of the Wall at different places, I'd appreciate it," Ev said. "And samples of the plaster."

Carson nodded. "Anything else we can do?"

Ev looked up at the heli. "You've already done quite a bit." He shook his head, grinning. "Crystal Falls," he said, looking at me. "I still think we should've named it Heart's Desire."

He climbed up into the bay, and C.J. took off, dipping so close to the ground we both ducked.

"Maybe we did too much," Carson said. "I hope C.J. isn't so grateful she kills him."

"I wouldn't worry about it," I said. The heli circled the canyon like a shuttlewren and swooped down in front of the falls for a last look. They flew off, straight north across the plains, which meant we weren't going to get any aerials.

"We're just postponing the inevitable, you know," he said, looking after the heli. "Sooner or later Big Brother's going to figure out we've been having way too many dust storms, or Wulfmeier'll stumble onto that vein of silver in 246-73. If Bult doesn't figure out what he could get for this place and tell them first."

"I've been thinking about that," I said. "Maybe it wouldn't be as bad as we think. They didn't build the Wall, did you know that? They just moved in afterward, clunked the natives on the head, and took over. Bult'd probably own Starting Gate and half of Earth inside a year."

"And build a dam over the falls," he said.

"Not if it was a national park," I said. "You heard what Ev said about how he'd wanted to see the silvershims and the Wall, especially when they find out who built it. I figure people would come a long way to see something like this." I gestured at the falls. "Bult could charge admission."

"And fine them for leaving footprints," he said. "Speaking of which, what's to stop Bult from getting a crush on you once I tell him I'm not a female?"

"He thinks I'm a male. You said yourself, half the time you can't tell what sex I am."

"And you're never going to let me forget it, are you?"

"Nope," I said.

I went over to where Bult was sitting, watching the pop-up of Carson holding Skimpy Skirt's hand. "Come with me," Carson said.

"Come on, Bult," I said. "Let's get going."

Bult shut the pop-up and handed it to Carson.

"Congratulations," I said. "You're engaged."

Bult got out his log. "Disturbance of land surface," he said to me. "One-fifty."

I climbed up on Useless. "Let's go."

Carson was looking at the falls again. "I still think we should've named it Tssarrrah Falls," he said. He went over to his pony and started rummaging in his pack.

"What on hell are you doing now?" I said. "Let's go!"

"Inappropriate tone and manner," Bult said into his log.

"I wasn't talking to you," I said. "What are you looking for?" I said to Carson.

"The binocs," Carson said. "Have you got 'em?"

"I gave 'em to you," I said. "Now, come on."

He got on his pony and we started off down the slope after Bult. Out beyond the cliff the plain was turning purple in the late afternoon. The Wall curved down out of the Ponypiles and meandered across it, and beyond it you could see the mesas and rivers and cinder cones of uncharted territory, spread out before me like a present, like a bowerbird's treasures.

"You did not give the binocs back to me," Carson said. "If you lost 'em again—"

Remake

To Fred Astaire

acknowledgments

Special thanks to Scott Kippen and Sheryl Beck and all the rest of the UNC Sigma Tau Deltans

and to

my daughter Cordelia and her statistics classes

and to

my secretary Laura Norton

all of whom helped come up with chase scenes, tears, happy endings, and all the other movie references

"Not much is impossible."

—Steve Williams
Industrial Light and Magic

"The girl seems to have talent but the boy can do nothing."

—Vaudeville booking report
on Fred Astaire

HOUSE LIGHTS DOWN

Before Titles

I saw her again tonight. I wasn't looking for her. It was an early Spielberg liveaction, *Indiana Jones and the Temple of Doom,* a cross between a shoot-'em-up and a VR ride and the last place you'd expect tap shoes, and it was too late. The musical had kicked off, as Michael Caine so eloquently put it, in 1965.

This liveaction was made in '84, at the very beginning of the computer graphics revolution, and it had a few CG sections: digitized Thugees being thrown off a cliff and a pathetically clunky morph of a heart being torn out. It also had a Ford Tri-Motor plane, which was what I was looking for when I found her.

I needed the Tri-Motor for the big good-bye scene at the airport, so I'd accessed Heada, who knows everything, and she'd said she thought there was one in one of the liveaction Spielbergs, the second Indy maybe. "It's close to the end."

"How close?"

"Fifty frames. Or maybe it's in the third one. No, that's a dirigible. The second one. How's the remake coming, Tom?"

Almost done, I thought. Three years off the AS's and still sober.

"The remake's stuck on the big farewell scene," I said, "which is why I need the plane. So what do you know, Heada? What's the latest gossip? Who's ILMGM being taken over by this month?"

"Fox-Mitsubishi," she said promptly. "Mayer's frantic. And the word is Universal's head exec is on the way out. Too many addictive substances."

"How about you?" I said. "Are you still off the AS's? Still assistant producer?"

"Still playing Melanie Griffith," she said. "Does the plane have to be color?"

"No. I've got a colorization program. Why?"

"I think there's one in *Casablanca.*"

"No, there's not," I said. "That's a two-engine Lockheed."

She said, "Tom, I talked to a set director last week who was on his way to China to do stock shots."

I knew where this was leading. I said, "I'll check the Spielberg. Thanks," and signed off before she could say anything else.

The Ford Tri-Motor wasn't at the end, or in the middle, which had one of the worst mattes I'd ever seen. I worked my way back through it at 48 per, thinking it would have been easier to do a scratch construct, and finally found the plane almost at the beginning. It was pretty good—there were close-ups of the door and the cockpit, and a nice medium shot of it taking off. I went back a few frames, trying to see if there was a close-up of the propellers, and then said, "Frame 1-001," in case there was something at the very beginning.

Trademark Spielberg morph of the old Paramount Studios mountain into opening shot, this time of a man-sized silver gong. Cue music. Red smoke. Credits. And there she was, in a chorus line, wearing silver tap shoes and a silver-sequined leotard with tuxedo lapels. Her face was made up thirties style—red lips, Harlow eyebrows—and her hair was platinum blonde.

It caught me off guard. I'd already searched the eighties, looking in everything from *Chorus Line* to *Footloose,* and not found any sign of her.

I said, "Freeze!" and then "Enhance right half," and leaned forward to look at the enlarged image to make sure, as if I hadn't already been sure the instant I saw her.

"Full screen," I said, "forward realtime," and watched the rest of the number. It wasn't much—four lines of blondes in sequined top hats and ribboned tap shoes doing a simple chorus routine that could have been lifted from *42nd Street,* and was about as good. There must not have been any dancing teachers around in the eighties either.

The steps were simple, mostly trenches and traveling steps, and I thought it had probably been one of the very first ones Alis did. She had been this good when I saw her practicing in the film hist classroom. And it was too Berkeleyesque. Near the end of the number it went to angles and a pan shot of red scarves being pulled out of tuxedo pockets, and Alis disappeared. The Digimatte couldn't have matched that many switching shots, and I doubted if Alis had even tried. She had never had any patience with Busby Berkeley.

"It isn't dancing," she'd said, watching the kaleidoscope scene in *Dames* that first night in my room.

"I thought he was famous for his choreography," I'd said.

"He is, but he shouldn't be. It's all camera angles and stage sets. Fred Astaire always insisted his dances be shot full-length and one continuous take."

"Frame ten," I said so I wouldn't have to put up with the mountain morph again, and started through the routine again. "Freeze."

The screen froze her in midkick, her foot in the silver tap shoe extended the way Madame Dilyovska of Meadowville had taught her, her arms outstretched. She was supposed to be smiling, but she wasn't. She had a look of intentness, of careful concentration under the scarlet lipstick, the penciled brows, the look she had worn that first night, watching Ginger Rogers and Fred Astaire on the freescreen.

"Freeze," I said again, even though the image hadn't moved, and sat there for a long time, thinking about Fred Astaire and looking at her face, that face I had seen under endless wigs, in endless makeups, that face I would have known anywhere.

TITLE UP

Opening Credits
and Dissolve to
Pan Shot of Party Scene

MOVIE CLICHE #14: The Party. Disjointed snatches of bizarre conversation, excessive AS consumption, assorted outrageous behavior.

SEE: ***Notorious, Greed, The Graduate, Risky Business, Breakfast at Tiffany's, Dance, Fools, Dance, The Party.***

She was born the year Fred Astaire died. Hedda told me that the first time I met Alis. It was at one of the dorm parties the studios sponsor. There's one every week, ostensibly to show off their latest CG innovations and try to tempt hackate film-school seniors into a life of digitizing and indentured servitude, really so their execs can score some chooch (of which there is never enough) and some popsy (of which there is plenty, all of it in white halter dresses and platinum hair). Hollywood at its finest, which is why I stay away, but this one was being sponsored by ILMGM, and Mayer had promised me he'd be there.

I'd been doing a paste-up for him, digitizing his studio exec boss's popsy into a River Phoenix movie. I wanted to give Mayer the opdisk and get paid before the boss found a new face. I'd already done the paste-up twice and fed in the feedback bypasses three times because he'd switched girlfriends, and this last time the new face had insisted on a scene *with* River Phoenix, which meant I'd had to watch every River Phoenix movie ever made, of which there are a lot—he was one of the first actors copyrighted. I wanted to get the money before Mayer's boss changed partners again. The money and some AS's.

The party was crammed into the dorm lounge, like always—freshies and faces and hackates and hangers-on. The usual suspects. There was a big fibe-op freescreen in the middle of the room. I glanced up at it, hoping to God it wasn't the new River Phoenix movie, and was surprised to see Fred Astaire and Ginger Rogers, dancing up a flight of stairs. Fred was wearing tails, and Ginger was in a white dress that flared into black at the hem. I couldn't hear the music over the party din, but it looked like the Continental.

I couldn't see Mayer. There was a guy in an ILMGM baseball cap and a beard—the hackates' uniform—standing under the freescreen with a remote, holding forth to a couple of CG majors. I scanned the crowd, looking for suits and/or somebody I knew who'd give me some chooch.

"Hi," one of the faces said breathily. She had platinum hair, a white halter dress, and a beauty mark, and she was very splatted. Her eyes weren't focusing at all.

"Hi," I said, still scanning the crowd. "And who are you supposed to be? Jean Harlow?"

"Who?" she said, and I wanted to believe that that was because of whatever AS she was doing, but it probably wasn't. Ah, Hollywood, where everybody wants to be in the movies and nobody's ever bothered to watch one.

"Jeanne Eagles?" I said. "Carole Lombard? Kim Basinger?"

"No," she said, trying to focus. "Marilyn Monroe. Are you a studio exec?"

"Depends. Do you have any chooch?"

"No," she said sadly. "All gone."

"Then I'm not a studio exec," I said. I could see an exec, though, over by the stairs, talking to another Marilyn. The Marilyn was wearing a white halter dress just like the one I was talking to had on.

I've never understood why the faces, who have nothing to sell but an original personality, an original face, all try to look like somebody else. But I guess it makes sense. Why should they be different from everybody else in Hollywood, which has always been in love with sequels and imitations and remakes?

"Are you in the movies?" my Marilyn persisted.

"Nobody's in the movies," I said, and started toward the studio exec through the crush.

It was harder work than hauling the *African Queen* through the reeds. I edged my way between a group of faces talking about a rumor that Columbia Tri-Star was hiring warmbodies, and then a couple of geekates in data helmets at some other party altogether, and over to the stairs.

I couldn't tell it wasn't Mayer till I got close enough to hear the exec's voice—studio execs are as bad as Marilyns. They all look alike. And have the same line.

". . . looking for a face for my new project," he was saying. The new project was a remake of *Back to the Future* starring, natch, River Phoenix. "It's a perfect time to rerelease," he said, leaning down the Marilyn's halter top. "They say we're *this* close"—he held his thumb and forefinger together, almost touching—"to getting the real thing."

"The real thing?" the Marilyn said, in a fair imitation of Marilyn Monroe's breathy voice. She looked more like her than mine had, though she was a little thick in the waist. But the faces don't worry about that as much as they used to. A few extra pounds can be didged out. Or in. "You mean time travel?"

"I mean time travel. Only it won't be in a DeLorean. It'll be in a time machine that looks like the skids. We've already come up with the graphics. The only thing we don't have is an actress to play opposite River. The director wanted to go with Michelle Pfeiffer or Lana Turner, but I told him I think we should go with an unknown. Somebody with a new face, somebody special. You interested in being in the movies?"

I'd heard this line before. In *Stage Door*. 1937.

I waded back into the party and over to the freescreen, where the baseball-cap-and-beard was holding forth to some freshies. ". . . programmed for any shots you want. Dolly shots, split-screens, pans. Say you want a close-up of this guy." He pointed up at the screen with the remote.

"Fred Astaire," I said. "That guy is Fred Astaire."

"You punch in 'close-up'—"

Fred Astaire's face filled the screen, smiling.

"This is ILMGM's new edit program," the baseball cap said to me. "It picks angles, combines shots, makes cuts. All you need is a full-length base shot to work from, like this one." He hit a button on the remote, and a full-length shot of Fred and Ginger replaced Fred's face. "Full-length shots are hard to come by. I had to go all the way back to the b-and-w's to find anything long enough, but we're working on that."

He hit another button, and we were treated to a view of Fred's mouth, and then his hand. "You can do any edit program you want," Baseball Cap said, watching the screen. Fred's mouth again, the white carnation in his lapel, his hand. "This one takes the base shot and edits it using the shot sequence of the opening scene from *Citizen Kane*."

A medium-shot of Ginger, and then of the carnation. I wondered which one was supposed to be Rosebud.

"It's all preprogrammed," Baseball Cap said. "You don't have to do a thing. It does everything."

"Does it know where Mayer is?" I asked.

"He *was* here," he said, looking vaguely around, and then back at the screen, where Fred was going through his paces. "It can extrapolate long shots, aerials, two-shots."

"Have it extrapolate somebody who knows where Mayer is," I said, and went back over the side and into the water. The party was getting steadily more crowded. The only ones with any room at all to move were Fred and Ginger, swirling up and down the staircase.

The exec I'd seen before was in the middle of the room, pitching to the same Marilyn, or a different one. Maybe he knew where Mayer was. I started toward him, and then spotted Hedda in a pink strapless sheath and diamond bracelets. *Gentlemen Prefer Blondes.*

Hedda knows everything, all the news, all the gossip. If anybody knew where Mayer was, it'd be Hedda. I waded my way over to her, past the exec, who was explaining time travel to the Marilyn. "It's the same principle as the skids," he said. "The Casimir effect. The randomized electrons in the walls create a negative-matter region that produces an overlap interval."

He must have been a hackate before he morphed into an exec.

"The Casimir effect lets you overlap space to get from one skids station to another, and the same thing's theoretically possible for getting from one parallel timefeed to another. I've got an opdisk that explains it all," he said, running his hand down her haltered neck. "How about if we go up to your room and take a look at it?"

I squeezed past him, hoping I wouldn't come up covered with leeches, and hauled myself out next to Hedda. "Mayer here?" I asked.

"Nope," she said, her platinum head bent over an assortment of cubes and capsules in her pink-gloved hand. "He was here for a few minutes, but he left with one of the freshies. And when the party started there was a guy from Disney nosing around. The word is Disney's scouting a takeover of ILMGM."

Another reason to get paid now. "Did Mayer say if he was coming back?"

She shook her head, still deep in her study of the pharmacy.

"Any chooch in there?" I said.

"I think these are," she said, handing me two purple-and-white capsules. "A face gave me this stuff, and he told me which was which, but I can't remember. I'm pretty sure those are the chooch. I took some. I can let you know in a minute."

"Great," I said, wishing I could take them now. Mayer's leaving with a freshie might mean he was pimping again, which meant another paste-up. "What's the word on Mayer's boss? His new girlfriend dump him yet?"

She looked instantly interested. "Not that I know of. Why? Did you hear something?"

"No." And if Hedda hadn't either, it hadn't happened. So Mayer'd just taken the freshie up to her dorm room for a quick pop or a quicker line or two of flake, and he'd be back in a few minutes, and I might actually get paid.

I grabbed a paper cup from a Marilyn swaying past and downed the capsules.

"So, Hedda," I said, since talking to her was better than to the baseball cap or the time-travel exec, "what other gossip you putting in your column this week?"

"Column?" she said, looking blank. "You always call me Hedda. Why? Is she a movie star?"

"Gossip columnist," I said. "Knew everything that was going on in Hollywood. Like you. So what is? Going on?"

"Viamount's got a new automatic foley program," she said promptly. "ILMGM's getting ready to file copyrights on Fred Astaire *and* Sean Connery, who finally died. And the word is Pinewood's hiring warmbodies for the new *Batman* sequel. And Warner's—" She stopped in midword and frowned down at her hand.

"What's the matter?"

"I don't think it's chooch. I'm getting a funny . . ." She peered at her hand. "Maybe the yellow ones were the chooch." She fished through her hand. "This feels more like ice."

"Who gave them to you?" I said. "The Disney guy?"

"No. This guy I know. A face."

"What does he look like?" I asked. Stupid question. There are only two varieties: James Dean and River Phoenix. "Is he here?"

She shook her head. "He gave them to me because he was leaving. He said he wouldn't need them anymore, and besides, he'd get arrested in China for having them."

"China?"

"He said they've got a liveaction studio there, and they're hiring stunt doubles and warmbodies for their propaganda films."

And I thought doing paste-ups for Mayer was the worst job in the world.

"Maybe it's redline," she said, poking at the capsules. "I hope not. Redline always makes me look like shit the next day."

"Instead of like Marilyn Monroe," I said, looking around the room for Mayer. He still wasn't back. The time-travel exec was edging toward the door with a Marilyn. The data-helmet geekates were laughing and snatching at air, obviously at a much better party than this one. Fred and Ginge were demonstrating another editing program. Rapid-fire cuts of Ginger, the ballroom curtains, Ginger's mouth, the curtains. It must be the shower scene from *Psycho.*

The program ended and Fred reached for Ginger's outstretched hand, her black-edged skirt flaring with momentum, and spun her into his arms. The edges of the freescreen started going to soft-focus. I looked over at the stairs. They were blurring, too.

"Shit, this isn't redline," I said. "It's klieg."

"It is?" she said, sniffing at it.

It is, I thought disgustedly, and what was I supposed to do now? Flashing on klieg wasn't any way to do a meeting with a sleaze like Mayer, and the damned stuff isn't good for anything else. No rush, no halluces, not even a buzz. Just blurred vision and then a flash of indelible reality. "Shit," I said again.

"If it is klieg," Hedda said, stirring it around with her gloved finger, "we can at least have some great sex."

"I don't need klieg for that," I said, but I started looking around the room for somebody to pop. Hedda was right. Flashing during sex made for an unforgettable orgasm. Literally. I scanned the Marilyns. I could do the exec's casting couch number on one of the freshies, but there was no way to tell how long that would take, and it felt like I only had a few minutes. The Marilyn I'd talked to before was over by the freescreen listening to the studio exec's time-travel spiel.

I looked over at the door. A girl was standing in the doorway, gazing tentatively around at the party as if she were looking for somebody. She had curly light brown hair, pulled back at the sides. The doorway behind her was dark, but there had to be light coming from somewhere because her hair shone like it was backlit.

"Of all the gin joints in all the world . . ." I said.

"Joint?" Hedda said, deep in her pill assortment. "I thought you said it was klieg." She sniffed it.

The girl had to be a face, she was too pretty not to be, but the hair was wrong, and so was the costume, which wasn't a halter dress and wasn't white. It was black, with a green fitted weskit, and she was wearing short green gloves. Deanna Durbin? No, the hair was the wrong color. And it was tied back with a green hair ribbon. Shirley Temple?

"Who's that?" I muttered.

"Who?" Hedda licked her gloved finger and rubbed it in the powder the pills had left on her glove.

"The face over there," I said, pointing. She had moved out of the doorway, over against the wall, but her hair was still catching the light, making a halo of her light brown hair.

Hedda sucked the powder off her glove. "Alice," she said.

Alice who? Alice Faye? No, Alice Faye'd been a platinum blonde, like everybody else in Hollywood. And she wasn't given to hair ribbons. Charlotte Henry in *Alice in Wonderland?*

Whoever the girl had been looking for—the White Rabbit, probably—she'd given up on finding him, and was watching the freescreen. On it, Fred and Ginger were dancing around each other without touching, their eyes locked.

"Alice who?" I said.

Hedda was frowning at her finger. "Huh?"

"Who's she supposed to be?" I said. "Alice Faye? Alice Adams? *Alice Doesn't Live Here Anymore?*"

The girl had moved away from the wall, her eyes still on the screen, and was heading toward the baseball cap. He leaped forward, thrilled to have a new audience, and started into his spiel, but she wasn't listening to him. She was watching Fred and Ginge, her head tilted up toward the screen, her hair catching the light from the fibe-op feed.

"I don't think any of this stuff is what he told me," Hedda said, licking her finger again. "It's her name."

"What?"

"Alice," she said. "A-l-i-s. It's her name. She's a freshie. Film hist major. From Illinois."

Well, that explained the hair ribbon, though not the rest of the getup. It wasn't Alice Adams. The gloves were 1950s, not thirties, and her face wasn't angular enough to be trying for Katharine Hepburn. "Who's she supposed to be?"

"I wonder which one of these is ice," Hedda said, poking around in her hand again. "It's supposed to make the flash go away faster. She wants to dance in the movies."

"I think you've had enough pill potluck," I said, reaching for her hand.

She squeezed it shut, protecting the pills. "No, really. She's a dancer."

I looked at her, wondering how many unmarked pills she'd taken before I got here.

"She was born the year Fred Astaire died," she said, gesturing with her closed fist. "She saw him on the fibe-op feed and decided to come to Hollywood to dance in the movies."

"*What* movies?" I said.

She shrugged, intent on her hand again.

I looked over at the girl. She was still watching the screen, her face intent. "Ruby Keeler," I said.

"Huh?" Hedda said.

"The plucky little dancer in *42nd Street* who wants to be a star." Only she was about twenty years too late. But just in time for a little popsy, and if she was wide-eyed enough to believe she could make it in the movies, it ought to be a piece of cake getting her up to my room.

I shouldn't have to explain time travel to her, like the exec. He was talking earnestly to a Marilyn wearing black fringe and holding a ukelele. *Some Like It Hot.*

"See, you're turning me down in this timefeed," he was saying, "but in a parallel timefeed we're already popping." He leaned closer. "There are hundreds of thousands of parallel timefeeds. Who *knows* what we're doing in some of them?"

"What if I'm turning you down in all of them?" the Marilyn said.

I squeezed past her fringe, thinking she might work out if Ruby didn't, and started through the crowd toward the screen.

"Don't!" Hedda said loudly.

At least half the room turned to look at her.

"Don't what?" I said, coming back to her. She was looking past me at Alis, and her face had the bleak, slightly dazed look klieg produces.

"You just flashed, didn't you?" I said. "I told you it was klieg. And that means I'll be doing the same thing shortly, so if you'll excuse me—"

She took hold of my arm. "I don't think you should—" she said, still looking at Alis. "She won't . . ." She was looking worriedly at me. Mildred Natwick in *She Wore a Yellow Ribbon,* telling John Wayne to be careful.

"Won't what? Give me a pop? You wanta bet?"

"No," she said, shaking her head like she was trying to clear it. "You . . . she knows what she wants."

"So do I. And thanks to your Russian-roulette approach to pharmaceuticals, it promises to be an unforgettable experience. If I can get Ruby up to my room in the next ten minutes. Now, if there are no further objections . . ." I said, and started past her.

She started to put out her hand, like she was going to grab my sleeve, and then let it drop.

The exec was talking about negative-matter regions. I went around him and over to the screen, where Alis was looking up at Fred's face, the staircase, Ginger's black-edged skirt, Fred's hand.

She was as pretty in close-up as she had been in the establishing shot. Her caught-back hair was picking up the flickering light from the screen and her face had an intent, focused look.

"They shouldn't do that," she said.

"What? Show a movie?" I said. " 'You've got to show a movie at a party. It's a Hollywood law.' "

She turned and smiled delightedly at me. "I know that line. It's from *Singin' in the Rain,*" she said, pleased. "I didn't mean the movie. It's them editing it like that." She looked back up at the screen. Or down. It was doing an aerial now, and all you could see were the tops of Fred and Ginger's heads.

"I take it you don't like Vincent's edit program?" I said.

"Vincent?"

I nodded toward the baseball cap, who was off in a corner doing a line of illy. "Doesn't he remind you of Vincent Price in *House of Wax?*"

The edit program was back to quick cuts—the steps, Fred's face, close-up of a step. The baby carriage scene from *Potemkin.*

"In more ways than one," I said.

"Fred Astaire always insisted they shoot his dances in full-length shot and a continuous take," she said without taking her eyes off the screen. "He said it's the only way to film dancing."

"He did, huh? No wonder I like the original better." I looked at her. "I've got it up in my room."

And that made her turn away from Ginger's flashingly cut feet, shoulder, hair, and look at me. It was the same intent, focused look she had had watching the screen, and I felt the edges start to blur.

"No cuts, no camera angles," I said rapidly. "Nothing pre-programmed. Full-length and continuous take. Want to come up and take a look?"

She looked back at the freescreen. Fred's chest, his face, his knees. "Yes," she said. "You've got the real movie? Not colorized or anything?"

"The real thing," I said, and led her up the stairs.

RUBY KEELER: [*Nervously*] I've never been in a man's apartment before.
ADOLPHE MENJOU: [*Pouring champagne*] You've never been in Hollywood before. [*Handing her glass*] Here, my dear, this will relax you.
RUBY KEELER: [*Hovering near door*] You said you had a screen test application up here. Shouldn't I fill it out?
ADOLPHE MENJOU: [*Turning down lights*] Later, my dear, after we've had a chance to get to know each other.

I've got anything you could want," I told Alis on the way up. "All the ILMGMs and the Warner and Fox-Mitsubishi libraries, at least everything that's been digitized, which should be everything you'd want." I led her down the hall. "The Fred Astaire–Ginger Rogers movies were Warner, weren't they?"

"RKO," she said.

"Same thing." I keyed the door. "Here we are," I said, and opened it onto my room.

She took a trusting step inside and then stopped at the sight of the arrays covering three walls with their mirrored screens. "I thought you said you were a student," she said.

Now was not the time to tell her I hadn't been to class in over a semester. "I am," I said, leaning past her so she'd step forward into the room, and picking up a shirt. "Clothes all over the floor, bed's not made." I lobbed the shirt into the corner. *"Andy Hardy Goes to College."*

She was looking at the digitizer and the fibe-op feed hookup. "I thought only the studios had Crays."

"I do work for them to help pay for tuition," I said. And keep me in chooch.

"What kind of work?" she said, looking up at her own face's reflection in the silvered screens, and now was not the time to tell her I specialized in procuring popsy for studio execs either.

"Remakes," I said. I smoothed out the blankets. "Sit down."

She perched on the edge of the bed, knees together.

"Okay," I said, sitting down at the comp. I asked for the Warner library menu. "The Continental's in *Top Hat,* isn't it?"

"The Gay Divorcee," she said. "Near the end."

"Main screen, end frame and back at 96," I said. Fred and Ginge leaped onto the screen and up over a table. "Rew at 96 frames per sec," and they jumped down off the table and back through breakfast to the ballroom.

I rew'd to the beginning of the number and let it go. "Do you want sound?" I said.

She shook her head, her face already intent on the screen, and maybe this hadn't been such a great idea. She leaned forward, and the same concentrated look she'd had downstairs came into her face, as if she were trying to memorize the steps. I might as well not have been in the room, which hadn't exactly been the idea in bringing her up here.

"Menu," I said. "Fred Astaire and Ginger Rogers movies." The menu came up. "Aux screen one, *Swingtime,"* I said. There was usually a big dance finale in these things, wasn't there? "End frame and back at 96."

There was. On the top left-hand screen, Fred in tails spun Ginge in a silver dress. "Frame 102-044," I said, reading the code at the bottom. "Forward realtime to end and repeat. Continuous loop. Screen two, *Follow the Fleet,* screen three, *Top Hat,* screen four, *Carefree.* End frame and back at 96."

I started continuous loops on them and went through the rest of the Fred and Ginger list, filling most of the left-hand array with their dancing: turning, tapping, twirling, Fred in tails, sailor's uniform, riding tweeds, Ginger in long, slinky dresses that flared out below the knee in a froth of feathers and fur and glitter. Waltzing, tapping, gliding through the Carioca, the Yam, the Piccolino. And all of them full-length. All of them without cuts.

Alis was staring at the screens. The careful, intent look was gone, and she was smiling delightedly.

"Anything else?"

"Shall We Dance," she said. "The title number. Frame 87-1309."

I set it running on the bottom row. Fred in meticulous tails, dancing with a chorus of blondes in black satin and veils. They all held up masks of Ginger Rogers's face, and they put them up in front of their faces and flirted away from Fred, their masks as stiff as faces.

"Any other movies?" I said, calling up the menu again. "Plenty of screens left. How about *An American in Paris?"*

"I don't like Gene Kelly," she said.

"Okay," I said, surprised. "How about *Meet Me in St. Louis?"*

"There isn't any dancing in it except the 'Under the Banyan Tree' number with Margaret O'Brien. It's because of Judy Garland. She was a terrible dancer."

"Okay," I said, even more surprised. *"Singin' in the Rain?* No, wait, you don't like Gene Kelly."

"The 'Good Mornin' ' number's okay."

I found it, Gene Kelly with Debbie Reynolds and Donald O'Connor, tapping up steps and over furniture in wild exuberance. Okay.

I scanned the menu for movies that didn't have Gene Kelly or Judy Garland in them. *"Good News?"*

" 'The Varsity Drag,' " she said, nodding. "It's right at the end. Do you have *Seven Brides for Seven Brothers?"*

"Sure. Which number?"

"The barnraising," she said. "Frame 27-986."

I called it up. I looked for something with Ruby Keeler in it. *"42nd Street?"*

She shook her head. "It's a Busby Berkeley. There's no dancing in it except for one background shot of a rehearsal and about sixteen bars in the 'Pettin' in the Park' number. There's never any dancing in Busby Berkeleys. Do you have *On the Town?"*

"I thought you didn't like Gene Kelly."

"Ann Miller," she said. "The 'Prehistoric Man' number. Frame 28-650. She's technically pretty good when she sticks to tap."

I don't know why I was so surprised or what I'd expected. Starstruck adoration, I guess. Ruby Keeler gushing, "Gosh, Mr. Ziegfeld, a part in your show! That'd be wonderful!" Or maybe Judy Garland, gazing longingly at the photo of Clark Gable in *Broadway Melody of 1938.* But she didn't like Judy, and she'd dismissed Gene Kelly as airily as if he was an auditioning chorus girl in a Busby Berkeley. Who she didn't like either.

I filled out the array with Fred Astaire, who she *did* like, though none of his color movies were as good as the b-and-w's, and neither were his partners. Most of them just hung on while he swung them around, or struck a pose and let him dance circles, literally, around them.

Alis wasn't watching them. She'd gone back to the center screen and was watching Fred, full-length, swirling Ginger weightlessly across the floor.

"So that's what you want to do," I said, pointing. "Dance the Continental?"

She shook her head. "I'm not good enough yet. I only know a few routines. I could do that," she said, pointing at the Varsity Drag, and then at the cowboy number from *Girl Crazy.* "And maybe that. Chorus, not lead."

And that wasn't what I expected either. The one thing the faces have in common under their Marilyn beauty marks is the unshakeable belief they've got what it takes to be a star. Most of them don't—they can't act or show emotion, can't even do a reasonable imitation of Norma Jean's breathy voice and sexy vulnerability—but they all think the only thing standing between them and stardom is bad luck, not talent. I'd never heard any of them say, "I'm not good enough."

"I'm going to need to find a dancing teacher," Alis was saying. "You don't know of one, do you?"

In Hollywood? She was as likely to find one as she was to run into Fred Astaire. Less likely.

And what if she *was* smart enough to know how good she was? What if she'd studied the movies and criticized them? None of it was going to bring back musicals. None of it was going to make ILMGM start shooting liveactions again.

I looked up at the arrays. On the bottom row Fred was trying to find the real Ginger in among the masks. On the third screen, top row, he was trying to talk her into a pop—she twirled away from him, he advanced, she returned, he bent toward her, she leaned languorously away.

All of which I'd better get on with or I was going to flash with Alis still sitting there on the edge of the bed, clothes on and knees together.

I asked for sound on Screen Three and sat down next to Alis on the bed. "I think you're good enough," I said.

She glanced at me, confused, and then realized I was picking up on her "I'm not good enough" line. "You haven't seen me dance," she said.

"I wasn't talking about dancing," I said, and bent forward to kiss her.

The center screen flashed white. "Message," it said. "From Heada Hopper." She'd spelled Hedda with an "a." I wondered if Hedda'd had another revelatory flash and was interrupting to tell it to me.

"Message override," I said, and stood up to clear the screen, but it was too late. The message was already on the screen.

"Mayer's here," it read. "Shall I send him up? Heada."

The last thing I wanted was Mayer up here. I'd have to make a copy of the paste-up and take it down to him. "River Phoenix file," I said to the computer, and shoved in a blank opdisk. *"Where the Boys Are.* Record remake."

The dancing screens went blank, and Alis stood up. "Should I go?" she said.

"No!" I said, rummaging for a remote. The comp spit out the disk, and I snatched it up. "Stay here. I'll be right back. I've just got to give this to a guy."

I handed her the remote. "Here. Hit *M* for Menu, and ask for whatever you want. If the movie you want isn't on ILMGM, you can call up the other libraries by hitting File. I'll be back before the Continental's over. Promise."

I started out the door. I wanted to shut the door to keep her there, but it looked more like I'd be right back if I left it open. "Don't leave," I said, and tore downstairs.

Heada was waiting for me at the foot of the stairs. "Sorry," she said. "Were you popping her?"

"Thanks to you, no," I said, scanning the room for Mayer. The room had gotten even more crowded since Alis and I left. So had the screen—a dozen Fred and Gingers were running split-screen circles around each other.

"I wouldn't have interrupted you," Heada said, "but you asked before if Mayer was here."

"It's okay," I said. "Where is he?"

"Over there." She pointed in the direction of the Freds and Gingers. Mayer was under them, listening to Vincent explain his edit program and twitching from too much chooch. "He said he wanted to talk to you about a job."

"Great," I said. "That means his boss has got a new girlfriend, and I've got to paste on a new face."

She shook her head. "Viamount's taking over ILMGM and Arthurton's going to head Project Development, which means Mayer's boss is out, and Mayer's scrambling. He's got to distance himself from his boss *and* convince Arthurton he should keep him instead of bringing in his own team. So this job is probably a bid to impress Arthurton, which could mean a remake, or even a new project. In which case . . ."

I'd stopped listening. Mayer's boss was out, which meant the disk in my hand was worth exactly nothing, and the job he wanted to see me about was pasting Arthurton's girlfriend into something. Or maybe the girlfriends of the whole Viamount board of directors. Either way I wasn't going to get paid.

". . . in *which* case," Heada was saying, "his coming to you is a good sign."

"Golly," I said, clasping my hands together. " 'This could be my big break.' "

"Well, it could," she said defensively. "Even a remake would be better than these pimping jobs you've been doing."

"They're all pimping jobs." I started through the crush toward Mayer.

Heada squeezed through after me. "If it *is* an official project," she said, "tell him you want a credit."

Mayer had moved to the other side of the freescreen, probably trying to get away from Vincent, who was right behind him, still talking. Above them, the crowd on the screen was still revolving, but slower and slower, and the edges of the room were starting to soft-focus. Mayer turned and saw me, and waved, all in slow motion.

I stopped, and Heada crashed into me. "Do you have any slalom?" I said, and she started fumbling in her hand again. "Or ice? Anything to hold off a klieg flash?"

She held out the same assortment of capsules and cubes as before, only not as many. "I don't think so," she said, peering at them.

"Find me something, okay?" I said, and squeezed my eyes shut, hard, and then opened them again. The soft-focus receded.

"I'll see if I can find you some lude," she said. "Remember, if it's the real thing, you want a credit." She slipped off toward a pair of James Deans, and I went up to Mayer.

"Here you go," I said to Mayer, and tried to hand him the disk. I wasn't going to get paid, but it was at least worth a try.

"Tom!" Mayer said. He didn't take the disk.

Heada was right. His boss was out.

"Just the guy I've been looking for," he said. "What have you been up to?"

"Working for you," I said, and tried again to hand him the disk. "It's all done. Just what you ordered. River Phoenix, close-up, kiss. She's even got four lines."

"Great," he said, and pocketed the disk. He pulled out a palmtop and punched in numbers. "You want this in your online account, right?"

"Right," I said, wondering if this was some kind of bizarre pre-flashing symptom: actually getting what you wanted. I looked around for Heada. She wasn't talking to the James Deans anymore.

"I can always count on you for the tough jobs," Mayer said. "I've got a new project you might be interested in." He put a friendly arm around my shoulder and led me away from Vincent. "Nobody knows this," he said, "but there's a possibility of a merger between ILMGM and Viamount, and if it goes through, my boss and his girlfriends'll be a dead issue."

How does Heada do it? I thought wonderingly.

"It's still just in the talking stages, of course, but we're all very excited about the prospect of working with a great company like Viamount."

Translation: It's a done deal, and scrambling isn't even the word. I looked down at Mayer's hands, half expecting to see blood under his fingernails.

"Viamount's as committed as ILMGM is to the making of quality movies, but you know how the American public is about mergers. So our first job, *if* this thing goes through, is to send them the message: 'We care.' Do you know Austin Arthurton?"

Sorry, Heada, I thought, it's another pimping job.

"What's the job?" I said. "Didging in Arthurton's girlfriend? Boyfriend? German shepherd?"

"Jesus, no!" he said, and looked around to make sure nobody'd heard that. "Arthurton's totally straight, vegetarian, clean, a real Gary Cooper type. He's completely committed to convincing the public the studio's in responsible hands. Which is where you come in. We'll supply you with a memory upgrade and automatic print-and-send, and I'll have you paid on receipt through the feed." He waved the disk of his old boss's girlfriend at me. "No more having to track me down at parties." He smiled.

"What's the job?"

He didn't answer. He looked around the room, twitching. "I see a lot of new faces," he said, smiling at a Marilyn in yellow feathers. *There's No Business Like Show Business.* "Anything interesting?"

Yes, up in my room, and I want to flash on her, not you, Mayer, so get to the point.

"ILMGM's taken some flack lately. You know the rap: violence, AS's, negative influence. Nothing serious, but Arthurton wants to project a positive image—"

And he's a real Gary Cooper type. I was wrong about its being a pimping job, Heada. It's a slash-and-burn.

"What does he want out?" I said.

He started to twitch again. "It's not a censorship job, just a few adjustments here and there. The average revision won't be more than ten frames. Each one'll take you maybe fifteen minutes, and most of them are simple deletes. The comp can do those automatically."

"And I take out what? Sex? Chooch?"

"AS's. Twenty-five a movie, and you get paid whether you have to change anything or not. It'll keep you in chooch for a year."

"How many movies?"

"Not that many. I don't know exactly."

He reached in his suit pocket and handed me an opdisk like the one I'd given him. "The menu's on here."

"Everything? Cigarettes? Alcohol?"

"All addictive substances," he said, "visuals, audios, and references. But the Anti-Smoking League's already taken the nicotine out, and most of the movies on the list have only got a couple of scenes that need to be reworked. A lot of them are already clean. All you'll have to do is watch them, do a print-and-send, and collect your money."

Right. And then feed in access codes for two hours. A wipe was easy, five minutes tops, and a superimpose ten, even working from a vid. It was the accesses that were murder. Even my River Phoenix–watching marathon was nothing compared to the hours I'd spend reading in accesses, working my way past authorization guards and ID-locks so the fibe-op source wouldn't automatically spit out the changes I'd made.

"No, thanks," I said, and tried to hand him back the disk. "Not without full access."

Mayer looked patient. "You know why the authorization codes are necessary."

Sure. So nobody can change a pixel of all those copyrighted movies, or harm a hair on the head of all those bought-and-paid-for stars. Except the studios.

"Sorry, Mayer. Not interested," I said, and started to walk away.

"Okay, okay," he said, twitching. "Fifty per and full exec access. I can't do anything about the fibe-op-feed ID-locks and the Film Preservation Society registration. But you can have complete freedom on the changes. No preapproval. You can be creative."

"Yeah," I said. "Creative."

"Is it a deal?" he said.

Heada was sidling past the screen, looking up at Fred and Ginger. They were in close-up, gazing into each other's eyes.

At least the job would pay enough for my tuition and my own AS's, instead of having to have Heada mooch for me, instead of taking klieg by mistake and having to worry about flashing on Mayer and carrying an indelible image of him around in my head forever. And they're all pimping jobs, in or out. Or official.

"Why not?" I said, and Heada came up. She took my hand and slipped a lude into it.

"Great," Mayer said. "I'll give you a list. You can do them in any order. A minimum of twelve a week."

I nodded. "I'll get right on it," I said, and started for the stairs, popping the lude as I went.

Heada pursued me to the foot of the stairs. "Did you get the job?"

"Yeah."

"Was it a remake?"

I didn't have time to listen to what she'd say when she found out it was a slash-and-burn. "Yeah," I said, and sprinted back up the stairs.

There really wasn't any hurry. The lude would give me half an hour at least and Alis was already on the bed. If she was still there. If she hadn't gotten her fill of Fred and Ginge and left.

The door was half-open the way I'd left it, which was either a good or a bad sign. I looked in. I could see the near bank. The array was blank. Thanks, Mayer. She's gone, and all I've got to show for it is a Hays Office list. If I'm lucky I'll get to flash on Walter Brennan taking a swig of rotgut whiskey.

I started to push the door open, and stopped. She was there, after all. I could see her reflection in the silvered screens. She was sitting on the bed, leaning forward, watching something. I pushed the door farther open so I could see what. The door scraped a little against the carpet, but she didn't move. She was watching the center screen. It was the only one on. She must not have been able to figure out the other screens from my hurried instructions, or maybe one screen was all she was used to back in Bedford Falls.

She was watching with that focused look she had had downstairs, but it wasn't the Continental. It wasn't even Ginger dancing side by side with Fred. It was Eleanor Powell. She and Fred were tap-dancing on a dark polished floor. There were lights in the background, meant to look like stars, and the floor reflected them in long, shimmering trails of light.

Fred and Eleanor were in white—him in a suit, no tails, no top hat this time, her in a white dress with a knee-length skirt that swirled out when she swung into the turns. Her light brown hair was the same length as Alis's and was pulled back with a white headband that glittered, catching the light from the reflections.

Fred and Eleanor were dancing side by side, casually, their arms only a little out to the sides for balance, their hands not even close to touching, matching each other step for step.

Alis had the sound off, but I didn't need to hear the taps, or the music, to know what this was. *Broadway Melody of 1940,* the second half of the "Begin the Beguine" number. The first half was a tango, formal jacket and long white dress, the kind of stuff Fred did with all his partners, except that he didn't have to cover for Eleanor Powell or maneuver fancy steps around her. She could dance as well as he did.

And the second half was this—no fancy dress, no fuss, the two of them dancing side by side, full-length shot and one long, unbroken take. He tapped a combination, she echoed it, snapping the steps out in precision time, he did another, she answered, neither of them looking at the other, each of them intent on the music.

Not intent. Wrong word. There was no concentration in them at all, no effort, they might have made up the whole routine just now as they stepped onto the polished floor, improvising as they went.

I stood there in the door, watching Alis watch them as she sat there on the edge of the bed, looking like sex was the farthest thing from her mind. Heada was right—this had been a bad idea. I should go back down to the party and find some face who wasn't locked at the knees, whose big ambition was to work as a warmbody for Columbia Tri-Star. The lude I'd just taken would hold off any flash long enough for me to talk one of the Marilyns into coming on cue.

And Ruby Keeler'd never miss me—she was oblivious to everything but Fred Astaire and Eleanor Powell, doing a series of rapid-fire tap breaks. She probably wouldn't even notice if I brought the Marilyn back up to the bed to pop. Which is what I should do, while I still had time.

But I didn't. I leaned against the door, watching Fred and Eleanor and Alis, watching Alis's reflection in the blank screens of the right-hand array. Fred and Eleanor were reflected in the screens, too, their images superimposed on Alis's intent face on the silver screens.

And intent wasn't the right word for her either. She had lost that alert, focused look she'd had watching the Continental, counting the steps, trying to memorize the combinations. She had gone beyond that, watching Fred and Eleanor dance side by side, their hands not touching, and they weren't counting either, they were lost in the effortless steps, in the easy turns, lost in the dancing, and so was Alis. Her face was absolutely still watching them, like a freeze frame, and Fred Astaire and Eleanor Powell were somehow still, too, even as they danced.

They tapped, turning, and Eleanor danced Fred back across the floor, facing him now but still not looking at him, her steps reflections of his, and then they were side by side again, swinging into a tap cadenza, their feet and the swirling skirt and the fake stars reflected in the polished floor, in the screens, in Alis's still face.

Eleanor swung into a turn, not looking at Fred, not having to, the turn perfectly matched to his, and they were side by side again, tapping in counterpoint, their hands almost touching, Eleanor's face as still as Alis's, intent, oblivious. Fred tapped out a ripple, and Eleanor repeated it, and glanced sideways over her shoulder and smiled at him, a smile of awareness and complicity and utter joy.

I flashed.

The klieg usually gives you at least a few seconds warning, enough time to do something to hold it off or at least close your eyes, but not this time. No warning, no telltale soft-focus, nothing.

One minute I was leaning against the door, watching Alis watch Fred and Eleanor tippity-tapping away, and the next: freeze frame, Cut! Print and Send, like a flashbulb going off in your face, only the afterimage is as clear as the picture, and it doesn't fade, it doesn't go away.

I put my hand up in front of my eyes, like somebody trying to shield themselves from a nuclear blast, but it was too late. The image was already burned into my neocortex.

I must've staggered back against the door, too, and maybe even cried out, because when I opened my eyes, she was looking at me, alarmed, concerned.

"Is something wrong?" she said, scrambling off the bed and taking my arm. "Are you okay?"

"I'm fine," I said. Fine. She was holding the remote. I took it away from her and clicked the comp off. The screen went silver, blank except for the reflection of the two of us standing there in the door. And superimposed on the reflection another reflection—Alis's face, rapt, absorbed, watching Fred and Eleanor in white, dancing on the starry floor.

"Come on," I said, and grabbed Alis's hand.

"Where are we going?"

Someplace. Anyplace. A theater where some other movie is showing. "Hollywood," I said, pulling her out into the hall. "To dance in the movies."

Camera whip-pans to medium-shot: LAIT station sign. Diamond screen, "Los Angeles Instransit" in hot pink caps, "Westwood Station" in bright green.

We took the skids. Mistake. The back section was closed off but they were still practically empty—a few knots of tourates on their way home from Universal Studios clumped together in the middle of the room, a couple of druggates asleep against the back wall, three others over by the far side wall, laying out three-card monte hands on the yellow warning strip, one lone Marilyn.

The tourates were watching the station sign anxiously, like they were afraid they'd miss their stop. Fat chance. The time between Instransit stations may be inst, but it takes the skids a good ten minutes to generate the negative-matter region that produces the transit, and another five afterwards before they turn on the exit arrows, during which time nobody was going anywhere.

The tourates might as well relax and enjoy the show. What there was of it. Only one of the side walls was working, and half of it was running a continuous loop of ads for ILMGM, which apparently didn't know it'd been taken over yet. In the center of the wall, a digitized lion roared under the studio trademark in glowing gold: "Anything's Possible!" The screen blurred and went to swirling mist, while a voice-over said, "ILMGM! More Stars Than There Are in Heaven," and then announced names while said stars appeared out of the fog. Vivien Leigh tripping toward us in a huge hoop skirt; Arnold Schwarzenegger roaring in on a motorcycle; Charlie Chaplin twirling his cane.

"Constantly working to bring you the brightest stars in the firmament," the voice-over said, which meant the stars currently in copyright litigation. Marlene Dietrich, Macaulay Culkin at age ten, Fred Astaire in top hat and tails, strolling effortlessly, casually toward us.

I'd dragged Alis out of the dorm to get away from mirrors and the Beguine and Fred, tippity-tapping away on my frontal lobe, to find something different to look at if I flashed again, but all I'd done was exchange my screen for a bigger one.

The other wall was even worse. It was apparently later than I'd thought. They'd shut the ads off for the night, and it was nothing but a long expanse of mirror. Like the polished floor Fred Astaire and Eleanor Powell had danced on, side by side, their hands nearly—

I focused on the reflections. The druggates looked dead. They'd probably taken capsules Heada told them were chooch. The Marilyn was practicing her pout in the mirror, flinching forward with a look of open-mouthed surprise, and splaying her hand against her white pleated skirt to keep it from billowing up. The steam grating scene from *The Seven Year Itch.*

The tourates were still watching the station sign, which read La Brea Tar Pits. Alis was watching it, too, her face intent, and even in the fluorescents and the flickering light of ILMGM upcoming remakes, her hair had that curious backlit look. Her feet were apart, and she held her hands out, braced for sudden movement.

"No skids in Riverwood, huh?" I said.

She grinned. "Riverwood. That's Mickey Rooney's hometown in *Strike Up the Band,"* she said. "We only had a little one in Galesburg. And it had seats."

"You can squeeze more people in during rush hour without seats. You don't have to stand like that, you know."

"I know," she said, moving her feet together. "I just keep expecting us to move."

"We already did," I said, glancing at the station sign. It had changed to Pasadena. "For about a nanosecond. Station to station and no in-between. It's all done with mirrors."

I stood on the yellow warning strip and put my hand out toward the side wall. "Only they're not mirrors. They're a curtain of negative matter you could put your hand right through. You need to get a studio exec on the make to explain it to you."

"Isn't it dangerous?" she said, looking down at the yellow warning strip.

"Not unless you try to walk through them, which ravers sometimes try to do. There used to be barriers, but the studios made them take them out. They got in the way of their promos."

She turned and looked at the far wall. "It's so big!"

"You should see it during the day. They shut off the back part at night. So the druggates don't piss on the floor. There's another room back there," I pointed at the rear wall, "that's twice as big as this."

"It's like a rehearsal hall," Alis said. "Like the dance studio in *Swing-time.* You could almost dance in here."

" 'I won't dance,' " I said. " 'Don't ask me.' "

"Wrong movie," she said, smiling. "That's from *Roberta.*"

She turned back to the mirrored side wall, her skirt flaring out, and her reflection called up the image of Eleanor Powell next to Fred Astaire on the dark, polished floor, her hand—

I forced it back, staring determinedly at the other wall, where a trailer for the new *Star Trek* movie was flashing, till it receded, and then turned back to Alis.

She was looking at the station sign. Pasadena was flashing. A line of green arrows led to the front, and the tourates were following them through the left-hand exit door and off to Disneyland.

"Where are we going?" Alis said.

"Sight-seeing," I said. "The homes of the stars. Which should be Forest Lawn, only they aren't there anymore. They're back up on the silver screen working for free."

I waved my hand at the near wall, where a trailer for the remake of *Pretty Woman,* starring, natch, Marilyn Monroe, was showing.

Marilyn made an entrance in a red dress, and the Marilyn stopped practicing her pout and came over to watch. Marilyn flipped an escargot at a waiter, went shopping on Rodeo Drive for a white halter dress, faded out on a lingering kiss with Clark Gable.

"Appearing soon as Lena Lamont in *Singin' in the Rain,*" I said. "So tell me why you hate Gene Kelly."

"I don't hate him exactly," she said, considering. "*American in Paris* is awful, and that fantasy thing in *Singin' in the Rain,* but when he dances with Donald O'Connor and Frank Sinatra, he's actually a good dancer. It's just that he makes it look so *hard.*"

"And it isn't?"

"No, it *is.* That's the point." She frowned. "When he does jumps or complicated steps, he flails his arms and puffs and pants. It's like he wants you to know how hard it is. Fred Astaire doesn't do that. His routines are lots harder than Gene Kelly's, the steps are *terrible,* but you don't see any of that on the screen. When he dances, it doesn't look like he's working at all. It looks easy, like he just that minute made it up—"

The image of Fred and Eleanor pushed forward again, the two of them in white, tapping casually, effortlessly, across the starry floor—

"And he made it look so easy you thought you'd come to Hollywood and do it, too," I said.

"I know it won't be easy," she said quietly. "I know there aren't a lot of liveactions—"

"Any," I said. "There aren't *any* liveactions being made. Unless you're in Bogota. Or Beijing. It's all CGs. No actors need apply."

Dancers either, I thought, but didn't say it. I was still hoping to get a pop out of this, if I could hang onto her till the next flash. If there was a next flash. I was getting a killing headache, which wasn't supposed to be a side-effect.

"But if it's all computer graphics," Alis was saying earnestly, "then they can do whatever they want. Including musicals."

"And what makes you think they want to? There hasn't been a musical since 1996."

"They're copyrighting Fred Astaire," she said, gesturing at the screen. "They must want him for something."

Something is right, I thought. The sequel to *The Towering Inferno.* Or snuffporn movies.

"I said I knew it wouldn't be easy," she said defensively. "You know what they said about Fred Astaire when he first came to Hollywood? Everybody said he was washed up, that his sister was the one with all the talent, that he was a no-talent vaudeville hoofer who'd never make it in movies. On his screen test somebody wrote, 'Thirty, balding, can dance a little.' They didn't think he could do it either, and look what happened."

There were movies for him to dance in, I didn't say, but she must have seen it in my face because she said, "He was willing to work really hard, and so am I. Did you know he used to rehearse his routines for weeks before the movie even started shooting? He wore out six pairs of tap shoes rehearsing *Carefree.* I'm willing to practice just as hard as he did," she said. "I know I'm not good enough. I need to take ballet, too. All I've had is jazz and tap. And I don't know very many routines yet. And I'm going to have to find somebody to teach me ballroom."

Where? I thought. There hasn't been a dancing teacher in Hollywood in twenty years. Or a choreographer. Or a musical. CGs might have killed the liveaction, but they hadn't killed the musical. It had died all by itself back in the sixties.

"I'll need a job to pay for the dancing lessons, too," she was saying. "The girl you were talking to at the party—the one who looks like Marilyn Monroe—she said maybe I could get a job as a face. What do they do?"

Go to parties, stand around trying to get noticed by somebody who'll trade a pop for a paste-up, do chooch, I thought, wishing I had some.

"They smile and talk and look sad while some hackate does a scan of them," I said.

"Like a screen test?" Alis said.

"Like a screen test. Then the hackate digitizes the scan of your face and puts it into a remake of *A Star Is Born* and you get to be the next Judy Garland. Only why do that when the studio's already got Judy Garland? And Barbra Streisand. And Janet Gaynor. And they're all copyrighted, they're already stars, so why would the studios take a chance on a new face? And why take a chance on a new movie when they can do a sequel or a copy or a remake of something they already own? And while we're at it, why not *star* remakes in the remake? Hollywood, the ultimate recycler!"

I waved my hand at the screen where ILMGM was touting coming attractions. *"The Phantom of the Opera,"* the voice-over said. "Starring Anthony Hopkins and Meg Ryan."

"Look at that," I said. "Hollywood's latest effort—a remake of a remake of a silent!"

The trailer ended, and the loop started again. The digitized lion did its digitized roar, and above it a digitized laser burned in gold: "Anything's Possible!"

"Anything's possible," I said, "if you have the digitizers and the Crays and the memory and the fibe-op feed to send it out over. And the copyrights."

The golden words faded into fog, and Scarlett simpered her way out of it towards us, holding up her hoop skirt daintily.

"Anything's possible, but only for the studios. They own everything, they control everything, they—"

I broke off, thinking, there's no way she'll give me a pop after that little outburst. Why didn't you just tell her straight out her little dream's impossible?

But she wasn't listening. She was looking at the screen, where the copyright cases were being trotted out for inspection. Waiting for Fred Astaire to appear.

"The first time I ever saw him, I knew what I wanted," she said, her eyes on the wall. "Only 'wanted' isn't the right word. I mean, not like you want a new dress—"

"Or some chooch," I said.

"It's not even that kind of wanting. It's . . . there's a scene in *Top Hat* where Fred Astaire's dancing in his hotel room and Ginger Rogers has the room below him, and she comes up to complain about the noise, and he tells her that sometimes he just finds himself dancing, and *she* says—"

" 'I suppose it's a kind of affliction,' " I said.

I'd expected her to smile at that, the way she had at my other movie quotes, but she didn't.

"An affliction," she said seriously. "Only that isn't it either, exactly. It's . . . when he dances, it isn't just that he makes it look easy. It's like all the steps and rehearsing and the music are just practice, and what he does is the real thing. It's like he's gone beyond the rhythm and the time steps and the turns to this other place. . . . If I could get there, do that . . ."

She stopped. Fred Astaire was sauntering toward us out of the mist in his top hat and tails, tipping his top hat jauntily forward with the end of his cane. I looked at Alis.

She was looking at him with that lost, breathless look she had had in my room, watching Fred and Eleanor, side by side, dressed in white, turning and yet still, silent, beyond motion, beyond—

"Come on," I said, and yanked on her hand. "This is our stop," and followed the green arrows out.

SCENE: ***Hollywood premiere night at Grauman's Chinese Theatre. Searchlights crisscrossing the night sky, palm trees, screaming fans, limousines, tuxedos, furs, flashbulbs popping.***

We came out on Hollywood Boulevard, on the corner of Chaos and Sensory Overload, the worst possible place to flash.

It was a DeMille scene, as usual. Faces and tourates and freelancers and ravers and thousands of extras, milling among the vid places and VR caves. And among the screens: drops and freescreens and diamonds and holos, all showing trailers edited à la *Psycho* by Vincent.

Trump's Chinese Theater had two huge dropscreens in front of it, running promos of the latest remake of *Ben-Hur.* On one of them, Sylvester Stallone in a bronze skirt and digitized sweat was leaning over his chariot, whipping the horses.

You couldn't see the other. There was a vid-neon sign in front of it that said Happy Endings, and a holoscreen showing Scarlett O'Hara in the fog, saying, "But, Rhett, I love you."

"Frankly, my dear—I love you, too," Clark Gable said, and crushed her in his arms. "I've always loved you!"

"The cement has stars in it," I said to Alis, pointing down. It was too crowded to see the sidewalk, let alone the stars. I led her out into the street, which was just as crowded, but at least it was moving, and down toward the vid places.

Hawkers from the VR caves crushed flyers into our hands, two dollars off reality, and River Phoenix pushed up. "Drag? Flake? A pop?"

I bought some chooch and popped it right there, hoping it would stave off a flash till we got back to the dorm.

The crowd thinned out a little, and I led Alis back onto the sidewalk and past a VR cave advertising, "A hundred percent body hookup! A hundred percent realistic!"

A hundred percent realistic, all right. According to Heada, who knows everything, simsex takes more memory than most of the VR caves can afford, and half of them slap a data helmet on the customer, add some noise to make it look like a VR image, and bring in a freelancer.

I towed Alis around the VR cave and straight into a herd of tourates standing in front of a booth called A Star Is Born and gawking at a vid-pitch. "Make your dreams come true! Be a movie star! $89.95, including disk. Studio-licensed! Studio-quality digitizing!"

"I don't know, which one do you think I should do?" a fat female tourate was saying, flipping through the menu.

A bored-looking hackate in a white lab coat and James Dean pompadour glanced at the movie she was pointing at, handed her a plastic bundle, and motioned her into a curtained cubicle.

She stopped halfway in. "I'll be able to watch this on the fibe-op feed, won't I?"

"Sure," James Dean said, and yanked the curtain across.

"Do you have any musicals?" I asked, wondering if he'd lie to me like he had to the tourate. She wasn't going to be on the fibe-op feed. Nothing gets on except studio-authorized changes. Paste-ups and slash-and-burns. She'd get a tape of the scene and orders not to make any copies.

He looked blank. "Musicals?"

"You know. Singing? Dancing?" I said, but the tourate was back wearing a too-short white robe and a brown wig with braids looped over her ears.

"Stand up here," James Dean said, pointing at a plastic crate. He fastened a data harness around her large middle and went over to an old Digimatte compositor and switched it on.

"Look at the screen," he said, and the tourates all moved so they could see it. Storm troopers blasted away, and Luke Skywalker appeared, standing in a doorway over a dropoff, his arm around a blank blue space in the screen.

I left Alis watching and pushed through the crowd to the menu. *Stagecoach, The Godfather, Rebel without a Cause.*

"Okay, now," James Dean said, typing onto a keyboard. The female tourate appeared on the screen next to Luke. "Kiss him on the cheek and step off the box. You don't have to jump. The data harness'll do everything."

"Won't it show in the movie?"

"The machine cuts it out."

They didn't have any musicals. Not even Ruby Keeler. I worked my way back to Alis.

"Okay, roll 'em," James Dean said. The fat tourate smooched empty air, giggled, and jumped off the box. On the screen, she kissed Luke's cheek, and they swung out across a high-tech abyss.

"Come on," I said to Alis and steered her across the street to Screen Test City.

It had a multiscreen filled with stars' faces, and an old guy with the pinpoint eyes of a redliner. "Be a star! Get your face up on the silver screen! Who do you want to be, popsy?" he said, leering at Alis. "Marilyn Monroe?"

Ginger Rogers and Fred Astaire were side by side on the bottom row of the screen. "That one," I said, and the screen zoomed till they filled it.

"You're lucky you came tonight," the old guy said. "He's going into litigation. What do you want? Still or scene?"

"Scene," I said. "Just her. Not both of us."

"Stand in front of the scanner," he said, pointing, "and let me get a still of your smile."

"No, thank you," Alis said, looking at me.

"Come on," I said. "You said you wanted to dance in the movies. Here's your chance."

"You don't have to do anything," the old guy said. "All I need's an image to digitize from. The scanner does the rest. You don't even have to smile."

He took hold of her arm, and I expected her to wrench away from him, but she didn't move.

"I want to dance in the movies," she said, looking at me, "not get my face digitized onto Ginger Rogers's body. I want to dance."

"You'll be dancing," the old guy said. "Up there on the screen for everybody to see." He waved his free hand at the milling cast of thousands, none of whom were looking at his screen. "And on opdisk."

"You don't understand," she said to me, tears welling up in her eyes. "The CG revolution—"

"Is right there in front of you," I said, suddenly fed up. "Simsex, paste-ups, snuffshows, make-your-own remakes. Look around, Ruby. You want to dance in the movies? This is as close as you're going to get!"

"I thought you understood," she said bleakly, and whirled before either of us could stop her, and plunged into the crowd.

"Alis, wait!" I shouted, and started after her, but she was already far ahead. She disappeared into the entrance to the skids.

"Lose the girl?" a voice said, and I turned and glared. I was opposite the Happy Endings booth. "Get dumped? Change the ending. Make Rhett come back to Scarlett. Make Lassie come home."

I crossed the street. It was all simsex parlors on this side, promising a pop with Mel Gibson, Sharon Stone, the Marx Brothers. A hundred percent realistic. I wondered if I should do a sim. I stuck my head in the promo data helmet, but there wasn't any blurring. The chooch must be working.

"You shouldn't do that," a female voice said.

I pulled my head out of the helmet. A freelancer was standing there, blond, in a torn net leotard and a beauty mark. *Bus Stop.* "Why go for a virtual imitation when you can have the real thing?" she breathed.

"Which is what?" I said.

The smile didn't fade, but she looked instantly on guard. Mary Astor in *The Maltese Falcon.* "What?"

"This real thing. What is it? Sex? Love? Chooch?"

She half put up her hands, like she was being arrested. "Are you a narc? 'Cause I don't know what you're talking about. I was just making a comment, okay? I just don't think people should settle for VRs, is all, when they could talk to somebody real."

"Like Marilyn Monroe?" I said, and wandered on down the sidewalk past three more freelancers. Marilyn in a white halter dress, Madonna in brass cones, Marilyn in pink satin. The real thing.

I scored some more chooch and a line of tinseltown from a James Dean too splatted to remember he was supposed to be selling the stuff, and ate it, walking on past the snuffshows, but somewhere I must have gotten turned around because I was back at Happy Endings, watching the holoscreen. Scarlett ran into the fog after Rhett, Butch and Sundance leaped forward into a hail of gunfire, Humphrey Bogart and Ingrid Bergman stood in front of an airplane looking at each other.

"Back again, huh?" the hawker said. "Best thing for a broken heart. Kill the bastards. Get the girl. What'll it be? *Lost Horizon? Terminator 9?*"

Ingrid was telling Bogie she wanted to stay, and Bogie was telling her it was impossible.

"What happy endings do people come up with for this?" I asked him.

"Casablanca?" He shrugged. "The Nazis show up and kill the husband, Ingrid and Bogart get married."

"And honeymoon in Auschwitz," I said.

"I didn't say the endings were any good."

On the screen Bogie and Ingrid were looking at each other. Tears welled up in her eyes, and the edges of the screen went to soft-focus.

"How about *Shadowlands?*" the guy said, but I was already shoving through the crowd, trying to reach the skids before I flashed.

I almost made it. I was past the chariot race when a Marilyn crashed into me and I went down, and I thought, natch, I'm going to flash on cement, but I didn't.

The sidewalk blurred and then went blinding, and there were stars in it, and Fred and Eleanor, all in white, danced easily, elegantly through the milling crowd, and superimposed across them was Alis, watching them, her face lost and sorrowful. Like Ingrid's.

Fade to Black

MONTAGE: ***No sound, HERO, seated at comp, punches keys and deletes AS's as scene on screen changes. Western saloon, elegant nightclub, fraternity house, waterfront bar.***

Whatever effect my Judge Hardy lecture had had on Alis, it didn't make her give up on her dream and head back to Meadowville. She was at the party again the next week.

I wasn't. I'd gotten Mayer's list and a notice that my scholarship had been canceled due to "nonperformance," and I was working on Mayer's list just to stay in the dorm. And in chooch.

I didn't miss anything, though. Heada came up to my room halfway through the party to fill me in. "The takeover's definitely on," she said. "Mayer's boss's been moved to Development, which means he's on the way out. Warner's filing a countersuit on Fred Astaire. It goes to court tomorrow."

Alis should have had her face pasted onto Ginger's while she had the chance. She'd never get a chance to dance with him now.

"Vincent's at the party," she said. "He's got a new decay morph."

"What a pity I've got to miss that," I said.

"What are you doing up here anyway?" she said, fishing. "You've never missed a party before. Everybody's down there. Mayer, Alis—" she paused, watching my face.

"Mayer, huh?" I said. "I've got to talk to him about a raise. Do you know who drinks in the movies? Everybody." I took a swig of scotch to illustrate. "Even Gary Cooper."

"Should you be doing that stuff?" Heada said.

"Are you kidding? It's cheap, it's legal, *and* I know what it is." And it was pretty good at keeping me from flashing.

"Is it safe?" Heada, who thought nothing of snorting white stuff she found on the floor, was reading the bottle warily.

"Of course it's safe. *And* endorsed by W. C. Fields, John Barrymore, Bette Davis, and E.T. And the major studios. It's in every movie on Mayer's list. *Camille, The Maltese Falcon, Gunga Din.* Even *Singin' in the Rain.* Champagne at the party after the premiere." The one where Donald O'Connor said, "You have to show a movie at a party. It's a Hollywood law."

I finished off the bottle. "Also *Oklahoma!* Poor Judd is dead. Dead drunk."

"Mayer was hitting on Alis at the party," she said, still looking at me.

Yeah, well, that was inevitable.

"Alis was telling him how she wanted to dance in the movies."

That was inevitable, too.

"I hope they'll be very happy," I said. "Or is he saving her to give to Gary Cooper?"

"She can't find a dancing teacher."

"Well, I'd love to stay and chat," I said, "but I've got to get back to the Hays Office." I called up *Casablanca* again and started deleting liquor bottles.

"I think you should help her," Heada said.

"Sorry," I said. " 'I stick my neck out for nobody.' "

"That's a quote from a movie, isn't it?"

"Bingo," I said. I deleted the crystal decanter Humphrey Bogart was pouring himself a drink out of.

"I think you should find her a dancing teacher. You know a lot of people in the business."

"There *aren't* any people in the business. It's all CGs, it's all ones and zeros and didge-actors and edit programs. The studios aren't even hiring warmbodies anymore. The only *people* in the business are dead, along with the liveaction. Along with the musical. Kaput. Over. 'The end of Rico.' "

"That's a quote from the movies, too, isn't it?"

"Yes," I said, "which are also dead in case you couldn't tell from Vincent's decay morph."

"You could get her a job as a face."

"Like the one you've got?"

"Well, then, a job as a hackate, as a foley, or a location assistant or something. She knows a lot about movies."

"She doesn't want to hack," I said, "and even if she did, the only movies she knows about are musicals. A location assistant's got to know everything, stock shots, props, frame numbers. Be a perfect job for you, Heada. Now I really have to get back to playing Lee Remick."

Heada looked like she wanted to ask if that was a movie, too.

"Hallelujah Trail," I said. "Temperance leader, battling demon rum." I tipped the bottle up, trying to get the last drops out. "You have any chooch?"

She looked uncomfortable. "No."

"Well, what have you got? Besides klieg. I don't need any more doses of reality."

"I don't have anything," she said, and blushed. "I'm trying to taper off a little."

"You?!" I said. "What happened? Vincent's decay morph get to you?"

"No," she said defensively. "The other night, when I was on the klieg, I was listening to Alis talk about wanting to be a dancer, and I suddenly realized there was nothing I wanted, except chooch and getting popped."

"So you decided to go straight, and now you and Alis are going to tap-dance your way to stardom. I can see it now, your names up in lights—Ruby Keeler and Una Merkel in *Gold Diggers of 2018!"*

"No," she said, "but I decided I'd like to be like her, that I'd like to want something."

"Even if that something is impossible?"

I couldn't make out her expression. "Yeah."

"Well, giving up chooch isn't the way to do it. If you want to figure out what it is you want, the way to do it is to watch a lot of movies."

She looked defensive again.

"How do you think Alis came up with this dancing thing? From the movies. She doesn't just want to dance in the movies, she wants to be Ruby Keeler in *42nd Street*—the plucky little chorus girl with a heart of gold. The odds are stacked against her, and all she's got is determination and a pair of tap shoes, but don't worry. All she has to do is keep hoofing and hoping, and she'll not only make it big, she'll save the show *and* get Dick Powell. It's all right there in the script. You didn't think Alis came up with it on her own, did you?"

"Came up with what?"

"Her *part,"* I said. "That's what the movies do. They don't entertain us, they don't send the message: 'We care.' They give us lines to say, they assign us parts: John Wayne, Theda Bara, Shirley Temple, take your pick."

I waved at the screen, where the Nazi commandant was ordering a bottle of Veuve Cliquot '26 he wasn't going to get to drink. "How about

Claude Rains sucking up to the Nazis? No, sorry, Mayer's already playing that part. But don't worry, there are enough parts to go around, and everybody's got a featured role, whether they know it or not, even the faces. They think they're playing Marilyn, but they're not. They're doing Greta Garbo as Sadie Thompson. Why do you think the execs keep doing all these remakes? Why do they keep hiring Humphrey Bogart and Bette Davis? It's because all the good parts have already been cast, and all we're doing is auditioning for the remake."

She looked at me so intently I wondered if she'd lied about giving up AS's and was doing klieg. "Alis was right," she said. "You do love the movies."

"What?"

"I never noticed, the whole time I've known you, but she's right. You know all the lines and all the actors, and you're always quoting from them. Alis says you act like you don't care, but underneath you really love them, or you wouldn't know them all by heart."

I said, in my best Claude Rains, " 'Ricky, I think that underneath that cynical shell you are quite the sentimentalist.' Ruby Keeler does Ingrid Bergman in *Spellbound.* Did Dr. Bergman have any other psychiatric observations?"

"She said that's why you do so many AS's, because you love movies and you can't stand seeing them being butchered."

"Wrong," I said. "You don't know everything, Heada. It's because I pushed Gregory Peck onto a spiked fence when we were kids."

"See?" she said wonderingly. "Even when you're denying it, you do it."

"Well, this has been fun, but I have to get back to work butchering," I said, "and you have to get back to deciding whether you want to play Sadie Thompson or Una Merkel." I turned back to the screen. Peter Lorre was clutching Humphrey Bogart's lapels, begging him to save him.

"You said everybody's playing a part, whether they know it or not," Heada said. "What part am I playing?"

"Right now? Thelma Ritter in *Rear Window.* The meddling friend who doesn't know when to keep her nose out of other people's business," I said. "Shut the door when you leave."

She did, and then opened it again and stood there watching me. "Tom?"

"Yeah?" I said.

"If I'm Thelma Ritter and Alis is Ruby Keeler, what part are you playing?"

"King Kong."

Heada left, and I sat there for a while, watching Humphrey Bogart stand by and let Peter Lorre get arrested, and then got up to see if there were any AS's on the premises. There was klieg in the medicine cabinet, just what I needed, and a bottle of champagne from one time when Mayer brought a face up to watch me paste her into *East of Eden.* I took a swig. It was flat, but better than nothing. I poured some in a glass and ff'd to the "Play it again, Sam" scene.

Bogart slugged down a drink, the screen went to soft-focus, and he was pouring Ingrid Bergman champagne in front of a matte that was supposed to be Paris.

The door opened.

"Forget to give me some gossip, Heada?" I said, taking another swallow.

It was Alis. She was wearing a pinafore and puffed sleeves. Her hair was darker, and had a big bow in it, but it had that same backlit look to it, framing her face with radiance.

Fred Astaire tapped a ripple on the polished floor, and Eleanor Powell repeated it and turned to smile at him—

I downed the rest of the champagne in one gulp, and poured some more. "Well, if it isn't Ruby Keeler," I said. "What do you want?"

She stayed in the doorway. "The musicals you showed me the other night, Heada said you might be willing to loan me the opdisks."

I took a drink of champagne. "They aren't on disk. It's a direct fibe-op feed," I said, and sat down at the comp.

"Is that what you do?" she said from behind me. She was standing looking over my shoulder at the screen. "You ruin movies?"

"That's what I do," I said. "I protect the movie-going public from the evils of demon rum and chooch. Mostly demon rum. There aren't all that many movies with drugs in them. *Valley of the Dolls, Postcards from the Edge,* a couple of Cheech and Chongs, *The Thief of Bagdad.* I also remove nicotine if the Anti-Smoking League didn't get there first." I deleted the champagne glass Ingrid Bergman was raising to her lips. "What do you think? Cocoa or tea?"

She didn't say anything.

"It's a big job. Maybe you could do the musicals. Want me to access Mayer and see if he'll hire you?"

She looked stubborn. "Heada said you could make opdisks for me off the feed," she said stiffly. "I just need them to practice with. Till I can find a dancing teacher."

I turned around in the chair to look at her. "And then what?"

"If you don't want to lend them to me, I could watch them here and copy down the steps. When you're not using the comp."

"And then what?" I said. "You copy down the steps and practice the routines and then what? Gene Kelly pulls you out of the chorus—no, wait, I forgot, you don't like Gene Kelly—Gene Nelson pulls you out of the chorus and gives you the lead? Mickey Rooney decides to put on a show? What?"

"I don't know. When I find a dancing teacher—"

"There *aren't* any dancing teachers. They all went home to Meadowville fifteen years ago, when the studios switched to computer animation. There aren't any soundstages or rehearsal halls or studio orchestras. There aren't any *studios,* for God's sake! All there is is a bunch of geekates hacking away on Crays and a bunch of corporation execs telling 'em what to do. Let me show you something." I twisted back around in the chair. "Menu," I said. *"Top Hat.* Frame 97-265."

Fred and Ginge came up on the screen, spinning around in the Piccolino. "You want to bring musicals back. We'll do it right here. Forward at five." The screen slowed to a sequence of frames. Kick and. Turn and. Lift.

"How long did you say Fred had to practice his routines?"

"Six weeks," she said tonelessly.

"Too long. Think of all that rehearsal-hall rent. And all those tap shoes. Frame 97-288 to 97-631, repeat four times, then 99-006 to 99-115, and continuous loop. At twenty-four." The screen slid into realtime, and Fred lifted Ginge, lifted her again, and again, effortlessly, lightly. Lift, and lift, and kick and turn.

"Does that kick look high enough to you?" I said, pointing at the screen. "Frame 99-108 and freeze." I fiddled with the image, raising Fred's leg till it touched his nose. "Too high?" I eased it back down a little, smoothed out the shadows. "Forward at twenty-four."

Fred kicked, his leg sailing into the air. And lift. And lift. And lift. And lift.

"All right," Alis said. "I get the point."

"Bored already? You're right. This should be a production number." I hit multiply. "Eleven, side by side," I said, and a dozen Fred Astaires kicked in perfect synch, lift, and lift, and lift, and lift. "Multiply rows," I said, and the screen filled with Fred, lifting, kicking, tipping his top hat.

I turned around to look at Alis. "Why would they want you when they can have Fred Astaire? A hundred Fred Astaires? A thousand? And none of them have trouble learning a step, none of them get blisters on their feet or throw temper tantrums or have to be paid or get old or—"

"Get drunk," she said.

"You want Fred drunk?" I said. "I can do that, too. Frame 97-412 and freeze." Fred Astaire stopped in midturn, smiling. "Frame 97—" I said, and the screen went silver and then to legalese. "The character of Fred Astaire is currently unavailable for fibe-op transmission. Copyright ownership suit *ILMGM* v. *RKO-Warner* . . ."

"Oops. Fred's in litigation. Too bad. You should have taken that paste-up while you had the chance."

She wasn't looking at the screen. She was looking at me, her gaze alert, focused, the way it had been on the Piccolino. "If you're so sure what I want is impossible, why are you trying so hard to talk me out of it?"

Because I don't want to see you down on Hollywood Boulevard in a torn-net leotard. I don't want to have to stick your face in a River Phoenix movie so Mayer's boss can pop you.

"You're right," I said. "Why the hell am I?" I turned to the comp and said, "Print accesses, all files." I ripped the hardcopy out of the printer. "Here. Take my fibe-op accesses and make all the disks you want. Practice till your little feet bleed." I thrust it at her.

She didn't take it.

"Go on," I said, and pressed it into her unresponsive hand. "Who am I to stand in your way? In the immortal words of Leo the Lion, anything's possible. Who cares if the studios have got all the copyrights and the fibe-op sources and the digitizers and the accesses? We'll sew our own costumes. We'll build our own sets. And then, right before we open, Bebe Daniels'll break her leg and you'll have to go on for her!"

She crumpled up the hardcopy, looking like she'd like to throw it at me. "How would you know what's possible and impossible? You don't even *try.* Fred Astaire—"

"Is tied up in court, but don't let that stop you. There's still Ann Miller. And *Seven Brides for Seven Brothers.* And Gene Kelly. Oh, wait, I forgot, you're too good for Gene Kelly. Tommy Tune. And don't forget Ruby Keeler."

She threw it.

I picked the hardcopy up and uncrumpled it. " 'Temper, temper, Scarlett,' " I drawled, smoothing it out. I tucked it in the pocket of her pinafore and patted it. "Now get out there on that stage. It's show time! The whole cast's counting on you. Remember you're going out there a youngster, but you've got to come back a star."

Her hand clenched, but she didn't throw the hardcopy again. She wheeled, skirt flaring like Eleanor's white one. I had to close my eyes against the sudden image of Fred and Eleanor dancing on the polished floor, the phony stars shimmering in endless ripples, and missed Alis's exit.

She slammed the door behind her, and the image receded. I opened it and leaned out. "Be so good you'll make me hate you," I called after her, but she was already gone.

SCENE: ***Busby Berkeley production number. Giant revolving fountain with chorus girls in gold lamé on each level, filling champagne glasses in the flowing fountain. Move in to close-up of champagne glass, then to close-up of bubbles, inside each bubble a chorus girl in gold-sequined tap pants and halter top, tap-dancing.***

Alis didn't come back again after that. Heada went out of her way to keep me posted—she hadn't found a dancing teacher, the Viamount takeover was a done deal, Columbia Tri-Star was doing a remake of *Somewhere in Time.*

"There was this Columbia exec at the party," Heada told me, perched on my bed. "He said they've been doing experiments with images projected into negative matter regions, and there's a measurable lag. He says they're *this* close"—she did the thumb-and-forefinger bit—"to inventing time travel."

"Great," I said. "Alis can go back to the thirties and take dancing lessons from Busby Berkeley himself."

Only she didn't like Busby Berkeley, and after taking all the AS's out of *Footlight Parade* and *Gold Diggers of 1933,* neither did I.

She was right about there not being any dancing in his movies. There was a glimpse of tapping feet in *42nd Street,* a rehearsal going on in the background of a plot exposition scene, a few bars in "Pettin' in the Park" for Ruby, who danced about as well as Judy Garland. Otherwise it was all neon violins and revolving wedding cakes and fountains and posed platinum-haired chorus girls, every one of whom had probably been a studio exec's popsy. Overhead kaleidoscope shots and pans and low-angle shots from underneath chorus girls' spread-apart legs that would have given the Hays Office fits. But no dancing.

Lots of drinking, though—speakeasies and backstage parties and silver flasks stuck in chorus girls' garters. Even a production number in a bar, with Ruby Keeler as Shanghai Lil, a popsy who'd done a lot of hooch and a lot of sailors. A hymn to alcohol's finer qualities.

Of which there were many. It was cheap, it didn't do as much damage as redline, and if it didn't give you the blessed forgetfulness of chooch, it stopped the flashing and put a nice soft-focus on things in general. Which made it easier to work on Mayer's list.

It also came in assorted flavors—martinis for *Topper,* elderberry wine for *Arsenic and Old Lace,* a nice Chianti for *Silence of the Lambs.* In between I drank champagne, which had apparently been in every movie ever made, and cursed Mayer, and deleted beakers and laboratory flasks from the cantina scene in *Star Wars.*

I went to the next party, and the one after that, but Alis wasn't there. Vincent was, demonstrating another program, and the studio exec, still pitching time travel to the Marilyns, and Heada.

"That stuff wasn't klieg after all," she told me. "It was some designer chooch from Brazil."

"Which explains why I keep hearing the Beguine," I said.

"Huh?"

"Nothing," I said, looking around the room. Vincent's program must be a weeper simulator. Jackie Cooper was up on the screen, in a battered top hat and a polka-dot tie, blubbering over his dead dog.

"She's not here," Heada said.

"I was looking for Mayer," I said. "He's going to have to pay me double for *The Philadelphia Story.* The thing's full of alcohol. Sherry before lunch, martinis out by the pool, champagne, cocktails, hangovers, ice packs. Cary Grant, Katharine Hepburn, Jimmy Stewart. The whole cast's stinking."

I took a swig from the crème de menthe I had left over from *Days of Wine and Roses.* "The visuals will take at least three weeks, and that doesn't include the lines. 'I have the hiccups. I wonder if I might borrow a drink.' "

"She was here earlier," Heada said. "One of the execs was hitting on her."

"No, no, *I* say, 'I wonder if I might borrow a drink,' and *you* say, 'Certainly. Coals to Newcastle.' " I took another drink.

"Should you be doing so much alcohol?" Heada, the chooch queen, said.

"I have to," I said. "It's the bad effect of watching all these movies. Thank goodness ILMGM's remaking them so no one else will be corrupted." I drank some more crème de menthe.

Heada looked at me sharply, like she'd been doing klieg again.

"ILMGM's doing a remake of *Time After Time.* The exec told Alis he thought he could get her a part in it."

"Great," I said, and went over to look at Vincent's program.

Audrey Hepburn was up on the screen now, standing in the rain and sobbing over her cat.

"This is our new tears program," Vincent said. "It's still in the experimental stage."

He said something to his remote, and the screen split. A computerized didge-actor sobbed alongside Audrey, clutching what looked like a yellow rug. Tears weren't the only thing in the experimental stage.

"Tears are the most difficult form of water simulation to do," Vincent said. The Tin Woodman was up there now, rusting his joints. "It's because tears aren't really water. They've got mucoproteins and lysozymes and a high salt content. It affects the index of refraction and makes them hard to reproduce," he said, sounding defensive.

He should. The didge-woodman's tears looked like Vaseline, oozing out of digitized eyes. "You ever program VRs?" I said. "Of, say, a movie scene like the one you used for the edit program a couple of weeks ago? The Fred Astaire and Ginger Rogers scene?"

"A virtual? Sure. I can do helmet and full-body data. Is this something you're working on for Mayer?"

"Yeah," I said. "Could you have the person take, say, Ginger Rogers's place, so she's dancing with Fred Astaire?"

"Sure. Foot and knee hookups, nerve stimulators. It'll feel like she's really dancing."

"Not feel like," I said. "Can you make it so she actually dances?"

He thought about it awhile, frowning at the screen. The Tin Woodman had disappeared. Ingrid Bergman and Humphrey Bogart were at the airport saying good-bye.

"Maybe," Vincent said. "I guess. We could put on some sole-sensors and rig a feedback enhance to exaggerate her body movements so she could shuffle her feet back and forth."

I looked at the screen. There were tears welling up in Ingrid's eyes, glimmering like the real thing. They probably weren't. It was probably the eighth take, or the eighteenth, and a makeup girl had come out with glycerine drops or onion juice to get the right effect. It wasn't the tears that did it anyway. It was the face, that sweet, sad face that knew it could never have what it wanted.

"We could do sweat enhancers," Vincent said. "Armpits, neck."

"Never mind," I said, will watching Ingrid. The screen split and a didge-actress stood in front of a didge-airplane, oozing baby oil.

"How about a directional sound hookup for the taps and endorphins?" Vincent said. "She'll swear she was really dancing with Gene Kelly."

I drank the rest of the crème de menthe and handed him the empty bottle and then went back up to my room and hacked away at *The Philadelphia Story* for two more days, trying to think of a good reason for Jimmy Stewart to carry Katharine Hepburn and sing "Somewhere Over the Rainbow" without being sloshed, and pretending I needed one.

Mayer would hardly care, and neither would his tight-assed boss. And nobody else watched liveactions. If the plot didn't make sense, the hackates who did the remake could worry about it. They'd probably remake the remake anyway. Which was also on the list.

I called it up. *High Society.* Bing Crosby and Grace Kelly. Frank Sinatra playing Jimmy Stewart. I ff'd through the last half of it, searching for inspiration, but it was even more awash with AS's. *And* it was a musical. I went back to *Story* and tried again.

It was no use. Jimmy Stewart had to be drunk in the swimming pool scene to tell Katharine Hepburn he loved her. Katharine had to be drunk for her fiancé to dump her and for her to realize she still loved Cary Grant.

I gave up on the scene and went back to the one before it. It was just as bad. There was too much exposition to cut it, and most of it was in Jimmy Stewart's badly slurred voice. I rewound to the beginning of the scene and turned the sound up, getting a match so I could overdub his dialogue.

"You're still in love with her, aren't you?" Jimmy Stewart said, leaning belligerently toward Cary Grant.

"Mute," I said, and watched Cary Grant say something imperturbable, his face revealing nothing.

"Insufficient," the comp said. "Additional match data needed."

"Yeah." I turned the sound up again.

"Liz says you are," Jimmy Stewart said.

I rew'd to the beginning of the scene and froze it for the frame number, and then went through the scene again.

"You're still in love with her, aren't you?" Jimmy Stewart said. "Liz says you are."

I blanked the screen, and accessed Heada. "I need to find out where Alis is," I said.

"Why?" she said suspiciously.

"I think I've found her a dancing teacher," I said. "I need her class schedule."

"Sorry," she said. "I don't know it."

"Come on, you know everything," I said. "What happened to 'I think you should help her'?"

"What happened to, 'I stick my neck out for nobody'?"

"I told you, I found her somebody to teach her to dance. An old woman out in Palo Alto. Ex–chorus girl. She was in *Finian's Rainbow* and *Funny Girl* back in the seventies."

She was still suspicious, but she gave it to me. Alis was taking Movie-making 101, basic comp graphics stuff, and a film hist class, The Musical 1939–1980. It was clear out in Burbank.

I took the skids and a bottle of *Public Enemy* gin and went out to find her. The class was in an old studio building UCLA had bought when the skids were first built, on the second floor.

I opened the door a crack and looked in. The prof, who looked like Michael Caine in *Educating Rita,* a movie with way too many AS's in it, was standing in front of a blank, old-fashioned comp monitor with a remote, holding forth to a scattering of students, mostly hackates taking it for their movie content elective, some Marilyns, Alis.

"Contrary to popular belief, the computer graphics revolution didn't kill the musical," the prof said. "The musical kicked off," he paused to let the class titter, "in 1965."

He turned to the monitor, which was no bigger than my array screens, and clicked the remote. Behind him, cowboys appeared, leaping around a train station. *Oklahoma.*

"The musicals, with their contrived story lines, unrealistic song-and-dance sequences, and simplistic happy endings, no longer reflected the audience's world."

I glanced at Alis, wondering how she was taking this. She wasn't. She was watching the cowboys, with that intent, focused look, and her lips were moving, counting the beats, memorizing the steps.

". . . which explains why the musical, unlike *film noir* and the horror movie, has not been revived in spite of the availability of such stars as Judy Garland and Gene Kelly. The musical is irrelevant. It has nothing to say to modern audiences. For example, *Broadway Melody of 1940* . . ."

I retreated up the uneven steps and sat there, working on the gin and waiting for him to finish. He did, finally, and the class trickled out. A trio of faces, talking about a rumor that Disney was going to use warmbodies in *Grand Hotel,* a couple of hackates, the prof, snorting flake on his way down the steps, another hackate.

I finished off the gin. Nobody else came out, and I wondered if I'd somehow missed Alis. I went to see. The steps had gotten steeper and more uneven while I sat there. I slipped once and grabbed onto the banister, and then stood there a minute, listening. There was a clatter and then a thunk from inside the room, and the faint sound of music. The janitor?

I opened the door and leaned against it.

Alis, in a sky-blue dress with a bustle, and a flowered hat, was dancing in the middle of the room, a blue parasol perched on her shoulder. A song was coming from the comp monitor, and Alis was high-stepping in time with a line of bustled, parasoled girls on the monitor behind her.

I didn't recognize the movie. *Carousel,* maybe? *The Harvey Girls?* The girls were replaced by high-stepping boys in derbies and straw hats, and Alis stopped, breathing hard, and pulled the remote out of her high-buttoned shoe. She rewound, stuck the remote back in her shoe, and propped the parasol against her shoulder. The girls appeared again, and Alis pointed her toe and did a turn.

She had piled the desks in stacks on either side of the room, but there still wasn't enough room. When she swung into the second turn, her outstretched hand crashed into them, nearly knocking them over. She reached for the remote again, rew'd, and saw me. She clicked the screen off and took a step backward. "What do you want?"

I waggled my finger at her. "Give you a little advice. 'Don't want what you can't have.' Michael J. Fox, *For Love or Money.* Bar scene, party, nightclub, three bottles of champagne. Only not anymore. Yours truly has done his job. Right down the sink."

I swung my arm to demonstrate, like James Mason in *A Star Is Born,* and the chairs went over.

"You're splatted," she said.

" 'Nope.' " I grinned. "Gary Cooper in *The Plainsman.*" I walked toward her. "Not splatted. Boiled, pickled, soused, sozzled. In a word, drunk as a skunk. It's a Hollywood tradition. Do you know how many movies have drinking in them? All. Except the ones I've taken it out of. *Dark Victory, Citizen Kane, Little Miss Marker.* Westerns, gangster movies, weepers. It's in all of them. Every one. Even *Broadway Melody of 1940.* Do you know why Fred got to dance the Beguine with Eleanor? Because George Murphy was too tanked up to go on. Forget dancing," I said, making another sweeping gesture that nearly hit her. "What you need to do is have a drink."

I tried to hand her the bottle.

She took another protective step toward the monitor. "You're drunk."

"Bingo," I said. " 'Very drunk indeed,' as Audrey Hepburn would say. *Breakfast at Tiffany's.* A movie with a happy ending."

"Why'd you come here?" she said. "What is it you want?"

I took a swig out of the bottle, remembered it was empty, and looked at it sadly. "Came to tell you the movies aren't real life. Just because you want something doesn't mean you can have it. Came to tell you to go home before they remake you. Audrey should've gone home to Tulip, Texas. Came to tell you to go home to Carval." I waited, swaying, for her to get the reference.

"Andy Hardy Has Too Much to Drink," she said. "He's the one who needs to go home."

The screen faded to black for a few frames, and then I was sitting halfway down the steps, with Alis leaning over me. "Are you all right?" she said, and tears were glimmering in her eyes like stars.

"I'm fine," I said. " 'Alcohol is the great level-el-ler,' as Jimmy Stewart would say. Need to pour some on these steps."

"I don't think you should take the skids in your condition," she said.

"We're all on the skids," I said. "Only place left."

"Tom," she said, and there was another fade to black, and Fred and Ginger were on both walls, sipping martinis by the pool.

"That'll have to go," I said. "Have to send the message 'We care.' Gotta sober Jimmy Stewart up. So what if it's the only way he can get up the courage to tell her what he really thinks? See, he knows she's too good for him. He knows he can't have her. He has to get drunk. Only way he can ever tell her he's in love with her."

I put out my hand to her hair. "How do you do that?" I said. "That backlighting thing?"

"Tom," she said.

I let my hand drop. "Doesn't matter. They'll ruin it in the remake. Not real anyway."

I waved my hand grandly at the screen like Gloria Swanson in *Sunset Boulevard.* "All a 'lusion. Makeup and wigs and fake sets. Even Tara. Just a false front. FX and foleys."

"I think you'd better sit down," Alis said, taking hold of my arm.

I shook it off. "Even Fred. Not the real thing at all. All those taps were dubbed in afterwards, and they aren't really stars. In the floor. It's all done with mirrors."

I lurched toward the wall. "Only it's not even a mirror. You can put your hand right through it."

After which things went to montage. I remember trying to get out at Forest Lawn to see where Holly Golightly was buried and Alis yanking on my arm and crying big jellied tears like the ones in Vincent's program. And something about the station sign beeping Beguine, and then we were back in my room, which looked funny, the arrays were on the wrong side of the room, and they all showed Fred carrying Eleanor over to the pool, and I said, "You know why the musical kicked off? Not enough drinking. Except Judy Garland," and Alis said, "Is he splatted?" and then answered herself, "No, he's drunk." And I said, " 'I don't want you to think I have a drinking problem. I can quit anytime. I just don't want to,' " and waited, grinning foolishly, for the two of them to get the reference, but they didn't. "*Some Like It Hot,* Marilyn Monroe," I said, and began to cry thick, oily tears. "Poor Marilyn."

And then I had Alis on the bed and was popping her and watching her face so I'd see it when I flashed, but the flash didn't come, and the room went to soft-focus around the edges, and I pounded harder, faster, nailing her against the bed so she couldn't get away, but she was already gone and I tried to go after her and ran into the arrays, Fred and Eleanor saying good-bye at the airport, and put my hand up and it went right through and I lost my balance. But when I fell, it wasn't into Alis's arms or into the arrays. It was into the negative-matter regions of the skids.

LEWIS STONE: [*Sternly*] I hope you've learned your lesson, Andrew. Drinking doesn't solve your problems. It only makes them worse.
MICKEY ROONEY: [*Hangdog*] I know that now, Dad. And I've learned something else, too. I've learned I should mind my own business and not meddle in other people's affairs.
LEWIS STONE: [*Doubtfully*] I hope so, Andrew. I certainly hope so.

In *The Philadelphia Story,* Katharine Hepburn's getting drunk solved everything: her stuffed-shirt fiancé broke off the engagement, Jimmy Stewart quit tabloid journalism and started the serious novel his faithful girlfriend had always known he had in him, Mom and Dad reconciled, and Katharine Hepburn finally admitted she'd been in love with Cary Grant all along. Happy endings all around.

But the movies, as I had tried so soddenly to tell Alis, are not Real Life. And all I had done by getting drunk was to wake up in Heada's dorm room with a two-day hangover and a six-week suspension from the skids.

Not that I was going anywhere. Andy Hardy learns his lesson, forgets about girls, and settles down to the serious task of Minding His Own Business, a job made easier by the fact that Heada wouldn't tell me where Alis was because she wasn't speaking to me.

And by Heada's (or Alis's) pouring all my liquor down the drain like Katharine Hepburn in *The African Queen* and Mayer's putting a hold on my account till I turned in last week's dozen. Last week's dozen consisted of *The Philadelphia Story,* which I was only halfway through. So it was heigh-ho, heigh-ho, off to work we go to find twelve squeaky-cleans I could claim I'd already edited, and what better place to look than Disney?

Only *Snow White* had a cottage full of beer tankards and a dungeon full of wine goblets and deadly potions. *Sleeping Beauty* was no better—it had a splatted royal steward who'd drunk himself literally under the table—and *Pinocchio* not only drank beer but smoked cigars the Anti-Smoking League had somehow missed. Even *Dumbo* got drunk.

But animation wipes are comparatively easy, and all *Alice in Wonderland* had was a few smoke rings, so I was able to finish off the dozen and replenish *my* stock of deadly potions so at least I didn't have to watch *Fantasia* cold sober. And a good thing, too. The *Pastorale* sequence in *Fantasia* was so full of wine it took me five days to clean it up, after which I went back to *The Philadelphia Story* and stared at Jimmy Stewart, trying to think of some way to salvage him, and then gave up and waited for my skids suspension to be over.

As soon as it was, I went out to Burbank to apologize to Alis, but more time must have gone by than I realized because there was a CG class cramming the unstacked chairs, and when I asked one of the hackates where Michael Caine and the film hist class had gone, he said, "That was last semester."

I stocked up on chooch and went to the next party and asked Heada for Alis's class schedule.

"I don't do chooch anymore," Heada said. She was wearing a tight sweater and skirt and black-framed glasses. *How to Marry a Millionaire.* "Why can't you leave her alone? She's not hurting anybody."

"I want—" I said, but I didn't know what I wanted. No, that wasn't true. What I wanted was to find a movie that didn't have a single AS in it. Only there weren't any.

"The Ten Commandments," I said, back in my room again.

There was drinking in the golden-calf scene and assorted references to "the wine of violence," but it was better than *The Philadelphia Story.* I laid in a supply of grappa and asked for a list of biblical epics, and went to work playing Charlton Heston—deleting vineyards and calling a halt to Roman orgies. Vengeance is mine, saith the Lord.

SCENE: ***Exterior of the Hardy house in summer. Picket fence, maple tree, flowers by front door. Slow dissolve to Autumn. Leaves falling. Tight focus on a leaf and follow it down.***

La-la-land is a lot like the skids. You stand still and stare at a screen, or, worse, your own reflection, and after a while you're somewhere else.

The parties continued, packed with Marilyns and studio execs. Fred Astaire stayed in litigation, Heada avoided me, I drank. In excellent company. Gangsters drank, Navy lieutenants, little old ladies, sweet young things, doctors, lawyers, Indian chiefs. Fredric March, Jean Arthur, Spencer Tracy, Susan Hayward, Jimmy Stewart. And not just in *The Philadelphia Story.* The all-American, "shucks, wah-ah-all," do-the-honorable-thing boy next door got regularly splatted. Aquavit in *The Man Who Shot Liberty Valance,* brandy in *Bell, Book, and Candle,* "likker" straight from the jug in *How the West Was Won.* In *It's a Wonderful Life,* he got drunk enough to get thrown out of a bar and ran his car into a tree. In *Harvey,* he spent the entire film pleasantly tipsy, and what in hell was I supposed to do when I got to that movie? What in hell was I supposed to do in general?

Somewhere in there, Heada came to see me. "I've got a question," she said, standing in the door.

"Does this mean you're over being mad at me?" I said.

"Because you practically broke my arms? Because you thought the whole time you were popping me I was somebody else? What's to be mad about?"

"Heada . . ." I said.

"It's okay. Happens to me all the time. I should open a simsex parlor." She came in and sat down on the bunk. "I've got a question."

"I'll answer yours if you answer mine," I said.

"I don't know where she is."

"You know everything."

"She dropped out. The word is, she's working down on Hollywood Boulevard."

"Doing what?"

"I don't know. Probably not dancing in the movies, which should make you happy. You were always trying to talk her out of—"

I cut in with, "What's your question?"

"I watched that movie you told me I was playing a part in. *Rear Window?* Thelma Ritter? And all the meddling you said she did, telling him to mind his own business, telling him not to get involved. It was good advice. She was just trying to help."

"What's your question?"

"I watched this other movie. *Casablanca.* It's about this guy who has a bar in Africa someplace during World War II, and his old girlfriend shows up, only she's married to this other guy—"

"I know the plot," I said. "What part don't you understand?"

"All of it," she said. "Why the bar guy—"

"Humphrey Bogart," I said.

"Why Humphrey Bogart drinks all the time, why he says he won't help her and then he does, why he tells her she can't stay. If the two of them are so splatted about each other, why can't she stay?"

"There was a war on," I said. "They both had work to do."

"And this work was more important than the two of them?"

"Yeah," I said, but I didn't believe it, in spite of Rick's whole "hill of beans" speech. Ilsa's lending moral support to her husband, Rick's fighting in the Resistance weren't more important. They were a substitute. They were what you did when you couldn't have what you wanted. "The Nazis would get them," I said.

"Okay," she said doubtfully. "So they can't stay together. But why can't he still pop her before she leaves?"

"Standing there at the airport?"

"No," she said, very serious. "Before. Back at the bar."

Because he can't have her, I thought. And he knows it.

"Because of the Hays Office," I said.

"In real life she would have given him a pop."

"That's a comforting thought," I said. "But the movies aren't real life. And they can't tell you how people feel. They've got to show you. Valentino rolling his eyes, Rhett sweeping Scarlett off her feet, Lillian

Gish clutching her heart. Bogie loves Ingrid and can't have her." I could see her looking blank again. "The bar owner loves his old girlfriend, so they have to *show* you by not letting him touch her or even give her a good-bye kiss. He has to just stand there and look at her."

"Like you drinking all the time and falling off the skids," she said.

Now it was my turn to look blank.

"The night Alis brought you back to my room, the night you were so splatted."

I still didn't get it.

"Showing the feelings," Heada said. "You trying to walk through the skids screen and nearly getting killed and Alis pulling you out."

SCENE: ***Exterior. The Hardy house. Wind whirls the dead leaves. Slow dissolve to a bare-branched tree. Snow. Winter.***

I'd apparently had quite a night that night. I had tried to walk through the skids wall like a druggate on too much rave and then popped the wrong person. A wonderful performance, Andrew.

And Alis had saved me. I took the skids down to Hollywood Boulevard to look for her, checking at Screen Test City and at A Star Is Born, which had a River Phoenix lookalike working there. The Happy Endings booth had changed its name to Happily Ever After and was featuring *Dr. Zhivago,* Omar Sharif and Julie Christie in the field of flowers, smiling and holding a baby. A knot of half-interested tourates were watching it.

"I'm looking for a face," I said.

"Take your pick," the guy said. "Lara, Scarlett, Marilyn—"

"We were down here a few months ago," I said, trying to jog his memory. "We talked about *Casablanca. . . .*"

"I got *Casablanca,"* he said. "I got *Wuthering Heights, Love Story—"*

"This face," I interrupted. "She's about so high, light brown hair—"

"Freelancer?" he said.

"No," I said. "Never mind."

I walked on. There was nothing else on this side except VR caves. I stood there and thought about them, and about the simsex parlors farther down and the freelancers hustling out in front of them in torn net leotards, and then went back to Happily Ever After.

"Casablanca," I said, pushing in front of the tourates, who'd decided to get in line. I slapped down my card.

The guy led me inside. "You got a happy ending for it?" he asked.

"You bet."

He sat me down in front of the comp, an ancient-looking Wang.

"Now what you do is push this button, and your choices'll come up on the screen. Push the one you want. Good luck."

I rotated the airplane forty degrees, flattened it to two-dimensional, and made it look like the cardboard it had been. I'd never seen a fog machine. I settled for a steam engine, spewing out great belching puffs of cloud, and ff'd to the three-quarters' shot of Bogie telling Ingrid, "We'll always have Paris."

"Expand frame perimeter," I said, and started filling in their feet, Ingrid in flats and Bogie in lifts, big chunky blocks of wood strapped to his shoes with pieces of—

"What in hell do you think you're doing?" the guy said, bursting in.

"Just trying to inject a little reality into the proceedings," I said.

He shoved me out of the chair and started pushing keys. "Get out of here."

The tourates who'd been ahead of me were standing in front of the screen, and a little crowd had formed around them.

"The plane was cardboard and the airplane mechanics were midgets," I said. "Bogie was only five four. Fred Astaire was the son of an immigrant brewery worker. He only had a sixth-grade education."

The guy emerged from the booth steaming like my fog machine.

" 'Here's looking at you, kid' took seventeen takes," I said, heading toward the skids. "None of it's real. It's all done with mirrors."

SCENE: ***Exterior. The Hardy house in winter. Dirty snow on roof, lawn, piled on either side of front walk. Slow dissolve to spring.***

I don't remember whether I went back down to Hollywood Boulevard again. I know I went to the parties, hoping Alis would show up in the doorway again, but not even Heada was there.

In between, I raped and pillaged and looked for something easy to fix. There wasn't anything. Sobering up the doctor in *Stagecouch* ruined the giving birth scene. *D.O.A.* went dead on arrival without Dana Andrews slugging back shots of whiskey, and *The Thin Man* disappeared altogether.

I called up the menu again, looking for something AS-free, something clean-cut and all-American. Like Alis's musicals.

"Musicals," I said, and the menu chopped itself into categories and put up a list. I scrolled through it.

Not *Carousel.* Billy Bigelow was a lush. So was Ava Gardner in *Showboat* and Van Johnson in *Brigadoon. Guys and Dolls?* No dice. Marlon Brando'd gotten a missionary splatted on rum. *Gigi?* It was full of liquor and cigars, not to mention "The Night They Invented Champagne."

Seven Brides for Seven Brothers? Maybe. It didn't have any saloon scenes or "Belly Up To The Bar, Boys" numbers. Maybe some applejack at the barnraising or in the cabin, nothing that couldn't be taken out with a simple wipe.

"Seven Brides for Seven Brothers," I said to the comp and poured myself some of the bourbon I'd bought for *Giant.* Howard Keel rode into town, married Jane Powell, and they started up into the mountains in his wagon. I could ff over this whole section—Howard was hardly likely to pull out a jug and offer Jane a swig, but I let it run at regular speed while she twittered on to Howard about her hopes and plans. Which were going to be smashed as soon as she found out she was supposed to cook and clean for his six mangy brothers. Howard giddyapped the make-believe horses and looked uncomfortable.

"That's right, Howard. Don't tell her," I said. "She won't listen to you anyway. She's got to find out for herself."

They arrived at the cabin. I'd expected at least one of the brothers to have a corncob pipe, but they didn't. There was some roughhousing, another song, and then a long stretch of pure wholesomeness till the barnraising.

I poured myself another bourbon and leaned forward, watching for homespun dissipation. Jane Powell handed pies and cakes out of the wagon, and a straw-covered jug I'd have to turn into a pot of beans or something, and they went into the barnraising number Alis had asked for the night I met her. "Ff to end of music," I said, and then, "Wait," which wasn't a command, and they continued galloping through the dance, finished, and started in on raising the barn in record time.

"Stop," I said. "Back at 96," I said, and rew'd to the beginning of the dance. "Forward realtime," I said, and there she was. Alis. In a pink gingham dress and white stockings, with her backlit hair pulled back into a bun.

"Freeze," I said.

It's the booze, I thought. Ray Milland in *Lost Weekend,* seeing pink elephants. Or some effect of the klieg, a delayed flash or something, superimposing Alis's face over the dancers like it had been over the figures of Fred Astaire and Eleanor Powell dancing on the polished floor.

And how often was this going to happen? Every time somebody went into a dance routine? Every time a face or a hair ribbon or a flaring skirt reminded me of that first flash? Deboozing Mayer's movies was bad enough. I didn't think I could take it if I had to look at Alis, too.

I turned the screen off and then on again, like I was trying to debug a program, but she was still there.

I watched the dance again, looking at her face carefully, and then triple-timed to the scene where the brides get kidnapped. The dancer, her light brown hair covered by a bonnet, looked like Alis but not *like* her. I triple-timed to the next dance number, the girls doing ballet steps in their pantaloons and white stockings this time, no bonnets, but whatever it was, her hair or the music or the flare of her skirt, had passed, and she was just a girl who looked like Alis. A girl, who, unlike Alis, had gotten to dance in the movies.

I ff'd through the rest of the movie, but there weren't any more dance numbers and no sign of Alis, and this was all Another Lesson, Andrew, in not mixing bourbon with *Rio Bravo* tequila.

"Beginning credits," I said, and went back and wiped the bottle in the boardinghouse scene and then triple-timed to the barnraising again to turn the jug into a pan of corn bread, and then thought I'd better watch the rest of the scene to make sure the jug wasn't visible in any of the other shots.

"Print and send," I said, "and forward realtime."

And there she was again. Dancing in the movies.

MOVIE CLICHE #15: The Hangover. (Usually follows #14: The Party.) Headache, jumping at loud noises, flinching at daylight.

SEE: *The Thin Man, The Tender Trap, After the Thin Man, McLintock!, Another Thin Man, The Philadelphia Story, Song of the Thin Man.*

I accessed Heada, no visual. "Do you know of anything that can sober me up?"

"Fast or painless?"

"Fast."

"Ridigaine," she said promptly. "What's up?"

"Nothing's up," I said. "Mayer's bugging me to work harder on his movies, and I decided the AS's are slowing me down. Do you have any?"

"I'll have to ask around," she said. "I'll get some and bring it over."

That's not necessary, I wanted to say, which would only make her more suspicious. "Thanks," I said.

While I was waiting for her I called up the credits. They weren't much help. There were seven brides, after all, and the only ones I knew were Jane Powell and Ruta Lee, who'd been in every B-picture made in the seventies. Dorcas was Julie Newmeyer, who'd later changed her name to Julie Newmar. When I went back and looked at the barnraising scene again, it was obvious which one she was.

I watched it, listening for the other characters' names. The little blonde Russ Tamblyn was in love with was named Alice, and Dorcas was the tall brunette. I ff'd to the kidnapping scene and matched the other girls to their characters' names. The one in the pink dress was Virginia Gibson.

Virginia Gibson. "Screen Actors' Guild directory," I said, and gave it the name.

Virginia Gibson had been in an assortment of movies, including *Athena* and something called *I Killed Wild Bill Hickok.*

"Musicals," I said, and the list shrank to five. No, four. *Funny Face* had Fred Astaire in it, which meant it was in litigation.

There was a knock on the door. I blanked the screen, then decided that would be a dead giveaway. *"Notorious,"* I said, and then chickened out. What if Ingrid Bergman had Alis's face, too? "Cancel," I said, and tried to think of another movie, any movie. Except *Athena.*

"Tom, are you okay?" Heada called through the door.

"Coming," I said, staring at the blank screen. *Saratoga Trunk?* No, that had Ingrid in it, too, and anyway, if this was going to happen all the time, I'd better know it before I took anything else.

"Notorious," I said softly, "Frame 54-119," and waited for Ingrid's face to come up.

"Tom!" Heada shouted. "Is something wrong?"

Cary Grant went out of the ballroom, and Ingrid gazed after him, looking anxious and like she was about to cry. And looking like Ingrid, which was a relief.

"Tom!" Heada said, and I opened the door.

Heada came in and handed me some blue capsules. "Take two. With water. Why didn't you answer the door?"

"I was getting rid of the evidence," I said, pointing at the screen. "Thirty-four champagne bottles."

"I watched that movie," she said, going over to the screen. "It's set in Brazil. It's got stock shots of Rio de Janeiro and Sugar Loaf."

"Right as always," I said, and then, casually, "Speaking of which, you know everything, Heada. Do you know if Fred Astaire's been copyrighted yet?"

"No," she said. "ILMGM's appealing."

"How long before these ridigaine take effect?" I said before she could ask why I wanted to know about Fred Astaire.

"Depends on how much you've got in your system," she said. "The way you've been popping it, six weeks."

"Six *weeks?"*

"I'm kidding," she said. "Four hours, maybe less. Are you sure you want to do this? What if you start flashing again?"

I didn't ask her how she knew I'd been flashing. This was, after all, Heada.

She handed me the glass. "Drink lots of water. And pee as much as you can," she said. "What's really up?"

"Slashing and burning," I said, turning back to the frozen screen. I cut out another champagne bottle.

She leaned over my shoulder. "Is this the scene where they run out of champagne, and Claude Rains goes down to the wine cellar and catches Cary Grant?"

"Not when I get through with it," I said. "The champagne's going to be ice cream. What do you think, should the uranium be hidden in the ice-cream freezer or the bag of rock salt?"

She looked at me seriously. "I *think* there's something wrong. What is it?"

"I'm four weeks behind on Mayer's list, and he's twitching down my neck, that's what's wrong. Are you sure these are ridigaine?" I said, peering at the capsules. "They aren't marked."

"I'm sure," she said, still looking suspiciously at me.

I popped the capsules in my mouth and reached for the bourbon.

Heada snatched it out of my hand. "You take them with *water.*" She went in the bathroom, and I could hear the gurgle of the bourbon being poured down the drain.

She came out of the bathroom and handed me a glass of water. "Drink as much as you can. It'll help flush your system faster. No alcohol." She opened the closet, felt around inside, pulled out a bottle of vodka.

"No alcohol," she said, unscrewing the cap, and went back in the bathroom to pour it out. "Any other bottles?"

"Why?" I said, sitting down on the bed. "You decide to switch over from chooch?"

"I told you, I quit," she said. "Stand up."

I did, and she knelt down and started fishing under the bed.

"Which is how I know how the ridigaine's going to make you feel," she said, pulling out a bottle of champagne. "You'll want a drink, but don't. You'll just toss it. And I mean toss it." She fumbled with the cork on the bottle. "So don't drink. And don't try to do anything. Lie down as soon as you start feeling anything, headache, shakes. And stay there. You might have halluces. Snakes, monsters . . ."

"Six-foot-tall rabbits named Harvey," I said.

"I'm not kidding," she said. "I felt like I was going to die when I took it. And chooch is a lot easier to quit than alcohol."

"So why'd you quit?" I said.

She gave me a wry look and went back to messing with the cork. "I thought it would make somebody notice me."

"And did they?"

"No," she said, and went back to messing with the cork. "Why did you call and ask me to bring you some ridigaine?"

"I told you," I said. "Mayer—"

She popped the cork. "Mayer's in New York, pimping support for his new boss, who, the word has it, is on the way out. The rumor is the ILMGM execs don't like his high-handed moralizing. At least when it applies to them." She poured out the champagne and came back in the room. "Any other champagne?"

"Lots," I said, and went over to the comp. "Next frame," I said, and a tubful of champagne bottles came up on the screen. "You want to pour these out, too?" I turned, grinning.

She was looking at me seriously. "What's really up?"

"Next frame," I said. The screen shifted to Ingrid, looking anxious, her hair like a halo. I took the champagne glass out of her hand.

"You saw her again, didn't you?" she said.

Everything.

"Who?" I said, even though it was hopeless. "Yeah," I said. "I saw her." I shut off *Notorious.* "Come here," I said, "I want you to look at something."

"Seven Brides for Seven Brothers," I said to the comp. "Frame 25-118."

The screen lit Jane Powell, sitting in the wagon, holding a basket.

"Forward realtime," I said, and Jane Powell handed the basket to Julie Newmar.

"I thought this was going into litigation," Heada said over my shoulder.

"Over who?" I said. "Jane Powell or Howard Keel?"

"Russ Tamblyn," she said, pointing at him. He'd climbed on the wagon and was gazing soulfully at the little blonde, Alice. "Virtusonic's been using him in snuffporn movies, and ILMGM doesn't like it. They're claiming copyright abuse."

Russ Tamblyn, looking young and innocent, which was probably the point, went off with Alice, and Howard Keel lifted Jane Powell down off the buckboard.

"Stop," I said to the computer. "I want you to look at this next scene," I said to Heada. "At the faces. Forward realtime," I said, and the dancers formed two lines and bowed and curtsied to each other.

I don't know what I'd expected Heada to do—gasp and clutch her heart like Lillian Gish maybe. Or turn to me halfway through and ask, "What exactly is it I'm supposed to be looking for?"

She didn't do either. She watched the entire scene, still and silent, her face almost as focused on the screen as Alis's had been, and then said quietly, "I didn't think she'd do it."

For a moment I couldn't register what she said for the roaring in my head, the roaring that was saying, "It *is* her. It's not a flash. It *is* her."

"All that talk about finding a dance teacher," Heada was saying. "All that stuff about Fred Astaire. I never thought she'd—"

"Never thought she'd do what?" I said blankly.

"This," she said, waving her hand vaguely at the screen, where the sides of the barn were going up. "That she'd end up as somebody's popsy," she said. "That she'd sign on. Give up. Sell out." She gestured at the screen again. "Did Mayer say which of the studio execs you were doing it for?"

"I didn't do it," I said.

"Well, *somebody* did it," she said. "Mayer must've asked Vincent or somebody. I thought you said she didn't want her face pasted on somebody else's."

"She didn't. She doesn't," I said. "This isn't a paste-up. It's her, dancing."

She looked at the screen. A cowboy brought his hammer down hard on Russ Tamblyn's thumb.

"She wouldn't sell out," I said.

"To quote a friend of mine," she said, "everybody sells out."

"No," I said. "People sell out to get what they want. Getting her face pasted onto somebody else's body isn't what she wanted. She wanted to dance in the movies."

"Maybe she needed the money," Heada said, looking at the screen. Someone whacked Howard Keel with a board, and Russ Tamblyn took a poke at him.

"Maybe she figured out she couldn't have what she wanted."

"No," I said, thinking about her standing there on Hollywood Boulevard, her face set. "You don't understand. No."

"Okay," she said placatingly. "She didn't sell out. It isn't a paste-up." She waved at the screen. "So what is it? How'd she get on there if somebody didn't paste her in?"

Howard Keel shoved a pair of brawlers into the corner, and the barn fell apart, collapsing into a clatter of boards and chagrin. "I don't know," I said.

We both stood there a minute, looking at the wreckage.

"Can I see the scene again?" Heada said.

"Frame 25-200, forward realtime," I said, and Howard Keel reached up again to lift Jane Powell down. The dancers formed their lines. And there was Alis, dancing in the movies.

"Maybe it isn't her," Heada said. "That's why you asked me to bring over the ridigaine, wasn't it, because you thought it might be the alcohol?"

"You see her, too."

"I know," she said, frowning, "but I'm not really sure I know what she looks like. I mean, the times I saw her I was pretty splatted, and so were you. And it wasn't all that many times, was it?"

That party, and the time Heada sent her to ask me for the access, and the episode of the skids. Memorable occasions, all.

"No," I said.

"So it could be it's just somebody else who looks like her. Her hair's darker than that, isn't it?"

"A wig," I said. "Wigs and makeup can make you look really different."

"Yeah," Heada said, as if that proved something. "Or really alike. Maybe this person's wearing a wig and makeup that makes her look like Alis. Who is it anyway? In the movie?"

"Virginia Gibson," I said.

"Maybe this Virginia Gibson and Alis just look alike. Was she in any other movies? Virginia Gibson, I mean? If she was, we could look at them and see what she looks like, and if this is her or not." She looked concernedly at me. "You'd better let the ridigaine work first, though. Are you having any symptoms yet? Headache?"

"No," I said, looking at the screen.

"Well, you will in a few minutes." She pulled the blankets off the bed. "Lie down, and I'll get you some water. Ridigaine's fast, but it's rough. The best thing is if you can—"

"Sleep it off," I said.

She brought a glass of water in and set it by the bed. "Access me if you get the shakes and start seeing things."

"According to you, I already am."

"I didn't *say* that. I just said you should check out this Virginia Gibson before you jump to any conclusions. *After* the ridigaine does its stuff."

"Meaning that when I'm sober, it won't look like her."

"Meaning that when you're sober, you'll at least be able to see her." She looked steadily at me. "Do you want it to be her?"

"I think I will lie down," I said to get her to leave. "My head aches." I sat down on the bed.

"It's starting to work," she said triumphantly. "*Access* me if you need anything."

"I will," I said, and lay back.

She looked around the room. "You don't have any more liquor in here, do you?"

"Gallons," I said, gesturing toward the screen. "Bottles, flasks, kegs, decanters. You name it, it's in there."

"It'll just make it worse if you drink anything."

"I know," I said, putting my hand over my eyes. "Shakes, pink elephants, six-foot-tall rabbits, 'and how are you, Mr. Wilson?' "

"Access me," she said, and left, finally.

I waited five minutes for her to come back and tell me to be sure and piss, and then another five for the snakes and rabbits to show up, or worse, Fred and Eleanor, dressed in white and dancing side by side. And thinking about what Heada'd said. If it wasn't a paste-up, what was it? And it couldn't be a paste-up. Heada hadn't heard Alis talking about wanting to dance in the movies. She hadn't seen her, that night down on Hollywood Boulevard, when I offered her a chance at one. She could have been digitized that night, been Ginger Rogers, Ann Miller, anybody she wanted. Even Eleanor Powell. Why would she have suddenly changed her mind and decided she wanted to be a dancer nobody'd ever heard of? An actress who'd only appeared in a handful of movies. One of which starred Fred Astaire.

"We're *this* close to having time travel," the exec had said, his thumb and finger almost touching.

And what if Alis, who was willing to do anything to dance in the movies, who was willing to practice in a cramped classroom with a tiny monitor and work nights in a tourate trap, had talked one of the time-travel hackates into letting her be a guinea pig? What if Alis had talked him into sending her back to 1954, dressed in a green weskit and short gloves, and then, instead of coming back like she was supposed to, had changed her name to Virginia Gibson and gone over to MGM to audition for a part in *Seven Brides for Seven Brothers?* And then gone on to be in six other movies. One of which was *Funny Face.* With Fred Astaire.

I sat up, slowly, so I wouldn't turn my headache into anything worse, and went over to the terminal and called up *Funny Face.*

Heada had said Fred Astaire was still in litigation, and he was. I put a watch-and-warn on both the movie and Fred in case the case got settled. If Heada was right—and when wasn't she?—Warner would turn around and file immediately, but if there was a glitch or Warner's lawyers were busy with Russ Tamblyn, there might be a window. I set the watch-and-warn to beep me and called up the list of Virginia Gibson's musicals again.

Starlift was a World War II b-and-w, which wouldn't give me as clear an image as color, and *She's Back on Broadway* was in litigation, too, for someone I'd never heard of. That left *Athena, Painting the Clouds with Sunshine,* and *Tea for Two,* none of which I could remember ever seeing.

When I called up *Athena,* I could see why. It was a cross between *One Touch of Venus* and *You Can't Take It with You,* with lots of floating chiffon and health-food eccentrics and almost no dancing. Virginia Gibson, in green chiffon, was supposed to be Niobe, the goddess of jazz and tap or something. Whatever she was, it wasn't Alis. It looked like her, especially with her hair pulled back in a Greek ponytail. "And with a fifth of bourbon in you," Heada would have said. And a double dose of ridigaine. Even then, it didn't look as much like her as the dancer in the barnraising scene. I called up *Seven Brides,* and the screen stayed silver for a long moment and then started scrolling legalese. "This movie currently in litigation and unavailable for viewing."

Well, that settled that. By the time the courts had decided to let Russ Tamblyn be sliced and diced, I'd be chooch free and able to see it was just somebody who looked like her, or not even that. A trick of lights and makeup.

And there was no point in slogging through any more musicals to drive the point home. Any resemblance was purely alcoholic, and I should do what Doc Heada said, lie down and wait for it to pass. And then go back to slicing and dicing myself. I should call up *Notorious* and get it over with.

"Tea for Two," I said.

Tea was a Doris Day pic, and I wondered if she was on Alis's bad-dancer list. She deserved to be. She smirked her way toothily through a tap routine with Gene Nelson, set in a rehearsal hall Alis would have killed for, all floor space and mirrors and no stacks of desks. There was a terrible Latin version of "Crazy Rhythm," Gordon MacRae singing "I Only Have Eyes for You," and then Virginia Gibson's big number.

And there was no question of her being Alis. With her hair down, she didn't even look that much like her. Or else the ridigaine was kicking in.

The routine was Hollywood's idea of ballet, more chiffon and a lot of twirling around, not the kind of routine Alis would have bothered with. *If* she'd had ballet back in Meadowville, and not just jazz and tap, but she hadn't, and Virginia obviously had, so Alis wasn't Virginia, and I was sober, and it was back to the bottles.

"Forward 64," I said, and watched Doris smirk her way through the title number and an unnecessary reprise. The next number was a big production number. Virginia wasn't in it, and I started to ff again and then stopped.

"Rew to music cue," I said, and watched the production number, counting the frame numbers. A blond couple stepped forward, did a series of toe slides, and stepped back again, and a dark-haired guy and a redhead in a white pleated skirt kicked forward and went into a side-by-side Charleston. She had curly hair and a tied-in-front blouse, and the two of them put their hands on their knees and did a series of cross kicks. "Frame 75-004, forward 12," I said, and watched the routine in slow motion.

"Enhance quadrant 2," and watched the red hair fill the screen, even though there wasn't any need for an enhancement, or for the slowmo, either. No question at all of who it was.

I had known the instant I saw her, the same way I had in the barn-raising scene, and it wasn't the booze (of which there was at least fifteen minutes' worth less in my system) or klieg, or a passing resemblance enhanced with rouge and eyebrow pencil. It was Alis. Which was impossible.

"Last frame," I said, but this was the Good Old Days when the chorus line didn't get into the credits, and the copyright date had to be deciphered. MCML. 1950.

I went back through the movie, going to freeze frame and enhance every time I spotted red hair, but I didn't see her again. I ff'd to the Charleston number and watched it again, trying to come up with a theory.

Okay. The hackate had sent her to 1950 (scratch that—the copyright was for the release date—had sent her to 1949) and she had waited around for four years, dancing chorus parts and palling around with Virginia Gibson, waiting for her chance to clunk Virginia on the head, stuff her behind a set, and take her place in *Brides.* So she could impress the producer of *Funny Face* with her dancing so that he'd offer her a part, and she'd finally get to dance with Fred, if only in the same production number.

Even splatted on chooch, I couldn't have bought that one. But it was her, so there had to be an explanation. Maybe in between chorus jobs Alis had gotten a job as a warmbody. They'd had them back then. They were called stand-ins, and maybe she got to be Virginia Gibson's because they looked alike, and Alis had bribed her to let her take her place, just for one number, or had connived to have Virginia miss a shooting session. Anne Baxter in *All About Eve.* Or maybe Virginia had an AS problem, and when she'd showed up drunk, Alis had had to take her place.

That theory wasn't much better. I called up the menu again. If Alis had gotten one chorus job, she might have gotten others. I scanned through the musicals, trying to remember which ones had chorus numbers. *Singin' in the Rain* did. That party scene I'd taken all that champagne out of.

I called up the record of changes to find the frame number and ff'd through the nonchampagne, to Donald O'Connor's saying, "You gotta show a movie at a party. It's a Hollywood law," through said movie, to the start of the chorus number.

Girls in skimpy pink skirts and flapper hats ran onstage to the tune of "You Are My Lucky Star" and a bad camera angle. I was going to have to do an enhance to see their faces clearly. But there wasn't any need to. I'd found Alis.

And she might have managed to bribe Virginia Gibson. She might even have managed to stuff her and the *Tea for Two* redhead behind their respective sets. But Debbie Reynolds hadn't had an AS problem, and if Alis had crammed her behind a set, *somebody* would have noticed.

It wasn't time travel. It was something else, a comp-generated illusion of some kind in which she'd somehow managed to dance and get it on film. In which case, she hadn't disappeared forever into the past. She was still in Hollywood. And I was going to find her.

"Off," I said to the comp, grabbed my jacket, and flung myself out the door.

MOVIE CLICHE #419: The Blocked Escape. Hero/Heroine on the run, near escape with bad guys, eludes them, nearly home free, villain looms up suddenly, asks, "Going somewhere?"

SEE: ***The Great Escape, The Empire Strikes Back, North by Northwest, The Thirty-Nine Steps.***

Heada was standing outside the door, arms folded, tapping her foot. Rosalind Russell as the Mother Superior in *The Trouble with Angels.*

"You're supposed to be lying down," she said.

"I feel fine."

"That's because the alcohol isn't out of your system yet," she said. "Sometimes it takes longer than others. Have you peed?"

"Yes," I said. "Buckets. Now if you'll excuse me, Nurse Ratchet . . ."

"Wherever you're going, it can wait till you're clean," she said, blocking my way. "I mean it. Ridigaine's not anything to fool with." She steered me back into the room. "You need to stay here and rest. Where were you going anyway? To see Alis? Because if you were, she's not there. She's dropped all her classes and moved out of her dorm."

And in with Mayer's boss, she meant. "I wasn't going to see Alis."

"Where *were* you going?"

It was useless to lie to Heada, but I tried it anyway. "Virginia Gibson was in *Funny Face.* I was going out to try to find a copy of it."

"Why can't you get it off the fibe-op?"

"Fred Astaire's in it. That's why I asked you if he was out of litigation." I let that sink in for a couple of frames. "You said it might just be a likeness. I wanted to see if it's Alis or just somebody who looks like her."

"So you were going out to look for a pirated copy?" Heada said, as if she almost believed me. "I thought you said she was in six musicals. They aren't all in litigation, are they?"

"There weren't any close-ups in *Athena,*" I said, and hoped she wouldn't ask why I couldn't enhance. "And you know how she is about Fred Astaire. If she's going to be in anything, it'd be *Funny Face.*"

None of this made any sense, since the idea was supposedly to find something Virginia Gibson was in, not Alis, but Heada nodded when I mentioned Fred Astaire. "I can get you one," she said.

"Thanks," I said. "It doesn't even have to be digitized. Tape'll work." I led her to the door. "I'll stay here and lie down and let the ridigaine do its stuff."

She crossed her arms again.

"I swear," I said. "I'll give you my key. You can lock me in."

"You'll lie down?"

"Promise," I lied.

"You won't," she said, "and you'll wish you had." She sighed. "At least you won't be on the skids. Give me the key."

I handed her the card.

"Both of them," she said.

I handed her the other card.

"Lie *down,*" she said, and shut the door and locked me in.

MOVIE CLICHE #86: Locked In.

SEE: ***Broken Blossoms, Wuthering Heights, The Phantom Foe, The Palm Beach Story, The Man with the Golden Arm, The Collector.***

Well, I needed more proof anyway before I confronted Alis, and I was starting to feel the headache I'd lied to Heada about having. I went into the bathroom and followed orders and then laid down on the bed and called up *Singin' in the Rain.*

There weren't any telltale matte lines or pixel shadows, and when I did a noise check, there weren't any signs of uneven degradation. Which didn't prove anything. *I* could do undetectable paste-ups with a fifth of William Powell's *Thin Man* rye in me.

I needed more data. Preferably something full-length and a continuous take, but Fred was still in litigation. I called up the list of musicals again. Alis had been wearing a bustle the day I went out to see her, which meant a period piece. Not *Meet Me in St. Louis.* She had said there wasn't any dancing in it. *Showboat,* maybe. Or *Gigi.*

I went through both of them, looking for parasols and backlit hair, but it took forever, and ff'ing made me dizzy.

"Global search," I said, pressing my hand to my eyes, "dance routines," and spent the next ten minutes explaining to the comp what a dance routine was. "Forward at 40," I said, and took it through *Carousel.*

The program worked okay, though this was still going to take forever. I debated eliminating ballet, decided the comp wouldn't have any more idea than Hollywood did of what it was, and added an override instead.

"Instant to next routine, cue," I said. "Next, please," and called up *On Moonlight Bay.*

Bay was another Doris Day toothfest, so even with the override it took far too long to get through it, but at least I could "next, please," when I saw there weren't any bustles.

"Vernon and Irene Castle," I said. No, that was a Fred Astaire. *The Harvey Girls?*

I got more legalese. Was everybody in litigation? I called up the menu, scanning it for period pieces.

"In the Good Old Summertime," I said, and then was sorry. It was a Judy Garland, and Alis had been right, there wasn't any dancing in Judy Garland movies. I tried to remember what else she'd said that night in my room and what movies she'd asked for. *On the Town.*

It wasn't in litigation. But her nemesis, Gene Kelly, was in it, leaping around in a white sailor suit and making it look hard. "Next, please," I said, and Ann Miller appeared in a low-cut dress, apple cheeks, and Marilyn figure, tapping her way between dinosaur skeletons. Even with makeup and digital padding, Alis couldn't have been mistaken for her, and I had the feeling that was important, but the clatter of Ann's taps was making my head pound. I "next, please" 'd to the Meadowville number Alis had said she liked, Vera-Ellen and the overenergetic Gene Kelly in a softshoe. Vera-Ellen was a lot more Alis's size, she even had a hair ribbon, but she wasn't Alis either. "Next, please."

Gene Kelly did one of his overblown ballets, Frank Sinatra and Betty Garrett danced a tango with an Empire State Building telescope, and Ann Miller, in an even more low-cut dress, showed up, and then Vera-Ellen. Wearing the green weskit and black skirt Alis had worn to the party that first night. I sat up.

Vera-Ellen took Gene Kelly's hand and spun away from the camera. "Freeze," I said. "Enhance," and there was no mistaking that backlit hair, and sure enough, when she spun back out of the turn, it was Alis, reaching her hand out, smiling delightedly at Gene.

I asked for a menu of Vera-Ellen movies. *"Belle of New York,"* I said.

Legalese. Fred Astaire. Ditto *Three Little Words.* I finally got *The Kid from Brooklyn,* and went through it number by number, but Alis wasn't in it, and there must be some other logic at work here. What? Gene Kelly? He'd been in both *Singin' in the Rain* and *On the Town.*

"Anchors Aweigh," I said.

Gene's costars were Kathryn Grayson and Jose Iturbi, neither of whom were noted for their dancing ability, so I didn't expect there to be any production numbers. There weren't. Gene Kelly danced with Frank Sinatra, with a chorus line of sailors, with a cartoon mouse.

It was another of his overblown fantasy numbers, this time with an animated background and Tom and Jerry and a lot of pre-CG special effects, but he and Tom the Mouse danced a soft-shoe side by side, hand and paw nearly touching, and it almost looked like the real thing.

I accessed Vincent, decided I didn't want this on the feed, and punched in a key override, wishing there was a way I could find out whether Heada was standing guard without opening the door.

There wasn't, but it was okay. She wasn't there. I locked the door in case she came back, and went down to the party. Vincent was demonstrating a new program to a trio of breathless Marilyns.

"Give it a command," Vincent said, pointing at the screen, where Clint Eastwood, dressed in a striped poncho and a concho-banded hat, was sitting in a chair, his hands at his sides like a puppet's. "Go ahead."

The Marilyns giggled. "Stand," one of them said daringly. Clint got woodenly to his feet.

"Take two steps backward," another Marilyn said.

"Mother, may I?" I said. "Vincent, I need to talk to you." I got between him and the Marilyns. "I need to bluescreen some liveaction into a scene. How do I do that?"

"It's easier to do a scratch construct," he said, looking at the screen where Clint was standing, waiting for orders. "Or a paste-up. What kind of liveaction? Human?"

"Yeah, human," I said, "but a paste-up won't work. So how do I bluescreen it in?"

He shrugged. "Set up a pixar and compositor. Maybe an old Digimatte, if you can find one. The tourate traps use them sometimes. The hard part's the patching—lights, perspective, camera angles, edges."

I'd stopped listening. The A Star Is Born place down on Hollywood Boulevard had had a Digimatte. And Heada'd said Alis had gotten a job down there.

"It still won't be as good as a graphic," he was saying. "But if you've got an expert melder, it's possible."

And a pixar, *and* the comp know-how, *and* the accesses. None of which Alis had. "What if you didn't have accesses? Say you wanted to do it without anyone knowing about it?"

"I thought you had full studio access," he said, suddenly interested. "Did Mayer fire you?"

"This is *for* Mayer. I'm taking the AS's out of a hackate movie," I said glibly. "*Rising Sun.* There are too many visual references to do a wipe. I've got to do a whole new scene, and I want it to be authentic."

I was counting on his not having seen the movie, or knowing it was made before accesses, a good bet with somebody who'd turn Clint Eastwood into a marionette. "The hero superimposes a fake image over a real one. To catch a criminal."

He was frowning vaguely. "Somebody breaks into the fibe-op feed in this movie?"

"Yeah," I said. "So how do I make it look like the real thing?"

"Source piracy? You don't," he said. "You have to have studio access."

Nowhere fast. "I don't have to show anything illegal," I said, "just talk about how he finds a bypass around the encryptions or breaks into the authorization guards," but he was already shaking his head.

"It doesn't work like that," he said. "The studios have paid too much for their properties and actors to let source piracy happen, and encryptions, authorization guards, navajos, all those can be gotten around. That's why they went to the fibe-op loop. What goes out comes back in."

Up on the screen Clint had started moving. I glanced up. He was walking in a figure-eight pattern, hands down, head down. Looping.

"The fibe-op feed sends the signal out and back again in a continuous loop. It's got an ID-lock built in. The lock matches the signal coming in against the one that went out, and if they don't match, it rejects the incoming and substitutes the old one."

"Every frame?" I said, thinking maybe the lock only checked every five minutes, enough time to squeeze in a dance routine.

"Every frame."

"Doesn't that take a ton of memory? A pixel-by-pixel match?"

"Brownian check," he said, but that wasn't much better. The lock would check random pixels and see if they matched, and there'd be no way to know in advance which ones. The only thing you'd be able to change the image to was another one exactly like it.

"What about when you have accesses?" I said, watching Clint make the circuit, around and around. Boris Karloff in *Frankenstein.*

"In that case, the lock checks the altered image for authorization and then allows it past."

"And there's no way to get a fake access?" I said.

He was looking at the screen irritatedly, as if I was the one who'd set Frankenstein in motion. "Sit," he said. Clint sat.

"Stay," I said.

Vincent glared at me. "What movie did you say this was for?"

"A remake," I said, looking over at the door. Heada was coming in. "Maybe I'll just stay with the wipe," I said, and ducked off toward the stairs.

"I still don't see why you insist on doing it by hand," he called after me. "There's no point. I've got a search-and-destroy program—"

I skidded upstairs and punched in the override, cursing myself for locking the door in the first place, opened it, got in bed, remembered the door was supposed to be locked, locked it, and flung myself back on the bed.

Hurrying had not been a good idea. My head had started to pound like the drums in the Latin number in *Tea for Two.*

I closed my eyes and waited for Heada, but it must not have been her in the doorway, or else she had gotten waylaid by Vincent and his dancing dolls. I called up *Three Sailors and a Girl,* but all the "next, please" 's made me faintly seasick. I closed my eyes, waiting for the queasiness to pass, and then opened them again and tried to come up with a theory that didn't belong in a movie.

Alis couldn't have bluescreened herself in like Gene Kelly's mouse. She didn't know anything about comps—she'd been taking Basic CG 101 last fall when I got her class schedule out of Heada. And even if she had somehow mastered melds and shading and rotoscoping, she still didn't have the accesses.

Maybe she'd gotten somebody to help her. But who? The undergrad hackates didn't have accesses either, and Vincent wouldn't have understood why she insisted on doing it by hand.

So it had to be a paste-up. And why not? Maybe Alis had finally realized dancing in the movies was impossible, or maybe Mayer'd promised to find her a dancing teacher if she'd pop his boss. She wouldn't be the first face to come to Hollywood and end up on a casting couch.

But if that were the case, she wouldn't have looked like she did. I called up *On the Town* again and peered at it through my headache. Alis leaped lightly around the Empire State Building, animated and happy. I turned it off and tried to sleep.

If it was a paste-up, she wouldn't have had that focused, intent look. Vincent, programs or no programs, could never have captured that smile.

Slow pan from comp screen to clock, showing 11:05, and back to screen. Shot of sailors dancing. Slow pan to clock, showing 3:45.

Somewhere in the middle of the night it occurred to me that there was another reason Mayer couldn't have done a paste-up of Alis. The best reason of all: Heada didn't know about it.

She knew everything, every bit and piece of popsy, every studio move, every takeover rumor. There wasn't anything that got by her. If Alis had given in to Mayer, Heada would have known about it before it happened. And reported it to me, as if it was what I wanted to hear.

And wasn't it? I had told Alis she couldn't have what she wanted, that dancing in the movies was impossible, and it was a paste-up or nothing, and everybody likes to be proved right, don't they?

Especially if they are right. You can't just walk through a movie screen like Mia Farrow in *The Purple Rose of Cairo* and take Virginia Gibson's place. You can't just walk through a looking glass like Charlotte Henry and find yourself dancing with Fred Astaire.

Even if that's what it looks like you're doing. It's a trick of lighting, that's all, and makeup, and too much liquor, too much klieg; and the only cure for that was to follow Heada's orders, piss, drink lots of water, try to sleep.

"*Three Sailors and a Girl,*" I said, and waited for the trick to be revealed.

Slow pan from comp screen to clock, showing 4:58, and back to screen. Shot of sailors dancing. Slow pan to clock, showing 7:22.

Feeling better?" Heada said. She was sitting on the bed, holding a glass of water. "I told you ridigaine was rough."

"Yeah," I said, closing my eyes against the glare from the glass.

"Drink this," she said, and stuck a straw in my mouth. "How's the craving? Bad?"

I didn't want to drink anything, including water. "No."

"You sure?" she said suspiciously.

"I'm sure," I said. I opened my eyes again, and when that went okay, I tried to sit up. "What took you so long?"

"After I found *Funny Face,* I went and talked to one of the ILMGM execs. You were right about it's not being Mayer. He's sworn off popsy. He's trying to convince Arthurton he's straight and narrow."

She stuck the straw under my nose again. "I talked to one of the hackates, too. He says there's no way to get liveaction stuff onto the fibe-op source without studio access. He says there are all kinds of securities and privacies and encryptions. He says there are so many, nobody, not even the best hackates, can get past them."

"I know," I said, leaning my head back against the wall. "It's impossible."

"Do you feel good enough to look at the disk?"

I didn't, and there was no point, but Heada put it in and we watched Fred dance circles around Audrey Hepburn and Paris.

The ridigaine was good for something, anyway. Fred was doing a series of swing turns, his feet tapping easily, carelessly, his arms extended, but there wasn't a quiver of a flash or even a soft-focus. My head still ached, but the drumming was gone, replaced by a bleak silence that felt like the aftermath of a flash and had its sharp clarity, its certainty.

I was certain Alis wouldn't have danced in this movie, with its modern dance and its duets, carefully choreographed by Fred to make Audrey Hepburn look like a better dancer than she was. Certain that when Virginia Gibson appeared, she'd be Virginia Gibson, who looked a lot like Alis.

And certain that when I called up *On the Town* and *Tea for Two* and *Singin' in the Rain,* it would still be Alis, no matter how secure the fibe-op loops, no matter how impossible.

Virginia Gibson came on in a gaggle of Hollywood's idea of fashion designers. "You don't see her, do you?" Heada said anxiously.

"No," I said, watching Fred.

"This Virginia Gibson person really does look a lot like Alis," Heada said. "Do you want to try *Seven Brides for Seven Brothers* again, just to make sure?"

"I'm sure," I said.

"Good," she said, standing up briskly. "Now, the main thing now that you're clean is to keep busy so you won't think about the craving, and anyway, you need to catch up on Mayer's list before he gets back, and I was thinking maybe I could help you. I've been watching a lot of movies, and I could tell you which ones have AS's in them and where it is. *The Color Purple* has a roadhouse scene where—"

"Heada," I said.

"And *after* you finish the list, maybe you and I could get Mayer to assign us a real remake. I mean, now that we're both clean. You said one time I'd make a great location assistant, and I've been watching a lot of movies. We'd make a great team. You could do the CGs—"

"I need you to do something for me," I said. "There was an ILMGM exec who used to come to the parties who was always using time travel as a line. I need you to find out his name."

"Time travel?" Heada said blankly.

"He said they were *this* close to discovering time travel," I said. "He kept talking about parallel timefeeds."

"You said it wasn't her in *Funny Face,*" she said slowly.

"He kept talking about doing a remake of *Time After Time.*"

She said, still blankly, "You think Alis went back in time?"

"I don't *know,*" I said, and the last word was a shout. "Maybe she found a pair of ruby slippers, maybe she walked up onto the screen like Buster Keaton in *Sherlock Holmes, Jr.* I don't *know!*"

Heada was looking at me, her eyes full of tears. "But you're going to keep looking for her, aren't you? Even though it's impossible," she said bitterly. "Just like John Wayne in *The Searchers.*"

"And he found Natalie Wood, didn't he?" I said. "Didn't he?" but she was already gone.

MONTAGE: ***No sound.*** **HERO,** ***seated at comp, chin on hand, saying, "Next, please," as routine on screen changes. Hula, Latin number, clambake, Hollywood's idea of ballet, hobo number, water ballet, doll dance.***

I didn't have all the alcohol out of my system yet. Half an hour after Heada left, my headache came back with a vengeance. I called up *Two Sailors and a Girl* (or was it *Two Girls and a Sailor?)* and slept for two days straight.

When I got up, I pissed several gallons and then checked to see if Heada had accessed me. She hadn't. I tried to access her, and then Vincent, and started through the movies again.

Alis was in *I Love Melvin,* playing, natch, a chorus girl trying to break into the movies, and in *Let's Dance* and *Two Weeks with Love.* I found her in two Vera-Ellen movies, which I watched twice, convinced that I was somehow missing an important clue, and in *Painting the Clouds with Sunshine,* taking Virginia Gibson's place again in a side-by-side tap routine with Gene Nelson and Virginia Mayo.

I accessed Vincent and asked him about parallel timefeeds. "Is this for *Rising Sun?"* he asked suspiciously.

"The Time Machine," I said. "Paul Newman and Julia Roberts. What *is* a parallel timefeed?" and got an earful of probability and causality and side-by-side universes.

"Every event has a dozen, a hundred, a thousand possible outcomes," he said. "The theory is there's a universe in which every single outcome actually exists."

A universe in which Alis gets to dance in the movies, I thought. A universe in which Fred Astaire's still alive and the CG revolution never happened.

I had been looking exclusively through musicals made during the fifties. But if there were parallel timefeeds, and Alis had somehow found a way to get in and out of those other universes, there was no reason she couldn't be in movies made later. Or earlier.

I started through the Busby Berkeleys, short as they were on dancing, and found her tapping without music in *Gold Diggers of 1935* and in the big finale of *42nd Street,* but that was it. I did better (and apparently so had she) in non-Busbys. *Hats Off,* wearing a hat, natch, and *Show of Shows* and *Too Much Harmony,* "Buckin' the Wind" in a number made for Marilyn, in garters and a white skirt that blew up around her stockinged legs. She was in *Born to Dance,* too, but in the chorus, and I couldn't find her in any other Eleanor Powell movies.

It took me a week to finish the b-and-w's, during which time I couldn't get through to Heada, and she didn't access me. When my comp finally did beep, I didn't wait for her to come on. "Did you find out anything?" I said.

"I found out all right!" Mayer said, twitching. "You haven't sent in a movie in three weeks! I was planning to give the whole package to my boss at next week's meeting, and you're wasting time with *Rising Sun,* which isn't even on the list!"

Which meant Vincent was costarring in the role of Joe Spinell as snitch in *The Godfather II.*

"I needed to replace a couple of scenes," I said. "There were too many visuals to do wipes. One of them's a dance number. You don't know anybody who can dance, do you?" I watched him, looking for some sign, some indication that he remembered Alis, knew her, had wanted to pop her badly enough that he'd pasted her face in over a dozen dancers'. Nothing. Not even a pause in the twitches.

"There was a face at a couple of the parties a while back," I said. "Pretty, light brown hair, she wanted to dance in the movies."

Nothing. It wasn't Mayer.

"Forget dancers," he said. "Forget *The Time Machine.* Just take the damned alcohol *out!* I want the rest of that list done by Monday, or you'll never work for ILMGM again!"

"You can count on me, Mr. Potter," I said, and let him tell me he was shutting down my credit.

"I want you sober!" he said.

Which, oddly enough, I was.

I took "Moonshine Lullaby" out of *Annie Get Your Gun* and the hookahs out of *Kismet* to show him I'd been listening, and started through the forties, looking for alcohol and Alis, two birds with one ff. She was in *Yankee Doodle Dandy,* and in the hoedown number in *Babes on Broadway,* wearing the pinafore she'd had on the night she'd come to ask me for the disk.

Heada came in while I was watching *Three Little Girls in Blue,* which had an assortment of bustles and Vera-Ellen, but no Alis.

"I found the exec," she said. "He's working for Warner now. He says they're looking at ILMGM as a possible takeover."

"What's his name?" I said.

"He wouldn't tell me anything. He said the reason they haven't rereleased *Somewhere in Time* is because they couldn't decide whether to cast Vivien Leigh or Marilyn Monroe."

"I'll talk to him. What's his name?"

She hesitated. "I talked to the hackates, too. They said last year they were transmitting images through a negative-matter region and got some interference that they thought was a time discrepancy, but they haven't been able to duplicate the results, and now they think it was a transmission from another source."

"How big of a time discrepancy?" I said.

She looked unhappy. "I asked them if they could duplicate the results, could they send a person back into the past, and they said even if it worked, they were only talking about electrons, not atoms, and there was no way anything living could survive a negative-matter region."

Which eliminated parallel timefeeds, and there must be worse to come because Heada was still hovering by the door like Clara Bow in *Wings,* unwilling to tell me the bad news.

"Have you found her in any more movies?" she said.

"Six," I said. "And if it's not time travel, she must have walked up onto the screen like Mia Farrow. Because it's not a paste-up. And it's not Mayer."

"There's another explanation," she said unhappily. "You were pretty splatted there for a while. One of the movies I watched was about a guy who was an alcoholic."

"Lost Weekend," I said. "Ray Milland," and could already see where this was going.

"He had blackouts when he drank," she said. "He did things and couldn't remember them." She looked at me. "You knew what she looked like. And you had the accesses."

DANA ANDREWS: [*Standing over police sergeant's desk*] She didn't do it, I tell you.
BRODERICK CRAWFORD: Is that so? Then who did?
DANA ANDREWS: I don't know, but I know she couldn't have. She's not that kind of girl.
BRODERICK CRAWFORD: Well, somebody did it. [*Eyes narrowing suspiciously*] Maybe you did it. Where were you when Carson was killed?
DANA ANDREWS: I was out taking a walk.

It was the likeliest explanation. I was an expert at paste-ups. And I'd had her face stuck in my head ever since the moment I flashed. And I had full studio access. Motive and opportunity.

I had wanted her, and she had wanted to dance in the movies, and in the wonderful world of CGs, anything is possible. But if I had done it, I wouldn't have given her a two-minute bit in a production number. I'd have deleted Doris Day and her teeth and let Alis dance with Gene Nelson in front of those rehearsal-hall mirrors. If I'd known about the routine, which I hadn't. I'd never even seen *Tea for Two.*

Or I didn't *remember* seeing it. Right after the episode on the skids, Mayer had credited my account for half a dozen Westerns, none of which I remembered doing. But if I had done it, I wouldn't have dressed her in a bustle. I wouldn't have made her dance with Gene Kelly.

I'd put a watch-and-warn on Fred Astaire and *Funny Face.* I changed it to *Broadway Melody of 1940* and asked for a status report on the case. It was close to being settled, but a secondary suit was expected to be filed, and the FPS was considering proceedings.

The Film Preservation Society. Every change was automatically recorded with them, and the studios didn't have any control over them. Mayer hadn't been able to get me out of putting in those codes because they were part and parcel of the fibe-op feed. If it was a paste-up it would have to be listed in their records.

I called up the FPS's files and asked for the record for *Brides.*

Legalese. I'd forgotten it was in litigation. *"Singin' in the Rain,"* I said.

The champagne wipes I'd done in the party scene were listed, along with one I hadn't. "Frame 9-106," it read, and listed the coordinates and the data. Jean Hagen's cigarette holder. It had been done by the Anti-Smoking League.

"Tea for Two," I said, and tried to remember the frame numbers for the Charleston scene, but it didn't matter. The screen was empty.

Which left time travel. I went back to doing the musicals, saying, "Next, please!" to conga lines and male choruses and a horrible black-face number I was surprised nobody'd wiped before this. She was in *Can-Can* and *Bells Are Ringing,* both made in 1960, after which I didn't expect to find much. Musicals had gone big-budget around then, which meant buying up Broadway shows and casting box-office properties like Audrey Hepburn and Richard Harris in them who couldn't sing or dance, and then cutting out all the musical numbers to conceal the fact. And then musicals'd turned socially relevant. As if the coffin had needed any more nails pounded into it.

There was plenty of alcohol in the musicals of the sixties and seventies, though, even if there wasn't much dancing. A gin-soaked father in *My Fair Lady,* a gin-soaked popsy in *Oliver,* an entire gin-soaked mining camp in *Paint Your Wagon.* Also saloons, beer, whiskey, red-eye, and a falling-down-drunk Lee Marvin (who coudn't sing or dance, but then neither could Clint Eastwood or Jean Seberg, and who cares? There's always dubbing). The gin-soaked twenties in Lucille Ball's (who couldn't act either, a triple threat) *Mame.*

And Alis, dancing in the chorus in *Goodbye, Mr. Chips* and *The Boyfriend.* Doing the Tapioca in *Thoroughly Modern Millie,* high-stepping to "Put on Your Sunday Clothes" in *Hello Dolly!* in a sky-blue bustled dress and parasol.

I went out to Burbank. And maybe time travel was possible. At least two semesters had gone by, but the class was still there. And Michael Caine was still giving the same lecture.

"Any number of reasons have been advanced for the demise of the musical," he was intoning, "escalating production costs, widescreen technological complications, unimaginative staging. But the real reason lies deeper."

I stood against the door and listened to him give the eulogy while the class took respectful notes on their palmtops.

"The death of the musical was due not to directorial and casting catastrophes, but to natural causes. The world the musical depicted simply no longer existed."

The monitor Alis had used to practice with was still there, and so were the stacked-up chairs, only now there were a lot more of them. Michael Caine and the class were crammed into a space too narrow for a soft-shoe, and the chairs had been there awhile. They were covered with dust.

"The musical of the fifties depicted a world of innocent hopes and harmless desires." He muttered something to the comp, and Julie Andrews appeared, sitting on an Alpine hillside with a guitar and assorted children. An odd choice for his argument of "simpler times," since the movie'd been made in 1965, the year of the Vietnam buildup. Not to mention its being set in 1939, the year of the Nazis.

"It was a sunnier, less complicated time," he said, "a time when happy endings were still believable."

The screen skipped to Vanessa Redgrave and Franco Nero, surrounded by soldiers with torches and swords. *Camelot.* "That idyllic world died, and with it died the Hollywood musical, never to be resurrected."

I waited till the class was gone and he'd had his snort of flake and asked him if he knew where Alis was, even though I knew it was no use, he wouldn't have helped her, and the last thing Alis would have needed was somebody else to tell her the musical was dead.

He didn't remember her, even after I'd plied him with chooch, and he refused to give me the student list for her class. I could get it from Heada, but I didn't want her looking sympathetic and thinking I'd lost my mind. Charles Boyer in *Gaslight.*

I went back to my room and took Billy Bigelow's drinking and half the plot out of *Carousel,* and went to bed.

An hour later the comp woke me out of a sound sleep, making a racket like the reactor in *The China Syndrome,* and I staggered over and blinked at it for a good five minutes before I realized it was the watch-and-warn, and *Brides* must be out of litigation, and another minute to think what command to give.

It wasn't *Brides.* It was Fred Astaire, and the court decision was scrolling down the screen: "Intellectual property claim denied, irreproducible art form claim denied, collaborative property claim denied." Which meant Fred's estate and RKO-Warner must have lost, and ILMGM, where Fred had spent all those years covering for partners who couldn't dance, had won.

"Broadway Melody of 1940," I said, and watched the Beguine come up just like I remembered it, stars and polished floor and Eleanor in white, side by side with Fred.

I had never watched it sober. I had thought the silence, the raptness, the quality of still, centered beauty was the effect of the klieg, but it wasn't. They tapped easily, carelessly, across a dark, polished floor, their hands not quite touching, and were as still, as silent as they were that night I watched Alis watching them. The real thing.

And it had never existed, that harmless, innocent world. In 1940, Hitler was bombing the hell out of London and already hauling Jews off in cattle cars. The studio execs were lobbying against war and making deals, the real Mayer was running the studio, and starlets were going pop on a casting couch for a five-second walk-on. Fred and Eleanor were doing fifty takes, a hundred, in a hot airless studio, and going home to soak their bleeding feet.

It had never existed, this world of starry floors and backlit hair and easy, careless kick-turns, and the 1940 audience watching it knew it didn't. And that was its appeal, not that it reflected "sunnier, simpler times," but that it was impossible. That it was what they wanted and could never have.

The screen cut to legalese again, ILMGM's appeal already under way, and I hadn't seen the end of the routine, hadn't gotten it on tape or even backed it up.

It didn't matter. It was Eleanor, not Alis, and no matter what Heada thought, no matter how logical it was, I wasn't the one doing it. Because if I had been, litigation or no litigation, that was where I would have put her, dancing side by side with Fred, half turning to give him that delighted smile.

MONTAGE: ***Tight close-up comp screen. Title credits dissolve into one another:*** **South Pacific, Stand Up and Cheer, State Fair, Strike Up the Band, Summer Stock.**

Eventually I ran out of places to look. I went down to Hollywood Boulevard again, but nobody remembered her, and none of the places had Digimattes except A Star Is Born, and it was closed for the night, an iron gate pulled across the front. Alis's other classes had been fibe-op-feed lectures, and her roommate, very splatted, was under the impression Alis had gone back home.

"She packed up all her stuff," she said. "She had all this stuff, costumes and wigs and stuff, and left."

"How long ago?"

"I don't know. Last week, I think. Before Christmas."

I talked to the roommate five weeks after I'd seen Alis in *Brides.* At the end of six weeks, I ran out of musicals. There weren't that many, and I'd watched them all, except for the ones in litigation because of Fred. And Ray Bolger, who Viamount filed copyright on the day after I went out to Burbank.

The Russ Tamblyn suit got settled, beeping me awake in the middle of the night to tell me somebody'd won the right to rape and pillage him on the big screen, and I backed up the barnraising scene and then watched *West Side Story,* just in case. Alis wasn't there.

I watched the "On the Town" routine again and looked up *Painting the Clouds with Sunshine,* convinced there was something important there that I was missing. It was a remake of *Gold Diggers of 1933,* but that wasn't what was bothering me. I put all the routines up on the array in order, easiest to most difficult, as if that might give me some clue to what she'd do next, but it wasn't any help. *Seven Brides for Seven Brothers* was the hardest thing she'd done, and she'd done that six weeks ago.

I listed the movies by date, studio, and dancers, and ran a cross-tabulation on the data. And then I sat and stared at the nonresults for a while. And at the array.

There was a knock on the door. Mayer. I blanked the screen and tried to think of a nonmusical to call up, but my mind had gone blank. *"Philadelphia Story,"* I said finally. "Frame 115-010," and yelled, "Come on in."

It was Heada. "I came to tell you Mayer's going nuclear about your not sending any movies," she said, looking at the screen. It was the wedding scene. Everybody, Jimmy Stewart, Cary Grant, were gathered around Katharine Hepburn, who had a huge hat and a hangover.

"The word is Arthurton's bringing in a new guy, supposedly to head up Editing," Heada said, "but really to be his assistant, in which case Mayer's out."

Good, I thought, at least that'll put a stop to the carnage. But if Mayer got fired, I'd lose my access, and I'd never find Alis.

"I'm working on them right now," I said, and launched into an elaborate explanation of why I was still on *Philadelphia Story.*

"Mayer offered me a job," Heada said.

"So now that he's hired you as a warmbody, you've got a stake in his not getting fired, and you've come to tell me to get busy?"

"No," she said. "Not warmbody. Location assistant. I leave for New York this afternoon."

It was the last thing I expected. I looked over at her and saw she was wearing a blazer and skirt. Heada as studio exec.

"You're leaving?" I said blankly.

"This afternoon," she said. "I came to give you my access number." She took out a hardcopy. "It's asterisk nine two period eight three three," she said, and handed me the piece of paper.

I looked at it, expecting the number, but it was a list of movie titles.

"None of them have any drinking in them," she said. "There are about three weeks' worth. They should stall Mayer for a while."

"Thank you," I said wonderingly.

"Betsy Booth strikes again," she said.

I must have looked blank.

"Judy Garland. *Love Finds Andy Hardy,"* she said. "I told you I've been watching a lot of movies. That's why I got the job. Location assistant has to know all the sets and stock shots and props and be able to find them for the hackate so he doesn't have to digitize new ones. It saves memory."

She pointed at the screen. *"The Philadelphia Story*'s got a public library, a newspaper office, a swimming pool, and a 1936 Packard." She smiled. "Remember when you said the movies taught us how to act and gave us lines to say? You were right. But you were wrong about which part I was playing. You said it was Thelma Ritter, but it wasn't." She waved her hand at the screen, where the wedding party was assembled. "It was Liz."

I frowned at the screen, unable for a moment to remember who Liz was. Katharine Hepburn's precocious little sister? No, wait. The other reporter, Jimmy Stewart's long-suffering girlfriend.

"I've been playing Joan Blondell," Heada said. "Mary Stuart Masterson, Ann Sothern. The girl next door, the secretary who's in love with her boss, only he never notices her, he thinks she's just a kid. He's in love with Tracy Lord, but Joan Blondell helps him anyway. She'd do anything for him, even watch movies."

She stuck her hands in her blazer pockets, and I wondered when she had stopped wearing the halter dress and the pink satin gloves.

"The secretary stands by him," Heada said. "She picks up after him and gives him advice. She even helps him out with his romances, because she knows at the end of the movie he'll finally notice her, he'll realize he can't get along without her, he'll figure out Katharine Hepburn's all wrong for him and the secretary's the one he's been in love with all along." She looked up at me. "But this isn't the movies, is it?" she said bleakly.

Her hair wasn't platinum blonde anymore. It was light brown with highlights in it. "Heada," I said.

"It's okay," she said. "I already figured that out. It's what comes of taking too much klieg." She smiled. "In real life, Liz would have to get over Jimmy Stewart, settle for being friends. Audition for a new part. Joan Crawford maybe?"

I shook my head. "Rosalind Russell."

"Well, Melanie Griffith anyway," she said. "So, anyway, I leave this afternoon, and I just wanted to say good-bye and have you wish me luck."

"You'll be great," I said. "You'll own ILMGM in six months." I kissed her on the cheek. "You know everything."

"Yeah."

She started out the door. " 'Here's lookin' at you, kid,' " she said.

I watched her down the hall, and then went back in the room, looking at the list Heada'd given me. There were more than thirty movies here. Closer to fifty. The ones near the bottom had notes after them: "Frame 14-1968, bottle on table," and "Frame 102-166, reference to ale."

I should feed the first twelve in, send them to Mayer to calm him down, but I didn't. I sat on the bed, staring at the list. Next to *Casablanca,* she had written, "Hopeless."

"Hi," Heada said from the door. "It's Tess Trueheart again," and then stood there, looking uncomfortable.

"What is it?" I said, standing up. "Is Mayer back?"

"She's not in 1950," she said, not meeting my eyes. "She's down on Sunset Boulevard. I saw her."

"On Sunset Boulevard?"

"No. On the skids."

Not in a parallel timefeed. Or some never-never-land where people walked through the screen into the movies. Here. On the skids. "Did you talk to her?"

She shook her head. "It was morning rush hour. I was coming back from Mayer's, and I just caught a glimpse of her. You know how rush hour is. I tried to get through the crowd to her, but by the time I made it, she'd gotten off."

"Why would she get off at Sunset Boulevard? Did you see her get off?"

"I told you, I just got a glimpse of her through the crowd. She was lugging all this equipment. But she had to have gotten off at Sunset Boulevard. It was the only station we passed."

"You said she was carrying equipment. What kind of equipment?"

"I don't know. Equipment. I *told* you, I—"

"Just got a glimpse of her. And you're sure it was her?"

She nodded. "I wasn't going to tell you, but Betsy Booth's a tough role to shake. And it's hard to hate Alis, after everything she's done." She gestured at her reflections in the array. "Look at me. Chooch free, klieg free." She turned and looked at me. "I always wanted to be in the movies and now I am."

She started down the hall again.

"Heada, wait," I said, and then was sorry, afraid her face would be full of hope when she turned around, that there would be tears in her eyes.

But this was Heada, who knows everything.

"What's your name?" I said. "All I have is your access, and I've never called you anything but Heada."

She smiled at me knowingly, ruefully. Emma Thompson in *Remains of the Day.* "I like Heada," she said.

Camera whip-pans to medium-shot: LAIT station sign. Diamond screen, "Los Angeles Instransit" in hot pink caps, "Sunset Boulevard" in yellow.

I took the opdisk of Alis's routines and went down to the skids. There was nobody on them except a huddle of tourates in mouse ears, a very splatted Marilyn, and Elizabeth Taylor, Sidney Poitier, Mary Pickford, Harrison Ford, emerging one by one from ILMGM's golden fog. I watched the signs, waiting for Sunset Boulevard and wondering what Alis was doing there. There was nothing down there but the old freeway.

The Marilyn wove unsteadily over to me. Her white halter dress was stained and splotched, and there was a red smear of lipstick by her ear.

"Want a pop?" she said, looking not at me but at Harrison Ford behind me on the screen.

"No, thanks," I said.

"Okay," she said docilely. "How about you?" She didn't wait for me, or Harrison, to answer. She wandered off and then came back. "Are you a studio exec?" she asked.

"No, sorry," I said.

"I want to be in the movies," she said, and wandered off again.

I kept my eyes fixed on the screen. It went silver for a second between promos, and I caught sight of myself looking clean and responsible and sober. Jimmy Stewart in *Mr. Smith Goes to Washington.* No wonder she'd thought I was a studio exec.

The station sign for Sunset Boulevard came up and I got off. The area hadn't changed. There was still nothing down here, not even lights. The abandoned freeway loomed darkly in the starlight, and I could see a fire a long way off under one of the cloverleafs.

There was no way Alis was here. She must have spotted Heada and gotten off here to keep her from finding out where she was really going. Which was where?

There was another light now, a thin white beam wobbling this way. Ravers, probably, looking for victims. I got back on the skids.

The Marilyn was still there, sitting in the middle of the floor, her legs splayed out, fishing through an open palm full of pills for chooch, illy, klieg. The only equipment a freelancer needs, I thought, which at least means whatever Alis is doing it's not freelancing, and realized I'd been relieved ever since Heada told me about seeing Alis with all that equipment, even though I didn't know where she was. At least she hadn't turned into a freelancer.

It was half past two. Heada had seen Alis at rush hour, which was still four hours away. If Alis went the same place every day. If she hadn't been moving someplace, carrying her luggage. But Heada hadn't said luggage, she'd said equipment. And it couldn't be a comp and monitor because Heada would have recognized those, and anyway, they were light. Heada had said "lugging." What then? A time machine?

The Marilyn had stood up, spilling capsules everywhere, and was heading over the yellow warning strip for the far wall, which was still extolling ILMGM's cavalcade of stars.

"Don't!" I said, and grabbed for her, a foot from the wall.

She looked up at me, her eyes completely dilated. "This is my stop. I have to get off."

"Wrong way, Corrigan," I said, turning her around to face the front. The sign read Beverly Hills, which didn't seem very likely. "Where did you want to get off?"

She shrugged off my arm, and turned back to the screen.

"The way out's that way," I said, pointing to the front.

She shook her head and pointed at Fred Astaire emerging out of the fog. "Through there," she said, and sank down to sitting, her white skirt in a circle. The screen went silver, reflecting her sitting there, fishing through her empty palm, and then to golden fog. The lead-in to the ILMGM promo.

I stared at the wall, which didn't look like a wall, or a mirror. It looked like what it was, a fog of electrons, a veil over emptiness, and for a minute it all seemed possible. For a minute I thought, Alis didn't get off at Sunset Boulevard. She didn't get off the skids at all. She stepped through the screen, like Mia Farrow, like Buster Keaton, and into the past.

I could almost see her in her black skirt and green weskit and gloves, disappearing into the golden fog and emerging on a Hollywood Boulevard full of cars and palm trees and lined with rehearsal halls full of mirrors.

"Anything's Possible," the voice-over roared.

The Marilyn was on her feet again and weaving toward the back wall.

"Not that way," I said, and sprinted after her.

It was a good thing she hadn't been headed for the screens this time—I'd never have made it. By the time I got to her, she was banging on the wall with both fists.

"Let me off!" she shouted. "This is my stop!"

"The way off's this way," I said, trying to turn her, but she must have been doing rave. Her arm was like iron.

"I have to get off here," she said, pounding with the flat of her hands. "Where's the door?"

"The door's that way," I said, wondering if this was how I had been the night Alis brought me home from Burbank. "You can't get off this way."

"She did," she said.

I looked at the back wall and then back at her. "Who did?"

"*She* did," she said. "She went right through the door. I saw her," and puked all over my feet.

MOVIE CLICHE #12: The Moral. A character states the obvious, and everybody gets the point.

SEE: *The Wizard of Oz, Field of Dreams, Love Story, What's New, Pussycat?*

I got the Marilyn off at Wilshire and took her to rehab, by which time she'd pretty much pumped her own stomach, and waited to make sure she checked in.

"Are you sure you've got time to do this?" she said, looking less like Marilyn and more like Jodie Foster in *Taxi Driver.*

"I'm sure." There was plenty of time, now that I knew where Alis was.

While she was filling out paperwork, I accessed Vincent. "I have a question," I said without preamble. "What if you took a frame and substituted an identical frame? Could that get past the fibe-op ID-locks?"

"An identical frame? What would be the point of that?"

"Could it?"

"I guess," he said. "Is this for Mayer?"

"Yeah," I said. "What if you substituted a new image that matched the original? Could the ID-locks tell the difference?"

"Matched?"

"A different image that's the same."

"You're splatted," he said, and signed off.

It didn't matter. I already knew the ID-locks couldn't tell the difference. It would take too much memory. And, as Vincent had said, what would be the point of changing an image to one exactly like it?

I waited till the Marilyn was in a bed and getting a ridigaine IV and then got back on the skids. After LaBrea there was nobody on them, but it took me till three-thirty to find the service door to the shut-off section and past five to get it open.

I was worried for a while that Alis had braced it shut, which she had, but not intentionally. One of the fibe-op feed cables was up against it, and when I finally got the door open a crack, all I had to do was push.

She was facing the far wall, looking at the screen that should have been blank in this shut-off section. It wasn't. In the middle of it, Peter Lawford and June Allyson were demonstrating the Varsity Drag to a gymnasium full of college students in party dresses and tuxes. June was wearing a pink dress and pink heels with pompoms, and so was Alis, and their hair was curled under in identical blond pageboys.

Alis had set the Digimatte on top of its case, with the compositor and pixar beside it on the floor, and snaked the fibe-op cable along the yellow warning strip and around in front of the door to the skids feed. I pushed the cable out from the door, gently, so it wouldn't break the connection, and opened the door far enough so I could see, and then stood, half-hidden by it, and watched her.

"Down on your heels," Peter Lawford instructed, "up on your toes," and went into a triple step. Alis, holding a remote, ff'd past the song and stopped where the dance started, and watched it, her face intent, counting the steps. She rew'd to the end of the song. She punched a button and everyone froze in midstep.

She walked rapidly in the silly high-heeled shoes to the rear of the skids, out of reach of the frame, and pressed a button. Peter Lawford sang, "—that's how it goes."

Alis set the remote down on the floor, her full-skirted dress rustling as she knelt, and then hurried back to her mark and stood, obscuring June Allyson except for one hand and a tail of the pink skirt, waiting for her cue.

It came, Alis went down on her heels, up on her toes, and into a Charleston, with June behind her from this angle like a twin, a shadow. I moved over to where I could see her from the same angle as the Digimatte's processor. June Allyson disappeared, and there was only Alis.

I had expected June Allyson to be wiped from the screen the way Princess Leia had been for the tourates' scene at A Star Is Born, but Alis wasn't making vids for the folks back home, or even trying to project her image on the screen. She was simply rehearsing, and she had only hooked the Digimatte up to feed the fibe-op loop through the processor because that was the way she'd been taught to use it at work. I could see, even from here, that the "record" light wasn't on.

I retreated to the half-open door. She was taller than June Allyson, and her dress was a brighter pink than June's, but the image the Digimatte was feeding back into the fibe-op loop was the corrected version, adjusted for color and focus and lighting. And on some of these routines, practiced for hours and hours in these shut-off sections of the skids, done and redone and done again, that corrected image had been so close to the original that the ID-locks didn't catch it, so close Alis's image had gotten past the guards and onto the fibe-op source. And Alis had managed the impossible.

She flubbed a turn, stopped, clattered over to the remote in her pompomed heels, rew'd to the middle section just before the flub, and froze it. She glanced at the Digimatte's clock and then punched a button and hurried back to her mark.

She only had another half hour, if that, and then she would have to dismantle this equipment and take it back to Hollywood Boulevard, set it up, open up shop. I should let her. I could show her the opdisk another time, and I had found out what I wanted to know. I should shut the door and leave her to rehearse. But I didn't. I leaned against the door, and stood there, watching her dance.

She went through the middle section three more times, working the clumsiness out of the turn, and then rew'd to the end of the song and went through the whole thing. Her face was intent, alert, the way it had been that night watching the Continental, but it lacked the delight, the rapt, abandoned quality of the Beguine.

I wondered if it was because she was still learning the routine, or if she would ever have it. The smile June Allyson turned on Peter Lawford was pleased, not joyful, and the "Varsity Drag" number itself was only so-so. Hardly Cole Porter.

It came to me then, watching her patiently go over the same steps again and again, as Fred must have done, all alone in a rehearsal hall before the movie had even begun filming, that I had been wrong about her.

I had thought that she believed, like Ruby Keeler and ILMGM, that anything was possible. I had tried to tell her it wasn't, that just because you want something doesn't mean you can have it. But she had already known that, long before I met her, long before she came to Hollywood. Fred Astaire had died the year she was born, and she could never, never, never, in spite of VR and computer graphics and copyrights, dance the Beguine with him.

And all this, the costumes and the classes and the rehearsing, were simply a substitute, something to do instead. Like fighting in the Resistance. Compared to the impossibility of what Alis was unfortunate enough to want, breaking into a Hollywood populated by puppets and pimps must have seemed a snap.

Peter Lawford took June Allyson's hand, and Alis misjudged the turn and crashed into empty air. She picked up the remote to rew, glanced toward the station sign, and saw me. She stood looking at me for a long moment, and then walked over and shut off the Digimatte.

"Don't—" I said.

"Don't what?" she said, unhooking connections. She shrugged a white lab coat on over the pink dress. "Don't waste your time trying to find a dancing teacher because there aren't any?" She buttoned up the coat and went over to the input and disconnected the feed. "As you can see, I've already figured that out. Nobody in Hollywood knows how to dance. Or if they do, they're splatted on chooch, trying to forget." She began looping the feed into a coil. "Are you?"

She glanced up at the station sign and then laid the coiled feed on top of the Digimatte and knelt next to the compositor, skirt rustling. "Because if you are, I don't have time to take you home and keep you from falling off the skids and fend off your advances. I have to get this stuff back." She slid the pixar into its case and snapped it shut.

"I'm not splatted," I said. "And I'm not drunk. I've been looking for you for six weeks."

She lifted the Digimatte down and into its case and began stowing wires. "Why? So you can convince me I'm not Ruby Keeler? That the musical's dead and anything I can do, comps can do better? Fine. I'm convinced."

She sat down on the case and unbuckled the pompomed heels. "You win," she said. "I can't dance in the movies." She looked over at the mirrored wall, shoe in hand. "It's impossible."

"No," I said. "I didn't come to tell you that."

She stuck the heels in one of the pockets of the lab coat. "Then what did you come to tell me? That you want your list of accesses back? Fine." She slid her feet into a pair of slip-ons and stood up. "I've learned just about all the chorus numbers and solos anyway, and this isn't going to work for partnered dancing. I'm going to have to find something else."

"I don't want the accesses back," I said.

She pulled off the blond pageboy and shook out her beautiful backlit hair. "Then what do you want?"

You, I thought. I want you.

She stood up abruptly and jammed the wig in her other pocket. "Whatever it is, it'll have to wait." She slung the coil of feed over her shoulder. "I've got a job to go to." She bent to pick up the cases.

"Let me help you," I said, starting toward her.

"No, thanks," she said, shouldering the pixar and hoisting the Digimatte. "I can do it myself."

"Then I'll hold the door for you," I said, and opened it.

She pushed through.

Rush hour. Packed mirror to mirror with Ray Milland and Rosalind Russell on their way to work, none of whom turned to look at Alis. They were all looking at the walls, which were going full blast: ILMGM, More Copyrights Than There Are in Heaven. A promo for *Beverly Hills Cop 15,* a promo for a remake of *The Three Musketeers.*

I pulled the door shut behind me, and a River Phoenix, squatting on the yellow warning strip, looked up from a razor blade and a palmful of powder, but he was too splatted to register what he was seeing. His eyes didn't even focus.

Alis was already halfway to the front of the skids, her eyes on the station sign. It blinked "Hollywood Boulevard," and she pushed her way toward the exit, with me following in her wake, and out onto the Boulevard.

It was still as dark as it gets, but everything was open. And there were still (or maybe already) tourates around. Two old guys in Bermuda shorts and vidcams were at the Happily Ever After booth, watching Ryan O'Neal save Ali MacGraw's life.

Alis stopped at the grille of A Star Is Born and fumbled with her key, trying to insert the card without putting any of her stuff down. The two tourates wandered over.

"Here," I said, taking the key. I opened the gate and took the Digimatte from her.

"Do you have Charles Bronson?" one of the oldates said.

"We're not open yet," I said. "I have something I have to show you," I said to Alis.

"What? The latest puppet show? An automatic rehearsal program?" She started setting up the Digimatte, plugging in the cables and fibe-op feed, shoving the Digimatte into position.

"I always wanted to be in *Death Wish,"* the oldate said. "Do you have that?"

"We're not *open,"* I said.

"Here's the menu," Alis said, switching it on for the oldate. "We don't have Charles Bronson, but we have got a scene from *The Magnificent Seven."* She pointed to it.

"You have to see this, Alis," I said, and shoved in the opdisk, glad I'd preset it and didn't have to call anything up. *On the Town* came up on the screen.

"I have customers to—" Alis said, and stopped.

I had set the disk to "Next, please" after fifteen seconds. *On the Town* disappeared, and *Singin' in the Rain* came up.

Alis turned angrily to me. "Why did you—"

"I didn't," I said. "You did." I pointed at the screen. *Tea for Two* came up, and Alis, in red curls, Charlestoned her way toward the front of the screen.

"It's not a paste-up," I said. "Look at them. They're the movies you've been rehearsing, aren't they? Aren't they?"

On the screen Alis was high-stepping with her blue parasol.

"You talked about *Singin' in the Rain* that night I met you. And I could have guessed some of the others. They're all full-length shot and continuous take." I pointed at her in her blue bustle. "But I didn't even know what movie that was from."

Hats Off came up. "And I'd never seen some of these."

"I didn't—" she said, looking at the screen.

"The Digimatte does a superimpose on the fibe-op image coming in and puts it on disk," I said, showing her. "That image goes back through the loop, too, and the fibe-op source randomly checks the pattern of pixels and automatically rejects any image that's been changed. Only you weren't trying to change the image. You were trying to duplicate it. And you succeeded. You matched the moves perfectly, so perfectly the Brownian check thought it was the same image, so perfectly it didn't reject it, and the image made it onto the fibe-op source." I waved my hand at the screen, where she was dancing to "42nd Street."

Behind us, the oldate said, "Who's in this *Magnificent Seven* scene?" but Alis didn't answer him. She was watching the shifting routines, her face intent. I couldn't read her expression.

"How many are there?" she said, still looking at the screen.

"I've found fourteen," I said. "You rehearsed more than that, right? The ones that got past the ID-locks are almost all dancers with the same shape of face and features you have. Did you do any Ann Millers?"

"Kiss Me Kate," she said.

"I thought you might have," I said. "Her face is too round. Your features wouldn't match closely enough to get past the ID-lock. It only works where there's already a resemblance." I pointed at the screen. "There are two others I found that aren't on the disk because they're in litigation. *White Christmas* and *Seven Brides for Seven Brothers."*

She turned to look at me. *"Seven Brides?* Are you sure?"

"You're right there in the barnraising scene," I said. "Why?"

She had turned back to the screen, frowning at Shirley Temple, who was dancing with Alis and Jack Haley in military uniforms. "Maybe—" she said to herself.

"I told you dancing in the movies was impossible," I said. "I was wrong. There you are."

As I said it, the screen went blank, and the oldate said loudly, "How about that guy who says, 'Make my day!' Do you have him?"

I reached to start the disk again, but Alis had already turned away.

"I'm afraid we don't have Clint Eastwood either. The scene from *Magnificent Seven* has Steve McQueen and Yul Brynner," she said. "Would you like to see it?" and busied herself punching in the access.

"Does he have to shave his head?" his friend said.

"No," Alis said, reaching for a black shirt and pants, a black hat. "The Digimatte takes care of that." She started setting up the tape equipment, showing the oldate where to stand and what to do, oblivious of his friend, who was still talking about Charles Bronson, oblivious of me.

Well, what had I expected? That she'd be overjoyed to see herself up there, that she'd fling her arms around me like Natalie Wood in *The Searchers?* I hadn't done anything. Except tell her she'd accomplished something she hadn't been trying to do, something she'd turned down standing on this very boulevard.

"Yul *Brynner,*" the oldate's friend said disgustedly, "and no Charles Bronson."

On the Town was on the screen again. Alis switched it off without a glance and called up *The Magnificent Seven.*

"You want Charles Bronson and they give you Steve McQueen," the oldate grumbled. "They always make you settle for second best."

That's what I love about the movies. There's always some minor character standing around to tell you the moral, just in case you're too dumb to figure it out for yourself.

"You never get what you want," the oldate said.

"Yeah," I said. " 'There's no place like home,' " and headed for the skids.

VERA MILES: [*Running out to corral, where RANDOLPH SCOTT is saddling horse*] You were going to leave, just like that? Without even saying good-bye?
RANDOLPH SCOTT: [*Cinching girth on horse*] I got a score to settle. And you got a young man to tend to. I got the bullet out of that arm of his, but it needs bandaging. [*RANDOLPH SCOTT steps in stirrup and swings up on horse*]
VERA MILES: Will I see you again? How will I know you're all right?
RANDOLPH SCOTT: I reckon I'll be all right. [*Tips hat*] You take care, ma'am. [*Wheels horse around and rides off into sunset*]
VERA MILES: [*Calling after him*] I'll never forget what you've done for me! Never!

I went home and started work. I did the ones that mattered first—restoring the double cigarette-lighting in *Now, Voyager,* putting the uranium back in the wine bottle in *Notorious,* reinebriating Lee Marvin's horse in *Cat Ballou.* And the ones I liked: *Ninotchka* and *Rio Bravo* and *Double Indemnity.* And *Brides,* which came out of litigation the day after I saw Alis. It was beeping at me when I woke up. I put Howard Keel's drink and whiskey bottle back in the opening scene, and then ff'd to the barnraising and turned the pan of corn bread back into a jug before I watched Alis.

It was too bad I couldn't have shown it to her, she'd seemed so surprised the number had made it onto film. She must have had trouble with it, and no wonder. All those lifts and no partner—I wondered what equipment she'd had to lug down Hollywood Boulevard and onto the skids to make it look like she was in the air. It would have been nice if she could see how happy she looked doing those lifts.

I put the barnraising dance on the disk with the others, in case Russ Tamblyn's estate or Warner appealed, and then erased all my transaction records, in case Mayer yanked the Cray.

I figured I had two weeks, maybe three if the Columbia takeover really went through. Mayer'd be so busy trying to make up his mind which way to jump he wouldn't have time to worry about AS's, and neither would Arthurton. I thought about calling Heada—she'd know what was happening—and then decided that was probably a bad idea. Anyway, she was probably busy scrambling to keep her job.

A week anyway. Enough time to give Myrna Loy back her hangover and watch the rest of the musicals. I'd already found most of them, except for *Good News* and *The Birds and the Bees.* I put the *dulce la leche* back in *Guys and Dolls* while I was at it, and the brandy back in *My Fair Lady* and made Frank Morgan in *Summer Holiday* back into a drunk. It went slower than I wanted it to, and after a week and a half, I stopped and put everything Alis had done on disk *and* tape, expecting Mayer to knock on the door any minute, and started in on *Casablanca.*

There was a knock on the door. I ff'd to the end where Rick's bar was still full of lemonade, took the disk of Alis's dancing and stuck it down the side of my shoe, and opened the door.

It was Alis.

The hall behind her was dark, but her hair, pulled into a bun, caught the light from somewhere. She looked tired, like she had just come from practicing. She still had on her lab coat. I could see white stockings and Mary Janes below it, and an inch or so of pink ruffle. I wondered what she'd been doing—the "Abba-Dabba Honeymoon" number from *Two Weeks with Love?* Or something from *By the Light of the Silvery Moon?*

She reached in the pocket of the lab coat and held out the opdisk I'd given her. "I came to bring this back to you."

"Keep it," I said.

She looked at it a minute, and then stuck it in her pocket. "Thanks," she said, and pulled it out again. "I'm surprised so many of the routines made it on. I wasn't very good when I started," she said, turning it over. "I'm still not very good."

"You're as good as Ruby Keeler," I said.

She grinned. "She was somebody's girlfriend."

"You're as good as Vera-Ellen. And Debbie Reynolds. And Virginia Gibson."

She frowned, and looked at the disk again and then at me, as if trying to decide whether to tell me something. "Heada told me about her job," she said, and that wasn't it. "Location assistant. That's great." She looked over at the array, where Bogart was toasting Ingrid. "She said you were putting the movies back the way they were."

"Not all the movies," I said, pointing at the disk in her hand. "Some remakes are better than the original."

"Won't you get fired?" she said. "Putting the AS's back in, I mean?"

"Almost certainly," I said. "But it is a fah, fah, bettah thing I do than I have evah done before. It is a—"

"Tale of Two Cities, Ronald Colman," she said, looking at the screens where Bogart was saying good-bye to Ingrid, at the disk, at the screens again, trying to work up to what she had to say.

I said it for her. "You're leaving."

She nodded, still not looking at me.

"Where are you going? Back to River City?"

"That's from *The Music Man,"* she said, but she didn't smile. "I can't go any farther by myself. I need somebody to teach me the heel-and-toe work Eleanor Powell does. And I need a partner."

Just for a moment, no, not even a moment, the flicker of a frame, I thought about what might have been if I hadn't spent those long splatted semesters dismantling highballs, if I had spent them out in Burbank instead, practicing kick-turns.

"After what you said the other night, I thought I might be able to use a positioning armature and a data harness for the lifts, and I tried it. It worked, I guess. I mean, it—"

Her voice cut off awkwardly like she'd intended to say something more, and I wondered what it was, and what it was I'd said to her. That Fred might be coming out of litigation?

"But the balance isn't the same as a real person," she said. "And I need experience learning routines, not just copying them off the screen."

So she was going someplace where they were still doing liveactions. "Where?" I said. "Buenos Aires?"

"No," she said. "China."

China.

"They're doing ten liveactions a year," she said.

And twenty purges. Not to mention provincial uprisings. And antiforeigner riots.

"Their liveactions aren't very good. They're terrible, actually. Most of them are propaganda films and martial-arts things, but a couple of them last year were musicals." She smiled ruefully. "They like Gene Kelly."

Gene Kelly. But it would be real routines. And a man's arm around her waist instead of a data harness, a man's hands lifting her. The real thing.

"I leave tomorrow morning," she said. "I was packing, and I found the disk and thought maybe you wanted it back."

"No," I said, and then, so I wouldn't have to tell her good-bye, "Where are you flying out of?"

"San Francisco," she said. "I'm taking the skids up tonight. And I'm still not packed." She looked at me, waiting for me to say my line.

And I had plenty to choose from. If there's anything the movies are good at, it's good-byes. From "Be careful, darling!" to "Don't let's ask for the moon when we have the stars," to "Come back, Shane!" Even, *"Hasta la vista,* baby."

But I didn't say them. I stood there and looked at her, with her beautiful, backlit hair and her unforgettable face. At what I wanted and couldn't have, not even for a few minutes.

And what if I said "Stay"? What if I promised to find her a teacher, get her a part, put on a show? Right. With a Cray that had maybe ten minutes of memory, a Cray I wouldn't have as soon as Mayer found out what I'd been doing?

Behind me on the screen, Bogart was saying, "There's no place for you here," and looking at Ingrid, trying to make the moment last forever. In the background, the plane's propellers were starting to turn, and in a minute the Nazis would show up.

They stood there, looking at each other, and tears welled up in Ingrid's eyes, and Vincent could mess with his tears program forever and never get it right. Or maybe he would. They had made *Casablanca* out of dry ice and cardboard. And it was the real thing.

"I have to go," Alis said.

"I know," I said, and smiled at her. "We'll always have Paris."

And according to the script, she was supposed to give me one last longing look and get on the plane with Paul Henreid, and why is it I still haven't learned that Heada is always right?

"Good-bye," Alis said, and then she was in my arms, and I was kissing her, kissing her, and she was unbuttoning the lab coat, taking down her hair, unbuttoning the pink gingham dress, and some part of me was thinking, "This is important," but she had the dress off, and the pantaloons, and I had her on the bed, and she didn't fade, she didn't morph into Heada, I was on her and in her, and we were moving together, easily, effortlessly, our outstretched hands almost but not quite touching on the tangled sheets.

I kept my gaze on her hands, flexing and stretching in passion, knowing if I looked at her face it would be freeze-framed on my brain forever, klieg or no klieg, afraid if I did she might be looking at me kindly, or, worse, not be looking at me at all. Looking through me, past me, at two dancers on a starry floor.

"Tom!" she said, coming, and I looked down at her. Her hair was spread out on the pillow, backlit and beautiful, and her face was intent, the way it had been that night at the party, watching Fred and Ginge on the freescreen, rapt and beautiful and sad. And focused, finally, on me.

MOVIE CLICHE #1: The Happy Ending. Self-explanatory.

SEE: ***An Officer and a Gentleman, An Affair to Remember, Sleepless in Seattle, The Miracle of Morgan's Creek, Shall We Dance, Great Expectations.***

It's been three years, during which time China has gone through four provincial uprisings and six student riots, and Mayer has gone through three takeovers and eight bosses, the next to last of whom moved him up to Executive Vice-President.

Mayer didn't tumble to my putting the AS's back in for nearly three months, by which time I'd finished the whole *Thin Man* series, *The Maltese Falcon,* and all the Westerns, and Arthurton was on his way out.

Heada, still costarring as Joan Blondell, talked Mayer out of killing me and into making a stirring speech about Censorship and Deep Love for the Movies and getting himself spectacularly fired just in time for the new boss to hire him back as "the only moral person in this whole poppated town."

Heada got promoted to set director and then (that next-to-last boss) to Assistant Producer in Charge of New Projects, and promptly hired me to direct a remake. Happy endings all around.

In the meantime, I programmed happy endings for Happily Ever After and graduated and looked for Alis. I found her in *Pennies from Heaven,* and in *Into the Woods,* the last musical ever made, and in *Small Town Girl.* I thought I'd found them all. Until tonight.

I watched the scene in the Indy again, looking at the silver tap shoes and the platinum wig and thinking about musicals. *Indiana Jones and the Temple of Doom* isn't one. "Anything Goes" is the only number in it, and it's only there because one of the scenes takes place in a nightclub, and they're the floor show.

And maybe that's the way to go. The remake I'm working on isn't a musical either—it's a weeper about a couple of star-crossed lovers—but I could change the hotel dining room scene into a nightclub. And then, the boss after next, do a remake with a nightclub setting, and put Fred (who's bound to be out of litigation by then) in it, just in one featured number. That was all he was in *Flying Down to Rio,* a featured number, thirtyish, slightly balding, who could dance a little. And look what happened.

And before you know it, Mayer will be telling everybody the musical's coming back, and I'll get assigned the remake of *42nd Street* and find out where Alis is and book the skids and we'll put on a show. Anything's possible.

Even time travel.

I accessed Vincent the other day to borrow his edit program, and he told me time travel's a bust. "We were *this* close," he said, his thumb and forefinger almost touching. "Theoretically, the Casimir effect should work for time as well as space, but they've sent image after image into a negative-matter region, and nothing. No overlap at all. I guess maybe there are some things that just aren't possible."

He's wrong. The night Alis left, she said, "After what you said the other night, I thought maybe I could use a data harness for the lifts," and I had wondered what it was I'd said, and when I showed her the opdisk, she'd said, *"Seven Brides for Seven Brothers?* Are you sure?"

"It's not on the disk," I'd said, "it's in litigation," and it had stayed in litigation till the next day. And when I checked, it had been in litigation the whole time I looked for her.

And for eight months before that, in a National Treasure suit the Film Preservation Society had brought. The night I saw *Brides,* it had been out of litigation exactly two hours. And had gone back in an hour later.

Alis had only been working at A Star Is Born for six months. *Brides* had been in litigation the whole time. Until after I found her. Until after I told her I'd seen her in it. And when I told her, she'd said, *"Seven Brides for Seven Brothers?* Are you sure?" and I'd thought she was surprised because the jumps and lifts were so hard, surprised because she hadn't been trying to superimpose her image on the screen.

Brides hadn't come out of litigation till the next day.

And a week and a half later Alis came to me. She came straight from the skids, straight from practicing with the harness and the armature that she'd thought might work, "after what you said the other night." And it had worked. "—I guess," she'd said. "I mean—"

She'd come straight from practice, wearing Virginia Gibson's pink gingham dress, Virginia Gibson's pantaloons, wearing her costume for the barnraising dance she'd just done. The barnraising dance I'd seen her in six weeks before she ever did it. And my theory about her having somehow gone back in time was right after all, even if it was only her image, only pixels on a screen. She hadn't been trying to discover time travel either. She had only been trying to learn routines, but the screen she'd been rehearsing in front of wasn't a screen. It was a negative-matter region, full of randomized electrons and potential overlaps. Full of possibilities.

Nothing's impossible, Vincent, I think, watching Alis do kick-turns in her sequined leotard. Not if you know what you want.

Heada is acccssing me. "I was wrong. The Ford Tri-Motor's at the beginning of the second one. *Indiana Jones and the Temple of Doom.* Beginning with frame—"

"I found it," I say, frowning at the screen where Alis, in her platinum wig, is doing a brush step.

"What's wrong?" Heada says. "Isn't it going to work?"

"I'm not sure," I say. "When's the Fred Astaire suit going to be settled?"

"A month," she says promptly. "But it's going right back in. Sofracima-Rizzoli's claiming copyright infringement."

"Who the hell is Sofracima-Rizzoli?"

"The studio that owns the rights to a movie Fred Astaire made in the seventies. *The Purple Taxi.* I figure they'll settle. Three months. Why?" she says suspiciously.

"The plane in *Flying Down to Rio.* I've decided that's what I want."

"A biplane? You don't have to wait for that. There are tons of other movies with biplanes in them. *The Blue Max, Wings, High Road to China—*" She stops, looking unhappy.

"Do they have skids in China?" I say.

"Are you kidding? They're lucky to have bicycles. And enough to eat. Why?" she says, suddenly interested. "Have you found out where Alis is?"

"No."

Heada hesitates, trying to decide whether to tell me something. "The assistant set director's back from China. He says the word is, it's Cultural Revolution 3. Book burnings, reeducation, they've shut at least one studio down and arrested the whole film crew."

I should be worried, but I'm not, and Heada, who knows everything, pounces immediately.

"Is she back?" she says. "Have you had word from her?"

"No," I say, because I have finally learned how to lie to Heada, and because it's true. I don't know where she is, and I haven't had word from her. But I've gotten a message.

Fred Astaire has been out of litigation twice since Alis left, once between copyright suits for exactly eight seconds, the other time last month when the AFI filed an injunction claiming he was a historic landmark.

That time I was ready. I had the Beguine number on opdisk, backup, and tape, and was ready to check it before the watch-and-warn had even stopped beeping.

It was the middle of the night, as usual, and at first I thought I was still asleep or having one last flash.

"Enhance upper left," I said, and watched it again. And again. And the next morning.

It looked the same every time, and the message was loud and clear: Alis is all right, in spite of uprisings and revolutions, and she's found a place to practice and somebody to teach her Eleanor Powell's heel-and-toe steps. And she's going to come back, because China doesn't have skids, and when she does, she's going to dance the Beguine with Fred Astaire.

Or maybe she already has. I saw her in the barnraising number in *Brides* six weeks before she did it, and it's been four since I saw her in *Melody.* Maybe she's already back. Maybe she's already done it.

I don't think so. I've promised the current A Star Is Born James Dean a lifetime supply of chooch to tell me if anybody touches the Digimatte, and Fred's still in litigation. And I don't know how far back in time the overlap goes. Six weeks before she did it was only when I *saw* her in *Brides.* There's no telling how long before that her image was there. Under two years, because it wasn't in *42nd Street* when I watched it the first time, when I was first starting Mayer's list, and yeah, I know I was splatted and might have missed her. But I didn't. I would know her face anywhere.

So under two years. And Heada, who knows everything, says Fred will be out of litigation in three months.

In the meantime, I keep busy, doing remakes and trying to make them good, getting Mayer to talk ILMGM into copyrighting Ruby Keeler and Eleanor Powell, working for the Resistance. I have even come up with a happy ending for *Casablanca.*

It is after the war, and Rick has come back to Casablanca after fighting with the Resistance, after who knows what hardships. The Café Américain has burned down, and everybody's gone, even the parrot, even Sam, and Bogie stands and looks at the rubble for a long time, and then starts picking through the mess, trying to see what he can salvage.

He finds the piano, but when he tips it upright, half the keys fall out. He fishes an unbroken bottle of scotch out of the rubble and sets it on the piano and starts looking around for a glass. And there she is, standing in what's left of the doorway.

She looks different, her hair's pulled back, and she looks thinner, tired. You can see by looking at her that Paul Henreid's dead and she's gone through a lot, but you'd know that face anywhere.

She stands there in the door, and Bogie, still trying to find a glass, looks up and sees her.

No dialogue. No music. No clinch, in spite of Heada's benighted ideas. Just the two of them, who never thought they'd see each other again, standing there looking at each other.

When I'm done with my remake, I'll put my *Casablanca* ending in Happily Ever After's comp for the tourates.

In the meantime, I have to separate my star-crossed lovers and send them off to suffer assorted hardships and pay for their sins. For which I need a plane.

I put the "Anything Goes" number on disk and backup, in case Kate Capshaw goes into litigation, and then ff to the Ford Tri-Motor and save that, too, in case the biplane doesn't work.

"High Road to China," I say, and then cancel it before it has a chance to come up. "Simultaneous display. Screen one, *Temple of Doom.* Two, *Singin' in the Rain.* Three, *Good News . . ."*

I go through the litany, and Alis appears on the screens, one after the other, in tap pants and bustles and green weskits, ponytails and red curls and shingled bobs. Her face looks the same in all of them, intent, alert, concentrating on the steps and the music, unaware that she is conquering encryptions and Brownian checks and time.

"Screen Eighteen," I say, *"Seven Brides for Seven Brothers,"* and she twirls across the floor and leaps into the arms of Russ Tamblyn. And he has conquered time, too. They all have, Gene and Ruby and Fred, in spite of the death of the musical, in spite of the studio execs and the hackates and the courts, conquering time in a turn, a smile, a lift, capturing for a permanent moment what we want and can't have.

I have been working on weepers too long. I need to get on with the business at hand, pick a plane, save the sentiment for my lovers' Big Farewell.

"Cancel, all screens," I say. "Center screen, *High Road to—"* and then stop and stare at the silver screen, like Ray Milland craving a drink in *The Lost Weekend.*

"Center screen," I say. "Frame 96-1100. No sound. *Broadway Melody of 1940,"* and sit down on the bed.

They are tapping side by side, dressed in white, lost in the music I cannot hear and the time steps that took them weeks to practice, dancing easily, without effort. Her light brown hair catches the light from somewhere.

Alis swings into a turn, her white skirt swirling out in the same clear arc as Eleanor's—check and Brownian check—and that must have taken weeks, too.

Next to her, casual, elegant, oblivious to copyrights and takeovers, Fred taps out a counterpoint ripple, and Alis answers it back, and turns to smile over her shoulder.

"Freeze," I say, and she stops, still turning, her hand outstretched and almost touching mine.

I lean forward, looking at the face I have seen ever since that first night watching her from the door, that face I would know anywhere. We'll always have Paris.

"Forward three frames and hold," I say, and she flashes me a delighted, an infinitely promising, smile.

"Forward realtime," I say, and there is Alis, as she should be, dancing in the movies.

THE END

Roll credits

Bellwether

To John
From Abigail

"Yours—yours—yours—"

acknowledgment

Special thanks to the girls at Margie's Java Joint, who make the best caffè latte and conversation in the world, and without whom I wouldn't have made it through the last months of this novel!

1. beginning

Brothers, sisters, husbands, wives—
Followed the Piper for their lives.
From street to street he piped advancing,
And step by step they followed dancing.

robert browning

hula hoop (march 1958—june 1959)

The prototype for all merchandising fads and one whose phenomenal success has never been repeated. Originally a wooden exercise hoop used in Australian gym classes, the Hula Hoop was redesigned in gaudy plastic by Wham-O and sold for $1.98 to adults and kids alike. Nuns, Red Skelton, geishas, Jane Russell, and the Queen of Jordan rotated them on their hips, and lesser beings dislocated hips, sprained necks, and slipped disks. Russia and China banned them as "capitalist," a team of Belgian explorers took twenty of them along to the South Pole (to give the penguins?), and over fifty million were sold worldwide. Died out as quickly as it had spread.

It's almost impossible to pinpoint the beginning of a fad. By the time it starts to look like one, its origins are far in the past, and trying to trace them back is exponentially harder than, say, looking for the source of the Nile.

In the first place, there's probably more than one source, and in the second, you're dealing with human behavior. All Speke and Burton had to deal with were crocodiles, rapids, and the tsetse fly. In the third, we know something about how rivers work, like, they flow downhill. Fads seem to spring full-blown out of nowhere and for no good reason. Witness bungee-jumping. And Lava lamps.

Scientific discoveries are the same way. People like to think of science as rational and reasonable, following step by step from hypothesis to experiment to conclusion. Dr. Chin, last year's winner of the Niebnitz

Grant, wrote, "The process of scientific discovery is the logical extension of observation by experimentation."

Nothing could be further from the truth. The process is exactly like any other human endeavor—messy, haphazard, misdirected, and heavily influenced by chance. Look at Alexander Fleming who discovered penicillin when a spore drifted in the window of his lab and contaminated one of his cultures.

Or Roentgen. He was working with a cathode-ray tube surrounded by sheets of black cardboard when he caught a glimpse of light from the other side of his lab. A sheet of paper coated with barium platinocyanide was fluorescing, even though it was shut off from the tube. Curious, he stuck his hand between the tube and the screen. And saw the shadow of the bones of his hand.

Look at Galvani, who was studying the nervous systems of frogs when he discovered electrical currents. Or Messier. He wasn't looking for galaxies when he discovered them. He was looking for comets. He only mapped them because he was trying to get rid of a nuisance.

None of which makes Dr. Chin any the less deserving of the Niebnitz Grant's million-dollar endowment. It isn't necessary to understand how something works to do it. Take driving. And starting fads. And falling in love.

What was I talking about? Oh, yes, how scientific discoveries come about. Usually the chain of events leading up to them, like that leading up to a fad, follows a course too convoluted and chaotic to follow. But I know exactly where one started and who started it.

It was in October. Monday the second. Nine o'clock in the morning. I was in the stats lab at HiTek, struggling with a box of clippings on hair-bobbing. I'm Sandra Foster, by the way, and I work in R&D at HiTek. I had spent all weekend going through yellowed newspapers and 1920s copies of *The Saturday Evening Post* and *The Delineator,* trudging upstream to the beginnings of the fad of hair-bobbing, looking for what had caused every woman in America to suddenly chop off her "crowning glory," despite social pressure, threatening sermons, and four thousand years of long hair.

I had clipped endless news items; highlighted references, magazine articles, and advertisements; dated them; and organized them into categories. Flip had stolen my stapler, I had run out of paper clips, and Desiderata hadn't been able to find any more, so I had had to settle for stacking them, in order, in the box, which I was now trying to maneuver into my lab.

The box was heavy and had been made by the same people who manufacture paper sacks for the supermarket, so when I'd dumped it just outside the lab so I could unlock the door, it had developed a major rip down one side. I was half-wrestling, half-dragging it over next to one of the lab tables so I could lift the stacks of clippings out when the whole side started to give way.

An avalanche of magazine pages and newspaper stories began to spill out through the side before I could get it pushed back in place, and I grabbed for them and the box as Flip opened the door and slouched in, looking disgusted. She was wearing black lipstick, a black halter, and a black leather micro-skirt and was carrying a box about the size of mine.

"I'm not *supposed* to have to deliver packages," she said. "You're *supposed* to pick them up in the mail room."

"I didn't know I had a package," I said, trying to hold the box together with one hand and reach a roll of duct tape in the middle of the lab table with the other. "Just set it down anywhere."

She rolled her eyes. "You're *supposed* to get a notice saying you have a package."

Yes, well, and you were probably supposed to deliver it, I thought, which explains why I never got it. "Could you reach me that duct tape?" I said.

"Employees aren't supposed to ask interdepartmental assistants to run personal errands or make coffee," Flip said.

"Handing me a roll of tape is not a personal errand," I said.

Flip sighed. "I'm *supposed* to be delivering the interdepartmental mail." She tossed her hair. She had shaved her head the week before but had left a long hank along the front and down one side expressly for flipping when she feels put-upon.

Flip is my punishment for having tried to get her predecessor, Desiderata, fired. Desiderata was mindless, clueless, and completely without initiative. She misdelivered the mail, wrote down messages wrong, and spent all her free time examining her split ends. After two months and a wrong phone call that cost me a government grant, I went to Management and demanded she be fired and somebody, anybody else be hired, on the grounds that nobody could possibly be worse than Desiderata. I was wrong.

Management moved Desiderata to Supply (nobody ever gets fired at HiTek except scientists and even we don't get pink slips. Our projects just get canceled for lack of funding) and hired Flip, who has a nose ring, a tattoo of a snowy owl, and the habit of sighing and rolling her eyes when you ask her to do anything at all. I am afraid to get her fired. There is no telling who they might hire next.

Flip sighed loudly. "This package is really heavy."

"Then set it down," I said, stretching to reach the tape. It was just out of reach. I inched the hand holding the side of the box shut higher and leaned farther across the lab table. My fingertips just touched the tape.

"It's breakable," Flip said, coming over to me, and dropped the box. I grabbed to catch it with both hands. It thunked down on the table, the side gave way on *my* box, and the clippings poured out of the box and across the floor.

"Next time you're going to have to pick it up yourself," Flip said, walking on the clippings toward the door.

I shook the box, listening for broken sounds. There weren't any, and when I looked at the top, it didn't say FRAGILE anywhere. It said PERISHABLE. It also said DR. ALICIA TURNBULL.

"This isn't mine," I said, but Flip was already out the door. I waded through a sea of clippings and called to her. "This isn't my package. It's for Dr. Turnbull in Bio."

She sighed.

"You need to take this to Dr. Turnbull."

She rolled her eyes. "I have to deliver the rest of the interdepartmental mail *first,*" she said, tossing her hank of hair. She slouched on down the hall, dropping two pieces of said departmental mail as she went.

"Make sure you come back and get it as soon as you're done with the mail," I shouted after her down the hall. "It's perishable," I shouted, and then, remembering that illiteracy is a hot trend these days and *perishable* is a four-syllable word, "That means it'll spoil."

Her shaved head didn't even turn, but one of the doors halfway down the hall opened, and Gina leaned out. "What did she do now?" she asked.

"Duct tape now qualifies as a personal errand," I said.

Gina came down the hall. "Did you get one of these?" she said, handing me a blue flyer. It was a meeting announcement. Wednesday. Cafeteria. All HiTek staff, including R&D. "Flip was supposed to deliver one to every office," she said.

"What's the meeting about?"

"Management went to another seminar," she said. "Which means a sensitivity exercise, a new acronym, and more paperwork for us. I think I'll call in sick. Brittany's birthday's in two weeks, and I need to get the party decorations. What's in these days in birthday parties? Circus? Wild West?"

"Power Rangers," I said. "Do you think they might reorganize the departments?" The last seminar Management had gone to, they'd created Flip's job as part of CRAM (Communications Reform Activation

Management). Maybe this time they'd eliminate interdepartmental assistants, and I could go back to making my own copies, delivering my own messages, and fetching my own mail. All of which I was doing now.

"I *hate* the Power Rangers," Gina said. "Explain to me how they ever got to be so popular."

She went back to her lab, and I went back to work on my bobbed hair. It was easy to see how it had become popular. No long hair to put up with combs and pins and pompadour puffs, no having to wash it and wait a week for it to dry. The nurses who'd served in World War I had had to cut their hair off because of lice, and had liked the freedom and the lightness short hair gave them. And there were obvious advantages when it came to the other fads of the day: bicycling and lawn tennis.

So why hadn't it become a fad in 1918? Why had it waited another four years and then suddenly, for no apparent reason, hit so big that barber shops were swamped and hairpin companies went bankrupt overnight? In 1921, hair-bobbing was still unusual enough to make front-page news and get women fired. By 1925, it was so common every graduation picture and advertisement and magazine illustration showed short hair, and the only hats being sold were bell-shaped cloches, which were too snug to fit over long hair. What had happened in the interim? What was the trigger?

I spent the rest of the day re-sorting the clippings. You'd think magazine pages from the 1920s would have turned yellowish and rough, but they hadn't. They'd slid like eels out onto the tile floor, fanning out across and under each other, mixing with the newspaper clippings and obliterating their categories. Some of the paper clips had even come off.

I did the re-sorting on the floor. One of the lab tables was full of clippings about pogs that Flip was supposed to have taken to be copied and hadn't, and the other one had all my jitterbug data on it. And neither one was big enough for the number of piles I needed, some of which overlapped: entire article devoted to hair-bobbing, reference within article devoted to flappers, pointed reference, casual reference, disapproving reference, humorous reference, shocked and horrified reference, illustration in advertisement, adoption by middle-aged women, adoption by children, adoption by the elderly, news items by date, news items by state, urban reference, rural reference, disparaging reference, reference indicating complete acceptance, first signs of waning of fad, fad declared over.

By 4:55 the floor of my whole lab was covered with piles and Flip still wasn't back. Stepping carefully among the piles, I went over and looked at the box again. Biology was clear on the other side of the complex, but there was nothing for it. The box said PERISHABLE, and even though irresponsibility is the hottest trend of the nineties, it hasn't worked its way through the whole society yet. I picked up the box and took it down to Dr. Turnbull.

It weighed a ton. By the time I'd maneuvered it down two flights and along four corridors, the reasons why irresponsibility had caught on had become very clear to me. At least I was getting to see a part of the building I ordinarily was never in. I wasn't even exactly sure where Bio was except that it was down on the ground floor. But I must be heading in the right direction. There was moisture in the air and a faint sound of zoo. I followed the sound down yet another staircase and into a long corridor. Dr. Turnbull's office was, of course, at the very end of it.

The door was shut. I shifted the box in my arms, knocked and waited. No answer. I shifted the box again, propping it against the wall with my hip, and tried the knob. The door was locked.

The last thing I wanted to do was lug this box all the way back up to my office and then try to find a refrigerator. I looked down the hall at the line of doors. They were all closed, and, presumably, locked, but there was a line of light under the middle one on the left.

I repositioned the box, which was getting heavier by the minute, lugged it down to the light, and knocked on the door. No answer, but when I tried the knob, the door opened onto a jungle of video cameras, computer equipment, opened boxes, and trailing wires.

"Hello," I said. "Anybody here?"

There was a muffled grunt, which I hoped wasn't from an inmate of the zoo. I glanced at the nameplate on the door. "Dr. O'Reilly?" I said.

"Yeah?" a man's voice from under what looked like a furnace said.

I walked around to the side of it and could see two brown corduroy legs sticking out from under it, surrounded by a litter of tools. "I've got a box here for Dr. Turnbull," I said to the legs. "She's not in her office. Could you take it for her?"

"Just set it down," the voice said impatiently.

I looked around for somewhere to set it that wasn't covered with video equipment and coils of chicken wire.

"Not on the equipment," the legs said sharply. "On the floor. *Carefully.*"

I pushed aside a rope and two modems and set the box down. I squatted down next to the legs and said, "It's marked 'perishable.' You need to put it in the refrigerator."

"All *right,*" he snapped. A freckled arm in a wrinkled white sleeve appeared, patting the floor around the base of the box.

There was a roll of duct tape lying just out of his reach. "Duct tape?" I said, putting it in his hand.

His hand closed around it and then just stayed there.

"You didn't want the duct tape?" I looked around to see what else he might have wanted. "Pliers? Phillips screwdriver?"

The legs and arm disappeared under the furnace and a head emerged from behind it. "Sorry," he said. His face was freckled, too, and he was wearing Coke-bottle-thick glasses. "I thought you were that mail person."

"Flip," I said. "No. She delivered the box to my office by mistake."

"Figures." He pulled himself out from under the furnace and stood up. "I really *am* sorry," he said, dusting himself off. "I don't usually act that rude to people who are trying to deliver things. It's just that Flip . . ."

"I know," I said, nodding sympathetically.

He pushed his hand through his sandy hair. "The last time she delivered a box to me she set it on top of one of the monitors, and it fell off and broke a video camera."

"That sounds like Flip," I said, but I wasn't really listening. I was looking at him.

When you spend as much time as I do analyzing fads and fashions, you get so you can spot them at first sight: ecohippie, jogger, Wall Street M.B.A., urban terrorist. Dr. O'Reilly wasn't any of them. He was about my age and about my height. He was wearing a lab coat and corduroy pants that had been washed so often the wale was completely worn off on the knees. They'd shrunk, too, halfway up his ankles, and there was a pale line where they'd been let down.

The effect, especially with the Coke-bottle glasses, should have been science geek, but it wasn't. For one thing, there were the freckles. For another, he was wearing a pair of once-white canvas sneakers with holes in the toes and frayed seams. Science geeks wear black shoes and white socks. He wasn't even wearing a pocket protector, though he should have been. There were two splotches of ballpoint ink and a puddle of Magic Marker on the breast pocket of the lab coat, and one of the patch pockets was out at the bottom. And there was something else, something I couldn't put my finger on, that made it impossible for me to categorize him.

I squinted at him, trying to figure out exactly what it was, so long he looked at me curiously. "I took the box to Dr. Turnbull's office," I said hastily, "but she's gone home."

"She had a grant meeting today," he said. "She's very good at getting grants."

"The most important quality for a scientist these days," I said.

"Yeah," he said, smiling wryly. "Wish I had it."

"I'm Sandra Foster," I said, sticking out my hand. "Sociology."

He wiped his hand on his corduroys and shook my hand. "Bennett O'Reilly."

And that was odd, too. He was my age. His name should be Matt or Mike or, God forbid, Troy. Bennett.

I was staring again. I said, "And you're a biologist?"

"Chaos theory."

"Isn't that an oxymoron?" I said.

He grinned. "The way I did it, yes. Which is why my project lost its funding and I had to come to work for HiTek."

Maybe that accounted for the oddness, and corduroys and canvas sneakers were what chaos theorists were wearing these days. No, Dr. Applegate, over in Chem, had been in chaos, and he dressed like everybody else in R&D: flannel shirt, baseball cap, jeans, Nikes.

And nearly everybody at HiTek's working out of their field. Science has its fads and crazes, like anything else: string theory, eugenics, mesmerism. Chaos theory had been big for a couple of years, in spite of Utah and cold fusion, or maybe because of it, but both of them had been replaced by genetic engineering. If Dr. O'Reilly wanted grant money, he needed to give up chaos and build a better mouse.

He was stooping over the box. "I don't have a refrigerator. I'll have to set it outside on the porch." He picked it up, grunting a little. "Jeez, it's heavy. Flip probably delivered it to you on purpose so she wouldn't have to carry it all the way down here." He boosted it up with his corduroy knee. "Well, on behalf of Dr. Turnbull and all of Flip's other victims, thanks," he said, and headed into the tangle of equipment.

A clear exit line, and, speaking of grants, I still had half those hair-bobbing clippings to sort into piles before I went home. But I was still trying to put my finger on what it was that was so unusual about him. I followed him through the maze of stuff.

"Is Flip responsible for this?" I said, squeezing between two stacks of boxes.

"No," he said. "I'm setting up my new project." He stepped over a tangle of cords.

"Which is?" I brushed aside a hanging plastic net.

"Information diffusion." He opened a door and stepped outside onto a porch. "It should keep cold enough out here," he said, setting it down.

"Definitely," I said, hugging my arms against a chilly October wind. The porch faced a large, enclosed paddock, fenced in on all sides by high walls and overhead with wire netting. There was a gate at the back.

"It's used for large-animal experiments," Dr. O'Reilly said. "I'd hoped I'd have the monkeys by July so they could be outside, but the paperwork's taken longer than I expected."

"Monkeys?"

"The project's studying information diffusion patterns in a troop of macaques. You teach a new skill to one of the macaques and then document its spread through the troop. I'm working with the rate of utilitarian versus nonutilitarian skills. I teach one of the macaques a nonutilitarian skill with a low ability threshold and multiple skill levels—"

"Like the Hula Hoop," I said.

He set the box down just outside the door and stood up. "The Hula Hoop?"

"The Hula Hoop, miniature golf, the twist. All fads have a low ability threshold. That's why you never see speed chess becoming a fad. Or fencing."

He pushed his Coke-bottle glasses up on his nose.

"I'm working on a project on fads. What causes them and where they come from," I said.

"Where do they come from?"

"I have no idea. And if I don't get back to work, I never will." I stuck out my hand again. "Nice to have met you, Dr. O'Reilly." I started back through the maze.

He followed me, saying thoughtfully, "I never thought of teaching them to do a Hula Hoop."

I was going to say I didn't think there'd be room in here, but it was almost six, and I at least had to get my piles up off the floor and into file folders before I went home.

I told Dr. O'Reilly goodbye and went back up to Sociology. Flip was standing in the hall, her hands on the hips of her leather skirt.

"I *came* back and you'd *left,*" she said, making it sound like I'd left her sinking in quicksand.

"I was down in Bio," I said.

"I had to come all the way back from Personnel," she said, tossing her hair. "You *said* to come back."

"I gave up on you and delivered the package myself," I said, waiting for her to protest and say delivering the mail was her job. I should have known better. That would have meant admitting she was actually responsible for something.

"I looked all over your office for it," she said virtuously. "While I was waiting for you, I picked up all that stuff you left on the floor and threw it in the trash."

the old curiosity shop (1840–41)

Book fad caused by serialization of Dickens's story about a little girl and her hapless grandfather, who are thrown out of their shop and forced to wander through England. Interest in the book was so great that people in America thronged the pier waiting for the ship from England to bring the next installment and, unable to wait for the ship to dock, shouted to the passengers aboard, "Did Little Nell die?" She did, and her death reduced readers of all ages, sexes, and degrees of toughness to agonies of grief. Cowboys and miners in the West sobbed openly over the last pages and an Irish member of Parliament threw the book out of a train and burst into tears.

The source of the Thames doesn't look like it. It looks like a pasture, and not even a soggy pasture. Not a single water plant grows there. If it weren't for an old well, filled up with stones, it would be impossible to even locate the spot. Cows, not being interested in stones, wander lazily across and around the source, munching buttercups and Queen Anne's lace, unaware that anything significant is beginning beneath their feet.

Science is even less obvious. It starts with an apple falling, a teakettle boiling. Alex Fleming, taking a last glance around his lab as he left for a long weekend, wouldn't have seen anything significant in the window left half open, in the sooty air from Paddington Station drifting in. Getting ready to gather up his notes, to tell his assistant to leave everything alone, to lock the door, he wouldn't have noticed that one of the petri dishes' lids had slid a fraction of an inch to the side. His mind would have already been on his vacation, on the errands he had to run, on going home.

So was mine. The only thing I was aware of was that Flip had thoughtfully crumpled each clipping into a wad before stuffing them into the trash can, and that there was no way I could get them all smoothed out tonight, and, as a result, I was not only oblivious to the first event in a chain of events that was going to lead to a scientific discovery, but I was about to miss the second one, too. And the third.

I set the trash can on the lab table on top of my jitterbug research, sealed the top with duct tape, stuck on a sign that said *"Do not* touch. This means you, Flip," and went out to my car. Halfway out of the parking lot I thought about Flip's ability to read, turned around, and went back to my office to get the trash can.

The phone was ringing when I opened the door. "Howdy," Billy Ray said when I picked it up. "Guess where I am."

"In Wyoming?" I said. Billy Ray was a rancher from Laramie I'd gone out with a while back when I was researching line dancing.

"In Montana," he said. "Halfway between Lodge Grass and Billings." Which meant he was calling me on his cellular phone. "I'm on my way to look at some Targhees," he said. "They're the hottest thing going."

I assumed they were also cows. During my line dancing phase, the hottest thing going had been Aberdeen Longhorns. Billy Ray is a very nice guy and a walking compendium of country-western fads. Two birds with one stone.

"I'm going to be in Denver this Saturday," he said through the stutter that meant his cellular phone was starting to get out of range. "For a seminar on computerized ranching."

I wondered idly what its acronym would be. Computerized Operational Wrangling?

"So I wondered if we could grab us some dinner. There's a new prairie place in Boulder."

And prairie was the latest thing in cuisine. "Sorry," I said, looking at the trash can on my lab table. "I've had a setback. I'm going to have to work this weekend."

"You should just feed everything onto your computer and let it do the work. I've got my whole ranch on my PC."

"I know," I said, wishing it were that simple.

"You need to get yourself one of those text scanners," Billy Ray said, the hum becoming more insistent. "That way you don't even have to type it in."

I wondered if a text scanner could read crumpled.

The hum was becoming a crackle. "Well, maybe next time," he sort of said, and passed into cellular oblivion.

I put down my noncellular phone and picked up the trash can. Under it, half buried in my jitterbug research, were the library books I should have taken back two days ago. I piled them on top of the stretched duct tape, which held, and carried them and the trash can out to the car and drove to the library.

Since I spend my working days studying trends, many of which are downright disgusting, I feel it's my duty after work to encourage the trends I'd like to see catch on, like signaling before you change lanes, and chocolate cheesecake. And reading.

Also, libraries are great places to observe trends in best-sellers, and library management. And librarian attire.

"What's on the reserve list this week, Lorraine?" I asked the librarian at the desk. She was wearing a black-and-white-mottled sweatshirt with the logo UDDERLY FANTASTIC on it, and a pair of black-and-white Holstein cow earrings.

"Led On by Fate," she said. "Still. The reserve list's a foot long. You are"—she counted down her computer screen—"fifth in line. You were sixth, but Mrs. Roxbury canceled."

"Really?" I said, interested. Book fads don't usually die out until the sequel comes out, at which point the readers realize they've been had. Witness *Oliver's Story* and *Slow Waltz at Cedar Bend.* Which is why the *Gone with the Wind* trend managed to last nearly six years, resulting in thousands of unhappy little boys having to live down the name of Rhett, or even worse, Ashley. If Margaret Mitchell'd come out with *Slow Waltz at Tara Bend* it would have been all over. Which reminded me, I should check to see if there'd been any dropoff in *Gone with the Wind*'s popularity since the publication of *Scarlett.*

"Don't get your hopes up about *Fate,"* Lorraine said. "Mrs. Roxbury only canceled because she said she couldn't bear to wait for it and bought her own copy." She shook her head, and her cows swung back and forth. "What *do* people see in it?"

Yes, well, and what did they see in *Little Lord Fauntleroy* back in the 1890s, Frances Hodgson Burnett's sickly sweet tale of a little boy with long curls who inherited an English castle? Whatever it was, it made the novel into a best-seller and then a hit play and a movie starring Mary Pickford (she already had the long curls), started a style of velvet suits, and became the bane of an earlier generation of little boys whose mothers inflicted lace collars, curlers, and the name Cedric on them and who would have been delighted to have only been named Ashley.

"What else is on the reserve list?"

"The new John Grisham, the new Stephen King, *Angels from Above, Brushed by an Angel's Wing, Heavenly Encounters of the Third Kind, Angels Beside You, Angels, Angels Everywhere, Putting Your Guardian Angel to Work for You,* and *Angels in the Boardroom.*"

None of those counted. The Grisham and the Stephen King were only best-sellers, and the angel fad had been around for over a year.

"Do you want me to put you on the list for any of those?" Lorraine asked. "*Angels in the Boardroom* is great."

"No, thanks," I said. "Nothing new, huh?"

She frowned. "I thought there was something . . ." She checked her computer screen. "The novelization of *Little Women,*" she said, "but that wasn't it."

I thanked her and went over to the stacks. I picked out F. Scott Fitzgerald's "Bernice Bobs Her Hair" and a couple of mysteries, which always have simple, solvable problems like "How did the murderer get into the locked room?" instead of hard ones like "What causes trends?" and "What did I do to deserve Flip?" and then went over to the eight hundreds.

One of the nastier trends in library management in recent years is the notion that libraries should be "responsive to their patrons." This means having dozens of copies of *The Bridges of Madison County* and Danielle Steel, and a consequent shortage of shelf space, to cope with which librarians have taken to purging books that haven't been checked out lately.

"Why are you throwing out Dickens?" I'd asked Lorraine last year at the library book sale, brandishing a copy of *Bleak House* at her. "You can't throw out Dickens."

"Nobody checked it out," she'd said. "If no one checks a book out for a year, it gets taken off the shelves." She had been wearing a sweatshirt that said A TEDDY BEAR IS FOREVER, and a pair of plush teddy bear earrings. "Obviously nobody read it."

"And nobody ever will because it won't be there for them to check out," I'd said. "*Bleak House* is a wonderful book."

"Then this is your chance to buy it," she'd said.

Well, and this was a trend like any other, and as a sociologist I should note it with interest and try to determine its origins. I didn't. Instead, I started checking out books. All my favorites, which I'd never checked out because I had copies at home, and all the classics, and everything with an old cloth binding that somebody might want to read someday when the current trends of sentimentality and schlock are over.

Today I checked out *The Wrong Box,* in honor of the day's events, and since I'd first seen Dr. O'Reilly with his legs sticking out from under a large object, *The Wizard of Oz,* and then went over to the Bs to look for Bennett. *The Old Wives' Tale* wasn't there (it had probably ended up in the book sale already), but right next to Beckett was Butler's *The Way of All Flesh,* which meant *The Old Wives' Tale* might just be misshelved.

I started down the shelves, looking for something chubby, clothbound, and untouched. Borges; *Wuthering Heights,* which I had already checked out this year; Rupert Brooke. And Robert Browning. *The Complete Works.* It wasn't Arnold Bennett, but it was both clothbound and fat, and it still had an old-fashioned pocket and checkout card in it. I grabbed it and the Borges and took them to the checkout desk.

"I remembered what else was on the reserve list," Lorraine said. "New book. *Guide to the Fairies.*"

"What is it, a children's book?"

"No." She took it off the reserve shelf. "It's about the presence of fairies in our daily lives."

She handed it to me. It had a picture of a fairy peeking out from behind a computer on the cover, and it fit one of the criteria for a book fad: It was only 80 pages long. *The Bridges of Madison County* was 192 pages, *Jonathan Livingston Seagull* was 93, and *Goodbye, Mr. Chips,* a huge fad back in 1934, was only 84.

It was also drivel. The chapter titles were "How to Get in Touch with Your Inner Fairy," "How Fairies Can Help Us Get Ahead in the Corporate World," and "Why You Shouldn't Pay Attention to Unbelievers."

"You'd better put me on the list," I said. I handed her the Browning.

"This hasn't been checked out in nearly a year," she said.

"Really?" I said. "Well, it is now." And took my Borges, Browning, and Baum and went to get some dinner at the Earth Mother.

poulaines [1350–1480]

Soft leather or cloth shoes with elongated points. Originating in Poland (hence *poulaine;* the English called them *crackowes* after Cracow), or more logically brought back from the Middle East by Crusaders, they became the craze at all the European courts. The pointed toes became more elaborate, stuffed with moss and shaped into lions' claws or eagles' beaks, and progressively longer, to the point that it was impossible to walk without tripping over them and completely impossible to kneel, and gold and silver chains had to be attached to the knees to hold up the ends. Translated into armor, the poulaine fad became downright dangerous: Austrian knights at the battle of Sempach in 1386 were riveted to the spot by their elongated iron shoes and were forced to strike off the points with their swords or be caught flat-footed, so to speak. Supplanted by the square-toed, ankle-strapped duck's-bill shoe, which promptly became ridiculously wide.

The Earth Mother has okay food and iced tea so good I order it all year round. Plus, it's a great place to study fads. Not only is its menu trendy (currently free-range vegetarian), but so are its waiters. Also, there's a stand outside with all the alternative newspapers.

I gathered them up and went inside. The door and entryway were jammed with people waiting to get in. Their iced tea must be becoming a trend. I presented myself to the waitress, who had a prison-style haircut, jogging shorts, and Tevas.

That's another trend, waitresses dressed to look as little as possible like waitresses, probably so you can't find them when you want your check. "Name and number in your party?" the waitress said. She was holding a tablet with at least twenty names.

"One, Foster," I said. "I'll take smoking or nonsmoking, whichever's quicker."

She looked outraged. "We don't *have* a smoking section," she said. "Don't you know what smoking can do to you?"

Usually get you seated quicker, I thought, but since she looked ready to cross out my name, I said, "*I* don't smoke. I was just willing to sit with people who do."

"Secondhand smoke is just as deadly," she said, and put an *X* next to my name that probably meant I would be seated right after hell froze over. "I'll call you," she said, rolling her eyes, and I certainly hoped *that* wasn't a trend.

I sat down on the bench next to the door and started through the papers. They were full of animal rights articles and tattoo removal ads. I turned to the personals. The personals aren't a fad. They were, in the late eighties, and then, like a lot of fads, instead of dying out, they settled into a small but permanent niche in society.

That happens to lots of fads: CBs were so popular for a few months that "Breaker, breaker" became a catchphrase and everyone had handles like "Red Hot Mama," and then went back to being used by truckers and speeding motorists. Bicycles, Monopoly, crossword puzzles, all were crazes that have settled into the mainstream. The personals took up residence in the alternative newspapers.

There can be trends within trends, though, and the personals go through fads of their own. Unusual varieties of sex was big for a while. Now it's outdoor activities.

The waitress, looking vastly disapproving, said, "Foster party of one," and led me to a table right in front of the kitchen. "We banned smoking two *years* ago," she said, and slapped down a menu.

I picked it up, glanced at it to see if they still had the sprouts and sun-dried tomatoes croissant, and settled down to the personals again. Jogging was out, and mountain biking and kayaking were in. And angels. One of the ads was headed HEAVENLY MESSENGER and another one said "Are your angels telling you to call me? Mine told me to write this ad," which I found unlikely.

Soul work was also in, and spirituality, and slashes. "S/DWF wanted," and "Into Eastern/Native American/personal growth," and "Seeking fun/possible life partner." Well, aren't we all?

A waiter appeared, also in jogging shorts, Tevas, and snit. He had apparently seen the *X*. I said, before he could lecture me on the dangers of nicotine, "I'll have the sprouts croissant and iced tea."

"We don't have that anymore."

"Sprouts?"

"Tea." He flipped the menu open and pointed to the right-hand page. "Our beverages are right here."

They certainly were. The entire page was devoted to them: espresso, cappuccino, caffè latte, caffè mocha, caffè cacao. But no tea. "I liked your iced tea," I said.

"No one drinks tea anymore," he said.

Because you took it off the menu, I thought, wondering if they'd used the same principle as the library, and I should have come here more often, or ordered more than one when I did come, and saved it from the ax. Also feeling guilty because I'd apparently missed the start of a trend, or at least a new stage in one.

The espresso trend's actually been around for several years, mostly on the West Coast and in Seattle, where it started. A lot of fads have come out of Seattle recently—garage bands, the grunge look, caffè latte. Before that, fads usually started in L.A., and before that, New York. Lately, Boulder's shown signs of becoming the next trend center, but the spread of espresso to Boulder probably has more to do with bottom lines than the scientific laws of fads, but I still wished I'd been around to watch it happen and see if I could spot the trigger.

"I'll have a caffè latte," I said.

"Single or double?"

"Double."

"Tall or short?"

"Tall."

"Chocolate or cinnamon on top?"

"Chocolate."

"Semisweet or dark?"

I'd been wrong when I told Dr. O'Reilly all fads had to have a low ability threshold.

After several more exchanges, concerning whether I wanted cubed sugar versus brown and nonfat versus two percent, he left, and I went back to the personals.

Honesty was out, as usual. The men were all "tall, handsome, and financially secure," and the women were all "gorgeous, slender, and sensitive." The G/Bs were all "attractive, sophisticated, and caring." Everyone had a "terrific sense of humor," which I also found unlikely. All of them were seeking sensitive, intelligent, ecological, romantic, articulate NSs.

NS. What was NS? Nordic skiing? Native American Shamanism? Natural sex? No sex? And here was NSO. No sexual orgasms? I flipped back to the translation guide. Of course. Nonsmoker only.

The buxom, handsome, caring people who place these things seem frequently to have confused the personals with the L. L. Bean catalog: I'd like Item D2481 in passion red. Size, small. And they frequently specify color, shape, and no pets. But the number of nonsmokings seemed to have radically increased since the last time I'd done a count. I got a red pen out of my purse and started to circle them.

By the time my sandwich and complex latte had arrived, the page was covered in red. I ate my sandwich and sipped my latte and circled.

The nonsmoking trend started way back in the late seventies, and so far it had followed the typical pattern for aversion trends, but I wondered if it was starting to reach another, more volatile level. "Any race, religion, political party, sexual preference okay," one of the ads read. "NO SMOKERS." In caps.

And "Must be adventurous, daring, nonsmoking risk-taker" and "Me: Successful but tired of being alone. You: Compassionate, caring, nonsmoking, childless." And my favorite: "Desperately seeking someone who marches to the beat of a different drummer, flouts convention, doesn't care what's in or out. Smokers need not apply."

Someone was standing over me. The waiter, probably, wanting to give me a nicotine patch. I looked up.

"I didn't know *you* came here," Flip said, rolling her eyes.

"I didn't know you came here either," I said. And now that I do I never will again, I thought. Especially since they don't serve iced tea anymore.

"The personals, huh?" she said, craning around to look at what I'd marked. "They're okay, I guess, if you're desperate."

I am, I thought, wondering wildly if she'd stopped on the way in to empty the trash and had I locked the car?

"*I* don't need artificial aids. *I* have Brine," she said, pointing at a guy with a shaved head, bovver boots, and studs in his nose, eyebrows, and lower lip, but I wasn't looking at him. I was looking at her extended arm, which had three wide gray armlets around it at wrist, mid-forearm, and just below the elbow. Duct tape.

Which explained her remark about it being a personal errand this afternoon. If this is the latest fad, I thought, I quit. "I have to go," I said, scooping up my newspapers and purse, and looking frantically around for my waiter, who I couldn't find since he was dressed like everybody else. I put down a twenty and practically ran for the exit.

"She doesn't appreciate me at all," I heard Flip telling Brine as I fled. "She could at least have thanked me for cleaning up her office."

I *had* locked my car, and, driving home, I began to feel almost cheerful about the duct tape armbands. Flip would, after all, have to take them off. I also thought about Brine and about Billy Ray, who wears a Stetson and boot-cut jeans and a pager, and about what an accomplishment Dr. O'Reilly's unstylishness really was.

Almost everything is in style for men these days: bomber jackets, bicycle pants, dashikis, *GQ* suits, jeans that are too big, tank shirts that are too small, deck shoes, hiking boots, Birkenstocks. And now with the addition of grunge's faded flannel shirts and thermal underwear, it's hard to find anything that looks bad enough to not be in style. But Dr. O'Reilly had managed it.

His hair was too long and his pants were too short, but it was more than that. One of the garage bands has a drummer who wears pedal pushers and braids onstage, and he looks like the ultimate in trendiness. And it wasn't his glasses. Look at Elton John. Look at Buddy Holly.

It was something else, something that had been nagging at me all evening. Maybe I should go back down to Bio and ask him if I could study him. Maybe if I followed him around while he taught his monkeys to Hula Hoop or whatever it was he was going to do, I could figure out how he managed to be trend-free. And by studying a nontrend, get some clue to its opposite. Or maybe I should go home, iron my clippings, and try to figure out what caused two million women to suddenly pick up their scissors in unison and whack off their Little Lord Fauntleroy curls.

I didn't do either one. Instead, I went home and read Browning. I read "The Pied Piper," a poem which, oddly enough, was about fads, and started *Pippa Passes,* a long poem about an Italian factory girl in Asolo who only got one day a year off (clearly she worked for the Italian branch of HiTek) and who spent it wandering past windows singing, among other things, "The lark's on the wing;/The snail's on the thorn," and inspiring everybody who heard her.

I wished she'd show up outside my window and inspire me, but it didn't seem likely. Inspiration was going to have to come the way it usually did in science, uncrumpling all those clippings and feeding the data into the computer. By experimenting and failing and trying again.

I was wrong. Inspiration had already happened. I just didn't know it yet.

quality circles [1980–85]

Business fad inspired by successful Japanese corporate practices. A committee of employees from all areas of the company would meet once a month, usually after work, to share experiences, communicate ideas, and make suggestions as to ways the corporation could be better run. Died out when it became apparent that none of those suggestions were being taken. Replaced by QIS, MBO, JIT, and hot groups.

Wednesday we had the all-staff meeting. I was nearly late to it. I'd been down in Supply, trying to wrestle a box of paper clips out of Desiderata, who didn't know where (or what) they were, and, as a result, every table in the cafeteria was filled when I got there.

Gina waved to me from across the room and pointed at an empty chair next to her, and I slid into it just as Management said, "We at HiTek never stop striving for excellence."

"What's going on?" I whispered to Gina.

"Management is proving beyond a shadow of a doubt they don't have enough to do," she murmured back. "So they've invented a new acronym. They're working up to it right now."

". . . principle of our exciting new management program is Initiative." He printed a large capital *I* on a flipchart with a Magic Marker. "Initiative is the cornerstone of a good company."

I looked around the room, trying to spot Dr. O'Reilly. Flip was slouched against the back wall, her arms swathed in duct tape, looking sullen.

"The cornerstone of Initiative is Resources," Management said. He printed an *R* in front of the *I*. "And what is HiTek's most valuable resource? You!"

I finally spotted Dr. O'Reilly standing near the trays and the silverware with his hands in his pockets. He looked a little more presentable today, but not much. He'd put a brown polyester blazer on that wasn't the same brown as his corduroy pants and a brown-and-white-checked shirt that didn't match either one.

"Resources and Initiative are worthless unless they're guided," Management said, sticking a *G* in front of the *R* and *I*. "Guided Resource Initiative Management," he said triumphantly, pointing to each letter in turn. "GRIM."

"Truer words," Gina muttered.

"The cornerstone of GRIM is Staff Input." Management wrote *SI* on the flipchart. "I want you to divide into brainstorming groups and list five objectives." He wrote a large *5* on the flipchart.

I looked over at Dr. O'Reilly, still standing by the silverware, wondering if I should invite him to join our brainstorming group, but Gina'd already grabbed Sarah from Chemistry and a woman from Personnel named Elaine who was wearing a sweatband and bicycle pants.

"Five objectives," Management said, and Elaine immediately got out a notebook and numbered a page from one to five, "for enhancing the work environment at HiTek."

"Fire Flip," I said.

"Do you know what she did to me the other day?" Sarah said. "She filed all my lab charts under *L* for lab."

"Should I write that down?" Elaine said.

"No," Gina said, "but I want you *all* to write this down. Brittany's birthday is on the eighteenth and you're all invited. Two o'clock. Presents, cake, and *no* Power Rangers. I put my foot down. You can have any kind of party you want, I told Brittany, but *not* Power Rangers."

Dr. O'Reilly had finally sat down at a table in the middle of the room and had taken off his jacket. It wasn't an improvement. All it meant was that you could see his tie, which was seriously out of style.

"Have you ever *seen* the Power Rangers?" Gina was saying.

"I can't come," Sarah said. "I'm running in a ten-K race with Paul Ottermeyer."

"In Safety? I thought you were going with Ted," Gina said.

"Ted has intimacy issues," Sarah said. "And until he learns to deal with them, there's no point in our trying to have a committed relationship."

"So you're settling for a ten-K race?" Gina said.

"You should try stair-walking," Elaine from Personnel said. "It gives you a much better full-body workout than running."

I leaned my chin on my hand and considered Dr. O'Reilly's tie. Ties are a lot like the rest of men's clothes. Almost everything's in. That wasn't true until recently. Each era had its own fashion in ties. Striped cravats were in in the 1860s and lavender ties in the 1890s. Bow ties were big in the twenties, hand-painted hula dancers in the forties, neon daisies in the sixties, and anything that wasn't in was out. But now all of the above are in, along with bolos, bandannas, and the ever-popular no tie at all. Bennett's tie wasn't any of those—it was just ugly.

"What are you looking at?" Gina asked.

"Dr. O'Reilly," I said, wondering if he was old enough to have bought the tie new.

"The geek down in Bio?" Elaine said, craning her neck.

"Bad tie," Gina said.

"And those glasses," Sarah said. "They're so thick you can't even tell what color his eyes are!"

"Gray," I said, but Elaine and Sarah had gone back to discussing stair-walking.

"The best stairs are up on campus," Elaine said. "The engineering building. Sixty-eight steps, but it's gotten pretty crowded. So I usually do the ones over on Clover."

"Ted lives on Iris," Sarah said. "He's got to acknowledge his male warrior spirit, or he'll never be able to embrace his female side."

"All right, fellow workers," Management said. "Do you have your five objectives? Flip, would you collect them?"

Elaine looked stricken. Gina snatched the list from her and wrote rapidly:

1. Optimize potential.
2. Facilitate empowerment.
3. Implement visioning.
4. Strategize priorities.
5. Augment core structures.

"How did you do that?" I said admiringly.

"Those are the five things I always write down," she said and handed the list to Flip as she slouched past.

"Before we go any further," Management said, "I want you all to stand up."

"Bathroom break," Gina murmured.

"We're going to do a sensitivity exercise," Management said. "Everybody find a partner."

I turned. Sarah and Elaine had already claimed each other, and Gina was nowhere to be seen. I hesitated, wondering if I could make it all the way over to Dr. O'Reilly in time, and saw a woman in a chic haircut and a red power suit moving purposefully through the crowd to me.

"I'm Dr. Alicia Turnbull," she said.

"Oh, right," I said, smiling. "Did you get your box okay?"

"Everybody got a partner?" Management boomed. "Now, face each other and raise both hands, palms outward."

We did. "You're all under arrest," I joked.

Dr. Turnbull raised an eyebrow.

"Okay, fellow workers," Management said, "now place your palms flat against the palms of your partner's hands."

Silliness has always been a dominant trend in America, but it has only recently invaded the workplace, although it has its origins in the efficiency experts of the twenties. Frank and Lillian Gilbreth, the founders of the *Cheaper by the Dozen* clan, who clearly did *not* spend all their time in the factory (twelve children, count 'em, twelve), popularized the ideas of motion study, psychology in the workplace, and the outside expert, and American business has been in decline ever since.

"Now, look *deep* in your partner's eyes," Management said, "and tell him or her three things you like about him or her. Okay. One."

"Where *do* they come up with this stuff?" I said, looking deep in Dr. Turnbull's eyes.

"Studies have shown sensitivity training significantly improves corporate workplace relations," she said frostily.

"Fine," I said. "You go first."

"That package clearly said 'perishable' on it," she said, pressing her palms against mine. "You should have delivered it to me immediately."

"You weren't there."

"Then you should have found out where I was."

"Two," Management said.

"That package contained valuable cultures. They could have spoiled."

She seemed to have lost sight of an important point here. "*Flip* was the one who was supposed to have delivered it to you."

"Then what was it doing in your office?"

"Three," Management said.

"Next time I'd appreciate it if you'd leave a message on my e-mail," she said. "Well? Aren't you going to tell me three things you like about me? It's your turn."

I like it that you work in Bio and that it's clear on the other end of the complex, I thought. "I like your suit," I said, "even though shoulder pads are terribly passé. And so is red. Too threatening. Feminine is what's in."

"Don't you feel better about yourself?" Management said, beaming. "Don't you feel closer to your fellow worker?"

Too close, in fact. I beat a hasty retreat back to my table and Gina. "Where did you go?" I demanded.

"To the bathroom," she said. "Meeting Survival Rule Number One. Always be out going to the bathroom during sensitivity exercises."

"Before we go any further," Management said, and I braced myself to make a break for the bathroom in case of another sensitivity exercise, but Management was moving right along to the increased paperwork portion of our program, which turned out to be procurement forms.

"We've had some complaints about Supply," Management said, "so we've instituted a new policy that will increase efficiency in that department. Instead of the old departmental supply forms, you'll use a new interdepartmental form. We've also restructured the funding allocation procedure. One of the most revolutionary aspects of GRIM is the way it streamlines funding. All applications for project funding will be handled by a central Allocations Review Committee, including projects which were previously approved. All forms are due Monday the twenty-third. All applications must be filed on the new simplified funding allocation application forms."

Which, if the stack of papers Flip was holding in her duct-taped arms as she passed among the crowd was any indication, were longer than the old funding application forms, and *they* were thirty-two pages.

"While the interdepartmental assistant's distributing the forms, I want to hear your input. What else can we do to make HiTek a better place?"

Eliminate staff meetings, I thought, but didn't say it. I may not be as well versed as Gina is in Meeting Survival, but I do know enough not to raise my hand. All it does is get you put on a committee.

Apparently everybody else knew it, too.

"Staff Input is the cornerstone of HiTek," he said.

Still nothing.

"Anybody?" Management said, looking GRIM. He brightened. "Ah, at last, someone who's not afraid to stand out in a crowd."

Everybody turned to look.

It was Flip. "The interdepartmental assistant has way too many duties," she said, flipping her hank of hair.

"You see," Management said, pointing at her. "That's the kind of problem-solving attitude that GRIM is all about. What solution do you suggest?"

"A different job title," Flip said. "And an assistant."

I looked across the room at Dr. O'Reilly. He had his head in his hands.

"Okay. Other ideas?"

Forty hands shot up. I looked at the waving hands and thought about the Pied Piper and his rats. And about hair-bobbing. Most hair fads are a clear case of follow-the-Piper. Bo Derek, Dorothy Hamill, Jackie Kennedy, had all started hairstyle fads, and they were by no means the first. Madame de Pompadour had been responsible for those enormous powdered wigs with sailing ships and famous artillery battles in them, and Veronica Lake for millions of American women being unable to see out of one eye.

So it was logical that hair-bobbing had been started by somebody, only who? Isadora Duncan had bobbed her hair in the early 1900s, and several suffragettes had bobbed theirs (and put on men's clothes) long before that, but neither had attracted any followers to speak of.

The suffragettes were obviously ahead of their time (and rather fearsomely formidable). Isadora, who leaped around the stage in skimpy chiffon tunics and bare feet, was too weird.

The obvious person was the ballroom dancer Irene Castle. She and her husband, Vernon (more miserable little boys), had set several dancing trends: the one-step, the hesitation waltz, the tango, the turkey trot, and, of course, the Castle Walk.

Irene was pretty, and almost everything she wore had become a fad, from white satin shoes to little Dutch caps. In 1913, at the height of their popularity, she'd had her hair cut short while she was in the hospital after an appendectomy, and she'd kept it short after she got better and had worn it with a wide band that clearly foreshadowed the flappers.

She was a known fashion-setter, and she'd definitely had followers. But if she was the source, why had it taken so long to catch on? When Bo Derek's corn-rowed hair hit movie screens in 1979, it was only a week before corn-rowed women started showing up everywhere. If Irene was the source, why hadn't hair-bobbing become a fad in 1913? Why had it waited for nine years and a world war to become a fad?

Maybe the movies were the key. No, Mary Pickford hadn't cut off her long curls until 1928. Had Irene and Vernon Castle done a silent film in, say, 1921?

Management was still calling on waving hands.

"I think we should have an espresso cart in the building," Dr. Applegate said.

"I think we should have a workout room," Elaine said.

"And some more stairs."

This could go on all day, and I wanted to check and see what movies had come out in 1922. I stood up, as unobtrusively as possible, snatched a form from Flip, who had skipped our table, and ducked out the back, leafing through the form to see how long it was.

Wonder of wonders, it was actually shorter than the original. Only twenty-two pages. And the type was only slightly smaller than— I crashed into someone and looked up.

It was Dr. O'Reilly, who must have been doing the same thing. "Sorry," he said. "I was thinking about this funding reapplication thing." He raised both hands, still holding the funding form in the right one, and faced his palms out. "Tell your partner three things you don't like about Management."

"Can it be more than three?" I said. "I suppose this means you won't get your macaques right away, Dr. O'Reilly."

"Call me Bennett," he said. "Flip's the only one with a title. I was supposed to get them this week. Now I'll have to wait till the twentieth. How about you? Does this affect your Hula Hoop project?"

"Hair-bobbing," I said. "The only effect is that I won't have any time to work on it because I'll be filling out this stupid form. I *wish* Management would find something to think about besides making up new forms."

"Shh," someone said fiercely from the door.

We moved farther down the hall, out of range.

"Paperwork is the cornerstone of Management," Bennett whispered. "They think reducing everything to forms is the key to scientific discovery. Unfortunately science doesn't work that way. Look at Newton. Look at Archimedes."

"Management would never have approved the funding for an orchard," I agreed, "or a bathtub."

"Or a river," Bennett said. "Which is why we lost our chaos theory funding and I had to come to work for GRIM."

"What were you working on?" I asked.

"The Loue. It's a river in France. It has its source in a grotto, which means it's a small, contained system with a comparatively limited number of variables. The systems scientists have tried to study before were huge—weather, the human body, rivers. They had thousands, even millions of variables, which made them impossible to predict, so we found . . ."

Up close his tie was even more nondescript than from a distance. It appeared to have some sort of pattern, though what exactly I couldn't make out. Not paisley (which had been popular in 1988), or polka dots (1970). It wasn't a nonpattern either.

". . . and measured the air temperature, water temperature, dimensions of the grotto, makeup of the water, plant life along the banks—" he said and stopped. "You're probably busy and don't have time to listen to all this."

"That's okay," I said. "I've got to go back to my office, but I'll walk you as far as the stairs."

"Okay, well, so my idea was that by precisely measuring every factor in a chaotic system, I could isolate the causes of chaos."

"Flip," I said. "The cause of chaos."

He laughed. "The *other* causes of chaos. I know talking about the causes of chaos sounds like a contradiction in terms, since chaotic systems are supposed to be systems where ordinary cause and effect break down. They're nonlinear, which means there are so many factors, operating in such an interconnected way, that they're impossible to predict."

Like fads, I thought.

"But there are laws governing them. We've mathematically defined some of them: entropy, interior instabilities, and iteration, which is—"

"The butterfly effect," I said.

"Right. A tiny variable feeds back into the system and then the feedback feeds back, until it influences the system all out of proportion to its size."

I nodded. "A butterfly flapping its wings in L.A. can cause a typhoon in Hong Kong. Or an all-staff meeting at HiTek."

He looked delighted. "You know something about chaos?"

"Only from personal experience," I said.

"Yeah," he said, "it does seem to be the order of the day around here. Well, so, anyway, my project was to calculate the effects of iteration and entropy and see if they accounted for chaos or if there was another factor involved."

"Was there?"

He looked thoughtful. "Chaos theorists think the Heisenberg uncertainty principle means that chaotic systems are inherently unpredictable. Verhoest believes that prediction is possible, but he's proposed there's another force driving chaos, an X factor that's influencing its behavior."

"Moths," I said.

"What?"

"Or locusts. Something other than butterflies."

"Oh. Right. But he's wrong. My theory is that iteration can account for everything that goes on in a chaotic system, once all the factors are known and properly measured. I never got the chance to find out. We were only able to do two runs before I got my funding cut. They didn't show an increase in predictability, which means either I was wrong or I didn't have all the variables." He stopped, his hand on a door handle, and I realized we were standing outside his door. I had apparently walked him all the way down to Bio.

"Well," I said, wishing I had more time to analyze his tie, "I guess I'd better get back to work. I've got to brace myself for Flip's new assistant. And fill out my funding allocation form." I looked at it ruefully. "At least it's short."

He peered blankly at me through his thick glasses.

"Only twenty-two pages," I said, holding it up.

"The funding forms aren't printed up yet," he said. "We're supposed to get them tomorrow." He pointed at the form I was holding. "That's the new simplified supply procurement form. For ordering paper clips."

2. bubblings

Mankind, of course, always has been and always will be, under the yoke of the butterflies in the matter of social rites, dress, entertainment, and the expenditure which these things involve.

hugh shetfield, the sovereignty of society, 1909

miniature golf [1927–31]

Recreation fad of small golf courses with eighteen very short holes complicated by windmills, waterfalls, and tiny sand traps. Its popularity was easily explainable. It was a cheap place to take a Depression date, had a low skill threshold with multiple achievement levels, and let you pretend for a couple of hours that you were part of the refined country-club set. Over forty thousand courses sprang up across the country, and at its height it was so popular it was even a threat to the movies, and the studios forbade their actors to be seen playing miniature golf. Died from overexposure.

The source of the Colorado River doesn't look like one either. It's in a glacier field up in the Green River Mountains, and what it looks like is tundra and snow and rock.

But even in deepest winter there's some melting, a drop here, a trickle there, a little film of water forming at the grubby edges of the glacier and spilling over onto the frozen ground. Falling and freezing, collecting, converging, so slowly you can't see it.

Scientific research is like that, too. "Eureka!"s like the one Archimedes had when he stepped in a bathtub and suddenly realized the answer to the problem of testing metals' density are few and far between, and mostly it's just trying and failing and trying something else, feeding in data and eliminating variables and staring at the results, trying to figure out where you went wrong.

Take Arno Penzias and Robert Wilson. Their goal was to measure the absolute intensity of radio signals from space, but first they had to get rid of the background noise in their detector.

They moved their detector to the country to get rid of city noise, radar stations, and atmospheric noise, which helped, but there was still background noise.

They tried to think what might be causing it. Birds? They went up on the roof and looked at the horn-shaped antenna. Sure enough, pigeons were nesting inside it, leaving droppings that might be causing the problem.

They evicted the pigeons, cleaned the antenna, and sealed every possible joint and crack (probably with duct tape). There was still background noise.

All right. So what else could it be? Streams of electrons from nuclear testing? If it was, the noise should be diminishing, since atomic tests had been banned in 1963. They ran dozens of tests on the intensity to see if it was. It wasn't.

And it seemed to be the same no matter which part of the heavens were overhead, which made no sense at all.

They tested and retested, taped and retaped, scraped off pigeon droppings, and despaired of ever getting to the point where they could perform their experiment on radio signal intensity for nearly five years before they realized what they had wasn't background noise at all. It was microwaves, the resounding echo of the Big Bang.

Friday Flip brought the new funding application. It was sixty-eight pages long and poorly stapled. Three pages fell out of it as Flip slouched in the door and two more as she handed it to me. "Thank you, Flip," I said, and smiled at her.

The night before I had read the last two thirds of *Pippa Passes,* during which Pippa had talked two murderously adulterous lovers into killing themselves, convinced a deceived young student to choose love over revenge, and reformed assorted ne'er-do-wells. And all just by chirping, "The year's at the spring,/And day's at the morn." Think what she could have accomplished if she'd had a library card.

"You can change the world," Browning was clearly saying. "By being perky and signaling before turning left, one person can have a positive effect on society," and it was obvious from "The Pied Piper" that he understood how trends worked.

I hadn't noticed any of these effects, but then neither had Pippa, who had presumably gone back to work at the silk factory the next day without any notion of all the good she'd done. I could see her at the staff meeting Management had called to introduce their new management system, PESTO. Right after the sensitivity exercise her coworker would lean over and whisper, "So, Pippa, what did you do on your day off?" and Pippa would shrug and say, "Nothing much. You know, hung out."

So I might be having more of an effect on literacy and left-turn signaling than I'd realized, and, by being pleasant and polite, could stop the downward trend to rudeness.

Of course, Browning had never met Flip. But it was worth a try, and I had the comfort of knowing I couldn't possibly make things worse.

So, even though Flip had made no effort to pick up the spilled pages and was, in fact, standing on one of them, I smiled at her and said, "How are you this morning?"

"Oh, just *great,*" she said sarcastically. "Perfectly *fine.*" She flopped down onto the hair-bobbing clippings on my lab table. "You will not *believe* what they expect me to do now!"

A little work? I thought uncharitably, and then remembered I was supposed to be following in Pippa's footsteps. "Who's they?" I said, bending to pick up the spilled pages.

*"Man*agement," she said, rolling her eyes. She was wearing a pair of neon-yellow tights, a tie-dyed T-shirt, and a very peculiar down vest. It was short and bunched oddly around the neck and armpits. "You know how I'm supposed to get a new job title and an assistant?"

"Yes," I said, continuing to smile. "Did you? Get a new job title?"

"Ye-es," she said. "I'm the interdepartmental communications liaison. But for my assistant, they expect me to be on a *search* committee. *After* work."

Along the bottom of the vest there was a row of snaps, a style I had never seen before. She's wearing it upside down, I thought.

"The whole *point* was I was overworked. That's why I have to have an assistant, isn't it? Hel*lo?"*

Wearing clothing some other way than was intended is an ever-popular variety of fad—untied shoelaces, backward baseball caps, ties for belts, slips for dresses—and one that can't be put down to merchandising because it doesn't cost anything. It's not new, either. High school girls in 1955 took to wearing their cardigan sweaters backward, and their mothers had worn unbuckled galoshes with short skirts and raccoon coats in the 1920s. The metal buckles had jangled and flapped, which is how the name *flapper* came about. Or, since there doesn't seem to be agreement on the source of anything where fads are concerned, they were named for the chickenlike flapping of their arms when they did the Charleston. But the Charleston didn't hit till 1923, and the word *flapper* had been used as early as 1920.

"Well," Flip said. "Do you want to hear this or not?"

It was no wonder Pippa had just gone singing past her clients' windows. If she'd had to put up with them, she wouldn't have been half as cheerful. I forced an interested expression. "Who else is on the committee?"

"*I* don't know. I told you, I don't have time to go to these things."

"But don't you want to make sure you get a good assistant?"

"Not if I have to stay after work," she said, irritably pulling clippings out from under her. "Your office is a mess. Don't you ever clean it?"

" 'The lark's on the wing;/The snail's on the thorn,' " I said.

"What?"

So Browning was wrong. "I'd love to talk," I said, "but I'd better get started on this funding form."

She didn't show any signs of moving. She was looking aimlessly through the clippings.

"I need you to make a copy of each of those. Now. Before you go to your search committee meeting."

Still nothing. I got a pencil, stuck the extra pages into the application, and tried to focus on the simplified funding form.

I never worry much about getting funding. It's true there are fads in both science and industry, but greed is always in style. HiTek would like nothing more than to know what causes fads so they could invent the next one. And stats projects are cheap. The only funding I was requesting was for a computer with more memory capacity. Which didn't mean I could forget about the funding form. It wouldn't matter if your project was a sure-fire method for turning lead into gold, if you don't have the forms filled out *and* turned in on time, Management will cancel you like a shot.

Project goals, experimental method, projected results, matrix analysis ranking. Matrix analysis ranking?

I flipped the page over to see if there were instructions, and the page came out altogether. There weren't any instructions, there or at the end of the application. "Were there instructions included with the form?" I asked Flip.

"How would I know?" she said, getting up. "What's this?" She stuck one of the clippings under my nose, an ad of a bobbed blonde standing next to a Hupmobile.

"The car?"

"No-o-o," she said, letting her breath out in a big sigh. "Her *hair.*"

"A bob," I said, and leaned closer to see if the hair was cut in an Eton bob or a shingle. It was crimped in even rows down the sides of her head. "A marcel wave," I said. "It was a permanent wave done with a special electrical metal-and-wires apparatus that was about as much fun as going to the dentist," but Flip had already lost interest.

"I think if they're going to make you stay after work or make you do extra jobs they should pay you overtime. Like stapling all these funding forms and delivering them to everybody. Some of them were supposed to go all the way down to Bio."

"Did you deliver one to Dr. O'Reilly?" I said, remembering her habit of dumping packages on closer offices.

"Of *course.* He didn't even thank me. What a swarb!"

"Swarb?" I said. Fads in language are impossible to keep up with, and I don't even try from a research standpoint, but I know most of the slang because that's how fads are described. But I'd never heard this one.

"You don't know what *swarb* means?" she said, in a tone that made me wish Pippa had gone around Italy slapping people. "No hots. No cutes. Cyber-ugg. Swarb." She flailed her duct-taped arms, trying to think of the word. *"Completely* fashion-impaired," she said, and flounced out in her duct tape and upside-down down. Without the clippings.

coffeehouse [1450–1554]

Middle Eastern fad that originated in Aden, then spread to Mecca and throughout Persia and Turkey. Men sat cross-legged on rugs and sipped thick, black, bitter coffee from tiny cups while listening to poets. The coffeehouses eventually became more popular than mosques and were banned by the religious authorities, who claimed they were frequented by people "of low costume and very little industry." Spread to London (1652), Paris (1669), Boston (1675), Seattle (1985).

Saturday morning the library called and told me my name had come up on the reserve list for *Led On by Fate,* so I went to Boulder to pick it up and buy a birthday present for Brittany.

"You can have *Angels, Angels Everywhere,* too, if you want," Lorraine told me at the library. She was wearing a sweatshirt with a dalmatian on it and red fireplug earrings. "We *finally* got two more copies now that nobody wants them."

I leafed through it while she swiped *Led On by Fate* with the light pen.

"Your guardian angel goes with you everywhere," it said. "It's always there, right beside you, wherever you go." There was a line drawing of an angel with large wings looming over a woman in a grocery checkout line. "You can ignore them, you can even pretend they don't exist, but that won't make them go away."

Until the fad's over, I thought.

I checked out *Led On by Fate* and a book on chaos theory and

Mandelbrot diagrams so I'd have a pretext for going down to Bio to see what Dr. O'Reilly was wearing, and went over to the Pearl Street Mall.

Lorraine was right. The bookstore had *Angel in My Condo* and *The Cherubim Cookbook* on a sale rack, and *The Angel Calendar* was marked fifty percent off. There was a big display up front for *Faerie Encounters of the Fourth Kind.*

I went upstairs to the kids' section and more fairies: *The Flower Fairies* (which had been a fad once before, back in the 1910s); *Fairies, Fairies Everywhere; More Fairies, Fairies Everywhere;* and *The Land of Faerie Fun.* Also Batman books, *Lion King* books, Power Rangers books, and Barbie books.

I finally managed to find a hardback copy of *Toads and Diamonds,* which I'd loved as a kid. It had a fairy in it, but not like those in *Fairies, Fairies, Etc.,* with lavender wings and bluebells for hats. It was about a girl who helps an ugly old woman who turns out to be a good fairy in disguise. Inner values versus shallow appearances. My kind of moral.

I bought it and went out into the mall. It was a beautiful Indian summer day, balmy and blue-skied. The Pearl Street Mall on a Saturday's a great place to analyze trends, since, one, there are hordes of people, and two, Boulder's almost terminally hip. The rest of the state calls it the People's Republic of Boulder, and it's got every possible kind of New Ager and falafel stand and street musician.

There are even fads in street music. Guitars were out and bongos were in again. (The first time was in 1958, at the height of the Beat movement. Very low ability threshold.) Flip's buzzcut-and-swag was very in, and so was the buzzcut-and-message. And duct tape. I saw two people with strips around their sleeves and one with dreadlocks and a bowler had a wide band of duct tape wrapped around his neck like the ones the French had worn during the *à la victime* fad after the Revolution.

Which was incidentally the last time women had cut their hair short until the 1920s, and it was a snap to trace that fad to its source. Aristocrats had had their hair chopped off to make it easier on the guillotine, and after the Empire was reinstated, relatives and friends had worn their hair short in sympathetic tribute. They'd also tied narrow red ribbons around their necks, but I doubted if that was what the dreadlocks person had had in mind. Or maybe it was.

Backpacks were out, and tiny, dangling wallets-on-a-string were in. Also Ugg boots, and kneeless jeans, and plaid flannel shirts. There wasn't an inch of corduroy anywhere. In-line skating with no regard for human life was very much in, as was walking slowly and obliviously four abreast. Sunflowers were out and violets were in. Ditto the Sinéad O'Connor look, and hair wraps. The long, thin strands of hair wrapped in brightly colored thread were everywhere.

Crystals and aromatherapy were out, replaced apparently by recreational ethnicity. The New Age shops were advertising Iroquois sweat lodges, Russian banya therapy, and Peruvian vision quests, $249 double occupancy, meals included. There were two Ethiopian restaurants, a Filipino deli, and a cart selling Navajo fry bread.

And half a dozen coffeehouses, which had apparently sprung up like mushrooms overnight: the Jumpstart, the Espresso Espress, the Caffe Lottie, the Cup o' Joe, and the Caffe Java.

After a while I got tired of dodging mimes and in-line skaters and went into the Mother Earth, which was now calling itself the Caffe Krakatoa (east of Java). It was as crowded inside as it had been out on the mall. A waitress with a swag haircut was taking names. "Do you want to sit at the communal table?" she was asking the guy in front of me, pointing to a long table with two people at it, one at each end.

That's a trend that's moved over here from England, where strangers have to share tables in order to keep up with the gossip on Prince Charles and Camilla. It hasn't caught on particularly over here, where strangers are more apt to want to talk about Rush Limbaugh or their hair implants.

I had sat at communal tables a few times when they were first introduced, thinking it was a good way to get exposure to trends in language and thought, but a taste was more than enough. Just because people are experiencing things doesn't mean they have any insight into them, a fact the talk shows (a trend that has reached the cancerous uncontrolled growth stage and should shortly exhaust its food supply) should have figured out by now.

The guy was asking, "If I don't sit at the communal table, how long a wait?"

The waitress sighed. *"I* don't know. Forty minutes?" and I certainly hoped that wasn't going to be a trend.

"How *many?"* she said to me.

"Two," I said, so I wouldn't have to sit at the communal table. "Foster."

"It has to be your first name."

"Why?" I said.

She rolled her eyes. "So I can *call* you."

"Sandra," I said.

"How do you spell that?"

No, I thought, please tell me Flip isn't becoming a trend. Please.

I spelled *Sandra* for her, grabbed up the alternative newspapers, and settled into a corner for the duration. There was no point in trying to do the personals till I was at a table, but the articles were almost as good. There was a new laser technology for removing tattoos, Berkeley had outlawed smoking outdoors, the must-have color for spring was postmodern pink, and marriage was coming back in style. "Living together is passé," assorted Hollywood actresses were quoted as saying. "The cool thing now is diamond rings, weddings, commitment, the whole bit."

"Susie," the waitress called.

No one answered.

"Susie, party of two," she said, flipping her rattail. *"Susie."*

I decided it was either me or somebody who'd given up and left. "Here," I said, and let a waiter with a Three Stooges haircut lead me to a knee-mashing table by the window. "I'm ready to order," I said before he could leave.

"I thought there were two in your party," he said.

"The other person will be here soon. I'll have a double tall caffè latte with skim milk and semisweet chocolate on top," I said brightly.

The waiter sighed and looked expectant.

"With brown sugar on the side," I said.

He rolled his eyes. "Sumatra, Yergacheffe, or Sulawesi?" he said.

I looked to the menu for help, but there was nothing there but a quote from Kahlil Gibran. "Sumatra," I said, since I knew where it was.

He sighed. "Seattle- or California-style?"

"Seattle," I said.

"With?"

"A spoon?" I said hopefully.

He rolled his eyes.

"What flavor *syrup?"*

Maple? I thought, even though that seemed unlikely. "Raspberry?" I said.

That was apparently one of the choices. He slouched off, and I attacked the personals. There was no point in circling the NSs. They were in virtually every ad. Two had it in their headline, and one, placed by a very intelligent, strikingly handsome athlete, had it listed twice.

Friends was out, and soul work was in. There were two references to fairies, and yet another abbreviation: GC. "JSDM seeks WSNSF. Must be GC. South of Baseline. West of Twenty-eighth." I circled it and turned back to the code book. Geographically compatible.

There weren't any other GCs, but there was a "Boulder mall area preferred," and one that specified, "Valmont or Pearl, 2500 block only."

Yes, in an eight-and-a-half narrow, and I'd like that delivered Federal Express to my door. It made me think fondly of Billy Ray, who was willing to drive all the way down from Laramie to take me out.

"This place is so *ridiculous,"* Flip said, sitting down across from me. She was wearing a babydoll dress, thigh-high pink stockings, and a pair of clunky Mary Janes, all of which she had on more or less right side up. "There's a forty-minute line."

Yes, I thought, and you should be in it. "There's a communal table," I said.

*"No*body sits together except swarbs and boofs," she said. "Brine made us sit at the communal table once." She bent over to pull up her thigh-highs.

There was no duct tape in evidence. Flip motioned the waiter over and ordered. "LattemarchianoskimtallJazula and not too much foam." She turned to look at me. "Brine ordered a latte with Su*ma*tra." She picked up my sack from the bookstore. "What's this?"

"A birthday present for Dr. Damati's little girl."

She had already pulled it out and was examining it curiously.

"It's a book," I said.

"Didn't they have the video?" She stuck it back in the sack. *"I* would've bought her a Barbie." She tossed her swath of hair, and I could see that she had a strip of duct tape across her forehead. There was a cut-out circle in the middle with what looked like a lowercase *i* tattooed right between her eyes.

"What's your tattoo?"

"It's not a tattoo," she said, brushing her hair back so I could see it better. It *was* a lowercase *i. "No*body wears tattoos anymore."

I started to draw her attention to her snowy owl and noticed that she was wearing duct tape there, too, a small circular patch right where the snowy owl had been.

"Tattoos are arti*ficial.* Sticking all those chemicals and cancerinogens under your skin," she said. "It's a brand."

"A brand," I said, wishing, as usual, that I hadn't started this.

"Brands are organic. You're not injecting something *into* your body. You're bringing out something that's already there in your natural body. Fire's one of the four elements, you know."

Sarah, over in Chem, would love to hear that.

"I've never seen one before," I said. "What does the *i* stand for?"

She looked confused. "Stand for? It doesn't stand for anything. It's *I.* You know, me. Who I am. It's a personal statement."

I decided not to ask her why her brand was lowercase, or if it had occurred to her that anyone seeing her with it would immediately assume it stood for *incompetent.*

"It's 'I,' " she said. "A person who doesn't need anybody else, especially not a *swarb* who would sit at the communal table and order Sumatra." She sighed deeply.

The waiter brought our lattes in Alice-in-Wonderland-sized cups, which might be a trend but was probably just a practical adjustment. Pouring steaming liquids into clear glass can have disastrous results.

Flip sighed again, a huge sigh, and licked the foam despondently off the back of her long-handled spoon.

"Do you ever feel com*plete*ly itch?"

Since I had no idea what *itch* was, I licked the back of my own spoon and hoped the question was rhetorical.

It was. "I mean, like take today. Here it is, the weekend, and I'm stuck sitting here with you." Here she rolled her eyes and sighed again. "Guys suck, you know."

By which I took it she meant Brine, of the bovver boots and assorted studs.

"*Life* sucks. You say to yourself, What am I doing in my job?"

Not much, I thought.

"So, everything sucks. You're not going anywhere, you're not accomplishing anything. I'm *twenty-two!*" She ate a spoonful of foam. "Like, why can't I ever meet a guy who isn't a swarb?"

It might be the forehead tattoo, I thought, and then remembered I wasn't any better off than Flip.

"It's just like Groupthink says." She looked at me expectantly, and then expelled so much air I thought she was going to deflate. "How can you not know about Groupthink? They're the most in band in Seattle. It's like their song says, 'Spinning my wheels on the launchpad, spitting I dunno and itch.' This is too bumming," she said, glaring at me like it was my fault. "I gotta get out of here."

She snatched up her check and slouched off through the crowd toward our waiter.

After a minute he came over and handed the check to me. "Your friend said you'd pay this," he said. "She said to tip me twenty percent."

alice blue [1902–4]

Color fad inspired by President Teddy Roosevelt's pretty and vivacious teenage daughter, of whom her father once said, "I can be President of the United States, or I can control Alice. I cannot possibly do both." Alice Roosevelt was one of the first "media stars"; her every move, comment, and outfit was copied by an eager public. When a dress was designed for her to match her gray-blue eyes, reporters dubbed it Alice blue, and the color became instantly popular. The musical comedy *Irene* featured a song called "Alice Blue Gown," shops marketed gray-blue fabric, hats, and hair ribbons, and hundreds of babies were named Alice and dressed not in the traditional pink but in Alice blue.

After Flip left I went back to the personals, but they seemed sad and a little desperate: "Lonely SWF seeks someone who really understands."

I wandered down the mall, looking at fairy T-shirts, fairy pillows, fairy soaps, and a cologne in a flower-shaped bottle called Elfmaiden. The Paper Doll had fairy greeting cards, fairy calendars, and fairy wrapping paper. The Peppercorn had a fairy teapot. The Quilted Unicorn, combining several trends, featured a caffè latte cup painted with a fairy dressed as a violet.

The sun had disappeared, and the day had turned gray and chilly. It looked as if it might even start to snow. I walked down past the Latte Lenya to the Fashion Front and went in to get warm and to see what color postmodern pink was.

Color fads are usually the result of a technological breakthrough. Mauve and turquoise, *the* colors of the 1870s, were brought about by a scientific breaththrough in the manufacture of dyes. So were the Day-Glo colors of the 1960s. And the new jewel-tone maroon and emerald car colors.

The fact that new colors are few and far between has never stopped fashion designers, though. They just give a new name to an old color. Like Schiaparelli's "shocking" pink in the 1920s, and Chanel's "beige" for what had previously been a nondescript tan. Or name a color after somebody, whether they wore it or not, like Victoria blue, Victoria green, Victoria red, and the ever-popular, and a lot more logical, Victoria black.

The clerk in the Fashion Front was talking on the phone to her boyfriend and examining her split ends. "Do you have postmodern pink?" I said.

"Yeah," she said belligerently, and turned back to the phone. "I have to go wait on this *woman,"* she said, slammed the phone down, and slouched over to the racks.

It is a fad, I thought, following her. Flip is a fad.

She shoved past a counter full of angel sweatshirts marked seventy-five percent off, and gestured at the rack. "And it's po-mo pink," she said, rolling her eyes. "Not postmodern."

"It's supposed to be the hot color for fall," I said.

"Whatever," she said, and slouched back to the phone while I examined "the hottest new color to hit since the sixties."

It wasn't new. It had been called ashes-of-roses the first time around in 1928 and dove pink the second in 1954.

Both times it had been a grim, grayish pink that washed out skin and hair, which hadn't stopped it from being hugely popular. It no doubt would be again in its present incarnation as po-mo pink.

It wasn't as good a name as ashes-of-roses, but names don't have to be enticing to be faddish. Witness flea, the winning color of 1776. And the hit of Louis XVI's court had been, I'm not kidding, puce. And not just plain puce. It had been so popular it'd come in a whole variety of appetizing shades: young puce, old puce, puce-belly, puce-thigh, and puce-with-milk-fever.

I bought a three-foot-long piece of po-mo pink ribbon to take back to the lab, which meant the clerk had to get off the phone *again.* "This is for hair wraps," she said, looking disapprovingly at my short hair, and gave me the wrong change.

"Do you like po-mo pink?" I asked her.

She sighed. "It's *the* boss color for fall."

Of course. And therein lay the secret to all fads: the herd instinct.

People wanted to look like everybody else. That was why they bought white bucks and pedal pushers and bikinis. But someone had to be the first one to wear platform shoes, to bob their hair, and that took the opposite of herd instinct.

I put my incorrect change and my ribbon in my shoulder bag (very passé) and went back out onto the mall. It had started to spit snow and the street musicians were shivering in their Birkenstocks and Ecuador shirts. I put on my mittens (com*plete*ly swarb) and walked back down toward the library, looking at yuppie shops and bagel stands and getting more and more depressed. I had no idea where any of these fads came from, even po-mo pink, which some fashion designer had come up with. But the fashion designer couldn't make people buy po-mo pink, couldn't make them wear it and make jokes about it and write editorials on the subject of "What is fashion coming to?"

The fashion designers could make it popular this season, especially since nobody would be able to find anything else in the stores, but they couldn't make it a fad. In 1971, they'd tried to introduce the long midiskirt and failed utterly, and they'd been predicting the "comeback of the hat" for years to no avail. It took more than merchandising to make a fad, and I didn't have any idea what that something more was.

And the more I fed in my data, the more convinced I was the answer wasn't in it, that increased independence and lice and bicycling were nothing more than excuses, reasons thought up afterward to explain what no one understood. Especially me.

I wondered if I was even in the right field. I was feeling so dissatisfied, as if everything I was doing was pointless, so . . . itch.

Flip, I thought. She did this to me with her talk about Brine and Groupthink. She's some kind of anti-guardian angel, following me everywhere, hindering rather than helping and putting me in a bad mood. And I'm not going to let her ruin my weekend. It's bad enough she ruins the rest of the week.

I bought a piece of chocolate cheesecake and went back to the library and checked out *The Red Badge of Courage, How Green Was My Valley,* and *The Color Purple,* but the mood persisted throughout the steely afternoon, and all the icy way home, making it impossible for me to work.

I tried reading the chaos theory book I'd checked out, but it just made me more depressed. Chaotic systems had so many variables it would have been nearly impossible to predict the systems' behavior if they acted in logical, straightforward ways. But they didn't.

Every variable interacted with every other, colliding and connecting in unexpected ways, setting up iteration loops that fed into the system again and again, crisscrossing and connecting the variables so many ways it wasn't surprising a butterfly could have a devastating effect. Or none at all.

I could see why Dr. O'Reilly had wanted to study a system with limited variables, but what was limited? According to the book, anything and everything was a variable: entropy, gravity, the quantum effects of an electron, or a star on the other side of the universe.

So even if Dr. O'Reilly was right and there weren't any outside X factors operating on the system, there was no way to compute all the variables or even decide what they were.

It all bore an uncomfortable resemblance to fads and made me wonder which variables I wasn't taking into account, so that when Billy Ray called, I clutched at him like a drowning man. "I'm so glad you called," I said. "My research went faster than I thought it would, so I'm free after all. Where are you?"

"On my way to Bozeman," he said. "When you said you were busy, I decided to skip the seminar and go pick up those Targhees I was looking at." He paused, and I could hear the warning hum of his cell phone. "I'll be back on Monday. How about dinner sometime next week?"

I wanted dinner tonight, I thought crabbily. "Great," I said. "Call me when you get back."

The hum crescendoed. "Sorry we missed each oth—" he said and went out of range.

I went and looked out the window at the sleet and then got into bed and read *Led On by Fate* cover to cover, which wasn't much of a feat. It was only ninety-four pages long, and so obviously wretchedly written it was destined to become a huge fad.

Its premise was that everything was ordained and organized by guardian angels, and the heroine was given to saying things like "Everything happens for a *reason,* Derek! You broke off our engagement and slept with Edwina and were implicated in her death, and I turned to Paolo for comfort and went to Nepal with him so that we'd learn the meaning of suffering and despair, without which true love is meaningless. All of it—the train wreck, Lilith's suicide, Halvard's drug addiction, the stock market crash—it was all so we could be together. Oh, Derek, there's a reason behind everything!"

Except, apparently, hair-bobbing. I woke up at three with Irene Castle and golf clubs dancing in my head. That happened to Henri Poincaré. He'd been working on mathematical functions for days and days, and one night he drank too much coffee (which probably had had the same effect as bad literature) and couldn't sleep, and mathematical ideas "rose in crowds."

And Friedrich Kekulé. He'd fallen into a reverie on top of a bus and seen chains of carbon atoms dancing wildly around. One of the chains had suddenly taken its tail in its mouth and formed a ring, and Kekulé had ended up discovering the benzene ring and revolutionizing organic chemistry.

All Irene Castle did with the golf clubs was the hesitation waltz, and after a while I turned on the light and opened Browning.

It turned out he had known Flip after all. He'd written a poem, "Soliloquy of the Spanish Cloister," about her. "G-r-r, you swine," he'd written, obviously after she crumpled up all his poems, and "There go, my heart's abhorrence." I decided to say it to Flip the next time she stuck me with the check.

hot pants [1971]

Fashion fad worn by everyone that only looked good on the very young and shapely. A successor to the miniskirt of the sixties, hot pants were a reaction to fashion designers' attempts to introduce the midcalf-length midiskirt. Hot pants were made out of satin or velvet, often with suspenders, and were worn with patent leather boots. Women wore them to the office, and they were even allowed in the Miss America pageant.

I spent the rest of the weekend ironing clippings and trying to decipher the simplified funding allocation form. What were Thrust Overlay Parameters? And my Efficiency Prioritization Ranking? And what did they mean by "List proprietary site bracket restrictions"? It made looking for the cause of hair-bobbing (or the source of the Nile) seem like a breeze in comparison.

Nobody else knew what EDI endorsements were either. When I went to work Monday, everybody I knew came up to the stats lab to ask about it.

"Do you have any idea how to fill this stupid funding form out?" Sarah asked, sticking her head in the door at mid-morning.

"Nope," I said.

"What do you suppose an expense gradation index is?" She leaned against the door. "Do you ever feel like you should just give up and start over?"

Yes, I thought, looking at my computer screen. I had spent most of the morning reading clippings, extracting what I hoped was the relevant information from them, typing it onto a disk, and designing statistical programs to interpret it. Or what Billy Ray had referred to as "sticking it on the computer and pushing a button."

I'd pushed the button, and surprise, surprise, there were no surprises. There was a correlation between the number of women in the workforce and the number of outraged references to hair-bobbing in the newspapers, an even stronger one between bobs and cigarette sales, and no correlation between the length of hair and the length of skirts, which I could have predicted. Skirts had dipped back to midcalf in 1926, while hair had gone steadily shorter all the way to the crash of '29, with the boyish shingle in 1925 and the even shorter Eton crop in 1926.

The strongest correlation of all was to the cloche hat, thus giving support to the cart-before-the-horse theory and proving beyond a shadow of a doubt that statistics isn't all that it's cracked up to be.

"Lately I've been feeling depressed about the whole thing," Sarah was saying. "I've always believed it was just a question of his having a higher relationship threshold than I do, but I've been thinking maybe this is just part of the denial structure that goes with codependent relationships."

Ted, I thought. We're talking about Ted, who doesn't want to get married.

"And this weekend, I got to thinking, What's the point? I'm following an intimacy path and he's into off-road detachment."

"Itch," I said.

"What?"

"What you're feeling," I said. "Like you're spinning your wheels on the launchpad. You didn't run into Flip this weekend, did you?"

"I saw her this morning," she said. "She brought me Dr. Applegate's mail."

An antiangel, wandering through the world spreading gloom and destruction.

"Well, anyway," Sarah said, "I'd better go see if I can find somebody in Management who can tell me what an expense gradation index is," and left.

I went back to my hair-bobbing data. I ran a geographical distribution for 1923 and then for 1922. They showed clusters in New York City and Hollywood, which were no surprise, and St. Paul, Minnesota, and Marydale, Ohio, which were. On a hunch, I asked for a breakdown of Montgomery, Alabama. It showed a cluster too small to be statistically significant but enough to explain the St. Paul one. Montgomery was where F. Scott Fitzgerald had met Zelda, and St. Paul was his hometown. The locals obviously were trying to live up to "Bernice Bobs Her Hair."

It didn't explain Marydale, Ohio. I ran a geographical distribution for 1921. It was still there.

"Here," Flip said, sticking my mail under my nose. Apparently nobody had told her po-mo pink was the in color for fall. She was wearing a brilliant bilious blue tunic and leggings and an assortment of duct tape.

"I'm glad you're here," I said, grabbing a stack of clippings. "You owe me two-fifty for your caffè latte and I need you to copy these for me. Oh, and wait." I went and got the personals I'd gone through Saturday, and two articles about angels. I handed them to Flip. "One copy of each."

"I don't believe in angels," she said.

Right on the cutting edge, as usual.

"I used to believe in them," she said, "but I don't anymore, not since Brine. I mean, if you really had a guardian angel, she'd cheer you up when you were bummed and get you out of committee meetings and stuff."

"What about fairies?" I asked.

"You mean like fairy godmothers?" she said. "Of course. Duh."

Of course.

I went back to my hair-bobbing. Marydale, Ohio. What could it have had to make it a hot spot of hair-bobbing? Hot, I thought. How about unusually hot weather in Ohio during the summer of 1921? So hot long hair would have clung sweatily to the back of the neck, and women would have said, "I can't take this anymore"?

I called up weather data for the state of Ohio for June through September and began looking for Marydale.

"Do you have a minute?" said a voice from the door. It was Elaine from Personnel. She was wearing a sweatband and a sour expression. "Do you have any idea what hiral implementation format rations are?" she asked.

"Not a clue. Did you try Management?"

"I've been up there twice and couldn't get in. There's a huge crowd." She took a deep breath. "I'm getting totally stressed. Do you want to go work out?"

"Stair-climbing?" I said dubiously.

She shook her head firmly. "Stair-climbing doesn't give a large-muscle workout. Wall-walking. Gym over on Twenty-eighth. They've got pitons and everything."

"No, thanks," I said. "I've got walls here."

She looked disapprovingly at them and went out, and I went back to my hair-bobbing. 1921 temps for Marydale had been slightly lower than normal, and it wasn't the hometown of either Irene Castle or Isadora Duncan.

I abandoned it for the moment and did a Pareto chart and then ran some more regressions. There was a weak correlation between church attendance and bobs, a strong correlation between bobs and Hupmobile sales, but not Packards or Model T Fords, and a very strong correlation between bobs and women in nursing careers. I called up a list of American hospitals in 1921. There wasn't one within a hundred miles of Marydale.

Gina came in, looking harassed.

"No, I don't know how to fill out the funding form," I said before she could ask, "and neither does anybody else."

"Really?" she said vaguely. "I haven't even looked at it yet. I've been spending all my time on the stupid search committee for Flip's assistant. What do *you* consider the most important quality in an assistant?"

"Being the opposite of Flip," I said, and then, when she didn't laugh, "Competence, cheerfulness, willingness to work?"

"Exactly," she said. "And if a person had those qualities, you'd hire them immediately, wouldn't you? And if they were as overqualified for the job as she is, you'd snap them right up. You wouldn't turn her down because of one little drawback and expect them to interview dozens of other people, especially when you've got other things to do. Fill out this ridiculous funding form, for one, *and* plan a birthday party. Do you know what Brittany picked, when I said she couldn't have the Power Rangers? *Barney.* And it isn't as if she isn't competent *and* cheerful *and* willing to work. Right?"

I was unclear as to whether she was talking about Brittany or the assistant applicant. "Barney is pretty awful," I said.

"Exactly," Gina said, as if I'd proved her point, whatever it was. "I'm hiring her," and she flounced out.

I went back and sat down in front of the computer. Cloche hats, Hupmobiles, and Marydale, Ohio. None of them seemed likely to be the trigger. What was? What had suddenly set the fad in motion?

Flip came in, carrying the stack of clippings and personals I'd just given her. "What did you want me to do with these again?"

mesmerism [1778–84]

Scientific fad resulting from new discoveries about magnetism, speculation about its medical possibilities, and greed. Paris society flocked to Dr. Mesmer to have "animal magnetism" treatments involving tubs of "magnetized water," iron rods, and Dr. Mesmer's lavender-robed assistants, who massaged the patients and looked deep into their eyes. The patients screamed, sobbed, sank into a deep trance, and paid Dr. Mesmer on leaving. Actually hypnotism, animal magnetism claimed to cure everything from tumors to consumption. Died out when a scientific investigation headed by Ben Franklin proved it did no such thing.

Tuesday Management called another meeting. "To explain the simplified funding forms," I said to Gina, walking down to the cafeteria.

"I hope so," she said, looking even more harassed than she had yesterday. "It would be nice to see somebody else on the defensive for a change."

I was going to ask her what she meant by that, but just then I spotted Dr. O'Reilly on the far side of the room talking to Dr. Turnbull. She was wearing a po-mo pink suit (sans shoulder pads), and he had on one of those print polyester shirts from the seventies. By the time I'd taken all that in, Gina was at our table with Sarah, Elaine, and a bunch of other people.

I walked over, bracing myself for a discussion of intimacy issues and power-walking, but they were apparently discussing Flip's new assistant.

"I didn't think it was possible to hire somebody worse than Flip," Elaine was saying. "How *could* you, Gina?"

"But she's very competent," Gina said defensively. "She's had experience with Windows and SPSS, and she knows how to repair a copy machine."

"All that's entirely irrelevant," a woman from Physics said, though it didn't sound irrelevant to me.

"Well, *I'm* not working with her," a man from Product Development said. "And don't tell me you didn't know she was one. You can tell just by looking at her."

Bigotry is one of the oldest and ugliest of trends, so persistent it only counts as a fad because the target keeps changing: Huguenots, Koreans, homosexuals, Muslims, Tutsis, Jews, Quakers, wolves, Serbs, Salem housewives. Nearly every group, so long as it's small and different, has had a turn, and the pattern never changes—disapproval, isolation, demonization, persecution. Which was one of the reasons it'd be nice to find the switch that turned fads on. I'd like to turn that one off for good.

"People like that shouldn't be allowed to work in a big company like HiTek," Sarah, who was actually a nice person in spite of her psychobabble about Ted, was saying.

And Dr. Applegate, who definitely should know better, added disgustedly, "I suppose if you fired her, she'd sue for discrimination. That's what's wrong with all this affirmative action stuff."

I wondered what small and different group Flip's new assistant had the misfortune to belong to: Hispanic, lesbian, NRA member?

"She's not setting foot in my lab," a woman wearing a turban said. "I'm not exposing myself to unnecessary health risks."

"But she won't be smoking on the job," Gina said. "She can keyboard a hundred words a minute."

"I can't believe I'm hearing this," Elaine said. "Haven't you read the FDA report on the dangers of secondhand smoke?"

On the other hand, there are moments when rather than reforming the human race I'd like to abandon it altogether and go become, say, one of Dr. O'Reilly's macaques, which have to have more sense.

I was about to say as much to Elaine when Dr. O'Reilly grabbed my arm. "Come sit with me," he said, and led me away. "I need you to be my partner in case Management springs another sensitivity thing." He looked at me uncertainly. "Unless you'd rather sit with your friends."

"No," I said, watching them surround Gina. "Not at the moment."

"Oh, good," he said. "The last sensitivity exercise, I got stuck with Flip." We sat down. "So how's your fads research coming?"

"It's not," I said. "I picked hair-bobbing because I wanted a fad that didn't have an obvious cause. Most fads are caused by a breakthrough in technology—nylons, waterbeds, light-up sneakers."

"Fallout shelters."

I nodded. "Or they're a marketing phenomena, like Trivial Pursuit and teddy bears."

"And fallout shelters."

"Right. Hair-bobbing didn't cost anything except the barber's fee, and if you didn't have that, all you needed to whack your hair off was a pair of scissors, which is a technology that's been around forever." I started to sigh and then realized I'd sound like Flip.

"So what's the problem?" Bennett asked.

"The problem is hair-bobbing doesn't have an obvious cause. Irene Castle looked like a possibility for a while, but it turned out she was following a Dutch bob fad that had been popular in Paris the year before. And none of the other sources has a direct correlation to the critical period. Have you ever heard of a place called Marydale, Ohio?"

"Good *morn*ing," Management said from the podium. He was wearing a polo shirt, Dockers, and a pleased smile. "We're really excited to see you all here."

"What's Management up to?" I whispered to Bennett.

"My guess is a new acronym," he whispered. "Departmental Unification Management Business." He wrote down the letters on his legal pad. "D.U.M.B."

"We have several items of business today," Management said happily. "First, some of you have been having minor difficulties filling out the simplified funding allocation forms. You'll be receiving a memo that answers all your questions. The interdepartmental communications liaison is in the process of making copies for each of you right now."

Bennett put his head down on the table.

"Secondly, I'd like to announce that HiTek is instituting a 'dress down' policy beginning this week. This is an innovative idea that all the best corporations are implementing. Casual dress induces a more relaxed workplace and stronger interemployee interfaces. So starting tomorrow I'll expect to see all of you in casual clothes."

I tuned him out and studied Bennett. He looked terrible. His polyester print shirt had little daisies on it in an assortment of browns, none of which came close to matching his brown cords. Over it he was wearing a pilled gray cardigan.

But it wasn't just the clothes. *The Brady Bunch Movie* had made seventies styles fashionable again. Flip had worn satin disco pants the other day, and platform shoes and gold chains were all over the Boulder mall. But Bennett didn't look "retro." He looked "swarb." I had the feeling that if he were wearing a bomber jacket and Nikes he'd still look that way. As if he were an antifaddist.

No, that wasn't right either. Any number of fads were started as a rejection of existing fads. The long hair of the sixties was a rejection of the crew cuts of the fifties, the short, flat, figureless flapper dresses a reaction to the exaggeratedly bustled and corseted Victorians.

Bennett wasn't rebelling. It was more like he was oblivious to the whole concept. No, that wasn't the right word either. Immune.

And if he could be immune to fads, did that mean they were caused by some kind of virus? I looked over at Gina's table, where Elaine and Dr. Applegate were earnestly whispering to her about emphysema and the surgeon general's warning. Was Bennett really immune to fads or just fashion-impaired, as Flip had said?

I opened my notebook and wrote, "They hired Flip's new assistant," and pushed it over in front of him.

He wrote back, "I know. I met her this morning. Her name's Shirl."

"Did you know she smokes?" I wrote and watched his expression when he read it. He looked neither surprised nor repelled.

"Flip told me," he wrote. "She said Shirl was going to pollute the workplace. The pot calling the kettle black."

I grinned.

"What does that *i* tattoo on Flip's forehead stand for?" he wrote.

"It's not a tattoo, it's a brand," I wrote back.

"Incompetent or *impossible?"*

"Initiative," Management said, and we both looked up guiltily. "Which brings me to our third item of business. How many of you know what the Niebnitz Grant is?"

I did, and even though nobody else raised their hand, I was willing to bet everybody else did, too. It's the largest research grant there is, even bigger than the MacArthur Grant, and with virtually no strings attached. The scientist gets the money and can apply it to any kind of research at all. Or retire to the Bahamas.

It's also the most mysterious research grant there is. Nobody knows who gives it, what they give it for, or even when it's given. There was one awarded last year, to Lawrence Chin, an artificial intelligence researcher, four the year before that, and none before that for over three years. The Niebnitz people (whoever they are) sweep down periodically like one of those Angels from Above on some unsuspecting scientist and make it so he never has to fill out another simplified funding allocation form.

There are no requirements, no application form, no particular field of study the grant favors. Of the four the year before last, one was a Nobel prize winner, one a graduate assistant, one a chemist at a French research institute, and one a part-time inventor. The only thing that's known for sure is the amount, which Management had just written on his flipchart: $1,000,000.

"The winner of the Niebnitz Grant receives one million dollars, to be spent on research of the recipient's choice." Management turned over a page of the flipchart. "The Niebnitz Grant is awarded for scientific sensibility." He wrote *science* on the flipchart. "Divergent thinking." He wrote *thought.* "And circumstantial predisposition to significant scientific breakthrough." He added *breakthrough* and then tapped all three words with his pointer. "Science. Thought. Breakthrough."

"What does this have to do with us?" Bennett whispered.

"Two years ago the Institut de Paris won a Niebnitz Grant," Management said.

"No, it didn't," I whispered. "A scientist *working* at the Institut won it."

"And *they* were using old-fashioned management techniques," Management said.

"Oh, no," I murmured. "Management expects us to win a Niebnitz Grant."

"How can they?" Bennett whispered. "Nobody even knows how they're awarded."

Management cast a cold eye in our direction. "The Niebnitz Grant Committee is looking for outstanding creative projects with the potential for significant scientific breakthroughs, which is what GRIM is all about. Now I'd like you to get in groups and write down five things you can do to win the Niebnitz Grant."

"Pray," Bennett said.

I grabbed a piece of paper and wrote down:

1. Optimize potential.
2. Facilitate empowerment.
3. Implement visioning.
4. Strategize priorities.
5. Augment core structures.

"What *is* that?" Bennett said, looking at the list. "Those make no sense."

"Neither does expecting us to win the Niebnitz Grant." I handed it in.

"Now let's get busy. You've got divergent thinking to do. Let's see some significant scientific breakthroughs."

Management marched out, his baton under his arm, but everyone just sat there, stunned, except Alicia Turnbull, who started taking rapid notes in her daybook, and Flip, who strolled in and started passing out pieces of paper.

"Projected Results: Significant Scientific Breakthrough," I said, shaking my head. "Well, bobbed hair certainly isn't it."

"Don't they know science doesn't work like that? You can't just order scientific breakthroughs. They happen when you look at something you've been working on for years and suddenly see a connection you never noticed before, or when you're looking for something else altogether. Sometimes they even happen by accident. Don't they know you can't get a scientific breakthrough just because you want one?"

"These are the people who gave Flip a promotion, remember?" I frowned. "What *is* 'circumstantial predisposition to significant scientific breakthrough'?"

"For Fleming it was looking at a contaminated culture and noticing the mold had killed the bacteria," Ben said.

"And how does Management know the Niebnitz Grant Committee gives the grant for creative projects with potential? How do they know there's a committee? For all we know, Niebnitz may be some old rich guy who gives money to projects that don't show any potential at all."

"In which case we're a shoo-in," Bennett said.

"For all we know, Niebnitz may give the grant to people whose names begin with *C,* or draw the names out of a hat."

Flip slouched over and handed one of her papers to Bennett. "Is this the memo explaining the simplified funding form?" he asked.

"No-*o-o-o,*" she said, rolling her eyes. "It's a petition. To make the cafeteria a one hundred percent smoke-free environment." She sauntered away.

"I know what the *i* stands for," I said. *"Irritating."*

He shook his head. *"Insufferable."*

coonskin caps [may 1955—december 1955]

Children's fad inspired by the Walt Disney television series *Davy Crockett,* about the Kentucky frontier hero who fought at the Alamo and "kilt a bar" at age three. Part of a larger merchandising fad that included bow-and-arrow sets, toy knives, toy rifles, fringed shirts, powder horns, lunchboxes, jigsaw puzzles, coloring books, pajamas, panties, and seventeen recorded versions of "The Ballad of Davy Crockett," to which every child in America knew all the verses. As a result of the fad, a shortage of coonskins developed, and an earlier fad, the raccoon coat of the twenties, was ripped up to make caps. Some boys even got their hair cut in the shape of a coonskin cap. The fad collapsed right before Christmas of 1955, leaving merchandisers with hundreds of unwanted caps.

It occurred to me the next day while ransacking my lab for the clippings I'd given Flip to copy that Bennett's remark about having already met her new assistant must mean she'd been assigned to Bio. But in the afternoon Gina, looking hunted, came in to say, "I don't care what they say. I did the right thing hiring her. Shirl just printed out and collated twenty copies of an article I wrote. Correctly. I don't care if I am breathing in second-secondhand smoke."

"Second-secondhand smoke?"

"That's what Flip calls the air smokers breathe out. But I don't care. It's worth it."

"Shirl's been assigned to you?" I said.

She nodded. "This morning she delivered my mail. *My* mail. You should get her assigned to you."

"I will," I said, but that was easier said than done. Now that Flip had an assistant, she (and my clippings) had disappeared off the face of the earth. I searched the entire building twice, including the cafeteria, where large NO SMOKING signs had been put on all the tables, and Supply, where Desiderata was trying to figure out what printer cartridges were, and found Flip finally in my lab, sitting at my computer and typing something in.

She deleted it before I could see what it was and leaped up. If she'd been capable of it, I would have said she looked guilty.

"*You* weren't using it," she said. "You weren't even *here.*"

"Did you make copies of those clippings I gave you Monday?" I said.

She looked blank.

"There was a copy of the personal ads on top of them."

She tossed her swag of hair. "Would you use the word *elegant* to describe me?"

She had added a hair wrap to her hank, a long thin strand of hair bound in bilious blue embroidery thread, and a band of duct tape across her forehead cut out to frame the *i*.

"No," I said.

"Well, nobody expects you to be all of them," she said, apropos of nothing. "Anyway, I don't know why you're so hooked on the personals. You've got that cowboy guy."

"What?"

"Billy Boy Somebody," she said, waving her hand at the phone. "He called and said he's in town for some seminar and you're supposed to meet him for dinner someplace. Tonight, I think. At the Nebraska Daisy or something. At seven o'clock."

I went over to my phone message pad. It was blank. "Didn't you write the message down?"

She sighed. "I can't do *everything.* That's why I was supposed to get an assistant, remember? So I wouldn't have to work so hard, only since she's a *smoker,* half the people I assigned her to don't want her in their labs, so I still have to copy all this stuff and go all the way down to Bio and stuff. I think smokers should be *forced* to give up cigarettes."

"Who all did you assign to her?"

"Bio and Product Development and Chem and Physics and Personnel and Payroll, and all the people who yell at me and make me do a lot of stuff. Or put in a camp or something where they couldn't expose the rest of us to all that smoke."

"Why don't you assign her to me? I don't mind that she smokes."

She put her hands on the hips of her blue leather skirt. "It causes cancer, you know," she said disapprovingly. "Besides, I'd never assign her to *you.* You're the only one who's halfway *nice* to me around here."

angel food cake [1880–90]

Food fad named to suggest the heavenly lightness and whiteness of the cake. Originated either at a restaurant in St. Louis, along the Hudson River, or in India. The secret of the cake was a dozen (or eleven, or fifteen) egg whites beaten into stiff glossy peaks. Difficult to bake, it inspired an entire folklore: The pan had to be ungreased, and no one could walk across the kitchen floor while it was baking. Supplanted by, of course, devil's food cake.

It was the Kansas Rose at five-thirty. "You got my message okay," Billy Ray said, coming out to meet me in the parking lot. He was wearing black jeans, a black-and-white cowboy shirt, and a white Stetson. His hair was longer than the last time I'd seen him. Long hair must be coming back in.

"Sort of," I said. "I'm here."

"Sorry it had to be so early," he said. "There's an evening workshop on 'Irrigation on the Internet' I don't want to miss." He took my arm. "This is supposed to be the trendiest place in town."

He was right. There was a half-hour wait, even with reservations, and every woman in line was wearing po-mo pink.

"Did you get your Targhees?" I asked him, leaning back against an ABSOLUTELY NO SMOKING sign.

"Yep, and they're great. Low maintenance, high tolerance for cold, and fifteen pounds of wool in a season."

"Wool?" I said. "I thought Targhees were cows."

"Nobody's raising cows anymore," he said, frowning as if I should know that. "The whole cholesterol thing. Lamb's got a lower cholesterol count, and shearling's supposed to be the hot new fashion fabric for winter."

"Bobby Jay," the hostess, who was wearing a red gingham pinafore and hair wraps, called out.

"That's us," I said.

"We don't want to sit anywhere close to where the smoking section used to be," Billy Ray said, and we followed her to the table.

The sunflower fad had apparently come here to die. They were entwined in the white picket fence around our table, framed on the wall, painted on the bathroom doors, embroidered on the napkins. A large artificial bunch was stuck in a Mason jar in the middle of our sunflowered tablecloth.

"Cool, huh?" Billy Ray said, opening his sunflower-shaped menu. "Everybody says prairie's going to be the next big fad."

"I thought shearling was," I muttered, picking up the menu. Prairie cuisine wasn't so much hot as substantial—chicken-fried steak, cream gravy, corn on the cob, all served family-style.

"Something to drink?" a waiter in buckskin and a knotted sunflower bandanna asked.

I looked at the menu. They had espresso, cappuccino, and caffè latte, also very big in prairie days. No iced tea.

"Iced tea's the Kansas state beverage," I told the waiter. "How can you not have it?"

He'd apparently been taking lessons from Flip. He rolled his eyes, sighed expertly, and said, "Iced tea is outré."

A word never uttered on the prairie, I thought, but Billy Ray was already ordering meat loaf, mashed potatoes, and cappuccino for both of us.

"So, tell me about this thing you're researching that's got you working weekends."

I did. "The problem is I've got causes coming out my ears," I said, after I'd explained what I'd been doing. "Female equality, bicycling, a French fashion designer named Poiret, World War One, and Coco Chanel, who singed her hair off when a heater exploded. Unfortunately, none of them seems to be the main source."

Our dinner arrived, on brown earthenware platters decorated with sunflowers. The coleslaw was garnished with fresh basil, which I didn't remember as being big on the prairie either, and the meat loaf was garnished with lemon slices.

Billy Ray told me about the merits of sheep-raising while we ate.

Sheep were healthy, profitable, no trouble to herd, and you could graze them anywhere, all of which I would have been more inclined to believe if he hadn't told me the same thing about raising longhorns six months ago.

"Dessert?" the waiter said, and brought over the pastry cart.

I figured a prairie dessert would probably be gooseberry pie or maybe canned peaches, but it was the usual suspects: crème brûlée, tiramisu, "and our newest dessert, bread pudding."

Well, that sounded like a Kansas dessert, all right, the sort of thing you were reduced to eating after the cow died and the grasshoppers ate up the crops.

"I'll have the tiramisu," I said.

"Me too," Billy Ray said. "I've always hated bread pudding. It's like eating leftovers."

"Everybody *raves* about our bread pudding," the waiter said reproachfully. "It's our most popular dessert."

The bad thing about studying trends is that you can't ever turn it off. You sit there across from your date eating tiramisu, and instead of thinking what a nice guy he is, you find yourself thinking about trends in desserts and how they always seem to be gooey and calorie-laden in direct proportion to the obsession with dieting.

Take tiramisu, which has chocolate and whipped cream and two kinds of cheese. And burnt-sugar cake, which was big in the forties, in spite of wartime rationing.

Pineapple upside-down cake was a fad in the twenties, a dessert I hope doesn't make a comeback anytime soon; chiffon cake in the fifties; chocolate fondue in the sixties.

I wondered if Bennett was immune to food trends, too, and what his ideas on bread pudding and chocolate cheesecake were.

"You thinking about hair-bobbing again?" Billy Ray said. "Maybe you're looking at too many things. This conference I'm at says you've got to niff."

"Niff?"

"NYF. Narrow Your Focus. Eliminate all the peripherals and focus in on the core variables. This hair-bobbing thing can only have one cause, right? You've got to narrow your focus to the likeliest possibilities and concentrate on those. It works, too. I tried it on a case of sheep mange. You're sure you won't come to my workshop with me?"

"I have to go to the library," I said.

"You should get the book. *Five Steps to Focusing on Success.*"

After dinner Billy Ray went off to niff, and I went over to the library to see about Browning. Lorraine wasn't there. A girl wearing duct tape, hair wraps, and a sullen expression was. "It's three weeks overdue," she said.

"That's impossible," I said. "I only checked it out last week. And I checked it in. On Monday." After I'd tried Pippa on Flip and decided Browning didn't know what he was talking about. I'd checked in Browning and checked out *Othello,* that other story about undue influences.

She sighed. "Our computer shows it as still checked out. Have you looked around at home?"

"Is Lorraine here?" I asked.

She rolled her eyes. "No-*o-o-o.*"

I decided it was the better part of valor to wait until she was and went over to the stacks to look for Browning myself.

The Complete Works wasn't there, and I couldn't remember the name of the book Billy Ray had suggested. I pulled out two books by Willa Cather, who knew what prairie cooking had actually been like, and *Far from the Madding Crowd,* which I remembered as having sheep in it, and then wandered around, trying to remember the name of Billy Ray's book and hoping for inspiration.

Libraries have been responsible for a lot of significant scientific breakthroughs. Darwin was reading Malthus for recreation (which should tell you something about Darwin), and Alfred Wegener was wandering around the Marburg University library, idly spinning the globe and browsing through scientific papers, when he got the idea of continental drift. But nothing came to me, not even the name of Billy Ray's book. I went over to the business section to see if I would remember the name of the book when I saw it.

Something about narrowing the focus, eliminating all the peripherals. "It can only have one cause, right?" Billy Ray had said.

Wrong. In a linear system it might, but hair-bobbing wasn't like sheep mange. It was like one of Bennett's chaotic systems. There were dozens of variables, and all of them were important. They fed into each other, iterating and reiterating, crossing and colliding, affecting each other in ways no one would expect. Maybe the problem wasn't that I had too many causes, but that I didn't have enough. I went over to the nine hundreds and checked out *Those Crazy Twenties; Flappers, Flivvers, and Flagpole-Sitters;* and *The 1920's: A Sociological Study,* and as many other books on the twenties as I could carry, and took them up to the desk.

"I show an overdue book for you," the girl said. "It's four weeks overdue."

I went home, excited for the first time that I was on the right track, and started work on the new variables.

The twenties had been awash in fads: jazz, hip flasks, rolled-down stockings, dance crazes, raccoon coats, mah-jongg, running marathons, dance marathons, kissing marathons, Stutz Bearcats, flagpole-sitting, tree-sitting, crossword puzzles. And somewhere in all those rouged knees and rain slickers and rocking-chair derbies was the trigger that had set off the hair-bobbing craze.

I worked until very late and then went to bed with *Far from the Madding Crowd.* I was right. It was about sheep. And fads. In Chapter Five one of the sheep fell over a cliff, and the others followed, plummeting one after the other onto the rocks below.

3. tributaries

"Please your honors," said he, "I'm able,
By means of a secret charm, to draw
All creatures living beneath the sun,
That creep or fly or run,
After me so as you never saw!"

robert browning

diorama wigs [1750–60]

Hair fad of the court of Louis XVI inspired by Madame de Pompadour, who was fond of dressing her hair in unusual ways. Hair was draped over a frame stuffed with cotton wool or straw and cemented with a paste that hardened, and the hair was powdered and decorated with pearls and flowers. The fad rapidly got out of hand. Frames grew as high as three feet tall, and the decorations became elaborate and then pictorial. Hairdos had waterfalls, cupids, and scenes from novels. Naval battles, complete with ships and smoke, were waged on top of women's heads, and one widow, overcome with mourning for her dead husband, had his tombstone erected in her hair. Died out with the advent of the French Revolution and the resultant shortage of heads to put wigs on.

Rivers are not just wide streams. They are drainage basins for dozens, sometimes hundreds of tributaries. The Lena River in Siberia, for example, drains an area of over a million square miles, including the Karenga, the Olekma, the Vitim, and the Aldan rivers, and a thousand smaller streams and brooks, some of which follow such distant, convoluted courses it would never occur to you they connected to the Lena, thousands of miles away.

The events leading up to a scientific breakthrough are frequently not only random but far afield from science. Take the measles. Einstein had them when he was four and his father was only trying to amuse a sick little boy when he gave him a pocket compass to play with. And the keys to the universe.

Fleming's life is a whole system of coincidences, beginning with his father, who was a groundskeeper on the Churchill estate. When ten-year-old Winston fell in the lake, Fleming's father jumped in and rescued him. The grateful family rewarded him by sending his son Alexander to medical school.

Take Penzias and Wilson. Robert Dicke, at Princeton University, talked to P.J.E. Peebles about calculating how hot the Big Bang was. He did, realized it was hot enough to be detectable as a residue of radiation, and told Peter G. Roll and David T. Wilkinson that they should look for microwaves.

Peebles (are you following this?) gave a talk at Johns Hopkins in which he mentioned Roll and Wilkinson's project. Ken Turner of the Carnegie Institute heard the lecture and mentioned it to Bernard Burke at MIT, a friend of Penzias. (Still with me?)

When Penzias called Burke on something else altogether (his daughter's birthday party probably), he told Burke about their impossible background noise. And Burke told him to call Wilkinson and Roll.

During the next week several things happened:

I fed flagpole-sitting and mah-jongg data into the computer, Management declared HiTek a smoke-free building, Gina's daughter, Brittany, turned five, and Dr. Turnbull, of all people, came to see me.

She was wearing a po-mo pink silk campshirt and pink jeans and a friendly smile. The jeans and campshirt meant she was following HiTek's dressing-down edict. I had no idea what the smile meant.

"Dr. Foster," she said, turning it on me full force, "just the person I wanted to see."

"If you're looking for a package, Dr. Turnbull," I said warily, "Flip hasn't been here yet."

She laughed, a merry, tinkling laugh I wouldn't have thought she was capable of. "Call me Alicia," she said. "No package. I just thought I'd drop by and chat with you. You know, so we could get to know each other better. We've really only talked a couple of times."

Once, I thought, and you yelled at me. What are you really here for?

"So," she said, sitting on one of the lab tables and crossing her legs. "Where did you go to school?"

"Getting to know you" at HiTek usually consists of "So, are you dating anybody?" or, in the case of Elaine, "Are you into high-impact aerobics?" but maybe this was Alicia's idea of small talk. "I got my doctorate at Baylor."

She smiled yet more brightly. "It was in sociology, wasn't it?"

"And stats," I said.

"A double major," she said approvingly. "Was that where you did your undergrad work?"

She couldn't be an industry spy. We worked for the same industry. And all this was up in Personnel's records anyway. "No," I said. "Where'd you do your graduate work?"

End of conversation. "Indiana," she said, as if I'd asked for something that was none of my business, and slid her pink rear off the table, but she didn't leave. She stood looking around the lab at the piles of data.

"You have so much stuff in here," she said, examining one of the untidy piles.

Maybe Management had sent her to spy on Workplace Organization. "I plan to get things straightened up as soon as I finish my funding forms," I said.

She wandered over to look at the flagpole-sitting piles. "I've already turned mine in."

Of course.

"And messiness is good. Susan Holyrood and Dan Twofeathers's labs were both messy. R. C. Mendez says it's a creativity indicator."

I had no idea who any of these people were or what was going on here. Something, obviously. Maybe Management had sent her to look for signs of smoking. Alicia had forgotten all about the friendly smile and was circling the lab like a shark.

"Bennett told me you're working on fads source analysis. Why did you decide to work with fads?"

"Everybody else was doing it."

"Really?" she said eagerly. "Who are the other scientists?"

"That was a joke," I said lamely, and set about the hopeless task of trying to explain it. "You know, fads, something people do just because everybody else is doing it?"

"Oh, I get it," she said, which meant she didn't, but she seemed more bemused than offended. "Wittiness can be a creativity indicator, too, can't it? What do *you* think the most important quality for a scientist is?"

"Luck," I said.

Now she did look offended. *"Luck?"*

"And good assistants," I said. "Look at Roy Plunkett. His assistant's using a silver gasket on the tank of chlorofluorocarbons was what led to the discovery of Teflon. Or Becquerel. He had the good luck to hire a young Polish girl to help him with his radiation therapy. Her name was Marie Curie."

"That's very interesting," she said. "Where did you say you did your undergrad work?"

"University of Oregon," I said.

"How old were you when you got your doctorate?"

We were back to the third degree. "Twenty-six."

"How old are you now?"

"Thirty-one," I said, and that was apparently the right answer because she turned the brights back on. "Did you grow up in Oregon?"

"No," I said. "Nebraska."

This, on the other hand, was *not.* Alicia switched off the smile, said, "I have a lot of work to do," and left without a backward glance. Whatever she'd wanted, apparently witty and messy weren't enough.

I sat there staring at the screen wondering what that had been all about, and Flip came in wearing an assortment of duct tape and a pair of backless clogs.

She should have used some of the duct tape on the clogs. They slopped off her feet with every step, and she had to half-shuffle her way down the hall to me. The clogs and the duct tape were both the bilious electric blue she'd worn the other day.

"What do you call that color?" I asked.

"Cerenkhov blue."

Of course. After the bluish radiation in nuclear reactors. How appropriate. In fairness, though, I had to admit it wasn't the first time a faddish color had been given a wretched name. Back in Louis XVI's day, color names had been downright nauseating. Sewerage, arsenic, smallpox, and Sick Spaniard had all been hit names for yellow-green.

Flip handed me a piece of paper. "You need to sign this," she said.

It was a petition to declare the staff lounge a nonsmoking area. "Where will people be allowed to smoke if they can't smoke in the lounge?" I said.

"They shouldn't smoke. It causes cancer," she said righteously. "I think people who smoke shouldn't be allowed to have jobs." She tossed her hank of hair. "And they should have to live someplace where their secondhand smoke can't hurt the rest of us."

"Really, Herr Goebbels," I said, forgetting that ignorance is the biggest trend of all, and handed the petition back to her.

"Second-secondhand smoke is dangerous," she said huffily.

"So is meanness." I turned back to the computer.

"How much does a crown cost?" she said.

It seemed to be my day for questions out of left field. "A crown?" I said, bewildered. "You mean, like a tiara?"

"No-o-o," she said. "A *crown.*"

I tried to picture a crown on top of Flip's hank of hair, with her hair wrap hanging down one side, and failed. But whatever she was talking about, I'd better pay attention because it was likely to be the next big fad. Flip might be incompetent, insubordinate, and generally insufferable, but she was right there on the cutting edge of fashion.

"A crown," I said. "Made out of gold?" I pantomimed placing one on my head. "With points?"

"Points?" she said, outraged. "It better not have points. A *crown."*

"I'm sorry, Flip," I said. "I don't know—"

"You're a *sci*entist," she said. "You're supposed to know scientific terms."

I wondered if *crown* had become a scientific term the way duct tape had become a personal errand.

"A *crown!"* she said, sighed enormously, and clopped out of the lab and down the hall.

It was my day for encounters I couldn't make heads or tails of, and that included my hair-bobbing data. I was sorry I'd ever gotten the idea of including the other fads of the day. There were way too many of them, and none of them made any sense.

Peanut-pushing, for instance, and flagpole-sitting, and painting knees with rouge. College kids had painted old Model T's with clever slogans like "Banana oil" and "Oh, you kid!", middle-aged housewives had dressed up like Chinese maidens and played mah-jongg, and fads had seemed to come out of the woodwork, superseding each other in months and sometimes weeks. The black bottom replaced mah-jongg, which had replaced King Tut, and the whole thing was so chaotic it was impossible to sort out.

Crossword puzzles were the only fad that was halfway reasonable, and even that was a puzzle. The fad had started in the fall of 1924, well after hair-bobbing, but crossword puzzles had been around since the 1800s, and the *New York World* had published a weekly crossword since 1913.

And reasonable, on closer examination, wasn't really the word. A minister had passed out crosswords during church that, on being solved, revealed the scripture lesson. Women had worn dresses decorated with black-and-white squares, and hats and stockings to match, and Broadway put on a revue called "Puzzles of 1925." People had cited crosswords as the cause of their divorces, secretaries wore pocket dictionaries around their wrists like bracelets, doctors warned of eyestrain, and in Budapest a writer left a suicide note in the form of a crossword puzzle, a puzzle, by the way, which the police never solved, probably because they were already consumed with the next fad: the Charleston.

Bennett stuck his head in the door. "Have you got a minute? I need to ask you a question." He came in. He had changed his checked shirt for a faded plaid one that was neither madras nor Ivy League, and he was carrying a copy of the simplified funding form.

"A two-letter word for an Egyptian sun god?" I said. "It's Ra."

He grinned. "No, I was just wondering if Flip had brought you a copy of the memo Management said they'd send around. Explaining the simplified funding form?"

"Yes and no," I said. "I had to get one from Gina." I fished it out from a pile of twenties books.

"Great," he said, "I'll go make a copy and bring this back."

"That's okay," I said. "You can keep it."

"You finished filling out your funding forms?"

"No," I said. "Read the memo."

He looked at it. " 'Page nineteen, Question forty-four-C. To find the primary extensional funding formula, multiply the departmental needs analysis by the fiscal base quotient, unless the project involves calibrated structuring, in which case the quotient should be calculated according to Section W-A of the accompanying instructions." He turned the paper over. "Where are the accompanying instructions?"

"No one knows," I said.

He handed the memo back to me. "Maybe I don't have to go to France to study chaos. Maybe I could study it right here," he said, shaking his head. "Thanks," and he started to leave.

"Speaking of which," I said, "how's your information diffusion project coming?"

"The lab's all ready," he said. "I can get the macaques as soon as I finish this stupid funding form, which should be in about"—he pulled a calculator out of his threadbare pants and punched in numbers—"six thousand years from now."

Flip slouched in and handed us each a stapled stack of papers.

"What's this?" Bennett said. "The accompanying instructions?"

"No-o-o," Flip said, tossing her head. "It's the FDA report on the health hazards of smoking."

dance marathon [1923–33]

Endurance fad in which the object was to dance the longest to earn money. Couples pinched and kicked each other to stay awake, and when that failed, took turns sleeping on their partner's shoulder for as long as 150 days. The marathons became a gruesome spectator sport, with people watching to see who would have hallucinations brought on by sleep deprivation, collapse, or, in the case of Homer Moorhouse, drop dead, and the New Jersey SPCA complained that the marathons were cruel to (human) animals. Persisted into the first years of the Depression simply because people needed the money, which worked out to a little over a penny an hour. If you won.

Tuesday I met the new assistant interdepartmental communications liaison. I'd decided I couldn't wait any longer for the accompanying instructions and was working on the funding forms when I noticed that the bottom of page 28 read, "List all," and the top of the next page read, "to the diversification quotient." I looked at the page number. It read "42."

I went down to see if Gina had the missing pages. She was sitting in a tangle of sacks, wrapping paper, and ribbons. "You *are* coming to Brittany's party, aren't you?" she said. "You have to come. There are going to be six five-year-olds and six mothers, and I don't know which is worse."

"I'll be there," I promised, and asked her about the missing pages.

"There are missing *pages?*" she said. "My funding form's at home.

When am I going to be able to fill out missing pages? I've still got to go buy plates and cups and decorations *and* fix the refreshments."

I escaped and went back to the lab. A gray-haired woman was sitting at the computer, rapidly typing in numbers.

"Sorry," she said as soon as I came in the room. "Flip said I could use your computer, but I don't want to get in your way." She began rapidly touching keys to save the file.

"Are you Flip's new assistant?" I asked, looking at her curiously. She was thin, with tan, leathery skin, like Billy Ray would have after another thirty years of riding the range.

"Shirl Creets," she said, shaking my hand. She had a grip like Billy Ray's, and her fingers were stained a yellowish brown, which explained how Sarah and Elaine had known she was a smoker "just by looking at her."

"Flip was using Dr. Turnbull's computer," she said, and her voice was hoarse, too, "and she told me to come up here and use yours, that you wouldn't mind. I'll be off this as soon as I save the file. I haven't been smoking," she added.

"You can smoke if you want," I said. "And you can use the computer. I've got to go over to Personnel anyway and pick up a different funding allocation form. This one's missing pages."

"I'll go get it for you," Shirl said, getting up immediately and taking the form from me. "Which pages is it missing?"

"Twenty-nine through forty-one," I said, "and maybe some at the end, I don't know. Mine only goes up to page sixty-eight. But you don't have to—"

"What are assistants *for?* Do you want me to make an extra copy so you can do a rough draft?"

"That would be nice, thank you," I said, in shock, and sat down at the computer.

I had been nice to Flip, and look what it had gotten me. I took it back that Browning knew anything about trends, Pied Piper or no Pied Piper.

The data Shirl had been typing in were still there. It was some kind of table. "Carbanks—48, Twofeathers—34," it read. "Holyrood—61, Chin—39." I wondered what project Alicia was working on now.

Shirl was back in five minutes flat, with a stack of neatly collated and stapled sheafs. "I put copies of the missing pages in your original, and made you two extra copies just in case." She set them gently down on the lab table and handed me another thick sheaf. "While I was in the copy room, I found these clippings. Flip didn't know who they belonged to. I thought they might be yours."

She held up a stack of clippings on dance marathons, neatly paper-clipped to a set of copies.

"I assumed you wanted copies," she said.

"Thank you," I said, astounded. "I don't suppose you could talk Flip into assigning you to me?"

"I doubt it," she said. "She seems to like you." She set the clippings on the lab table and began straightening the top of it. She fished the chaos theory book out of the mess.

"Mandelbrot diagrams," she said interestedly. "Is that what you're researching?"

"No," I said. "Fad origins. I was just reading that out of curiosity. They are connected, though. Fads are a facet of the chaotic system of society, with a number of variables contributing to them."

She stacked *Brave New World* and *All's Well that Ends Well* on top of the chaos theory book without comment and picked up *Flappers, Flivvers, and Flagpole-Sitters.* "What made you choose fads?" she said disapprovingly.

"You don't like fads?"

"I just think there are more direct ways of influencing society than starting a fad. I had a physics teacher who used to say, 'Pay no attention to what other people are doing. Do what you want, and you can change the world.' "

"Oh, I don't want to discover how to start them," I said. "I suppose HiTek does, and that's why they keep funding the project, although if the mechanism is as complex as it's beginning to look, they'll never be able to isolate the critical variable, at which point they'll probably stop funding me." I looked at the dance marathon notes. "What *I* want to do is understand what causes them."

"Why?" she said curiously.

"Because I just want to understand. Why do people act the way they do? Why do they all suddenly decide to play the same game or wear the same clothes or believe the same thing? In the 1920s smoking was a fad. Now it's *anti*smoking. Why? Is it instinctive behavior or societal influences? Or something in the air? The Salem witch trials were caused by fear and greed, but they're always around, and we don't burn witches all the time, so there must be something else going on.

"I just don't understand what," I said. "And it doesn't look like I will anytime soon. I don't seem to be getting anywhere. *You* don't happen to know what caused hair-bobbing, do you?"

"It's going slowly?" she said.

"Slow isn't the word," I said. I gestured with the marathon dancing copies. "I feel like *I'm* in a dance marathon contest. Most of the time it's not dancing at all, it's just putting one foot in front of the other, trying to hang on and stay awake. Trying to remember why you signed up in the first place."

"My physics teacher used to say that science was one percent inspiration and ninety-nine percent perspiration," she said.

"And fifty percent filling out nonsimplified funding forms," I said. I picked up one of the extra copies. "I'd better take one of these over to Gina."

"I've already taken one to Dr. Damati," she said. "Oh, and I need to get back there. I promised her I'd wrap Brittany's presents for her."

"You're *sure* you can't persuade Flip?" I said.

After she left, I started work on page 29, but it didn't make any more sense than when it had been missing, and I was starting to feel vaguely itch again. I took one of the extra copies and went down to Bio to Bennett's lab.

Alicia was there, head to head with Bennett at the computer, but he looked up immediately and smiled at me.

"Hi," he said. "Come on in."

"No, that's okay. I didn't mean to interrupt," I said, smiling at Alicia. She didn't smile back. "I just wanted to bring you a complete funding form." I handed him the funding form. "There were pages missing in the ones Flip passed out."

"Incompetent," he said. "Incorrigible. Incapacitating."

Alicia was actively glaring at me.

"Intruding," I said. "Which is what I'm doing on your meeting. I'll talk to you later." I headed for the door.

"No, wait," he said. "You'll be interested in this. Dr. Turnbull was just telling me about her project." He looked at Alicia. "Tell Dr. Foster what you've been doing."

"I've taken the data on all the previous Niebnitz Grant winners: scientific discipline, project area, educational background—"

That explained the third degree I'd gotten from her yesterday. She had been trying to determine if I fit the profile, and from the look she was giving me, I must not have even placed.

"—age, gender, ethnic group, political affiliation." She scrolled through several screens, and I recognized a chart like the one Shirl had just been working on. "I'm running regressions to determine the relevant characteristics and then analyzing those to construct a profile of the typical Niebnitz Grant recipient and the criteria the Niebnitz Grant Committee uses to make their choices."

The committee's criteria were originality of thought and creativity, I thought. Assuming there *is* a committee.

"I haven't completed the regressions yet, but some patterns are emerging." She called up a spreadsheet. "The grant is given at a median interval of one point nine years apart, but the closest two grants have ever been given is one point two years, which means the grant won't be given until May at the earliest."

It didn't mean any such thing, and I would have said so, but she was into it now.

"Distribution of the awards follows a cyclical pattern, with academic institutions, research labs, and commercial corporations alternating, the next one being a corporation, which gives us an advantage, *and"*—she switched to a different spreadsheet—"there is a definite bias toward scientists west of the Mississippi, which is also an advantage, *and* a bias toward the biological sciences. I haven't determined the specific area yet, but I should have that part of the profile by tomorrow."

All of which sounded suspiciously like science on demand. I looked at Bennett to see what he thought about all this, but he was watching the screen intently, abstractedly, as if he'd forgotten we were there.

Well, of course he was interested. Why wouldn't he be? If he could win the Niebnitz Grant, he could go back to the Loue River to work on chaos theory and forget all about forms and Flip and the uncertainties of funding.

Except science doesn't work like that. You can't handicap significant breakthroughs like they were a horse race.

But this wouldn't be the first time somebody'd convinced himself of something that wasn't true where money was involved. Take the stock market fad of the late twenties. Or the Dutch tulip craze of the 1600s. In 1634, the prices of tulips that were fancier or prettier or rarer than others started going up, and suddenly everybody—merchants, princes, peasants, brothers, sisters, husbands, wives—was buying and selling bulbs like mad. Prices skyrocketed, speculators made fortunes overnight, and people hocked their wooden shoes *and* the dike to buy a bulb that might cost as much as twelve annual incomes. And then for no reason, the market collapsed, and it was just like October 29, 1929, only with no skyscraper windows for Dutch stockholders to fling themselves out of.

Not to mention chain letters, pyramid schemes, and the Florida land boom.

"The other factor that needs to be considered is the name of the grant," Alicia was saying. "Niebnitz may refer either to Ludwig Niebnitz, who was an obscure eighteenth-century botanist, or to Karl Niebnitz von Drull, who lived in fifteenth-century Bavaria. If it's Ludwig, that would account for the biological bias. Von Drull was more famous. His area was alchemy."

"I have to go," I said, standing up. "If I'm going to switch my fads project to changing lead into gold, I'll need to get busy," and I walked out.

Bennett followed me out into the hall. "Thanks for bringing the funding form."

"We have to stick together against the forces of Flip," I said. "Have you met her new assistant?"

"Yeah, she's great," he said. "I wonder whatever possessed her to take a job like this?"

"NIEBNITZ may also be an acronym," Alicia said from the doorway. "In which case—"

I took my leave and went back up to my lab.

Flip was there, typing something on my computer. "How would you describe me?" she asked.

I looked around the lab. It was spotless. Shirl had cleaned off the lab tables and put all my clippings in folders. In alphabetical order.

Inescapable, I thought. Impacted. "Inextricable," I said.

"That sounds good," she said. "Does it have two *k*s or one?"

dr. spock (1945–65)

Child care fad, inspired by the pediatrician's book, *Baby and Child Care,* growing interest in psychology, and the fragmentation of the extended family. Spock advocated a more permissive approach than previous child care books and advised flexibility in feeding schedules and attention to child development, advice which far too many parents misinterpreted as letting the child do whatever it wanted. Died out when the first generation of Dr. Spock-raised children became teenagers, grew their hair down to their shoulders, and began blowing up administration buildings.

Wednesday I went to the birthday party. I'd arranged to leave early and was putting on my coat when Flip slouched in, wearing a laced bodice and duct-tape-decorated jeans, and handed me a piece of paper.

"I don't have time for any petitions," I said.

"It's not a petition," she said, tossing her hair. "It's a memo about the funding forms."

The memo said the funding forms were due on the twenty-third, which I already knew.

"You're supposed to turn the form in to me."

I nodded and handed it back to her. "Take this down to Dr. O'Reilly's lab," I said, pulling on my gloves.

She sighed. "He's never there. He's always in Dr. Turnbull's lab."

"Then take it to Dr. Turnbull's lab."

"They're always together. He's com*plete*ly raved about her, you know."

No, I thought, I didn't know that.

"They're always sitting at the computer together. I don't know what she sees in him. He's com*plete*ly swarb," Flip said, picking at the duct tape on the back of her hand. "Maybe she can make him not so fashion-impaired."

And if she does, I thought irritatedly, there goes his nonfadness, and I'll never figure out why he was immune to them.

"What does *sophisticated* mean?" Flip asked.

"Cosmopolitan," I said, "but you're not," and left for the party. The weather had turned colder. We usually get one big snowstorm in October, and it looked like the weather was gearing up for it.

Gina was nearly hysterical by the time I got there. "You won't believe what Brittany decided she wanted after I said she couldn't have Barney," she said, pointing to the decorations, which were a pink that bore no relation to postmodern.

"Barbie!" Brittany shouted. She was wearing a Little Mermaid dress and bright pink hair wraps. "Did you bring me a present?"

The other little girls were all wearing Pocahontas pinafores except for a sweet little blonde named Peyton, who was wearing a Lion King jumper and light-up sneakers.

"Are you married?" Peyton's mother said to me.

"No," I said.

She shook her head. "So many guys have intimacy issues these days. Peyton, we're not opening presents yet."

"Are you dating anyone?" Lindsay's mother said.

"We're going to open presents later, Brittany," Gina said. "First we're all going to play a game. Bethany, it's Brittany's birthday."

She attempted a game involving balloons with pink Barbies on them and then gave up and let Brittany open her presents.

"Open Sandy's first," Gina said, handing her the book. "No, Caitlin, these are Brittany's presents."

Brittany ripped the paper off *Toads and Diamonds* and looked at it blankly.

"That was my favorite fairy tale when I was little," I said. "It's about a girl who meets a good fairy, only she doesn't know it because the fairy's in disguise—" but Brittany had already tossed it aside and was ripping open a Barbie doll in a glittery dress.

"Totally Hair Barbie!" she shrieked.

"Mine," Peyton said, and made a grab that left Brittany holding nothing but Barbie's arm.

"She broke Totally Hair Barbie!" Brittany wailed.

Peyton's mother stood up and said calmly, "Peyton, I think you need a time-out."

I thought Peyton needed a good swat, or at least to have Totally Hair Barbie taken away from her and given back to Brittany, but instead her mother led her to the door of Gina's bedroom. "You can come out when you're in control of your feelings," she said to Peyton, who looked like she was in control to me.

"I can't believe you're still using time-outs," Chelsea's mother said. "Everybody's using holding now."

"Holding?" I asked.

"You hold the child immobile on your lap until the negative behavior stops. It produces a feeling of interceptive safety."

"Really," I said, looking toward the bedroom door. I would have hated trying to hold Peyton against her will.

"Holding's been totally abandoned," Lindsay's mother said. "We use EE."

"EE?" I said.

"Esteem Enhancement," Lindsay's mother said. "EE addresses the positive peripheral behavior no matter how negative the primary behavior is."

"Positive peripheral behavior?" Gina said dubiously.

"When Peyton took the Barbie away from Brittany just now," Lindsay's mother said, obviously delighted to explain, "you would have said, 'My, Peyton, what an assertive grip you have.' "

Brittany opened Swim 'n' Dive Barbie, Stick 'n' Peel Barbie, Barbie's City Nights cycle, and an elaborately coiffed and veiled Barbie in a wedding dress. "Romantic Bride Barbie," Brittany said, transported.

"Can we have cake now?" Lindsay said, and Peyton must have had her little ear to the door because she opened it, looking not particularly contrite, said, "I feel better about myself now," and climbed up to the table.

"No cake," Gina said. "Too much cholesterol. Frozen yogurt and Snapple," and all the little girls came running as if they'd heard the Pied Piper's flute.

The mothers and I picked up wrapping paper and ribbon, checking carefully for stray Barbie high heels and microscopic accessories. Danielle's mother smoothed down Romantic Bride Barbie's net overskirt. "I wonder if Lisa'd like a dress like this," she said. "She's trying to talk Eric into getting married sometime this summer."

"Are you going to be her matron of honor?" Chelsea's mother asked. "What colors is she going to have?"

"She hasn't decided. Black and white is really in, but she already did that the last time she got married."

"Postmodern pink," I said. "It's the new color for spring."

"I look washed out in pink," Danielle's mother said. "And she's still got to talk him into it. He says, why can't they just live together?"

Lindsay's mother picked up Romantic Bride Barbie and began fluffing up her bouffant sleeves. "I always said I'd never get married again, after that *jerk* Matt," she said. "But I don't know, lately I've been feeling sort of . . . I don't know . . ."

Itch? I thought.

The phone rang, and Gina went into the bedroom to get it, and everybody else adjourned to the kitchen.

There was a shriek from the kitchen, and everybody went in to enhance esteem. I picked up Romantic Bride Barbie and looked at the pink net rosebuds and white satin flounces, marveling. Barbie's a fad that should have lasted, at the most, for two seasons. Even the Shirley Temple doll had only been a fad for three.

Instead, Barbie's well into her thirties and more of a fad than ever, even in these days of feminism and non-gender-biased child-rearing. She'd be the perfect thing to study for what causes fads, but I wasn't sure I wanted to know. Barbie's one of those fads whose popularity makes you lose all faith in the human race.

Gina came out of the bedroom. "It's for you," she said, looking speculatively at me. "You can take it in the bedroom."

I put down Romantic Bride Barbie and stood up.

"It's *my* birthday!" Brittany shrieked.

"My, Peyton," Lindsay's mother said, "what a *creative* thing to do with your frozen yogurt."

Gina hurried into the kitchen, and I went into the bedroom.

It was done in violets, with a purple cordless phone. I picked it up.

"Howdy," Billy Ray said. "Guess where I'm calling from?"

"How did you find out I was here?"

"I called HiTek, and your assistant told me."

"*Flip* gave you the number?" I said. "Correctly?"

"I don't know what her name was. Raspy voice. Coughed a lot."

Shirl. She must be putting some more of Alicia's data on my computer.

"Well, so, listen, I'm on my way through the Rockies right now and—hang on. Tunnel coming up. Call you back as soon as I'm through it." There was a hum, and a click.

I hung up the phone and sat there on Gina's violet-covered bed, wondering how Billy Ray ever got any ranching done when he was never at the ranch, and pondering the appeal of Barbie.

Part of it must be that she's been able to incorporate other fads over the years. In the mid-sixties, Barbie had ironed hair and Carnaby Street clothes, in the seventies granny dresses, in the eighties leotards and leg warmers.

Nowadays there are astronaut Barbies and management Barbies, and even a doctor, though it's hard to imagine Barbie making it through junior high, let alone medical school.

Billy Ray had apparently forgotten all about me, and so had Peyton's mother. She opened the door, said, ". . . and I want you to stay in time-out until you've decided to relate to your peers," and ushered in a frozen yogurt-covered Peyton.

Neither of them saw me, especially not Peyton, who flung herself against the door, red-faced and whimpering, and then, when it was apparent that wasn't going to work, dropped to her hands and knees next to the bed and pulled out a tablet and crayons.

She sat down cross-legged in the middle of the floor, opened the box of crayons, selected a pink one, and began to draw.

"Hi," I said, and was happy to see her jump a foot. "What are you doing?"

"You're not supposed to talk in a time-out," she said righteously.

You're not supposed to color either, I thought, wishing Billy Ray would remember he was calling me back.

She selected a green crayon and bent over the tablet, drawing earnestly. I moved the phone around to the other side of the bed so I could see the picture.

"What are you drawing?" I asked. "A butterfly?"

She rolled her eyes. *"No-o-o,"* she said. "It's a story."

"A story?" I said, tilting my head around to see it better. "About what?"

"About *Bar*bie." She sighed, a dead ringer for Flip, and chose a bright blue crayon.

Why do only the awful things become fads? I thought. Eye-rolling and Barbie and bread pudding. Why never chocolate cheesecake or thinking for yourself?

I looked more closely at the picture. It looked more like a Mandelbrot diagram than a story. It appeared to be some sort of map, or maybe a diagram, with many lines of tiny lavender stars and pink zigzag symbols intersecting across the paper. Peyton had obviously been working on it during a number of time-outs.

"What's this?" I said, pointing at a row of purple zigzags.

"See," she said, bringing the tablet and the crayons up onto my lap, "Barbie went to her Malibu Beach House." She drew a scalloped blue line above the zigzags. "It's very far. They had to go in her Jaguar."

"And that's this line?" I said, pointing at the blue scallops.

"No-o-o," she said, irritated at all these interruptions. "That's to show what she was wearing. See, when she goes to the Malibu Beach House she wears her blue hat. So they all got to the Malibu Beach House," she said, walking her crayon like a doll across the paper, "and Barbie said, 'Let's go swimming,' and I said, 'Okay, let's,' and . . ." There was a pause while Peyton found an orange crayon. "And Barbie said, 'Let's go!' and we went swimming." She began drawing a row of rapid sideways zigzags.

"Is that her swimming suit?" I asked.

"No-o-o," she said. "That's Barbie."

Barbie? I thought, wondering what the symbolism of the zigzags was. Of course. Barbie's high heels.

"So the next day," Peyton said, selecting yellow orange and drawing spiky suns, "Barbie said, 'Let's go shopping,' and I said, 'Okay, let's,' and she said, 'Let's ride our mopeds,' and I said—"

Billy Ray came out of his tunnel, and I got the phone switched on almost before it rang. "So you're on your way to Denver?" I said.

"Nope. Other direction. Durango. Conference on teleconferences. I got to thinking about you and thought I'd call. Do you ever get to hankering for something besides what you're doing?"

"Yes," I said fervently, reading the names of the crayons Peyton had discarded. Periwinkle. Screamin' green. Cerulean blue.

"—so Barbie said, 'Hi, Ken,' and Ken said, 'Hi, Barbie, want to go on a date?' " Peyton said, busily drawing lines.

"Me too," Billy Ray said. "I've been thinking, is this really what I want?"

"Didn't the sheep work out?"

"The Targhees? No, they're doing fine. It's this whole ranching thing. It's so isolated."

Except for the fax and the net and the cell phone, I thought.

". . . so Barbie said, 'I don't want to be in time-out,' " Peyton said, wielding a black crayon. " 'Okay,' Barbie's mom said, 'you don't have to.' "

"Do you ever get to feeling . . . ," Billy Ray said, ". . . kinda . . . I don't know what to call it . . ."

I do, I thought. Itch. And does that mean this unsettled, dissatisfied feeling is some sort of fad, too, like tattoos and violets? And if so, how did it get started?

I sat up straighter on the bed. "When exactly did you start having this feeling?" I asked him, but there was already an ominous hum from the cell phone.

"Another tunnel," Billy Ray said. "We'll talk about it some more when I get back. I've got something I want to—" and the phone went dead.

Lindsay's mother had talked about feeling itch, and so had Flip, that day in the coffeehouse, and I had felt so vaguely longing I'd gone out with Billy Ray. Had I spread the feeling on to him, like some kind of virus, and was that how fads spread, by infection?

"Your turn," Peyton said, holding out a neon-red crayon. Radical red.

"Okay," I said, taking the crayon. "So Barbie decided to go to . . ." I drew a line of radical red high heels across the blue scallops. ". . . the barbershop. 'I want my hair bobbed,' she said to the barber." I started a line of aquamarine scissors. "And the barber said, 'Why?' And Barbie said, 'Because everybody else is doing it.' So the barber chopped off Barbie's hair and—"

"No-o," Peyton said, grabbing the aquamarine away from me and handing me laser lemon. *"This* is Cut 'n' Curl Barbie."

"Oh," I said. "Okay. So the barber said, 'But somebody had to do it first, and *they* couldn't do it because everybody else was doing it, so why did *they'—"*

There was a sound at the door, and Peyton snatched the laser lemon out of my hand, flipped the tablet shut, stowed them both under the bed with amazing speed, and was sitting on the edge of it with her hands folded in her lap when her mother opened the door.

"Peyton, we're watching a video now. Do—" she said, and stopped when she saw me. "You didn't talk to Peyton while she was in her time-out, did you?"

"Not a word," I said.

She turned back to Peyton. "Do you think you can exhibit positive peer behavior now?"

Peyton nodded wisely and tore out of the room, her mother following. I put the phone back on the nightstand and started after her, and then stopped and recovered the tablet from its hiding place and looked at it again.

It was a map, in spite of what Peyton had said. A combination map and diagram and picture, with an amazing amount of information packed onto one page: location, time elapsed, outfits worn. An amazing amount of data.

And it intersected in interesting ways, the lines crossing and recrossing to form elaborate intersections, radical red changing to lavender and orange in overlay. Barbie only rode her moped in the lower half of the picture, and there was a solid knot of stars in one corner. A statistical anomaly?

I wondered if a diagram-map-story like this would work for my twenties data. I'd tried maps and statistical charts and computational models, but never all three together, color-coded for date and vector and incidence. If I put it all together, what kinds of patterns would emerge?

There was a shriek from the living room. "It's *my* birthday!" Brittany wailed.

I tucked the tablet back under the bed.

"My, Peyton," Lindsay's mother said. "What a creative way to show your need for attention."

pyrography [1900–05]

Craft fad in which designs were burned into wood or leather with a hot iron. Flowers, birds, horses, and knights in armor were branded onto pin cases, pen trays, glove boxes, pipe racks, playing card cases, and other similarly useless items. Died out because its ability threshold was too high. Everyone's horses looked like cows.

Thursday the weather got worse. It was spitting snow when I got to work, and by lunch it was a full-blown blizzard. Flip had managed to break both copy machines, so I gathered up my flagpole-sitting clippings to be copied at Kinko's, but as I walked out to my car I decided they could wait, and I scuttled back to the building, my head down against the snow. And practically ran into Shirl.

She was huddled next to a minivan, smoking a cigarette. She had a brown mitten on the hand that wasn't holding the cigarette, her coat collar was turned up, a muffler was wrapped around her chin, and she was shivering.

"Shirl!" I shouted against the wind. "What are you doing out here?"

She clumsily fished a piece of paper out of her coat pocket with her mittened hand and handed it to me. It was a memo declaring the entire building smoke-free.

"Flip," I said, shaking snow off the already wet memo. "She's behind this." I crumpled the memo up and threw it on the ground. "Don't you have a car?" I said.

She shook her head, shivering. "I get a ride to work."

"You can sit in my car," I said, and thought of a better place. "Come on." I took hold of her arm. "I know someplace you can smoke."

"The whole building's been declared off-limits to smoking," she said, resisting.

"This place isn't in the building," I said.

She stubbed out her cigarette. "This is a kind thing to do for an old lady," she said, and we both scuttled back to the building through the driving snow.

We stopped inside the door to shake the snow off and take off our hats. Her leathery face was bright red with cold.

"You don't have to do this," she said, unwrapping her muffler.

"When you've spent as much time studying fads as I have, you develop a hearty dislike for them," I said. "Especially aversion fads. They seem to bring out the worst in people. And it's the principle of the thing. Next it might be chocolate cheesecake. Or reading. Come on."

I led her down the hall. "This place won't be warm, but it'll be out of the wind, and you won't get snowed on, at least. And this antismoking fad should be dying out by spring. It's reaching the extreme stage that inevitably produces a backlash."

"Prohibition lasted thirteen years."

"The law did. The fad didn't. McCarthyism only lasted four." I started down the stairs to Bio.

"Where exactly is this place?" Shirl asked.

"It's Dr. O'Reilly's lab," I said. "It's got a porch out back with an overhang."

"And you're sure he won't mind?"

"I'm sure," I said. "He never pays any attention to what other people think."

"He sounds like an extraordinary young man," Shirl said, and I thought, He really is.

He didn't fit any of the usual patterns. He certainly wasn't a rebel, refusing to go along with fads to assert his individuality. Rebellion can be a fad, too, as witness Hell's Angels and peace symbols. And yet he wasn't oblivious either. He was funny and intelligent and observant.

I tried to explain that to Shirl as we went downstairs to Bio. "It isn't that he doesn't care what other people think. It's just that he doesn't see what it has to do with him."

"My physics teacher used to say Diogenes shouldn't have wasted his time looking for an honest man," Shirl said, "he should have been looking for somebody who thought for himself."

I started down Bio's hall, and it suddenly occurred to me that Alicia might be in the lab. "Wait here a sec," I said to Shirl, and peeked in the door. "Bennett?"

He was hunched over his desk, practically hidden by papers.

"Can Shirl smoke out on the porch?" I said.

"Sure," he said without looking up.

I went out and got Shirl.

"You can smoke in here if you want," Bennett said when we came in.

"No, she can't. HiTek's made the whole building nonsmoking," I said. "I told her she could smoke out on the porch."

"Sure," he said, standing up. "Feel free to come down here anytime. I'm always here."

"Oh?" Shirl said. "You work on your project even during lunch?"

He told her he didn't have a project to work on and he had to wait for his funding to be approved before he could get his macaques, but I wasn't paying attention. I was looking at what he was wearing.

Flip had been right about Bennett. He was wearing a white shirt and a Cerenkhov blue tie.

"I've been working on this chaos thing," he said, straightening the tie.

"Did Alicia decide chaos theory was the optimum project to win the Niebnitz Grant?" I said, and couldn't keep the sharpness out of my voice.

"No," he said, frowning at me. "When she was talking about variables the other day, it gave me an idea about why my prediction rate didn't improve. So I refigured the data."

"And did it help?" I said.

"No," he said, looking abstracted, the way he had when Alicia'd been talking. "The more work I do on it, the more I think maybe Verhoest was right, and there is an outside force acting on the system." He said to Shirl, "You're probably not interested in this. Here, let me show you where the porch is." He led her through the habitat to the back door. "When my macaques come, you'll have to go around the side." He opened the door, and snow and wind whirled in. "Are you sure you don't want to smoke inside? You could stand in the door. Leave the door open at least so there's some heat."

"I was born in Montana," she said, wrapping her muffler around her neck as she went out. "This is a mild summer breeze," but I noticed she left the door open.

Bennett came back in, rubbing his arms. *"Brr,* it's freezing out there. What's the matter with people? Sending an old lady out in the snow in the name of moral righteousness. I suppose Flip was behind it."

"Flip is behind everything." I looked at the littered desk. "I guess I'd better let you get back to work. Thanks for letting Shirl smoke down here."

"No, wait," he said. "I had a couple of things I wanted to ask you about the funding form." He scrabbled through the stuff on his desk and came up with the form. He flipped through pages, looking. "Page fifty-one, section eight. What does *Documentation Scatter Method* mean?"

"You're supposed to put down *ALR-Augmented,"* I said.

"What does that mean?"

"I have no idea. It's what Gina told me to put."

He penciled it in, shaking his head. "These funding forms are going to be the death of me. I could have *done* the project in the time it's taken me to fill out this form. HiTek wants us to win the Niebnitz Grant, to make scientific breakthroughs. But name me one scientist who ever made a significant breakthrough while filling out a funding form. Or attending a meeting."

"Mendeleev," Shirl said.

We both turned around. Shirl was standing inside the door, shaking snow off her hat. "Mendeleev was on his way to a cheesemaking conference when he solved the problem of the periodic chart," she said.

"That's right, he was," Bennett said. "He stepped on the train and the solution came to him, just like that."

"Like Poincaré," I said. "Only he stepped on a bus."

"And discovered Fuchsian functions," Bennett said.

"Kekulé was on a bus, too, wasn't he, when he discovered the benzene ring," Shirl said thoughtfully. "In Ghent."

"He was," I said, surprised. "How do you know so much about science, Shirl?"

"I have to make copies of so many scientific reports, I figured I might as well read them," she said. "Didn't Einstein look at the town clock from a bus while he was working on relativity?"

"A bus," I said. "Maybe that's what you and I need, Bennett. We take a bus someplace and suddenly everything's clear—you know what's wrong with your chaos data and I know what caused hair-bobbing."

"That sounds like a great idea," Bennett said. "Let's—"

"Oh, good, you're here, Bennett," Alicia said. "I need to talk to you about the grant profile. Shirl, make five copies of this." She dumped a stack of papers into Shirl's arms. "Collated and stapled. And this time don't put them on my desk. Put them in my mailbox." She turned back to Bennett. "I need you to help me come up with additional relevant factors."

"Transportation," I said, and started for the door. "And cheese."

ironing hair [1965–68]

Hair fad inspired by Joan Baez, Mary Travers, and other folksingers. Part of the hippie fad, the lank look of long straight hair was harder to obtain than the male's general shagginess. Beauty parlors gave "antiperms," but the preferred method among teenagers was laying their heads on the ironing board and pressing their locks with a clothes iron. The ironing was done a few inches at a time by a friend (who hopefully knew what she was doing), and college girls lined up in dorms to take their turns.

During the next few days, nothing much happened. The simplified funding allocation forms were due on the twenty-third, and, after donating yet another weekend to filling them out, I gave mine to Flip to deliver and then thought better of it and took it up to Paperwork myself.

The weather turned nice again, Elaine tried to talk me into going white-water rafting with her to relieve stress, Sarah told me her boyfriend, Ted, was experiencing attachment aversion, Gina asked me if I knew where to find Romantic Bride Barbie for Bethany (who had decided she wanted one just like Brittany's and whose birthday was in November), and I got three overdue notices for Browning, *The Complete Works.*

In between, I finished entering all my King Tut and black bottom data and started drawing a Barbie picture. I didn't have a box of sixty-four crayons, but there was a paintbox on the computer. I called it up, along with my statistical and differential equations programs, and started coding the correlations and plotting the relationships to each other. I graphed skirt lengths in cerulean blue, cigarette sales in gray, plotted lavender regressions for Isadora Duncan and yellow ones for temps above eighty-five. White for Irene Castle, radical red for references to rouge, brown for "Bernice Bobs Her Hair."

Flip came in periodically to hand me petitions and ask me questions like, "If you had a fairy godmother, what would she look like?"

"An old lady," I said, thinking of *Toads and Diamonds,* "or a bird, or something ugly, like a toad. Fairy godmothers disguise themselves so they can tell if you're deserving of help by whether you're nice to them. What do you need one for?"

She rolled her eyes. "You're not supposed to ask interdepartmental communications liaisons personal questions. If they're in disguise, how do you know to be nice to them?"

"You're supposed to be nice in general—" I said and realized it was hopeless. "What's the petition for?"

"It's to make HiTek give us dental insurance, of course," she said.

Of course.

"You don't think it's my assistant, do you?" Flip said. "She's an old lady."

I handed her back the petition. "I doubt very much that Shirl is your fairy godmother in disguise."

"Good," she said. "There's no way I'm going to be nice to somebody who *smokes."*

I didn't see Bennett, who was busy preparing for the arrival of his macaques, or Shirl, who was doing all Flip's work, but I did see Alicia. She came up to the lab, wearing po-mo pink, and demanded to borrow my computer.

"Flip's using mine," she said irately, "and when I told her to get off, she *refused.* Have you ever met anyone who was that rude?"

That was a tough one. "How's the search for the Philosopher's Stone going?" I said.

"I've definitely eliminated circumstantial predisposition as a criterion," she said, shifting my data to the lab table. "Only two Niebnitz Grant recipients have ever made a significant scientific breakthrough subsequent to their winning of the award. And I've narrowed down the project approach to a cross-discipline-designed experiment, but I still haven't determined the personal profile. I'm still evaluating the variables." She popped my disk out and shoved her own in.

"Have you taken disease into account?" I said.

She looked irritated. "Disease?"

"Diseases have played a big part in scientific breakthroughs. Einstein's measles, Mendeleev's lung trouble, Darwin's hypochondria. The bubonic plague. They closed down Cambridge because of it, and Newton had to go back home to the apple orchard."

"I hardly see—"

"And what about their shooting skills?"

"If you're trying to be funny—"

"Fleming's rifle-shooting skills were why St. Mary's wanted him to stay on after he graduated as a surgeon. They needed him for the hospital rifle team, only there wasn't an opening in surgery, so they offered him a job in microbiology."

"And what exactly does Fleming have to do with the Niebnitz Grant?"

"He was circumstantially predisposed to significant scientific breakthroughs. What about their exercise habits? James Watt solved the steam engine problem while he was taking a walk, and William Rowan Hamilton—"

Alicia snatched up her papers and ejected her disk. "I'll use someone else's computer," she said. "It may interest you to know that statistically, fad research has absolutely no chance at all."

Yes, well, I knew that. Particularly the way it was going right now. Not only did my diagram not look nearly as good as Peyton's, but no butterfly outlines had appeared. Except the Marydale, Ohio, one, which was not only still there, but had been reinforced by the rolled-down stockings and crossword puzzle data.

But there was nothing for it but to keep slogging through the crocodile- and tsetse fly-infested tributaries. I calculated prediction intervals on Couéism and the crossword puzzle, and then started feeding in the related hairstyle data.

I couldn't find the clippings on the marcel wave. I'd given them to Flip a week and a half ago, along with the angel data and the personal ads. And hadn't seen any of it since.

I sorted through the stacks next to the computer on the off chance she'd brought it back and just dumped it somewhere, and then tracked Flip down in Supply, making long strands of Desiderata's hair into hair wraps.

"The other day I gave you a bunch of stuff to copy," I said to Flip. "There were some articles about angels and a bunch of clippings about hair-bobbing. What did you do with them?"

Flip rolled her eyes. "How would I know?"

"Because I gave them to you to copy. Because I *need* them, and they're not in my lab. There were some clippings about marcel waves," I persisted. "Remember? The wavy hairdo you liked?" I made a series of crimping motions next to my hair, hoping she'd remember, but she was wrapping Desiderata's wrappers with duct tape. "There was a page of personal ads, too."

That clearly rang a bell. She and Desiderata exchanged looks, and she said, "So now you're accusing me of stealing?"

"Stealing?" I said blankly. Angel articles and marcel wave clippings?

"They're public, you know. Anybody can write in."

I had no idea what she was talking about. Public?

"Just because you circled him doesn't mean he's yours." She yanked on Desiderata's hair. Desiderata yelped. "Besides, you already have that rodeo guy."

The personals, I thought, the light dawning. We're talking about the personal ads. Which explained her asking me about *elegant* and *sophisticated.* "You answered one of the personal ads?" I said.

"Like you didn't know. Like you and Darrell didn't have a big laugh over it," she said, and flung down the duct tape and ran out of the room.

I looked at Desiderata, who was trailing a long ragged end of duct tape from the hair wrap. "What was that all about?" I said.

"He lives on Valmont," she said.

"And?" I said, wishing I understood at least something that was said to me.

"Flip lives south of Baseline."

I was still looking blank.

Desiderata sighed. "Don't you *get* it? She's geographically incompatible."

She also has an *i* on her forehead, I thought, which somebody looking for elegant and sophisticated must have found daunting. "His name's Darrell?" I asked.

Desiderata nodded, trying to wind the end of the duct tape around her hair. "He's a dentist."

The crown, I thought. Of course.

"I think he's totally swarb, but Flip really likes him."

It was hard to imagine Flip liking anyone, and we were getting off the main issue. She had taken the personal ads, and done what with the rest of the articles? "You don't know where she might have put my marcel wave clippings, do you?"

"Gosh, no," Desiderata said. "Did you look in your lab?"

I gave up and went down to the copy room to try to find them myself. Flip apparently never copied anything. There were huge piles on both sides of the copier, on top of the copier lid, and on every flat surface in the room, including two waist-high piles on the floor, stacked in layers like sedimentary rock formations.

I sat down cross-legged on the floor and started through them: memos, reports, a hundred copies of a sensitivity exercise that started with "List five things you like about HiTek," a letter marked URGENT and dated July 6, 1988.

I found some notes I'd taken on Pet Rocks and the receipt from somebody's paycheck, but no marcel waves. I scooted over and started on the next stack.

"Sandy," a man's voice said from the door.

I looked up. Bennett was standing there. Something was clearly wrong. His sandy hair was awry and his face was gray under his freckles.

"What is it?" I said, scrambling to my feet.

He gestured, a little wildly, at the sheaf of papers in my hand. "You didn't find my funding allocation application in there, did you?"

"Your funding allocation form?" I said bewilderedly. "It had to be turned in Monday."

"I *know,*" he said, raking his hand through his hair. "I did turn it in. I gave it to Flip."

4. rapids

I suppose God could have made
a sillier animal than a sheep,
but it is very certain
that He never did. . . .

dorothy sayers

jitterbug (1938–45)

Dance fad of World War II, involving fancy footwork and athletic moves. Danced to big-band swing tunes, jitterbuggers flung their partners over their backs, under their legs, and into the air. GIs spread the jitterbug overseas wherever they were stationed. Replaced by the cha-cha.

Catastrophes can sometimes lead to scientific breakthroughs. A contaminated culture and a near drowning led to the discovery of penicillin, ruined photographic plates to the discovery of X rays. Take Mendeleev. His whole life was a series of catastrophes: He lived in Siberia, his father went blind, and the glass factory his mother started to make ends meet after his father died burned to the ground. But it was that fire that made his mother move to St. Petersburg, where Mendeleev was able to study with Bunsen and, eventually, come up with the periodic table of the elements.

Or take James Christy. He had a more minor catastrophe to deal with: a broken Star Scan machine. He'd just taken a picture of Pluto and was getting ready to throw it away because of a clearly wrong bulge at the edge of the planet when the Star Scan (obviously made by the same company as HiTek's copy machines) crashed.

Instead of throwing the photographic plate away, Christy had to call the repairman, who asked Christy to wait in case he needed help. Christy stood around for a while and then took another, harder look at the bulge and decided to check some of the earlier photographs. The very first one he found was marked "Pluto image. Elongated. Plate no good. Reject."

He compared it to the one in his hand. The plates looked the same, and Christy realized he was looking not at ruined pictures, but at a moon of Pluto.

On the whole, though, catastrophes are just catastrophes. Like this one.

Management cares about only one thing. Paperwork. They will forgive almost anything else—cost overruns, gross incompetence, criminal indictments—as long as the paperwork's filled out properly. And in on time.

"You gave your funding allocation form to *Flip?"* I said, and was instantly sorry.

He went even paler. "I know. Stupid, huh?"

"Your monkeys," I said.

"My ex-monkeys. I will not be teaching them the Hula Hoop." He went over to the stack I'd just been through and started through it.

"I've already been through those," I said. "It's not in there. Did you tell Management Flip lost it?"

"Yes," he said, picking up the papers on top of the copier. "Management said Flip says she turned in all the applications people gave her."

"And they *believed* her?" I said. Well, of course they believed her. They'd believed her when she said she needed an assistant. "Is anybody else's form missing?"

"No," he said grimly. "Of the three people stupid enough to let Flip turn their forms in, I'm the only one whose form she lost."

"Maybe . . . ," I said.

"I already asked them. I can't redo it and turn it in late." He set down the stack, picked it up, and started through it again.

"Look," I said, taking it from him. "Let's take this in an orderly fashion. You go through these piles." I set it next to the stack I'd gone through. "Stacks we've looked through on *this* side of the room." I handed him one of the worktable stacks. "Stuff we haven't on this side. Okay?"

"Okay," he said, and I thought a little of his color came back. He picked up the top of the stack.

I started through the recycling bin, into which somebody (very probably Flip) had dropped a half-full can of Coke. I grabbed a sticky armful of papers, sat down on the floor, and began pulling them apart. It wasn't in the first armload. I bent over the bin and grabbed a second, hoping the Coke hadn't trickled all the way to the bottom. It had.

"I knew better than to give it to Flip," Bennett said, starting on another stack, "but I was working on my chaos theory data, and she told me she was supposed to take them up to Management."

"We'll find it," I said, prying a Coke-gummed page free from the wad. Halfway through the papers I gave a yelp.

"Did you find it?" he said hopefully.

"No. Sorry." I showed him the sticky pages. "It's the marcel wave notes I was looking for. I gave them to Flip to copy."

The color went completely out of his face, freckles and all. "She threw the application away," he said.

"No, she didn't," I said, trying not to think about all those crumpled hair-bobbing clippings in my wastebasket the day I met Bennett. "It's here somewhere."

It wasn't. We finished the stacks and went through them even though it was obvious the form wasn't there.

"Could she have left it in your lab?" I said when I reached the bottom of the last stack. "Maybe she never made it out of there with it."

He shook his head. "I've already been through the whole place. Twice," he said, digging through the wastebasket. "What about your lab? She delivered that package to you. Maybe—"

I hated having to disappoint him. "I just ransacked it. Looking for these." I held up my marcel wave clippings. "It could be in somebody else's lab, though." I got up stiffly. "What about Flip? Did you ask her what she did with it? What am I thinking? This is Flip we're talking about."

He nodded. "She said, 'What funding form?' "

"All right," I said. "We need a plan of attack. You take the cafeteria, and I'll take the staff lounge."

"The cafeteria?"

"Yes, you know Flip," I said. "She probably misdelivered it. Like that package the day I met you," and I felt there was a clue there, something significant not to where his funding form might be, but to something else. The thing that had triggered hair-bobbing? No, that wasn't it. I stood there, trying to hold the feeling.

"What is it?" Bennett said. "Do you think you know where it is?"

It was gone. "No. Sorry. I was just thinking about something else. I'll meet you at the recycling bin over in Chem. Don't worry. We'll find it," I said cheerfully, but I didn't have much hope that we actually would. Knowing Flip, she could have left it anywhere. HiTek was huge. It could be in anybody's lab. Or down in Supply with Desiderata, the patron saint of lost objects. Or out in the parking lot. "Meet you at the recycling bin."

I started up to the staff lounge and then had a better idea. I went to find Shirl. She was in Alicia's lab, typing Niebnitz Grant data into the computer.

"Flip lost Dr. O'Reilly's funding form," I said without preamble.

I had somehow hoped she would say, "I know right where it is," but she didn't. She said, "Oh, dear," and looked genuinely upset. "If he leaves, that—" She stopped. "What can I do to help?"

"Look in here," I said. "Bennett's in here a lot, and anyplace you can think of where she might have put it."

"But the deadline's past, isn't it?"

"Yes," I said, angry that she was pointing out the thought I'd been trying to ignore, that Management, sticklers for deadlines that they were, would refuse to accept it even if we did find it, sticky with Coke and obviously mislaid. "I'll be up in the staff lounge," I said, and went up to look through the mailboxes.

It wasn't there, or in the stack of old memos on the staff table, or in the microwave. Or in Alicia's lab. "I looked all through it," Shirl said, sticking her head in. "What day did Dr. O'Reilly give it to Flip?"

"I don't know," I said. "It was due on Monday."

She shook her head grimly. "That's what I was afraid of. The trash comes on Tuesdays and Thursdays."

I was sorry I'd brought her into this. I went down to the recycling bin. Bennett was almost all the way inside it, his legs dangling in midair. He came up with a fistful of papers and an apple core.

I took half the papers, and we went through them. No funding form.

"All right," I said, trying to sound upbeat. "If it's not in here, it's in one of the labs. What shall we start with? Chem or Physics?"

"It's no use," Bennett said wearily. He sank back against the bin. "It's not here, and I'm not here for much longer."

"Isn't there some way to do the project without funding?" I said. "You've got the habitat and the computer and cameras and everything. Couldn't you substitute lab rats or something?"

He shook his head. "They're too independent. I need an animal with a strong herd instinct."

What about "The Pied Piper"? I thought.

"And even lab rats cost money," he said.

"What about the pound?" I said. "They've probably got cats. No, not cats. Dogs. Dogs have pack behavior, and the pound has lots of dogs."

He was looking almost as disgusted as Flip. "I thought you were an expert on fads. Haven't you ever heard of animal rights?"

"But you're not going to do anything to them. You're just going to observe them," I said, but he was right. I'd forgotten about the animal rights movement. They'd never let us use animals from the pound. "What about the other Bio projects? Maybe you could borrow some of their lab animals."

"Dr. Kelly's working with nematodes, and Dr. Riez is working with flatworms."

And Dr. Turnbull's working on ways to win the Niebnitz Grant, I thought.

"Besides," he said, "even if I had animals, I couldn't feed them. I didn't get my funding form in on time, remember? It's okay," he said at the look on my face. "This'll give me a chance to go back to chaos theory."

For which there isn't any funding, I thought, even if you do turn in the forms.

"Well," he said, standing up. "I'd better go start typing my résumé."

He looked at me seriously. "Thanks again for helping me. I mean it." He started down the hall.

"Don't give up yet," I said. "I'll think of something." This from someone who couldn't figure out what had caused the angels fad, let alone hair-bobbing.

He shook his head. "We're up against Flip here. It's bigger than both of us."

chain letters [spring 1935]

Moneymaking fad which involved sending a dime to the name at the top of a list, adding your name to the bottom, and sending five copies of the letter to friends, who, hopefully, were as gullible as you were. Caused by greed and a lack of understanding of statistics, the fad sprang up in Denver, deluging the post office with nearly a hundred thousand letters a day. It lasted three weeks in Denver, then moved on to Springfield, where dollar and five-dollar chains circulated for a frenzied two weeks before the inevitable collapse. Mutated into Circle of Gold (1978), which passed the letters in person, and various pyramid schemes.

I watched him go and then went back up to my lab. Flip was there on my computer. "How do you spell *adorable?*" she asked.

It took all my willpower not to shake her till her *i* rattled. *"What* did you do with Dr. O'Reilly's funding form?"

She tossed her assortment of hair appendages. "I *told* Desiderata you'd take it out on me for stealing your boyfriend. Which is not fair. You already have that cow guy."

"Sheep," I corrected automatically, and then gaped at her. Sheep.

"Telling an interdepartmental communications liaison who they can write letters to is ha*rass*ment," she said, but I didn't hear her. I was punching in Billy Ray's number.

"Boy, am I glad to hear your voice," Billy Ray said. "I've been thinking about you a lot lately."

"Could I borrow some sheep?" I said, not listening to him either.

"Sure," he said. "What for?"

"A learning experiment."

"How many do you need?"

"How many does it take before they act like a flock?"

"Three. When do you want them?"

He really was a very nice guy. "A couple of weeks," I said. "I'm not sure. I need to check some things out first. Like how big a flock we can have in the paddock." And I need to get Bennett to agree. And Management.

"Drawing a circle doesn't make somebody somebody's *prop*erty," Flip said.

I ran back down to Bio. Bennett wasn't typing up his résumé. He was sitting on a rock in the middle of the habitat, looking depressed.

"Ben," I said, "I have a proposition for you."

He almost smiled. "Thanks, but—"

"Listen," I said, "and don't say no till you hear the whole thing. I want us to combine our projects. No, wait, hear me out. I asked for funding for a higher-memory-capacity computer, but I could use yours. Flip's always on mine anyway. And then we could use my funding to buy the food and supplies."

"That still doesn't solve the problem of the macaques. Unless you asked for an awfully expensive computer."

"I have a friend who has a sheep ranch in Wyoming," I said.

"Yeah, I know," he said.

"He's willing to loan us as many sheep as we need, no cost, we just have to feed them." He looked like he was getting set to refuse, and I hurried on. "I know sheep don't have the social organization of macaques, but they do have a very strong following instinct. What one of them does, they all want to do. And they withstand cold, so they can be outside."

He was looking at me seriously through his thick glasses.

"I know it's not the project you wanted to do, but it would be something. It would keep you from leaving HiTek, and it'll probably only be a few months till Management comes up with a new acronym and a new funding procedure, and you can put in for your macaques again."

"I don't know anything about sheep."

"We can do all the background research while we're waiting for the paperwork to go through."

"And what do you get out of it, Sandy?" Ben said. "Sheep have their hair bobbed for them."

I couldn't very well tell him I thought his immunity to fads was part of the key to where fads came from. "A computer I can run these new diagrams I thought of on," I said. "And a different perspective. I'm not getting anywhere with my hair-bobbing project. Richard Feynman said if you're stuck on a scientific problem, you should work on something else for a while. It gives you a different angle on the problem. He took up the bongo drums. And a lot of scientists make their most significant scientific breakthroughs when they're working outside their own field. Look at Alfred Wegener, who discovered continental drift. He was a meteorologist, not a geologist. And Joseph Black, who discovered carbon dioxide, wasn't a chemist. He was a doctor. Einstein was a patent official. Working outside their fields makes scientists see connections they never would have seen before."

"Umm," Ben said. "And there definitely is a connection between sheep and people who follow fads."

"Right. Who knows? Maybe the sheep will start a fad."

"Flagpole-sitting?"

"The crossword puzzle. A three-letter word for a lab animal. *Ewe.*" I smiled at him. "And even if they don't, it'll be a positive relief to work with them. Except for Mary and her little lamb, sheep have never been a fad. So what do you think?"

He smiled sadly. "I think Management will never go for it."

"But if they did?"

"If they did, I can't think of anything I'd rather do than work with you. But they won't. And even if they did, it'll take months to fill out all the paperwork, let alone wait for it to go through."

"Then it would give us *both* a different perspective. Remember Mendeleev and the cheesemaking conference."

"How do you suggest we go about telling Management your proposition?" he said.

"You leave that part to me. You go to work on adapting the project to work with sheep. I'll go talk to an expert," I said, and went up to see Gina.

She was addressing bright pink Barbie invitations. "I still can't find a Romantic Bride Barbie anywhere. I've called five different toy stores."

I told her what had happened.

She shook her head sadly. "Too bad. I always liked him—even if he didn't have any fashion sense."

"I need your help," I said. I told her about combining the projects.

"So he gets your funding and Billy Ray's sheep," she said. "What do you get out of it?"

"A minor victory over Flip and the forces of chaos," I said. "It isn't fair for him to lose his funding just because Flip is incompetent."

She gave me a long, considering look, and then shook her head.

"Management'll never go for it. First, it's live-animal research, which is controversial. Management hates controversy. Second, it's something innovative, which means Management will hate it on principle."

"I thought one of the keystones of GRIM was innovation."

"Are you kidding? If it's new, Management doesn't have a form for it, and Management loves forms almost as much as they hate controversy. Sorry," she said. "I know you like him." She went back to addressing envelopes.

"If you'll help me, I'll find Romantic Barbie for you," I said.

She looked up from the invitations. "It has to be Romantic Bride Barbie. Not Country Bride Barbie or Wedding Fantasy Barbie."

I nodded. "Is it a deal?"

"I can't guarantee Management will go for it even if I help you," she said, shoving the invitations to the side and handing me a notepad and pencil. "All right, tell me what you were going to tell Management."

"Well, I thought I'd start by explaining what happened to the funding form—"

"Wrong," she said. "They'll know what you're up to in a minute. You tell them you've been working on this joint project thing since the meeting before last, when they said how important staff input and interaction were. Use words like *optimize* and *patterning systems.*"

"Okay," I said, taking notes.

"Tell them any number of scientific breakthroughs have been made by scientists working together. Crick and Watson, Penzias and Wilson, Gilbert and Sullivan—"

I looked up from my notes. "Gilbert and Sullivan weren't scientists."

"Management won't know that. And they might recognize the name. You'll need a two-page prospectus of the project goals. Put anything you think they'll think is a problem on the second page. They never read the second page."

"You mean an outline of the project?" I said, scribbling. "Explaining the experimental method we're going to use and describing the connection between trends analysis and information diffusion research?"

"No," she said, and turned around to her computer. "Never mind, I'll write it for you." She began typing rapidly. "You tell them integrated cross-discipline teaming projects are the latest thing at MIT. Tell them single-person projects are passé." She hit PRINT, and a sheet started scrolling through the printer.

"And pay attention to Management's body language. If he taps his forefinger on the desk, you're in trouble."

She handed me the prospectus. It looked suspiciously like her five all-purpose objectives, which meant it would probably work.

"And don't wear that." She pointed at my skirt and lab coat. "You're supposed to be dressing down."

"Thanks," I said. "Do you think this'll do it?"

"When it's live-animal research?" she said. "Are you kidding? Romantic Bride Barbie is the one with the pink net roses," she said. "Oh, and Bethany wants a brunette one."

mah-jongg (1922–24)

American game fad inspired by the ancient Chinese tiles game. As played by Americans, it was a sort of cross between rummy and dominoes involving building walls and then breaking them down, and "catching the moon from the bottom of the sea." There were enthusiastic calls of "Pung!" and "Chow!" and much clattering of ivory tiles. Players dressed up in Oriental robes (sometimes, if the players were unclear on the concept of China, these were Japanese kimonos) and served tea. Although superseded by the crossword puzzle craze and contract bridge, mah-jongg continued to be popular among Jewish matrons until the 1960s.

I had failed to include all the variables. It was true that Management values paperwork more than anything. Except for the Niebnitz Grant.

I had hardly started into my spiel in Management's white-carpeted office when Management's eyes lit up, and he said, "This would be a cross-discipline project?"

"Yes," I said. "Trends analysis combined with learning vectors in higher mammals. And there are certain aspects of chaos theory—"

"Chaos theory?" he said, tapping his forefinger on his expensive teak desk.

"Only in the sense that these are nonlinear systems which require a designed experiment," I said hastily. "The emphasis is primarily on information diffusion in higher mammals, of which human trends are a subset."

"Designed experiment?" he said eagerly.

"Yes. The practical value to HiTek would be better understanding of how information spreads through human societies and—"

"What was your original field?" he cut in.

"Statistics," I said. "The advantages of using sheep over macaques are—" and never got to finish because Management was already standing up and shaking my hand.

"This is exactly the kind of project that GRIM is all about. Interfacing scientific disciplines, implementing initiative and cooperation to create new workplace paradigms."

He actually talks in acronyms, I thought wonderingly, and almost missed what he said next.

"—exactly the kind of project the Niebnitz Grant Committee is looking for. I want this project implemented immediately. How soon can you have it up and running?"

"I—it—" I stammered. "There's some background research we'll need to do on sheep behavior. And there are the live-animal regulations that have to be—"

He waved an airy hand. "It'll be our problem to deal with that. I want you and Dr. O'Reilly to concentrate on that divergent thinking and scientific sensibility. I expect great things." He shook my hand enthusiastically. "HiTek is going to do everything we can to cut right through the red tape and get this project on line immediately."

And did.

Permissions were typed up, paperwork waived, and live-animal approvals filed for almost before I could get down to Bio and tell Bennett they'd approved the project.

"What does 'on line immediately' mean?" he said worriedly. "We haven't done any background research on sheep behavior, how they interact, what skills they're capable of learning, what they eat—"

"We'll have plenty of time," I said. "This is Management, remember?"

Wrong again. Friday Management called me on the white carpet again and told me the permissions had all been gotten, the live-animal approvals approved. "Can you have the sheep here by Monday?"

"I'll need to see if the owner can arrange it," I said, hoping Billy Ray couldn't.

He could, and did, though he didn't bring them down himself. He was attending a virtual ranching meeting in Lander. He sent instead Miguel, who had a nose ring, Aussie hat, headphones, and no intention of unloading the sheep.

"Where do you want them?" he said in a tone that made me peer under the brim of the Aussie hat to see if he had an *i* on his forehead.

We showed him the paddock gate, and he sighed heavily, backed the truck more or less up to it, and then stood against the truck's cab looking put-upon.

"Aren't you going to unload them?" Ben said finally.

"Billy Ray told me to deliver them," Miguel said. "He didn't say anything about unloading them."

"You should meet our mail clerk," I said. "You're obviously made for each other."

He tipped the Aussie hat forward warily. "Where does she live?"

Bennett had gone around to the back of the truck and was lifting the bar that held the door shut. "You don't suppose they'll all come rushing out at once and trample us, do you?" he said.

No. The thirty or so sheep stood on the edge of the truck bed, bleating and looking terrified.

"Come on," Ben said coaxingly. "Do you think it's too far for them to jump?"

"They jumped off a cliff in *Far from the Madding Crowd,"* I said. "How can it be too far?"

Nevertheless, Ben went to get a piece of plywood for a makeshift ramp, and I went to see if Dr. Riez, who had done an equine experiment before he turned to flatworms, had a halter we could borrow.

It took him forever to find a halter, and I figured by the time I got back to the lab it would no longer be needed, but the sheep were still huddled in the back of the truck.

Ben was looking frustrated, and Miguel, up by the front of the truck, was swaying to some unheard rhythm.

"They won't come," Ben said. "I've tried calling and coaxing and whistling."

I handed him the halter.

"Maybe if we can get one down the ramp," he said, "they'll all follow." He took the halter and went up the ramp. "Get out of the way in case they all make a mad dash."

He reached to slip the halter over the nearest sheep's head, and there was a mad dash, all right. To the rear of the truck.

"Maybe you could pick one up and carry it off," I said, thinking of the cover of one of the angel books. It showed a barefoot angel carrying a lost lamb. "A small one."

Ben nodded. He handed me the halter and went up the ramp, moving slowly so he wouldn't scare them. "Shh, shh," he said softly to a little ewe. "I won't hurt you. Shh, shh."

The sheep didn't move. Ben knelt and got his arms under the front and back legs and hoisted the animal up. He started for the ramp.

The angel had clearly doped the sheep with chloroform before picking it up. The ewe kicked out with four hooves in four different directions, flailing madly and bringing its muzzle hard up against Ben's chin. He staggered and the ewe twisted itself around and kicked him in the stomach. Ben dropped it with a thud, and it dived into the middle of the truck, bleating hysterically.

The rest of the sheep followed. "Are you all right?" I said.

"No," he said, testing his jaw. "What happened to 'little lamb, so meek and mild'?"

"Blake had obviously never actually met a sheep," I said, helping him down the ramp and over to the water trough. "What now?"

He leaned against the water trough, breathing heavily. "Eventually they have to get thirsty," he said, gingerly touching his chin. "I say we wait 'em out."

Miguel bopped over to us. "I haven't got all day, you know!" he shouted over whatever was blaring in his headphones, and went back to the front of the truck.

"I'll go call Billy Ray," I said, and did. His cellular phone was out of range.

"Maybe if we sneak up on them with the halter," Ben said when I got back.

We tried that. Also getting behind them and pushing, threatening Miguel, and several long spells of leaning against the water trough, breathing hard.

"Well, there's certainly information diffusion going on," Ben said, nursing his arm. "They've all decided not to get off the truck."

Alicia came over. "I've got a profile of the optimum Niebnitz Grant candidate," she said to Ben, ignoring me. "And I've found another Niebnitz. An industrialist. Who made his fortune in ore refining *and* founded several charities. I'm looking into their committee's selection criteria." She added, still to Ben, "I want you to come see the profile."

"Go ahead," I said. "You obviously won't miss anything. I'll go try Billy Ray again."

I did. He said, "What you have to do is—" and went out of range again.

I went back out to the paddock. The sheep were out of the truck, grazing on the dry grass. "What did you do?" Ben said, coming up behind me.

"Nothing," I said. "Miguel must have gotten tired of waiting," but he was still up by the front of the truck, grooving to Groupthink or whatever it was he was listening to.

I looked at the sheep. They were grazing peacefully, wandering happily around the paddock as if they'd always belonged there. Even when Miguel, still wearing his headphones, revved up the truck and drove off, they didn't panic. One of them close to the fence looked up at me with a thoughtful, intelligent gaze.

This is going to work, I thought.

The sheep stared at me for a moment longer, dropped its head to graze, and promptly got it stuck in the fence.

qiao pai [1977–95]

Chinese game fad inspired by the American card game bridge (a fad in the 1930s). Popularized by Deng Xiaoping, who learned to play in France, *qiao pai* quickly attracted over a million enthusiasts, who play mostly at work. Unlike American bridge, bidding is silent, players do not arrange their hands in order, and the game is extremely formalized. Superseded Ping-Pong.

Over the next few days it became apparent that there was almost no information diffusion in a flock of sheep. There were also hardly any fads.

"I want to watch them for a few days," Ben said. "We need to establish what their normal information diffusion patterns are."

We watched. The sheep grazed on the dry grass, took a step or two, grazed some more, walked a little farther, grazed some more. They would have looked almost like a pastoral painting if it hadn't been for their long, vacuous faces, and their wool.

I don't know who started the myth that sheep are fluffy and white. They were more the color of an old mop and just as matted with dirt.

They grazed some more. Periodically one of them would leave off chewing and totter around the perimeter of the paddock, looking for a cliff to fall off of, and then go back to grazing. Once one of them threw up. Some of them grazed along the fence. When they got to the corner they stayed there, unable to figure out how to turn it, and kept grazing, eating the grass right down to the dirt. Then, for lack of better ideas, they ate the dirt.

"Are you sure sheep are a higher mammal?" Ben asked, leaning with his chin on his hands on the fence, watching them.

"I'm so sorry," I said. "I had no idea sheep were this stupid."

"Well, actually, a simple behavior structure may work to our advantage," he said. "The problem with macaques is they're smart. Their behavior's complicated, with a lot of things going on simultaneously—dominance, familial interaction, grooming, communication, learning, attention structure. There are so many factors operating simultaneously the problem is trying to separate the information diffusion from the other behaviors. With fewer behaviors, it will be easier to see the information diffusion."

If there is any, I thought, watching the sheep.

One of them walked a step, grazed, walked two more steps, and then apparently forgot what it was doing and gazed vacantly into space.

Flip slouched by, wearing a waitress uniform with red piping on the collar and "Don's Diner" embroidered in red on the pocket, and carrying a paper.

"Did you get a job?" Ben asked hopefully.

Roll. Sigh. Toss. "No-o-o-o."

"Then why are you wearing a uniform?" I asked.

"It's *not* a uniform. It's a dress designed to *look* like a uniform. Because of how I have to do all the work around here. It's a *state*ment. You have to sign this," she said, handing me the paper and leaning over the gate. "Are these the sheep?"

The paper was a petition to ban smoking in the parking lot.

Ben said, "One person smoking one cigarette a day in a three-acre parking lot does not produce secondhand smoke in sufficient concentration to worry about."

Flip tossed her hair, her hair wraps swinging wildly. *"Not* secondhand smoke," she said disgustedly. "Air pol*lu*tion."

She slouched away, and we went back to observing. At least the lack of activity gave us plenty of time to set up our observation programs and review the literature.

There wasn't much. A biologist at William and Mary had observed a flock of five hundred and concluded that they had "a strong herd instinct," and a researcher in Indiana had identified five separate forms of sheep communication (the *baa*s were listed phonetically), but no one had done active learning experiments. They had just done what we were doing: watch them chew, totter, mill, and throw up.

We had a lot of time to talk about hair-bobbing and chaos theory.

"The amazing thing is that chaotic systems don't always stay chaotic," Ben said, leaning on the gate. "Sometimes they spontaneously reorganize themselves into an orderly structure."

"They suddenly become less chaotic?" I said, wishing that would happen at HiTek.

"No, that's the thing. They become more and more chaotic, until they reach some sort of chaotic critical mass. When that happens, they spontaneously reorganize themselves at a higher equilibrium level. It's called self-organized criticality."

We seemed well on the way to it. Management issued memos, the sheep got their heads stuck in the fence, the gate, and under the feed dispenser, and Flip came periodically to hang on the gate between the paddock and the lab, flip the latch monotonously up and down, and look lovesick.

By the third day it was obvious the sheep weren't going to start any fads. Or learn how to push a button to get feed. Ben had set up the apparatus the morning after we got the sheep and demonstrated it several times, getting down on all fours and pressing his nose against the wide flat button. Feed pellets clattered down each time, and Ben stuck his head into the trough and made chewing noises. The sheep watched impassively.

"We're going to have to force one of them to do it," I said. We'd watched the videotapes from the day they arrived and seen how they'd gotten off the truck. The sheep had jostled and backed until one was finally pushed off onto the ramp. The others had immediately tumbled after it in a rush. "If we can teach one of them, we know the others will follow it."

Ben went resignedly to get the halter. "Which one?"

"Not that one," I said, pointing at the sheep that had thrown up. I looked at them, sizing them up for alertness and intelligence. There didn't appear to be much. "That one, I guess."

Ben nodded, and we started toward it with the halter. It chewed thoughtfully a moment and then bolted into the far corner. The entire flock followed, leaping over each other in their eagerness to reach the wall.

" 'And out of the houses the rats came tumbling,' " I murmured.

"Well, at least they're all in one corner," Ben said. "I should be able to get the halter on one of them."

Nope, although he was able to grab a handful of wool and hold on nearly halfway across the paddock.

"I think you're scaring them," Flip said from the gate. She had been hanging on it half the morning, morosely flipping the latch up and down and telling us about Darrell the dentist.

"They're scaring me," Ben said, brushing off his corduroy pants, "so we're even."

"Maybe we should try coaxing them," I said. I squatted down. "Come here," I said in the childish voice people use with dogs. "Come on. I won't hurt you."

The sheep gazed at me from the corner, chewing impassively.

"What do shepherds do when they lead their flocks?" Ben asked.

I tried to remember from pictures. "I don't know. They just walk ahead of them, and the sheep follow them."

We tried that. We also tried sneaking up on both sides of a sheep and coming at the flock from the opposite side, on the off-chance they would run the other way and one of them would accidentally collide with the button.

"Maybe they don't like those feed pellet things," Flip said.

"She's right, you know," I said, and Ben stared at me in disbelief. "We need to know more about their eating habits and their abilities. I'll call Billy Ray and see what they do like."

I got Billy Ray's voice mail. "Press one if you want the ranchhouse, press two if you want the barn, press three if you want the sheep camp." Billy Ray wasn't at any of the three. He was on his way to Casper.

I went back to the lab, told Bennett and Flip I was going to the library, and drove in.

Flip's clone was at the desk, wearing a duct tape headband and an *i* brand.

"Do you have any books on sheep?" I asked her.

"How do you spell that?"

"With two *e*s." She still looked blank. *"S. H."*

"The Sheik of Araby," she read from the screen, *"Middle-Eastern Sheiks and—"*

"Sheep," I said. "With a *p."*

"Oh." She typed it in, backspacing several times. *"The Mystery of the Missing Sheep,"* she read. *"Six Silly Sheep Go Shopping, The Black Sheep Syndrome . . ."*

"Books *about* sheep," I said. "How to raise them and train them."

She rolled her eyes. "You *did*n't *say* that."

I finally managed to get a call number out of her and checked out *Sheep Raising for Fun and Profit; Tales of an Australian Shepherd;* Dorothy Sayers's *Nine Tailors,* which I seemed to remember had some sheep in it; *Sheep Management and Care;* and, remembering Billy Ray's sheep mange, *Common Sheep Diseases,* and took them up to be checked out.

"I show an overdue book for you," she said. *"Complete Words* by Robert Browning."

"Works," I said. *"Complete Works.* We went through this last time. I checked it in."

"I don't show a return," she said. "I show a fine of sixteen fifty. It shows you checked it out last March. Books can't be checked out when outstanding fines exceed five dollars."

"I checked the book in," I said, and slapped down twenty dollars.

"Plus you have to pay the replacement cost of the book," she said. "That's fifty-five ninety-five."

I know when I am licked. I wrote her a check and took the books back to Ben, and we started through them.

They were not encouraging. "In hot weather sheep will bunch together and smother to death," *Sheep Raising for Fun, Etc.* said, and "Sheep occasionally roll over on their backs and aren't able to right themselves."

"Listen to this," Ben said. " 'When frightened, sheep may run into trees or other obstacles.' "

There was nothing about skills except "Keeping sheep inside a fence is a lot easier than getting them back in," but there was a lot of information about handling them that we could have used earlier.

You were never supposed to touch a sheep on the face or scratch it behind the ears, and the Australian shepherd advised ominously, "Throwing your hat on the ground and stomping on it doesn't do anything except ruin your hat."

" 'A sheep fears being trapped more than anything else,' " I read to Ben.

"Now you tell me," he said.

And some of the advice apparently wasn't all that reliable. "Sit quietly," *Sheep Management* said, "and the sheep will get curious and come to see what you're doing."

They didn't, but the Australian shepherd had a practical method for getting a sheep to go where you wanted.

" 'Get down on one knee beside the sheep,' " I read from the book.

Ben complied.

" 'Place one hand on dock,' " I read. "That's the tail area."

"On the tail?"

"No. Slightly to the rear of the hips."

Shirl came out of the lab onto the porch, lit a cigarette, and then came over to the fence to watch us.

" 'Place the other hand under the chin,' " I read. " 'When you hold the sheep this way, he can't twist away from you, and he can't go forward or back.' "

"So far so good," Ben said.

"Now, 'Hold the chin firmly and squeeze the dock gently to make the sheep go forward.' " I lowered the book and watched. "You stop it by pushing on the hand that's under the chin."

"Okay," Ben said, getting up off his knee. "Here goes."

He gave the woolly rear of the sheep a gentle squeeze. The sheep didn't move.

Shirl took a long, coughing drag on her cigarette and shook her head.

"What are we doing wrong?" Ben said.

"That depends," she said. "What are you trying to do?"

"Well, eventually I want to teach a sheep to push a button to get feed," he said. "For now I'd settle for getting a sheep on the same side of the paddock as the feed trough."

He had been holding on to the sheep and squeezing the whole time he'd been talking, but the sheep was apparently operating on some sort of delayed mechanism. It took two docile steps forward and began to buck.

"Don't let go of the chin," I said, which was easier said than done. We both grabbed for the neck. I dropped the book and got a handful of wool. Ben got kicked in the arm. The sheep gave a mighty lunge and took off for the middle of the flock.

"They do that," Shirl said, blowing smoke. "Whenever they've been separated from the flock, they dive straight back into the middle of it. Group instinct reasserting itself. Thinking for itself is too frightening."

We both went over to the fence. "You know about sheep?" Ben said.

She nodded, puffing on her cigarette. "I know they're the orneriest, stubbornest, dumbest critters on the planet."

"We already figured that out," Ben said.

"How do you know about sheep?" I asked.

"I was raised on a sheep ranch in Montana."

Ben gave a sigh of relief, and I said, "Can you tell us what to do? We can't get these sheep to do anything."

She took a long drag on her cigarette. "You need a bellwether," she said.

"A bellwether?" Ben said. "What's that? A special kind of halter?"

She shook her head. "A leader."

"Like a sheepdog?" I said.

"No. A dog can harry and guide and keep the sheep in line, but it can't make them follow. A bellwether's a sheep."

"A special breed?" Ben asked.

"Nope. Same breed. Same sheep, only it's got something that makes the rest of the flock follow it. Usually it's an old ewe, and some people think it's something to do with hormones; other people think it's something in their looks. A teacher of mine said they're born with some kind of leadership ability."

"Attention structure," Ben said. "Dominant male monkeys have it."

"What do *you* think?" I said.

"Me?" she said, looking at the smoke from her cigarette twisting upward. "I think a bellwether's the same as any other sheep, only more so. A little hungrier, a little faster, a little greedier. It wants to get to the feed first, to shelter, to a mate, so it's always out there in front." She stopped to take a drag on her cigarette. "Not a lot. If it was a long way in front, the flock'd have to strike out on their own to follow, and that'd mean thinking for themselves. Just a little bit, so they don't even know they're being led. And the bellwether doesn't know it's leading."

She dropped her cigarette in the grass and stubbed it out. "If you teach a bellwether to push a button, the rest of the flock'll do it, too."

"Where can we get one?" Ben said eagerly.

"Where'd you get your sheep?" Shirl said. "The flock probably had one, and you just didn't get it in this batch. These weren't the whole flock, were they?"

"No," I said. "Billy Ray has two hundred head."

She nodded. "A flock that big almost always has a bellwether."

I looked at Ben. "I'll call Billy Ray," I said.

"Good idea," he said, but he seemed to have lost his enthusiasm.

"What's the matter?" I said. "Don't you think a bellwether's a good idea? Are you afraid it'll interfere with your experiment?"

"What experiment? No, no, it's a good idea. Attention structure and its effect on learning rate is one of the variables I wanted to study. Go ahead and call him."

"Okay," I said, and went into the lab. As I opened the door, the hall door slammed shut. I walked through the habitat and looked down the hall.

Flip, wearing overalls and Cerenkhov-blue-and-white saddle oxfords, was just disappearing into the stairwell. She must have been bringing us the mail. I was surprised she hadn't come out into the paddock and asked us if we thought she was captivating.

I went back in the lab. She'd left the mail on Ben's desk. Two packages for Dr. Ravenwood over in Physics, and a letter from Gina to Bell Laboratories.

flower child weddings (1968–75)

Rebellion fad made popular by people who didn't want to totally rebel against tradition and not get married at all. Performed in a meadow or on a mountaintop, the ceremony featured, "Feelings," played on a sitar and vows written by the participants with assistance from Kahlil Gibran. The bride generally wore flowers in her hair and no shoes. The groom wore a peace symbol and sideburns. Supplanted in the seventies by living together and lack of commitment.

Billy Ray brought the bellwether down himself. "I put it down in the paddock," he said when he came into the stats lab. "The gal down there said to just put it in with the rest of the flock."

He must mean Alicia. She'd spent all afternoon huddled with Ben, discussing the Niebnitz profile, which was why I'd come up to the stats lab to feed in twenties data. I wondered why Ben wasn't there.

"Pretty?" I said. "Corporate type? Wears a lot of pink?"

"The bellwether?" he said.

"No, the person you talked to. Dark hair? Clipboard?"

"Nope," he said. "Tattoo on her forehead."

"Brand," I said absently. "Maybe we'd better go check on the bellwether."

"She'll be fine," he said. "I brought her down myself so I could take you to that dinner we missed out on last week."

"Oh, good," I said. This would give me a chance to get some ideas of low-threshold skills we could teach the sheep. "I'll get my coat."

"Great," he said, beaming. "There's this great new place I want to take you to."

"Prairie?" I said.

"No, it's a Siberian restaurant. Siberian is supposed to be the hot new cuisine."

I hoped he meant *hot* in the sense of *warm.* It was freezing outside in the parking lot, and there was a bitter wind. I was glad Shirl didn't have to stand out there to have a cigarette.

Billy Ray led me to his truck and helped me in. As he started to pull out of the parking lot, I put my hand on his arm. "Wait," I said, remembering what Flip had done to my clippings. "Maybe we should check to make sure the bellwether's all right before we leave. What did she say exactly? The girl who was down there in the lab. She wasn't out in the paddock, was she?"

"Nope," he said. "I was looking for somebody to give the bellwether to, and she came in with some letters and said they were in Dr. Turnbull's lab and to just leave the bellwether in the paddock, so I did. She's fine. Got right off the truck and started grazing."

Which must mean she was really a bellwether. Things were looking up.

"She wasn't still there when you left, was she?" I said. "The girl, not the bellwether."

"Nope. She asked me whether I thought she had a good sense of humor, and when I said I didn't know, I hadn't heard her say anything funny, she kind of sighed and rolled her eyes and left."

"Good," I said. It was five-thirty already. Flip wouldn't have stayed a minute past five, and she usually left early, so the chances she would have come back to the lab to work mischief were practically nonexistent. And Ben was still there; he'd come back from Alicia's lab to check on things before he went home. If he wasn't too enamored of Alicia and the Niebnitz Grant to remember he had a flock of sheep.

"This place is great," Billy Ray said. "We'll have to stand in line an hour to get in."

"Sounds great," I said. "Let's go."

It was actually an hour and twenty minutes, and during the last half hour the wind picked up and it started to snow. Billy Ray gave me his sheepskin-lined jacket to put over my shoulders. He was wearing a band-collared shirt and cavalry pants. He'd let his hair grow out, and he had on yellow leather riding gloves. The Brad Pitt look. When I kept shivering, he let me wear the gloves, too.

"You'll love this place," he said. "Siberian food is supposed to be great. I'm really glad we were able to get together. There's something I've been wanting to talk to you about."

"I wanted to talk to you, too," I said through stiff lips. "What kinds of tricks can you teach sheep?"

"Tricks?" he said blankly. "Like what?"

"You know, like learning to associate a color with a treat or running a maze. Preferably something with a low ability threshold and a number of skill levels."

"Teach sheep?" he repeated. There was a long pause while the wind howled around us. "They're pretty good at getting out of fences they're supposed to stay inside of."

That wasn't exactly what I had in mind.

"I'll tell you what," he said. "I'll get on the Internet and see if anybody on there's ever taught a sheep a trick." He took off his hat, in spite of the snow, and turned it between his hands. "I told you I had something I wanted to talk to you about. I've had a lot of time to think lately, driving to Durango and everything, and I've been thinking a lot about the ranching life. It's a lonely life, out there on the range all the time, never seeing anybody, never going anywhere."

Except to Lodge Grass and Lander and Durango, I thought.

"And lately I've been wondering if it's all worth it and what am I doing it for. And I've been thinking about you."

"Barbara Rose," the Siberian waiter said.

"That's us," I said. I gave Billy Ray his coat and gloves back, and he put his hat on, and we followed the waiter to our table. It had a samovar in the middle of it, and I warmed my hands over it.

"I think I told you the other day I was feeling at loose ends and kind of dissatisfied," he said after we had our menus.

"Itch," I said.

"That's a good word for it. I've been itchy, all right, and while I was driving back from Lodgepole I finally figured out what I was itching for." He took my hand.

"What?" I said.

"You."

I yanked my hand back involuntarily, and he said, "Now, I know this is kind of a surprise to you. It was a surprise to me. I was driving through the Rockies, feeling out of sorts and like nothing mattered, and I thought, I'll call Sandy, and after I got done talking to you, I got to thinking, Maybe we should get married."

"Married?" I squeaked.

"Now I want to say right up front that whatever your answer is, you can have the sheep for as long as you want. No strings attached. And I know you've got a career that you don't want to give up. I've got that figured out. We wouldn't have to get married till after you've got this hair-bobbing thing done, and then we could set you up on the ranch with faxes and a modem and e-mail. You'd never even know you weren't right there at HiTek."

Except Flip wouldn't be there, I thought irrelevantly, or Alicia. And I wouldn't have to go to meetings and do sensitivity exercises. But married!

"Now, you don't have to give me your answer right away," Billy Ray went on. "Take all the time you want. I've had a couple of thousand miles to think about it. You can let me know after we have dessert. Till then, I'll leave you alone."

He picked up a red menu with a large Russian bear on it and began reading through it, and I sat and stared at him, trying to take this in. Married. He wanted me to marry him.

And, well, why not? He was a nice guy who was willing to drive hundreds of miles to see me, and I was, as I had told Alicia, thirty-one, and where was I going to meet anybody else? In the personals, with their athletic, caring NSs who weren't even willing to walk across the street to date somebody?

Billy Ray had been willing to drive all the way down from someplace on the off chance of taking me to dinner. And he'd loaned me a flock of sheep *and* a bellwether. And his gloves. Where was I going to meet anybody that nice? Nobody at HiTek was going to propose to me, that was for sure.

"What do you want?" Billy Ray asked me. "I think I'm going to have the potato dumplings."

I had borscht flavored with basil (which I hadn't remembered as being big in Siberian cuisine) and potato dumplings and tried to think. What did I want?

To find out where hair-bobbing came from, I thought, and knew that was about as likely as winning the Niebnitz Grant. In spite of Feynman's theory that working in a totally different field sparked scientific discovery, I was no closer to finding the source of fads than before. Maybe what I needed was to get away from HiTek altogether, out in the fresh air, on an isolated Wyoming ranch.

"Far from the madding crowd," I murmured.

"What?" Billy Ray said.

"Nothing," I said, and he went back to his dinner.

I watched him eat his dumplings. He really did look a little like Brad Pitt. He was awfully trendy, but maybe that would be an advantage for my project, and we wouldn't have to get married right away. He'd said I could wait until after I finished the project. And, unlike Flip's dentist, he wouldn't mind my being geographically incompatible while I worked on it.

Flip and her dentist, I thought, wondering uneasily if this was just another fad. That article had said marriage was in, and all the little girls were crazy for Romantic Bride Barbie. Lindsay's mother was thinking of getting married again in spite of that jerk Matt, Sarah was trying to talk Ted into proposing, and Bennett was letting Alicia pick out his ties. What if they were all part of a commitment fad?

I was being unfair to Billy Ray. He was in love with what was trendy, he might even stand in line in a blizzard for an hour and a half, but he wouldn't *marry* someone because marriage was in. And what if it was a trend? Fads aren't all bad. Look at recycling and the civil rights movement. And the waltz. And, anyway, what was wrong with going along with a trend once in a while?

"Time for dessert," Billy Ray said, looking at me from under the brim of his hat.

He motioned the waitress over, and she rattled off the usual suspects: crème brûlée, tiramisu, bread pudding.

"No chocolate cheesecake?" I said.

She rolled her eyes.

"What do you want?" Billy Ray said.

"Give me a minute," I said, breathing hard. "You go ahead."

Billy Ray smiled at the waitress. "I'll have the bread pudding," he said.

"Bread pudding?" I said.

The waitress said helpfully, "It's our most popular dessert."

"I thought you didn't like bread pudding," I said.

He looked up blankly. "When did I say that?"

"At that prairie cuisine place you took me to. The Kansas Rose. You had the tiramisu."

"Nobody eats tiramisu anymore," he said. "I love bread pudding."

virtual pets (fall 1994–spring 1996)

Japanese computer game fad featuring a programmed pet. The puppy or kitten grows when fed and played with, learns tricks (the dogs, presumably, not the cats), and runs away if neglected. Caused by the Japanese love of animals and an overpopulation problem that makes having pets impractical.

Ben met me in the parking lot the next morning. "Where's the bellwether?" he said.

"Isn't it in with the other sheep?" I scrambled out of the car. I *knew* I shouldn't have trusted Flip. "Billy Ray said he put it in the paddock."

"Well, if it's there, it looks just like all the other sheep."

He was right. It did. We did a quick count, and there was one more than usual, but which one was the bellwether was anybody's guess.

"What did it look like when your friend put it in the paddock?"

"I wasn't down here," I said, looking at the sheep, trying to detect one that looked different. "I knew I should have come down to check on it, but we were going out to dinner and—"

"Yeah," he said, cutting me off. "We'd better find Shirl."

Shirl was nowhere to be found. I looked in the copy room and in Supply, where Desiderata was examining her split ends, which were lying on the counter in front of her.

"What happened to you, Desiderata?" I said, looking at her hacked-off hair.

"I couldn't get the duct tape off," she said forlornly, holding up one of the still-wrapped hair strands. "It was worse than the rubber cement that time."

I winced. "Have you seen Shirl?"

"She's probably off smoking somewhere," she said disapprovingly. "Do you *know* how *bad* second-secondhand smoke is for you?"

"Almost as bad as duct tape," I said, and went down to Alicia's lab in case Shirl was feeding in stats for her.

She wasn't, but Alicia, wearing a po-mo pink silk blouse and palazzo pants, was. *"None* of the Niebnitz Grant winners was a smoker," she said when I asked her if she'd seen Shirl.

I thought about explaining that, given the percentage of nonsmokers in the general population and the tiny number of Niebnitz Grant recipients, the likelihood of their being nonsmokers (or anything else) was statistically insignificant, but the bellwether was still unidentified.

"Do you know where Shirl might be?" I said.

"I sent her up to Management with a report," she said.

But she wasn't there either. I went back down to the lab. Bennett hadn't found her either. "We're on our own," he said.

"Okay," I said. "It's a bellwether, so it's a leader. So we put out some hay and see what happens."

We did.

Nothing happened. The sheep near Ben scattered when he forked the hay in and then went on grazing. One of them wandered over to the water trough and got its head stuck between it and the wall and stood there bleating.

"Maybe he brought the wrong sheep," Ben said.

"Do you have the videotapes from last night?" I said.

"Yeah," he said and brightened. "Your friend's bringing the bellwether will be on it."

It was. Billy Ray let down the back of the truck, and the bellwether trotted meekly down the ramp and into the midst of the flock, and it was a simple matter of following its progress frame by frame right up to the present moment.

Or it would have been, if Flip hadn't gotten in the way. She completely blocked the view of the flock for at least ten minutes, and when she finally moved off to the side, the flock was in a completely different configuration.

"She wanted to know if Billy Ray thought she had a sense of humor," I said.

"Of course," Ben said. "What now?"

"Back it up," I said. "And freeze-frame it just before the bellwether gets off the truck. Maybe it's got some distinguishing characteristics."

He rewound, and we stared at the frame. The bellwether looked exactly the same as the other ewes. If she had any distinguishing characteristics, they were visible only to sheep.

"It looks a little cross-eyed," Ben said finally, pointing at the screen. "See?"

We spent the next half hour working our way through the flock, taking ewes by the chin and looking into their eyes. They were all a little cross-eyed and so vacant-looking they should have had an *i* stamped on their long, dirty-white foreheads for *impenetrable.*

"There's got to be a better way to do this," I said after a deceptively scrawny ewe had mashed me against the fence and nearly broken both my legs. "Let's try the videotapes again."

"Last night's?"

"No, this morning's. And keep a tape running. I'll be right back."

I ran up to the stats lab, keeping an eye out for Shirl on the way, but there was no sign of her. I grabbed the disk my vector programs were on and then started rummaging through my fad collection.

It had occurred to me on the way upstairs that if we did manage to identify the bellwether, we needed something to mark it with. I pulled out the length of po-mo pink ribbon I'd bought in Boulder and ran back down to the lab.

The sheep were gathered around the hay, chewing steadily on it with their large square teeth. "Did you see who led them to it?" I asked Ben.

He shook his head. "They all just seemed to gravitate toward it at once. Look." He switched on the videotape and showed me.

He was right. On the monitor, the sheep wandered aimlessly through the paddock, stopping to graze with every other step, paying no attention to each other or the hay, until, apparently by accident, they were all standing with their forefeet in the hay, taking casual mouthfuls.

"Okay," I said, sitting down at the computer. "Hook the tape in, and I'll see if I can isolate the bellwether. You're still taping?"

He nodded. "Continuous and backup."

"Good," I said. I rewound to ten frames before Ben had forked out the hay, froze the frame, and made a diagram of it, assigning a different colored point to each of the sheep, and did the same thing for the next twenty frames to establish a vector. Then I started experimenting to see how many frames I could skip without losing track of which sheep was which.

Forty. They grazed for a little over two minutes and then took an average of three steps before they stopped and ate some more. I started through at forty, lost track of three sheep within two tries, cut back to thirty, and worked my way forward.

When I had ten points for every sheep, I fed in an analysis program to calculate proximities and mean direction, and continued plotting vectors.

On the screen the movement was still random, determined by length of grass or wind direction or whatever it was in their tiny little thought processes that makes sheep move one way or the other.

There was one vector headed toward the hay, and I isolated it and traced it through the next hundred frames, but it was only a matted ewe determined to wedge itself into a corner. I went back to tracing all the vectors.

Still nothing on the screen, but in the numbers above it, a pattern started to emerge. Cerulean blue. I followed it forward, unconvinced. The sheep looked like she was grazing in a rough circle, but the proximities showed her moving erratically but steadily toward the hay.

I isolated her vector and watched her on the videotape. She looked completely ordinary and totally unaware of the hay. She walked a couple of steps, grazed, walked another step, turning slightly, grazed again, ending up always a little closer to the hay, and from halfway through the frames, the regression showed the rest of the flock following her.

I wanted to be sure. "Ben," I said. "Cover up the water trough and put a pan of water in the back gate. Wait, let me hook this up to the tape so I can trace it as it happens. Okay," I said after a minute. "Walk along the side so you don't block the camera."

I watched on the monitor as he maneuvered a sheet of plywood onto the trough, carried a pan out, and filled it with the hose, watching the sheep sharply to see if any of them noticed.

They didn't.

They stayed right by the hay. There was a brief flutter of activity as Ben carried the hose back and lifted the latch on the gate, and then the sheep went back to business as usual.

I tracked cerulean blue in real time, watching the numbers. "I've got her," I said to Bennett.

He came and looked over my shoulder. "Are you sure? She doesn't look too bright."

"If she was, the others wouldn't follow her," I said.

"I looked for you up*stairs,*" Flip said, "but you weren't there."

"We're busy, Flip," I said without taking my eyes off the screen.

"I'll get the slip halter and a collar," Ben said. "You direct me."

"It'll just take a *minute,*" Flip said. "I want you to look at something."

"It'll have to wait," I said, my eyes still fixed on the screen. After a minute, Ben appeared in the picture, holding the collar and halter.

"Which one?" he shouted.

"Go left," I shouted back. "Three, no four sheep. Okay. Now toward the west wall."

"This is about Darrell, isn't it?" Flip said. "He was in a news*pa*per. Anybody who read it had a right to answer it."

"Left one more," I shouted. "No, not that one. The one in front of it. Okay, now, don't scare it. Put your hand on its hindquarters."

"Besides," Flip said, "it said 'sophisticated and elegant.' Scientists aren't *el*egant, except Dr. Turnbull."

"Careful," I shouted. "Don't spook it." I started out to help him.

Flip blocked my way. "All I want is for you to look at something. It'll only take a minute."

"Hurry," Ben called. "I can't hold her."

"I don't have a minute," I said and brushed past Flip, praying that Ben hadn't lost the bellwether. He still had her, but just barely. He was hanging on to her tail with both hands, and was still holding the halter and the collar. There was no way he could let go to give them to me. I pulled the ribbon out of my pocket, wrapped it around the bellwether's straining neck, and tied it in a knot. "Okay," I said, spreading my feet apart, "you can let go."

The rebound nearly knocked me down, and the bellwether immediately began pulling away from me and the not-nearly-strong-enough ribbon, but Ben was already slipping the halter on.

He handed it to me to hold and got the collar on, just as the ribbon gave way with a loud rip. He grabbed on to the halter, and we both held on like two kids flying a wayward kite. "The . . . collar's . . . on," he said, panting.

But you couldn't see it. It was completely swallowed up in the bellwether's thick wool. "Hold her a minute," I said, and looped what was left of the ribbon under the collar. "Hold still," I said, tying it in a big, floppy bow. "Po-mo pink is *the* color for fall." I adjusted the ends. "There, you're the height of fashion."

Apparently she agreed. She stopped struggling and stood still. Ben knelt beside me and took the halter off. "We make a great team," he said, grinning at me.

"We do," I said.

"Well," Flip said from the gate. She clicked the latch up and down. "Do you have a minute *now?*"

Ben rolled his eyes.

"Yes," I said, laughing. I stood up. "I have a minute. What is it you wanted me to look at?"

But it was obvious, now that I looked at her. She had dyed her hair—hank, hair wraps, even the fuzz of her shaved skull—a brilliant, bilious Cerenkhov blue.

"Well?" Flip said. "Do you think he'll like it?"

"I don't know, Flip," I said. "Dentists tend to be kind of conservative."

"I *know,"* she said, rolling her eyes. "That's why I dyed it *blue.* Blue's a con*ser*vative color." She tossed her blue hank. *"You're* no help," she said, and stomped out.

I turned back to Ben and the bellwether, who was still standing perfectly still. "What next?"

Ben squatted next to the bellwether and took her chin in his hand. "We're going to teach you low-threshold skills," he said, "and you're going to teach your friends. Got it?"

The bellwether chewed thoughtfully.

"What would you suggest, Dr. Foster? Scrabble, Ping-Pong?" He turned back to the bellwether. "How'd you like to start a chain letter?"

"I think we'd better stick to pushing a button to open a feed trough," I said. "As you say, she doesn't look too bright."

He turned her head to one side and then the other, frowning. "She looks like Flip." He grinned at me. "All right, Trivial Pursuit it is. But first, I've got to go get some peanut butter. *Sheep Management and Care* says sheep love peanut butter," and left.

I tied a double knot in the bellwether's bow and then leaned on the gate and watched them. Their movements looked as random and directionless as ever. They grazed and took a step and grazed again, and so did she, indistinguishable from the rest of them except for her pallid pink bow, unnoticed and unnoticing. And leading.

She tore a piece of grass, chewed on it, took two steps, and stared blankly into space for a long minute, thinking about what? Having her nose pierced? The hot new exercise fad for fall?

"Here you are," Shirl said, carrying a stack of papers and looking irate. "You're not engaged to that Billy Ray person, are you? Because if you are, that changes my entire—" She stopped. "Well, are you?"

"No," I said. "Who told you I was?"

"Flip," she said disgustedly. She set down the papers and lit a cigarette. "She told Sarah you were getting married and moving to Nevada."

"Wyoming," I said, "but I'm not."

"Good," Shirl said, taking an emphatic drag on the cigarette. "You're a very talented scientist with a very bright future. With your

ability, good things are going to happen to you very shortly, and you have no business throwing it all away."

"I'm not," I said, and made an effort to change the subject. "Did you want to see me about something?"

"Yes," she said, gesturing toward the paddock. "When the bellwether gets here, be sure you mark it before you put it in with the other sheep so you can tell which one it is. And there's an all-staff meeting tomorrow." She picked up the memos and handed one to me. "Two o'clock."

"Not *another* meeting," I said.

She stubbed out her cigarette and left, and I went back to leaning on the fence, watching the sheep. They were grazing peacefully, the bellwether in the middle of them, indistinguishable except for her pink bow.

I should move the feeding trough out to the paddock and check the circuits, so it'd be ready when Ben got back, I thought, but I went back in to the computer, traced vectors for a while, and then sat and looked at the screen, watching them move, watching the bellwether move among them, and thinking about Robert Browning and bobbed hair.

mood rings [1975]

Jewelry fad consisting of a ring set with a large "stone" that was actually a temperature-sensitive liquid crystal. Mood rings supposedly reflected the wearer's mood and revealed his or her thoughts. Blue meant tranquillity; red meant crabbiness; black meant depression and doom. Since the ring actually responded to temperature, and after a while not even that, no one achieved the ideal "bliss" purple without a high fever, and everyone eventually sank into gloom and despair as their rings went permanently black. Superseded by Pet Rocks, which didn't respond to anything.

The bellwether could definitely make the flock do what she wanted. Getting the bellwether to do what we wanted her to do was another matter. She watched as we smeared peanut butter on the button she was supposed to push and then led the entire flock into a smothering jam-up in the back corner.

We tried again. Ben coaxed her with a rotten apple, which *Sheep Raising for Fun and Profit* had sworn they liked, and she trotted after him over to the trough. "Good girl," he said, and bent over to give her the apple, and she butted him smartly in the stomach and knocked the wind out of him.

We tried decayed lettuce next and then fresh broccoli, neither of which produced any results—"At least it didn't butt you," I said—and then gave up for the night.

When I got to work the next morning with a bag full of cabbage and kiwi fruit *(Tales of an Australian Shepherd)*, Ben was smearing molasses on the button.

"Well, there's definitely been information diffusion," he said. "Three other sheep have already butted me this morning."

We led the bellwether over to the trough using the chin-rump-halter method and a squirt gun, which *Sheep Management and Care* had suggested. "It's supposed to keep them from butting."

It didn't.

I helped him up. "*Tales of an Australian Shepherd* said only the rams butt, not the ewes." I dusted him off. "It's enough to make you lose faith in literature."

"No," he said, holding his stomach. "The poet had it right. 'The sheep is a perilous beast.' "

On the fifth try we got her to lick the molasses. Pellets obligingly chattered into the trough. The bellwether gazed interestedly at it for a long minute, during which Ben looked at me and crossed his fingers, and then she bucked, catching me smartly on both ankles and making me let go of the halter. She dived headlong into the flock, scattering it wildly. One of the ewes ran straight into Ben's leg.

"Look on the bright side," I said, nursing my ankles. "There's an all-staff meeting at two o'clock."

Ben limped over and retrieved the halter, which had come off. "They're supposed to like peanuts."

The bellwether didn't like peanuts, or celery or hat-stomping. She did, however, like bolting and backing and trying to shake her collar off. At a quarter to one Ben looked at his watch and said, "Almost time for the meeting," and I didn't even contradict him.

I limped to the stats lab, washed off what lanolin and dirt I could and went up to the meeting, hoping Management would think I was making a sterling effort to dress down.

Sarah met me at the door of the cafeteria. "Isn't it exciting?" she said, sticking her left hand in my face. "Ted asked me to *marry* him!"

Commitment-Aversion Ted? I thought. The one who had severe intimacy issues and a naughty inner child?

"We went ice-climbing, and he hammered his piton in and said, 'Here, I know you've been wanting this,' and handed a ring to me. I didn't even make him. It was *so* romantic!

"Gina, look!" she said, charging toward her next victim. "Isn't it exciting?"

I went on into the cafeteria. Management was standing at the front of the room next to Flip. He was wearing jeans with a crease in them. She was wearing Cerenkhov blue toreador pants and a slouch hat that was pulled down over her ears. They were both wearing T-shirts with the letters SHAM across the front.

"Oh, no," I murmured, wondering what this would mean to our project, "not another acronym."

"Systemized Hierarchial Advancement Management," Ben said, sliding into the chair next to me. "It's the management style nine percent of the companies whose scientists won the Niebnitz Grant were using."

"Which translates to how many?"

"One. And they'd only been using it three days."

"Does this mean we'll have to reapply for funding for our project?"

He shook his head. "I asked Shirl. They don't have the new funding forms printed yet."

"We've got a lot on the agenda today," Management boomed, "so let's get started. First, there've been some problems with Supply, and to rectify that we've instituted a new streamlined procurement form. The workplace message facilitation director"—he nodded at Flip, who was holding a massive stack of binders—"will pass those out."

"The workplace message facilitation director?" I muttered.

"Just be glad they didn't make her a vice president."

"Secondly," Management said, "I've got some excellent news to share with you regarding the Niebnitz Grant. Dr. Alicia Turnbull has been working with us on a game plan that we're going to implement today. But first I want all of you to choose a partner—"

Ben grabbed my hand.

"—and stand facing each other."

We stood and I put my hands up, palms facing out. "If we have to say three things we like about sheep, I'm quitting."

"All right, HiTekkers," Management said, "now I want you to give your partners a big hug."

"The next big trend at HiTek will be sexual harassment," I said lightly, and Ben took me in his arms.

"Come on, now," Management said. "Not everybody's participating. *Big* hug."

Ben's arms in the faded plaid sleeves pulled me close, enfolded me. My hands, caught up in that palms-out silliness, went around his neck. My heart began to pound.

"A hug says, 'Thank you for working with me,' " Management said. "A hug says, 'I appreciate your personness.' "

My cheek was against Ben's ear. He smelled faintly of sheep. I could feel *his* heart pounding, the warmth of his breath on my neck. My breath caught, like a hiccuping engine, and stalled.

"All right now, HiTekkers," Management said. "I want you to look at your partner—still hugging, don't let go—and tell him or her how much he or she means to you."

Ben raised his head, his mouth grazing my hair, and looked at me. His gray eyes, behind his thick glasses, were serious.

"I—" I said, and jerked out of his embrace.

"Where are you going?" Ben said.

"I have to—I just thought of something that ties into my hair-bobbing theory," I said desperately. "I've got to put it on the computer before I forget. About marathon dancing."

"Wait," he said, and grabbed my hand. "I thought marathon dancing wasn't until the thirties."

"It started in 1927," I said, and wrenched out of his grasp.

"But wasn't that still after the hair-bobbing craze?" he said, but I was already out the door and halfway up the stairs.

hair wreaths (1870–90)

Ghoulish Victorian handicraft fad in which the hair of a deceased loved one (or assortment of loved ones, preferably with different-colored hair) was made into flowers. The hair (obtained somehow or other) was braided and woven into bouquets and wreaths, and placed under a glass dome, or framed and hung on the wall. Supplanted by the suffrage movement, croquet, and Elinor Glyn. The hair wreath fad may have been a contributing factor in the hair-bobbing fad of the 1920s.

Significant breakthroughs have been triggered by all sorts of things—apples, frog legs, photographic plates, finches—but mine must be the only one ever triggered by one of Management's idiotic sensitivity exercises.

I didn't stop till I was inside the stats lab. I hugged my arms to my chest and leaned against the door, panting and murmuring, over and over again, "Stupid, stupid, stupid."

I was supposed to be such an expert at spotting trends, but it had taken me weeks to see where this one was leading. And all that time I'd thought it was his immunity to fads I was interested in. I'd taken notes on his cloth sneakers and ties. I'd even seriously considered Billy Ray's proposal. And all that time—

There was somebody coming down the hall. I hastily sat down in front of the computer, pulled up a program, and sat there, staring blindly at it.

"Busy?" Gina said, coming in.

"Yes," I said.

"Oh," and her expression plainly said, "You don't look busy." "I couldn't find you after the meeting. I took a bathroom break right before they started the sensitivity exercise, and when I got back, you were gone. I just wanted to bring you the list of toy stores I've already tried so you don't waste your time on them."

"Right," I said. "I'll go this weekend."

"Oh, no hurry. Bethany's birthday isn't for another two weeks, but it makes me kind of nervous that Toys "Я" Us was out of it. That's where Chelsea's mother found the one for Brittany, and she said it was the only place she could find one." She frowned. "Are you okay? You look like somebody who got sent to her room for a time-out."

A time-out. You'll just have to sit here quietly until you can get control of your feelings, young lady.

"I'm fine," I said. "I should have listened to your advice and taken a bathroom break, that's all."

She nodded. "Those sensitivity exercises'll do you in. Well, I'll let you get back to work. Or whatever." She patted me on the shoulder.

"And I'll deliver Romantic Bride Barbie. You don't have to worry. I'll find it," I said, and started sorting blindly through a stack of clippings.

As soon as she was gone I shut the door, and then went back and sat down at the computer and stared at the screen.

The file I'd called up was my hair-bobbing model. It sat there, with its crisscrossing colored lines and that anomalous cluster in Marydale, Ohio, like a reproach.

How could I hope to understand what had motivated women to cut their hair seventy years ago when I didn't even understand what motivated me?

I hadn't even had a clue. Until Ben put his arms around me and pulled me close, I'd honestly thought I was trying to salvage his project because I couldn't stand Flip. I'd even thought the reason I was irritated with Alicia was because she was trying to produce science-on-demand. And all the time—

I heard a noise in the hall and put my hands on the keyboard. I needed to look busy so no one else would come talk to me.

I stared at the model, with its intersecting patterns, its crisscrossing curves, every event impacting on every other, iterating and reiterating and leading inevitably to an outcome.

Like my downfall. And maybe what I should be doing was drawing that, graphing the events and interactions that had led me to this pass. I called up the paintbox and an empty file and started trying to reconstruct the whole debacle.

I had borrowed Billy Ray's sheep. No, it had started before that, with Management and GRIM. Management had ordered a new funding form, and Ben's had gotten lost, and I had suggested we work together. And Management had said yes because they wanted one of HiTek's scientists to win the Niebnitz Grant.

I started drawing in the connecting lines, from Management's meetings to the funding forms to Shirl, the new assistant, who had brought me extra copies of the missing pages, which I'd taken down to Ben, to Alicia, who wanted to collaborate with Bennett to win the Niebnitz Grant. And back to Management and GRIM. And Flip.

"You left the meeting *early,*" Flip said reprovingly, opening the door. She still had on the pulled-down hat, but she'd abandoned the SHAM T-shirt and was wearing a see-through dress over a bodysuit that appeared to be made of Cerenkhov blue duct tape.

"You didn't get your streamlined supply procurement processing form," she said, and handed me a binder. "And I *want*ed to ask you a question."

"I'm busy, Flip," I said.

"It'll *on*ly take a *min*ute," she said. "I know you're still mad about my answering the personal ad, but you're the only one I can ask. Desiderata and Shirl are both really nevved at me."

I *wonder* why, I thought. "I am really busy, Flip."

"It'll only take a *min*ute." She pulled a stool over next to the computer and perched on it. "How far should somebody go when they're really unbalanced about somebody?"

This was just what I needed, to discuss the sex life of a person with a pierced nose and duct tape underwear.

"I mean, if you thought you'd never see him again, do you think it's stupid to do something really swarb?"

I had talked Ben into combining our projects. I had borrowed a flock of sheep. Stupid, stupid, stupid.

"It's about my hair," she said, and pulled off her hat. "I cut it off."

She certainly had. Her hair was chopped to within an inch of her blue scalp. For a second I thought she'd had the same problem with the duct tape as Desiderata, but her flipping hank had been hacked off, too. She looked like a very cold plucked chicken.

I felt a sudden pang of empathy for her, in love with a dentist, of all people, who didn't know she existed, who was probably already engaged.

"So what I wondered," she said, "was whether it looks okay like this or whether I should add another brand." She pointed to her right temple, just below the scalped area.

"Of what?" I said faintly.

She sighed. "Of a strip of duct tape, of course."

Of course.

"I think it depends on how you're going to let your hair grow out," I said, hoping she was going to.

Apparently she was, because she put her hat back on again and said, "So you don't, then? Think it would be stupid?"

She apparently didn't expect an answer because she was already halfway out the door.

"Flip," I said, "would you do me a favor? Would you go down to Bio and tell Dr. O'Reilly I'm leaving early, and I'll talk to him tomorrow?"

"Bio is clear on the other side of the building," she said, outraged. "Anyway, I doubt if he's down there. When I left the meeting, he was talking to Dr. Turnbull. *Like* always. I bet he wishes he'd had her for a partner for that hug thing."

"I'm really busy, Flip," I said, and started typing to prove it. Flip. This was all Flip's fault. She had lost Bennett's funding forms *and* stolen my personal ads, which is why I'd been in the copy room when Bennett came in.

"Did you know Dr. Patton got engaged?" Flip said conversationally. "To that guy who didn't want to get married?"

"Yes," I said.

"I'll bet Dr. O'Reilly and Dr. Turnbull get married pretty soon."

I continued to type doggedly, and after a while Flip got bored and slouched off, but I didn't stop. I hadn't been kidding when I said this mess was all Flip's fault. She hadn't just lost the funding forms and stolen the personals. She had started the whole thing. If she hadn't delivered Dr. Turnbull's package to me in the first place, I would never even have met Ben. I never even got down to Bio, and at that first meeting he'd been clear on the other side of the room.

I kept adding lines, tracing the interconnecting events. She had thrown away six weeks' worth of research and stolen my stapler. And she'd left pages out of the funding forms. I'd had to take the missing pages to Ben. The prints of her Mary Janes and backless clogs were all over the place, making mischief.

She was like some Iago. Or some evil guardian angel. "Always there, right there beside you, wherever you go," was what *Angels, Angels Everywhere* had said. And it was true. She was everywhere, like some awful anti-Pippa, wandering past unsuspecting windows and wreaking havoc wherever she went.

I added more lines. Flip raising her hand and getting an assistant, Flip spearheading the antismoking campaign that had made me suggest the paddock to Shirl, who had told us about the bellwether. Flip getting me depressed that day in Boulder. If it hadn't been for her talking about feeling itch, I would never have gone out with Billy Ray, I would never have known Targhees were sheep, and I would never have come up with the idea of borrowing them.

And Ben would be off somewhere in France, studying chaos theory, I thought bleakly. I knew none of this was Flip's fault. I was the one who'd made up excuses to see Ben, to talk to him, from that very first day when I'd followed him out on the porch.

Flip wasn't the source. She might have precipitated things, but the outcome was my fault. I had been following the oldest trend of all. Right over the cliff.

Flip was back, standing and looking interestedly over my shoulder.

"I'm still busy, Flip," I said.

She tossed her nonexistent hank. "Dr. O'Reilly left. I bet he went out on a date with Dr. Turnbull."

A ghastly unlosable guardian angel. "Don't you have someplace you need to go?" I said.

"That's what I *came* to tell you," she said. "Bye."

And left. I pondered the screen, wondering how to graph that little encounter, but she was already back.

"Are there hats in Texas?" she said.

"Ten-gallon ones," I said.

She left again, this time apparently for good. I added a few more lines to my graph, and then just sat there and stared at the crisscrossing curves, the neatly plotted regressions.

"Seven o'clock," Gina said, sticking her head in the door. She had her coat on. "You can come out of time-out now."

I smiled. "Thanks, Mom," I said, but I didn't leave. I waited till I was sure everybody was gone and then went down and hung over the gate, watching the sheep as they moved and grazed and moved again, occasionally bleating, occasionally lost, impelled by bellwethers they didn't recognize, by instincts they didn't know they had.

kewpies (1909–15)

Doll fad derived from illustrated poems in the *Ladies' Home Journal.* Kewpie dolls looked like rosy-cheeked cherubs, with round tummies and a yellow curl on top of their heads. Wildly popular with adults and little girls, kewpies appeared as paper dolls, salt shakers, greeting cards, wedding cake decorations, and prizes at county fairs.

For the next two days I kept clear of the lab and Ben, straightening up *my* lab and entering miles of data about mah-jongg and Lindbergh's flight across the Atlantic.

This is ridiculous, I told myself on Thursday. You're not Peyton. You have to see him sometime. Grow up.

But when I got down to the lab, Alicia was there, leaning over the gate. Ben had the bellwether by her po-mo pink bow and was explaining the principle of attention structure. He was wearing his blue tie.

"This has *real* possibilities," Alicia was saying. "Thirty-one percent of all projects the Niebnitz Grant recipients were working on at the time of the award were cross-discipline collaborations. The thing is getting the *right* collaboration. The committee is obviously going for gender balance, which you're okay on, but chaos theory and statistics are both math-based disciplines. You need a biologist."

"Do you need me?" I said.

They both looked up.

"If not, I have some research I need to do at the library."

"No, go ahead," Ben said. "The bellwether's not in the mood to learn anything this morning." He rubbed his knee. "She's already butted me twice. While you're at the library, see if they've got anything on how to get a leader to follow."

"I will," I said, and started down the hall.

"Wait," Ben said, sprinting to catch up with me. "I wanted to talk to you. Did you have a breakthrough? With the dance marathon thing?"

Yes, I thought, looking at him forlornly. A breakthrough. "No," I said. "I thought there was a connection, but there wasn't," and I went to Boulder to look for Romantic Bride Barbie.

Gina had given me a list of toy stores, with the ones she'd already tried crossed off, which didn't leave all that many. I started at the top, determined to work my way down.

I had only thought I understood the Barbie fad. Not even Brittany's birthday party had prepared me for what I actually found.

There were Fashion Bright Barbies, Costume Ball Barbies, Bubble Angel Barbies, Sunflower Barbies, and even a Locket Surprise Barbie, whose plastic chest opened up to dispense lip gloss and rouge. There were multicultural Barbies, Barbies that lit up, remote-control Barbies, Barbies whose hair you could bob.

Barbie had a Porsche, a Jaguar, a Corvette, a Mustang, a speedboat, an RV, and a horse. Also a beauty bath, a Fun Fridge, a health spa, and a McDonald's. Not to mention the Barbie jewelry boxes, lunchboxes, workout tapes, audiotapes, videotapes, and pink nail polish.

But no Romantic Bride Barbie. The Toy Palace had Country Bride Barbie, with a pink-checked gingham sash and a bouquet of daisies. Toys "Я" Us had a Dream Wedding Barbie and Barbie's Wedding Fantasy, both of which I seriously considered in spite of Gina's injunctions.

The Cabbage Patch had four full aisles of Barbies and a clerk with an *i* stamped on her forehead. "We have Troll Barbie," she said, when I asked her about Romantic Bride. "And Pocahontas."

I made it through four toy stores and three discount stores and then drove over to the Caffe Krakatoa to see if there were any Barbies listed in the personals.

It was now calling itself Kepler's Quark, a bad sign.

"Don't tell me. You don't have latte anymore," I said to the waiter, who was wearing a black turtleneck, black jeans, and sunglasses.

"Caffeine's bad for you," he said, handing me the menu, which had grown to ten pages. "I'd suggest a smart drink."

"Isn't that an oxymoron?" I said. "Believing a beverage can increase your IQ?"

He tossed his head, revealing an *i* on his forehead.

Of course.

"Smart drinks are nonalcoholic beverages with neurotransmitters to enhance memory and alertness and increase brain function," he said. "I'd suggest the Brain Blast, which increases your math skills, or the Get Up and Van Gogh, which enhances your artistic ability."

"I'll have the Reality Check," I said, hoping it would enhance my ability to face facts.

I tried reading the personals, but they were too depressing: "To the blonde who eats lunch every day at Jane's Java Joint, you don't know me but I'm hopelessly in love with you. Please reply."

I switched to the articles.

A "harmonic bonding" therapist was offering duct tape soul alignments.

Two men in New York City had been arrested for operating the hot new fad, a "smoking speakeasy."

Po-mo pink had fizzled as a fad. A fashion designer was quoted as saying, "There's no accounting for the public's taste."

Truer words, I thought, and it was time I faced that, too. I was never going to discover the source of the hair-bobbing fad, no matter how much data I fed into my computer model. No matter how many different colored lines I drew.

Because it didn't have anything to do with suffrage or World War I or the weather. And even if I could ask Bernice and Irene and the rest of them why they'd done it, it still wouldn't help. Because they wouldn't know.

They were as benighted and blind as I had been, moved by feelings they weren't aware of, by forces they didn't understand. Right straight into the river.

My smart drink came. It was chartreuse, a color that had been a fad in the late twenties. "What's in it?" I said.

He sighed, a heavy sigh like someone out of Dostoyevsky. "Tyrosine, L-phenylalanine, and synergistic cofactors," he said. "And pineapple juice."

I took a sip of it. I didn't feel any smarter. "Why did you get your forehead branded?" I said.

Apparently he hadn't finished his smart drink. He stared at me blankly.

"Your *i* brand?" I said, pointing at it. "Why did you decide to have it done?"

"*Every*body has them," he said, and slouched off.

I wondered if he had gotten the brand to please his girlfriend or if he was rebelling against anti-intellectualism or his parents, or in love with somebody who didn't know he was alive.

I sipped my drink and kept reading. I didn't feel any smarter. Bantam Books had paid an eight-figure advance for *Getting in Touch with Your Inner Fairy Godmother.* Cerenkhov blue was the "cool/hot" color for winter, and men and women were smoking cigars in L.A., inspired by Rush Limbaugh or David Letterman or forces they didn't understand. Like sheep. Like rats.

None of which solved the problem of how I was going to go on working with Bennett. Or of where I was going to find Romantic Bride Barbie.

I went over to the library and checked out *Anna Karenina* and *Cyrano de Bergerac* and got the Denver phone book from the reference section. I copied down all the toy stores that weren't on Gina's list and all the department and discount stores, explained to Flip's clone that I had already paid the fine on Browning's *Complete Works,* and set out again, marking off stores as I went.

I eventually found Romantic Bride Barbie at a Target in Aurora—wedged in behind Barbie's Horse Stable Club—and took it up to the checkout.

The clerk was trying to make change for the man in front of me.

"It's eighteen seventy-eight," she said.

"I *know,*" the man said. "I gave you a twenty-dollar bill and then after you rang it up as eighteen seventy-eight, I gave you three cents. You owe me a dollar and a quarter."

She flipped her hair back, irritably, revealing an *i.*

Give up, I thought. It's no use.

"The register says one twenty-two," she said.

"I *know,*" he said. "That's why I gave you the three cents. Twenty-two plus three makes a quarter."

"A quarter of *what?*"

I set Romantic Bride Barbie on the end of the counter. I read the tabloid headlines and looked at the impulse items on the rack next to the counter. Duct tape in several widths, and bubble packs of Barbie high heels in assorted colors.

"All *right,* fine," the man said. "Give me back the three cents and give me one twenty-two."

I picked up a pack of high heels. "New! Cerenkhov blue," it read. I set it down next to the duct tape and as I did, I felt a strange sensation, as if I were on the verge of something important, like the final side of a Rubik's cube clicking into place.

"This doesn't have a price on it," the checkout clerk said. She was holding Romantic Bride Barbie. "I can't sell anything that doesn't have a price on it."

"It's thirty-eight ninety-nine," I said. "The manager said to ring it up under Miscellaneous."

"Oh," she said, and rang it up.

This is a fad I could actually learn to like, I thought, smiling at her *i.* Forewarned is forearmed.

"That'll be forty-one thirty-three," she said. I stood there, wallet in hand, looking at the boxes of crayons, trying to recapture the feeling I'd had. Something about Cerenkhov blue, and duct tape, or—

Whatever it was, it was gone. I hoped it hadn't been the cure for cholera.

"Forty-one thirty-*three,*" the clerk said.

I carefully counted out the exact change and left with Romantic Bride Barbie. On the way out, I stepped on something and looked down. It was a penny. Farther on there were two more. They looked like they had been flung down with some force.

prohibition (1895—january 16, 1920)

Aversion fad against alcohol fueled by the Women's Christian Temperance Union, Carry Nation's saloon-smashing, and the sad effects of alcoholism. Schoolchildren were urged to "sign the pledge" and women to swear not to touch lips that had touched liquor. The movement gained impetus and political support all through the early 1900s, with party candidates drinking toasts with glasses of water and several states voting to go dry, and finally culminated in the Volstead Act. Died out as soon as Prohibition was enacted. Replaced by bootleggers, speakeasies, bathtub gin, hip flasks, organized crime, and Repeal.

Gina couldn't believe I'd found Romantic Bride Barbie. She hugged me twice. "You're wonderful. You're a miracle worker!"

"Not quite," I said, trying to smile. "I don't seem to be having any luck finding the source of hair-bobbing."

"Speaking of which," she said, still admiring Romantic Bride Barbie, "Dr. O'Reilly was up here before, looking for you. He looked worried."

What's Flip lost now? I wondered, the bellwether? and started down to Bio. Halfway there, I ran into Ben. He grabbed my arm. "We were supposed to be in Management's office ten minutes ago."

"Why? What's this about?" I asked, trying to keep up. "Are we in trouble?"

Well, of course we were in trouble. The only time anybody got to see the inside of Management's office, Staff Input notwithstanding, was when they were getting transferred to Supply. Or having their funding cut.

"I hope it isn't the animal-rights activists," Ben said, coming to a stop outside Management's door. "Do you think I should have worn a jacket?"

"No," I said, remembering his jackets. "Maybe it's something minor. Maybe we didn't dress down enough."

The secretary in the outer office told us to go right in. "It's not something minor," Ben whispered, and reached for the doorknob.

"Maybe we're not in trouble," I said. "Maybe Management's going to commend us for cross-disciplinary cooperation."

He opened the door. Management was standing behind his desk with his arms folded.

"I don't think so," Ben murmured, and we went in.

Management told us to sit down, another bad sign. One of SHAM's Eight Efficiency Enhancers was "Holding meetings standing up encourages succinctness."

We sat.

Management remained standing. "An extremely serious matter has come to my attention concerning you and your project."

It is the animal-rights activists, I thought, and braced myself for what he was going to say next.

"The assistant workplace message facilitator was observed smoking in the area of the animal compound. She says she had permission to do so. Is that true?"

Smoking. This was about Shirl's smoking.

"Who gave her this permission?" Management demanded.

"I did," we both said. "It was my idea," I said. "I asked Dr. O'Reilly if it was all right."

"Are you aware that the HiTek building is a smoke-free zone?"

"It was outside," I said, and then remembered Berkeley. "I didn't think she should have to stand out in the middle of a blizzard to smoke."

"I didn't either," Ben said. "She didn't smoke inside. Just in the paddock."

Management looked even grimmer. "Are you aware of HiTek's guidelines for live-animal research?"

"Yes," Ben said, looking bewildered. "We followed the—"

"Live animals are required to have a healthy environment," Management said. "Are you aware of the dangers of atmospheric carcinogens, the FDA's report on the dangers of secondhand smoke? It can cause lung cancer, emphysema, high blood pressure and heart attacks."

Ben looked even more confused. "She didn't smoke anywhere near us, and it was outside. It—"

"Live animals are required to have a *healthy* environment," Management said. "Would you call smoke a healthy environment?"

Never underestimate the power of an aversion trend, I thought. The last one in this country ended in wholesale accusations of communist leanings, ruined reputations, destroyed careers.

" '. . . out of the houses the rats came tumbling,' " I murmured.

"What?" Management said, glaring at me.

"Nothing."

"Do you know what the effects of secondhand smoke on sheep are?" Management said.

No, I thought, and you don't either. You're just following the flock.

"Your blatant disregard for the health of the sheep has clearly made the project ineligible for serious consideration as a grant contender."

"She only smoked one cigarette a day," Ben said. "The compound where the sheep are is a hundred feet by eighty. The density of the smoke from a single cigarette would be less than one part per billion."

Give it up, Ben, I thought. Aversion trends have nothing to do with scientific logic, and we've not only exposed sheep to secondhand smoke, HiTek thinks we've jeopardized its chances of winning its heart's desire, the Niebnitz Grant.

I looked at Management. HiTek's actually going to fire somebody, I thought, and it's us.

I was wrong.

"Dr. Foster, you were the one who obtained the sheep, weren't you?"

"Yes," I said, resisting the urge to add "sir." "From a rancher in Wyoming."

"And is he aware that you intended exposing his sheep to harmful carcinogens?"

"No, but he won't object," I said, and then remembered the bread pudding. I had never asked him his views on smoking, but I knew what they were: whatever everyone else thought.

"As I recall, this project was your idea, too, Dr. Foster," Management said. "It was your idea to use sheep, in *spite* of Management's objections."

"She was only trying to help me save my project," Ben said, but Management wasn't listening.

"Dr. O'Reilly," he said, "this unfortunate situation is clearly not your fault. The project will have to be terminated, I'm afraid, but Dr. Turnbull is in need of a colleague for the project she is working on, and she specifically requested you."

"*What* project?" Ben said.

"That hasn't been decided yet," Management said. "She is looking into several possibilities. Whatever, I'm sure it will be an excellent project to be involved with. We feel it has a seventy-eight percent chance of winning the Niebnitz Grant." He turned back to me. "Dr. Foster, I'll hold you responsible for returning the sheep to their owner immediately."

The secretary came in. "I'm sorry to interrupt, Mr.—"

"A reprimand will be placed in your file, Dr. Foster," Management said, ignoring her, "and there will be a serious reexamination of your project at the next funding allocation period. In the meantime—"

"Sir, you need to come out here," the secretary said.

"I'm in the middle of a meeting," Management cut in. "I want a full report detailing your progress in trends research," he said to me.

"Now wait a minute," Ben said. "Dr. Foster was only—"

The secretary said, *"Excuse me,* Mr.—"

"What *is* it, Ms. Shepard?" Management said.

"The sheep—"

"Has the owner called to complain?" he said, shooting me a venomous glance.

"No, sir. It's the sheep. They're in the hall."

5. main channel

God's in his heaven—
All's right with the world.

robert browning

dancing mania [1374]

Northern European religious fad in which people danced uncontrollably for hours. They formed circles in streets and churches and leaped, screamed, and rolled on the ground, often shouting that they were possessed by demons and begging said demons to stop tormenting them. Caused by nervous hysteria and/or the wearing of pointed shoes.

The idea that chaos and significant scientific breakthroughs are connected was first proposed by Henri Poincaré, who had been unable to forget putting his foot on the omnibus step and having it all come clear. The pattern of his discovery, he told the Société de Psychologie, was one of unexpected insight arising out of frustration, confusion, and mental chaos.

Other chaos theorists have explained Poincaré's experience as the result of the conjunction of two distinct frames of reference. The chaotic circumstances—Poincaré's frustration with the problem, his insomnia, the distractions of packing for a trip, the change of scenery—created a far-from-equilibrium situation in which unconnected ideas shifted into new and startling conjunctions with each other and tiny events could have enormous consequences. Until chaos could be crystallized into a higher order of equilibrium by the simple act of stepping onto a bus. Or into a flock of sheep.

They weren't in the hall. They were in the outer office and on their way into Management's white-carpeted inner sanctum. The secretary flattened herself against the wall to let them pass, clutching her steno pad to her chest.

"Wait!" Management said, putting his hands up as if doing a sensitivity exercise. "You cannot come in here!"

Ben dived to head off the lead ewe, which must not have been the bellwether, because even though he got it stopped at the door and held it there, pushing against its shoulders like a football tight end, the other sheep simply swarmed past it and into Management's office. And maybe I had misjudged them and they did have brains. They had unerringly headed straight for the part of the building where they could do the most damage.

They did it, tracking in an amount of dirt I wouldn't have thought their little cloven hooves could carry, leaving a long smear of dirt-laden lanolin on the white walls and Management's secretary as they brushed past them.

Ben was still struggling with the ewe, which was eager to join the flock, now heading straight for Management's polished teak desk.

"Endangering the welfare of live animals," Management said, clambering up on top of it. "Providing inadequate project supervision."

The sheep were circling the desk like Indians riding around a wagon train.

"Failing to institute proper security measures!" Management said.

"Facilitating potential," I murmured, trying to get them moving in another direction, any direction.

"These animals should not be in here!" Management shouted from the top of his desk.

The same idea had apparently occurred to the sheep. They set up a pitiful bleating all at once, opening their mouths in a continuous, deafening *baa*.

I looked sharply at the sheep, trying to spot where the bleating had originated, but it had seemed to come from everywhere at once. Like hair-bobbing.

"Did you hear where the bleating started?" I shouted to Ben, who let go of the ewe, and the sheep were suddenly on the move again, milling randomly through the office and toward the door to the secretary's hall.

"Where are they going?" Ben said.

Management had clambered down off his desk and was shouting warnings again, looking slightly more dressed-down than before. "HiTek will not tolerate employee sabotage! If either of you or that *smoker* let these sheep out on purpose—"

"We didn't," Ben said, trying to get to the door. "They must have gotten out by themselves," and I had a sudden image of Flip leaning on the paddock gate, flipping the latch up and down, up and down.

Ben made it to the door as the last two sheep were squeezing through, bleating frantically at the thought of being left behind.

But once in the hall they began milling aimlessly around, looking lost but immovable.

"We have to find the bellwether," I said. I began to work my way through them, searching for the pink ribbon.

There was a yelp from the end of the hall and a "Blast you, you brainless critter!" It was Shirl, her arms full of papers. "Get out of my way, you fool animal!" she shouted. "How did you get—" She stopped short at the sight of the hallful of sheep. "Who let them out?"

"Flip," I said, feeling around a ewe's neck for the ribbon.

"She can't have," Shirl said, wading toward me through the sheep. "She's not here."

"What do you mean she's not here?" I said. Two ewes pushed past me on either side and nearly knocked me down.

"She quit," Shirl said, swatting at the one on the left with her papers. "Three days ago."

"I don't care," I said, pushing at the other one. "Somehow, somewhere, Flip is behind this. She's behind everything."

The sheep surged suddenly down the hall toward Personnel. "Where are they going now?" Ben said.

"They have no idea," I said. "Behold the American public."

Management emerged from his office, Dockers in disarray. "This sort of behavior is obviously a side effect of nicotine!"

"We have to find the bellwether," I said. "It's the key."

Ben stopped. He looked at me. "The key," he said.

Management bellowed, "When I find out who's causing this—this chaos—"

"Chaos," Ben said, almost to himself. "The key's the bellwether."

"Yes," I said. "It's the only way we can get them back to Bio. You start at this end, and I'll take the other end. Okay?"

He didn't answer me. He stood, transfixed, while the sheep milled around him, his mouth half open, his eyes squinting behind his Coke-bottle glasses. "A bellwether," he said softly.

"Yes, the bellwether," I said, and it took a long moment for his eyes to focus on me. "Find the bellwether. Think pink," and I started for the end of the hall. "Shirl, run down to the lab and get a halter and lead." Something suddenly struck me. "Did you say Flip quit?"

Shirl nodded. "That dentist she met in the personals. He moved, and she followed him. So they could be geographically compatible." She went back down the hall in the direction of Bio.

The sheep were in the stairwell, milling frightenedly at the edge of the top stair, and it was too bad it wasn't a cliff. Maybe they'd still fall down it and break their necks—but no such luck. They clambered lightly down a flight and into the hall to Stats. I ran back upstairs. "They're heading for Stats!" I shouted to Ben.

He wasn't there. I ran back down the stairs and stopped halfway. In a corner on the floor, thoroughly trampled and very dirty, was the pink ribbon. Wonderful, I thought, and looked up to see Alicia Turnbull glaring at me. "Dr. *Foster,*" she said disapprovingly.

"Don't tell me," I said. "None of the Niebnitz Grant winners were ever involved in livestock stampedes."

"Where is Dr. O'Reilly?" she demanded.

"I don't know," I said. I picked up the draggled ribbon. "I don't know where the bellwether is either. Or what sort of project will win the Niebnitz Grant. I do, however, have a good idea what those sheep are doing to Stats at this very minute, so if you'll excuse me—" I said, and pushed past her out of the stairwell and into the hall.

At least they can't do any damage in my lab, I thought, hoping the rest of the doors were shut.

The flock was still in the hall, so they must be. Gina was at the far end, coming out of the stats lab.

"Time for a bathroom break," she said as soon as she saw them, and ducked through a door.

I started through the sheep, leaning down to lift up their chins and look into their vacant faces for an expression that looked slightly cross-eyed or halfway intelligent.

The door opened again. "There's one in the bathroom," Gina said. She edged her way down the hall toward where I was gazing into the sheeps' eyes.

They all looked cross-eyed. I peered anxiously into their long faces, into their vacant eyes, that were born to have an *i* branded between them.

"There'd better not be one in my office," Gina said, and opened her door.

"Shut your door!" I said, but too late. A fat ewe was already through it. "*Shut* it," I said again, and she did.

The rest of the sheep congregated outside her door, milling and *baa*ing, desperately seeking someone to tell them what to do, where to go. Which must mean the ewe in Gina's office was the bellwether.

"Keep it there!" I shouted through the door. The ribbon wasn't strong enough for a leash, but I had a Davy Crockett jump rope that might be. I started for my lab, wondering what had happened to Ben. Probably Alicia had found him and was telling him about her Niebnitz sure thing.

There was a shriek from Gina's office, and her door opened.

"Don't—" I shouted. The ewe dived through the door and into the midst of the flock like a card disappearing into a deck. "Did you see where she went, Gina?"

"No," she said tightly. "I didn't." She was clutching a battered pink box. A torn white net ruffle trailed from one corner. "Look what that *sheep* did to Romantic Wedding Barbie!" she said, holding up a lock of brunette hair. "It was the last one in Boulder."

"In the greater Denver area," I said, and went into the stats lab.

All I need now is Flip, I thought, and was amazed she wasn't there in the stats lab, having quit or not. A sheep was, munching thoughtfully on a disk. I grabbed it out of her mouth, or most of it, pried her large square teeth apart, fished out the remaining piece, and looked squarely into her slightly crossed eyes.

"Listen to me," I said, holding on to her jaw. "I've had all I can take for one day. I've lost my job, I've lost the only person I've ever met who doesn't act like a sheep, I don't know where fads come from and I'm never going to find out, and I've *had* it. I want you to follow me, and I want you to follow me now." I threw the pieces of disk on the floor and turned and walked out of my lab.

And she must have been the bellwether, because she trotted after me all the way down two flights into Bio, and through the lab to the paddock, just like Mary and her little lamb. And the rest of the flock followed, wagging their tails behind them.

ostrich plumes [1890–1913]

Edwardian fashion fad inspired by Charles Darwin and related public interest in natural history. The curling plumes were dyed all colors and worn in the hair, on hats, fans, and even feather dusters. Related fads included trimming hats and dresses with lizards, spiders, toads, and centipedes. As a result of the fad, ostriches were hunted into extinction in Egypt, North Africa, and the Middle East. Recurred in 1960s with minidresses, wigs, and capes of ostrich plumes dyed neon orange and hot pink.

I called Billy Ray to come pick the sheep up.

"I'll send Miguel down with the truck right away," he said. "I'd come myself, but I've got to go down to New Mexico and talk to this rancher about ostriches."

"Ostriches," I said.

"They're the latest thing. Reba's raising fifty of them on a spread outside Gallup, and ostrich steak's selling like gangbusters. Lower in cholesterol than chicken and tastes better."

One of the sheep had gotten itself stuck in the corner of the fence again. It stood there, looking blankly at the fence post like it had no idea how it had gotten there.

"Plus you can sell the feathers and tan the skin for purses and boots," Billy Ray said. "Reba says they're going to be *the* livestock of the nineties."

The sheep butted its head against the post a couple of times and then gave up and stood there, bleating, a nice object lesson.

"I'm sorry the sheep thing didn't work out," Billy Ray said.

Me too, I thought. "You're getting out of range," I said. "I can't hear you," and hung up.

You can learn a lot from sheep. I went over to the corner and put my hands under its chin and on its rump. "You have to turn around," I said. "You have to go in another direction."

I dragged it around to face the other way. It immediately began to graze.

"You have to admit it's no use and go try something else," I said, and went back into the lab. Shirl was there. "Where's Dr. O'Reilly?" I said.

"He was in talking to Dr. Turnbull a minute ago," she said.

"Good," I said, and went back up to my stats lab to write up my report for Management.

"Sandra Foster: Project Report," I typed on a disk the ewe hadn't eaten.

Project goals:

1. Determine what triggers fads.
2. Determine the source of the Nile.

Project results:

1. Not found. Pied Piper may have something to do with it, for all I know. Or Italy.
2. Found. Lake Victoria.

Suggestions for further research:

1. Eliminate acronyms.
2. Eliminate meetings.
3. Study effect of antismoking fad on ability to think clearly.
4. Read Browning. And Dickens. And all the other classics.

I printed it out, and then gathered up my coat and non-wallet-on-a-string and went up to see Management.

Shirl was there, running a carpet cleaning machine. Management was dusting off his desk, which had been pushed against one corner.

"Don't step on the carpet," he said when I came in. "It's wet."

I walked squishily over to his desk. "The sheep are all in the paddock," I said over the sucking sound of the carpet steamer. "I've arranged for them to be sent back." I handed him my report.

"What's this?" he said.

"You said you wanted to reevaluate my project's goals," I said. "So do I."

"What's this?" he said, scowling at it. "Pied *Pip*er?"

"By Robert Browning," I said. "You know the story. Piper is hired to free Hamelin of rats, does so, but the town refuses to pay him. 'And as for our Corporation—shocking.' "

Management reared up behind his desk. "Are you threatening me, Dr. Foster?"

"No," I said, surprised. " 'Insulted by a lazy ribald?' " I quoted, " 'You threaten us, fellow? Do your worst,/Blow your pipe until you burst.' You should read more poetry. You can learn a lot from it. Do you have a library card?"

"A library—?" Management said, looking apoplectic.

"I'm not threatening you," I said. "Why would I? I didn't get rid of any rats *or* find out what causes hair-bobbing. I couldn't even locate a piper."

I stopped, thinking about that, and just like the night before, standing in line at Target with the late Romantic Bride Barbie, I felt like I was on the verge of something significant.

"Are you calling HiTek a rat?" Management said, and I waved him away impatiently, trying to focus on my elusive thought. A piper.

"Are you saying—" Management bellowed, and it was gone.

"I'm saying you hired me for the wrong reason. You shouldn't be looking for the secret to making people follow fads, you should be looking for the secret to making them think for themselves. Because that's what science is all about. And because the next fad may be the dangerous one, and you'll find it out with the rest of the flock on your way over the cliff. And no, I don't need a security escort back to my lab," I said, opening my purse so he could see inside. "I'm leaving. 'Up the Hill-side yonder, through the morning,' " and I squished my way back across the carpet. "Bye, Shirl," I called to her, "you can come smoke at my house anytime," and I went out to my car and drove to the library.

rubik's cube [1980–81]

Game fad involving a cube made up of smaller cubes of different colors that could be rotated to form different combinations. The object of the game (which more than a hundred million people tried to solve) was to twist the sides of the cube until each side was a solid color. The fad's skill threshold was somewhat too high—as witness the dozens of puzzle-help books published—and the fad died out with many people never having solved it even once.

Lorraine was back. "Do you want *Your Guardian Angel Can Change Your Life?*" she asked me. She was wearing a fairy godmother sweatshirt and sparkly magic wand earrings. "It came in, and so did your book on hair-bobbing."

"I don't want it," I said. "I don't know what caused it, and I don't care."

"We found that book on Browning. You had checked it in after all. Our media organization assistant shelved it with the cookbooks."

See, I told myself—walking over to Kepler's Quark and giving my first name to a waitress with chopped-off hair and a waitress uniform that probably wasn't a uniform—things are looking up already. They found Browning, you never have to read the personals again, and Flip can't slouch in here to ruin your day and stick you with the check.

The waitress seated me at a table by the window. See, I told myself again, she didn't seat you at the communal table. She isn't wearing duct tape. Definitely looking up.

But it didn't feel like it. It felt like I was out of a job. It felt like I was in love with somebody who didn't love me back.

He's totally fashion-impaired, I told myself. Look on the bright side. You no longer have to worry about what caused hair-bobbing. Which was a good thing, because I was pretty much out of ideas.

"Hi," Ben said, sitting down across from me.

"What are you doing here?" I said as soon as I was able to. "Shouldn't you be at work?"

"I quit," he said.

"You quit? Why? I thought you were going to work on Dr. Turnbull's project."

"You mean Alicia's statistically-thought-out, science-on-demand, sure-to-win-the-Niebnitz-Grant project? It's too late. The Niebnitz Grant has already been awarded."

He didn't look upset about it. He didn't look like somebody who'd just quit his job. He looked containedly excited, his eyes jubilant behind the Coke bottles. He's going to tell me he's engaged to Alicia, I thought.

"Who won it?" I said, to stop him. "The Niebnitz Grant. A thirty-eight-year-old designed experimenter from west of the Mississippi?"

Ben motioned the waitress over and said, "What have you got to drink that's not coffee?"

The waitress rolled her eyes. "There's our new drink. The Chinatasse. It's the latest thing."

"Two Chinatasses," he said, and I waited for the waitress to quiz him on whole vs. skim, white vs. brown, Beijing vs. Guangzhou, but Chinatasses apparently had a lower skill threshold than caffè latte. The waitress slouched off, and Ben said, "This came for you," and handed me a letter.

"How did you know where to find me?" I said, looking at the envelope. It was blank except for my name.

"Flip told me," he said.

"I thought she was gone."

"She told me a while back. She said you hung out here a lot. I came here three or four times, hoping I'd run into you, but I never did. She said you came here looking for guys in the personals."

"Flip," I said, shaking my head. "I was reading them for trends research. I wasn't trying . . . you did?"

He nodded, no longer jubilant. His gray eyes were serious behind the Coke-bottle glasses. "I stopped coming a couple of weeks ago because Flip told me you were engaged to the sheep guy."

"Ostrich," I said. "Flip told me you were crazy about Alicia, that that's why you wanted to work with her."

"Well, at least now we know what the *i* on her forehead stands for. *Interfering.* I don't want to work with Alicia. I want to work with you."

"I'm not engaged to the sheep guy," I said. I thought of something. "Why did you buy that Cerenkhov blue tie?"

"To impress you. Flip told me you'd never go out with me unless I got some new clothes, and this awful blue was the only thing I could find in the stores." He looked sheepish. "I also took out an ad in the personals."

"You did? What did it say?"

"Insecure, ill-dressed chaos theorist desires intelligent, insightful, incandescent trends researcher. Must be SC."

"SC?"

"Scientifically compatible." He grinned. "People do crazy things when they're in love."

"Like borrow a flock of sheep to keep somebody from losing their grant?"

The waitress plunked down two glasses in front of us, spilling Chinatasse everywhere.

"We need those to go," Ben said.

The waitress sighed loudly and stomped off with them.

"If we're going to be working together," Ben said to me, "we'd better get started."

"Wait a minute," I said. "We both quit, remember?"

"Well, the thing is, HiTek wants us back."

"They do?"

"All is forgiven." He nodded. "They say we can have anything we need—lab space, assistants, computers."

"But what about the sheep and the secondhand smoke?"

"Open the letter."

I did.

"Read it."

I did. "I don't understand," I said.

I turned the letter over. There wasn't anything on the back. I looked at the envelope again. It still only had my name on it. I looked at Ben, who looked jubilant again. "I don't understand," I said again.

"Me neither," he said. "Alicia was there when I opened mine. She had to recalculate all her percentages."

I read the letter again. "We won the Niebnitz Grant?"

"We won the Niebnitz Grant."

"But . . . we aren't . . . we don't . . ."

"Well, that's the thing," he said, leaning across the table and, finally, taking my hand. "I had this idea. You know how I told you chaotic systems could be predicted by measuring all the variables and calculating the iteration? Well, I think Verhoest was right after all. There *is* another factor at work. But it's not an outside factor. It's something already in the system. Remember how Shirl said the bellwether was the same as the other sheep, only a little greedier, a little faster, a little ahead? What if—"

"—instead of butterflies, there's a bellwether in chaotic systems?" I said.

"Exactly." He was holding both my hands now. "And it doesn't look any different from the other variables in the system, but it's the trigger for the iteration, it's the catalyst, it's—"

"Pippa," I said, clutching his hands. "There's this poem, *Pippa Passes,* by—"

"Browning," he said. "She sings at people's windows—"

"And changes their lives, and they never even see her. If you were making a computer model of the village of Asolo, you wouldn't even put her in it, but she's—"

"—the variable that sets the butterfly's wings in motion, the force behind the iteration, the trigger behind the trigger, the factor that causes—"

"—women to bob their hair in Hong Kong."

"Exactly. The trigger that causes your fads. The—"

"—source of the Nile."

The waitress came back with the same two glasses. "We don't have cups to go. It pollutes the environment." She set the glasses down and stomped off again.

"Like Flip," Ben said, thinking about it. "She misdelivered the package, and that's how I met you."

"Among other things," I said, and felt that feeling again of being on the verge of something, of the Rubik's cube starting to turn.

"Let's go," Ben said. "I want to see what happens when I add the bellwether into my chaos theory data."

"Wait—I want to drink my Chinatasse, in case it's the next fad. And there's something else . . . You didn't give HiTek our decision yet, did you, about staying?"

He shook his head. "I thought you'd want to be there."

"Good," I said. "Don't tell them no yet. There's something I want to check on."

"Okay. I'll meet you back at HiTek in a few minutes then," he said. "Okay?" and went out.

"Umm," I said, trying to catch the thought I'd had before. Something about trains, or was it buses? And something the waitress had said.

I took a thoughtful sip of the Chinatasse, and if I needed a sign that chaos was reattaining equilibrium at a new and higher level, this was it. It was the Earth Mother's wonderful spiced iced tea.

Which should inspire me if anything could. But I couldn't capture the thought. The idea that I should have gone back with Ben kept intruding, and that, except for that sensitivity exercise, and some incidental hand-holding, he had never touched me.

And apparently there was some kind of feedback loop operating in our system because he was back and pushing past the waitress, who wanted to write his name down, and through the tables and pulling me to my feet. And kissing me.

"Okay," he said, when we pulled apart.

"Okay," I said breathlessly.

"Wow!" the waitress said. "Did you meet him in the personals?"

"No," I said, wishing she would shut up and that Ben would kiss me again. "Through Flip."

"We were introduced by a bellwether," Ben said, putting his arms around me again.

"Wow!" the waitress said.

Couéism [1923]

Psychology fad inspired by Dr. Emile Coué, a French psychologist and the author of *Self-Mastery by Auto-Suggestion.* Coué's method of self-improvement consisted of knotting a piece of string and reciting over and over, "Every day in every way, I am getting better and better." Died out when it became apparent no one was.

Scientific breakthroughs have been triggered by the most minor of events: the sight of bathwater rising, the movement of a breeze, the pressure of a foot on a step. I had never heard of one being triggered by a kiss, though.

But it was a kiss that had the full weight of five weeks of chaotic turbulence behind it, shifting patterns of thought out of their accustomed positions, stirring up the variables, separating and mixing them again into new conjunctions, new possibilities. And when Ben had put his arms around me, it had been like the discovery of penicillin and the benzene ring and the Big Bang all rolled into one. Eureka to the tenth power. Like coming to the source of the Nile.

"This FLIP thing, where you met him," the waitress was saying, "is it like a recovery group?"

"*Dis*covery," I said, staring transfixed after Ben, wondering how I could have been so blind. It was all so clear: what triggered fads and how scientific breakthroughs happen and why we had won the Niebnitz Grant.

"Can anybody join this FLIP?" the waitress said. "I'm already in a latte recovery group, but there aren't any cute guys in it."

"I need my check," I said, fishing a twenty out of my purse and handing it to her so I could go back to HiTek and get all this on the computer.

"He already paid," she said, trying to hand me back the twenty.

"Keep it," I said, and grinned at her as something else hit me. "We're rich. We won the Niebnitz Grant!"

I hurried back to HiTek and up to the stats lab, and called up my hair-bobbing model.

Suppose fads were a form of self-organized criticality arising out of the chaotic system of the popular culture. And suppose that, like other chaotic systems, they were influenced by a bellwether. The independence of women, Irene Castle, outdoor sports, rebellion against the war, all of those would simply be variables in the system. They would require a catalyst, a butterfly to set them in motion.

I focused in on the bump in Marydale, Ohio. Suppose that wasn't a statistical anomaly. Suppose there'd been a girl in Marydale, Ohio, a girl just like everybody else, with flapping galoshes and rouged knees, indistinguishable from the rest of the flock, only a little greedier, a little faster, a little hungrier. A little ahead of the flock. A girl who had had a crush on a dentist on the other side of town and had walked into the barbershop and, with no idea she was starting a fad, that she was crystallizing chaos into criticality, told the barber to cut off her hair.

I called up the rest of the twenties data and asked for geographical breakdowns, and there was the anomaly again, for rolled-down stockings and the crossword puzzle, right over Marydale. And for the shimmy, even though the dance had originated in New York. But it hadn't become a fad until a bobbed-haired girl in Marydale, Ohio, had picked it up. A girl like Flip. A butterfly. A bellwether. The source of the Nile.

I called up the paintbox and traced the course of events at HiTek again, from Flip's misdelivering Dr. Turnbull's package to her fiddling with the latch on the gate, but this time I also fed in *Led On by Fate* and the bread pudding, Management's sensitivity exercises, the duct tape, Elaine's exercises, Shirl's smoking, Sarah's boyfriend, Romantic Bride Barbie, and the various skill levels of caffè latte.

All the variables I could think of and every one of Flip's actions, irrelevant or not, all of them feeding back into the system, adding turbulence, and leading not, as I'd thought after the sensitivity exercise, to disaster, but to the Niebnitz Grant, to love and to geographic compatibility and the source of hair-bobbing. To a new, higher state of equilibrium.

Flip had felt itch, and as a result I had told Billy Ray I'd go out with him, and he'd said he felt itch, too, and told me about the sheep, which I'd thought of when Flip lost Ben's funding form.

Flip. Her footprints, like Barbie's sharp little high heels, like the echoes of Pippa's voice, were all over the crime scene. She had told Ben I was engaged to Billy Ray, she had failed to copy pages 29 through 41, she had taught the bellwether to open the gate, she had told Management about Shirl's smoking, upping the level of chaos each time, mixing and separating the variables.

The screen filled with lines. I connected them, feeding in the iteration equations, and the lines became a tangle, the tangle a knot. The lost stapler, Browning's "Pied Piper," Billy Ray's cellular phone, po-mo pink. Flip had circulated a nonsmoking petition and Shirl had ended up out in the parking lot in a blizzard and I took her down to Ben's lab and she watched Ben and me struggle with the sheep and said, "You need a bellwether."

The screen went dark, layer on layer of events feeding back into each other, and then sprang suddenly into a new design. A beautiful, elaborate structure, vivid with radical red and cerulean blue.

Self-organized criticality. Scientific breakthrough.

I sat and looked at it for a while, marveling at its simplicity and thinking about Flip. I had been wrong. The *i* on her forehead didn't stand for *incompetence* or *itch.* Or even *influence.* It stood for *inspiration.* And she was Pippa after all, only instead of singing she was stirring up the variables, upping the level of chaos with every petition and misdelivered package until the system went critical.

I also thought about penicillin and Alexander Fleming, with his crowded, too-small lab, heaped with piles of moldy petri dishes. The institute he worked in had been right in the middle of chaos—half a block from Paddington Station on a noisy street. Add in the vacation and the August heat and the new research assistant he had had to make room for, and all those tributary details like his father and the rifle team. And water polo. At school he'd been on a team that played a water polo match against St. Mary's Hospital. Three years later, when he was getting ready to go to medical school, he picked St. Mary's because he remembered the name.

Add in that, and the soot and the open window of the lab above, and you had a real mess. Or did you?

David Wilson had called the discovery of penicillin "Quite one of the luckiest accidents that ever occurred in nature." But was it? Or was it a scientific discovery waiting to happen, a system so chaotic that all it would take to push it over the edge into self-organized criticality was a spore, drifting in through an open window like Pippa's song?

Poincaré had believed creative thought was a process of inducing inner chaos to achieve a higher level of equilibrium. But did it have to be inner?

I saved everything to disk, stuck it in my pocket, and went down to Bio.

"I need to know something," I asked Ben. "Your bellwether chaos theory. Did you figure it out little by little or did it hit you all at once?"

He frowned. "Both. I'd been thinking about Verhoest and his X factor, and that maybe he was right, and I started trying to think what form another factor might take."

"And that's when the apple hit you on the head?"

He shook his head. "Alicia came in to tell me her research showed the next Niebnitz Grant recipient would be a radio astronomer and that Management had called another meeting, and then we had the sensitivity hug and for a couple of days after that all I could think about was you and how you were engaged to that cowboy."

"Ostrich rancher," I corrected. "For a couple of weeks, at least. So the ideas were in there percolating, but do you remember what it was that put it all together?"

"You did," he said. "The sheep were milling around in the hall outside of Management, and you said, 'Flip did this. I know it,' and Shirl said she wasn't there, and you said, 'I don't care. Somehow she's behind this.' And I thought, No, she isn't. The bellwether is. And I remembered Flip leaning on the paddock gate, flipping the lock up and down, and I thought, The bellwether must have learned how to open it from her, and led the rest of the sheep into this chaos.

"And it hit me, just like that. Bellwethers cause chaos. They're the unseen factor."

"I *knew* it," I said. "I have to go find something. Just what I thought. You're wonderful. Be right back." I kissed him for inspiration, and went to find Flip.

I had forgotten she'd quit. "Three days ago," Elaine in Personnel said. She was wearing a pair of Cerenkhov blue Rollerblades. "In-in-line skating," she said, raising her leg to demonstrate. "It gives a much better full-body workout than wall-walking, and it helps you get around the office faster. Did you hear about Sarah and her boyfriend?"

"They broke up?" I said.

"No. They got *married!"*

I pondered the implications of that. "Did Flip leave a forwarding address?" I asked. "Or say where she was going?"

She shook her head. "She said to give her check to Desiderata down in Supply and she'd send it on to her."

"Can I see her file?"

"Personnel records are confidential," she said, suddenly businesslike.

"Call Management and ask them," I said. "Tell them it's me."

She did. "Management said to give you anything you want," she said bemusedly, hanging up. "Do you want the whole file?"

"Just her previous work record."

She skated over to the file cabinet, got it, and skated over to me, executing a neat toe stop.

It was what I'd expected. Flip had worked at a coffeehouse in Seattle, and before that at a Burger King in L.A. "Thanks," I said, handing it back to her, and then thought of something else. "Let me see her file a minute." I opened it and glanced at the top line, where it said "full name, last, first, middle initial."

"Orliotti," it said. "Philippa J."

tattoos [1691]

Self-mutilation fad which first became popular in Europe in the 1600s when explorers brought the practice back from the South Seas. The fad recurred as an upper-class craze in the Edwardian era. Jennie Jerome, Winston Churchill's mother, had a snake tattooed around her wrist. Tattooing became popular again in World War II, this time among servicemen and especially sailors, again in the sixties as part of the hippie movement, and yet again in the late eighties. Tattooing has the disadvantage of being a passing fad with permanent results.

I wrote down Flip's last name and made a note to find out her grandmother's maiden name and check to see if she was living anywhere near Marydale, Ohio, in 1921, and went down to Supply.

Desiderata couldn't find Flip's forwarding address. "She said she was going to someplace in Arizona," Desiderata said, looking in among the erasers. "Albuquerque, I think."

"Albuquerque is in New Mexico," I said.

"Oh," she said, frowning. "Then maybe it was Fort Worth. Wherever he went."

"Who?"

She rolled her eyes. "The *dentist* guy."

Of course. He had particularly specified geographic compatibility.

"Maybe she told Shirl," Desiderata said, rummaging through the pencils.

"I thought Shirl got fired," I said, "for smoking in the paddock."

"Hunh-unh," Desiderata said. "She quit. She said she was only going to stay till they hired a new workplace message facilitation director, and they did that this morning, so maybe she's already gone."

She wasn't. She was in the copy room, fixing the copy machine before she left, but Flip hadn't told Shirl where she was going either. "She mentioned something about this Darrell moving his practice to Prescott," Shirl said, leaning over the paper feed. "I heard you and Dr. O'Reilly won the Niebnitz Grant. That's wonderful."

"It is," I said, watching her yank a jammed sheet of paper out of the feed with her fingers. There were no signs of nicotine stains on them. "It's too bad I don't know who gives the grant. I had something I wanted to tell them."

Shirl pushed the feed into position and closed the lid. "I'm sure the committee wants to remain anonymous."

"If it is a committee," I said. "Committees are terrible at keeping secrets, and even Dr. Turnbull wasn't able to find out anything. I think it's one person."

"One very rich person," she said, her voice no longer raspy.

"Right. Somebody circumstantially predisposed to wealth, who thinks for herself and wants other people to, too. When did you quit smoking?"

"Flip converted me," she said. "Filthy habit. Hazardous to your health."

"Umm," I said. "Somebody extremely competent—"

"Speaking of which," she said, "have you run into Flip's replacement yet? It'll make you glad you don't work here anymore. I didn't think it was possible to hire somebody worse than Flip, but Management's succeeded."

"Somebody extremely competent," I repeated, looking steadily at her, "who travels around the country like Diogenes, looking for scientists with circumstantial predispositions to scientific discovery. Somebody no one would suspect."

"Interesting theory," Shirl said dismissively, centering the paper on the glass plate. "What was it you wanted to tell this person? If he or she is incognito, he or she probably doesn't want to be thanked." She hit a button and started to lower the lid.

"Oh, I wasn't going to thank her," I said. "I was going to tell her she's going about things all wrong."

The copy light flashed blindingly. Shirl blinked. "You're saying the Niebnitz people picked the wrong winners?"

"It's not the people you choose. It's the grant itself. A million dollars means the scientist can quit his job, get a lab all his own, pursue his work in complete peace and quiet."

"And that's a bad thing?"

"Maybe. Look at Einstein. He discovered relativity while he was working in a dinky patent office, full of papers and contraptions. When he tried to work at home, it was even worse. Wet laundry hanging everywhere, a baby squalling on one knee, his first wife yelling at him."

"And those seem like ideal working conditions to you?"

"Maybe. What if instead of being hindrances, the noise and the damp laundry and the cramped apartment all combined to create a situation in which new ideas could coalesce?" I held up two fingers. "Only *two* of the winners of the Niebnitz Grant have gone on to make significant discoveries. Why?"

"Scientific discoveries can't be produced on demand. They take long years of painstaking work—"

"And luck. And serendipity. A breeze blowing Galvani's frog legs against a railing and closing a circuit, a hand getting in the way of cathode rays, an apple falling. Fleming. Penzias and Wilson. Kekulé. Scientific breakthroughs involve combining ideas no one thought to connect before, seeing connections nobody saw before. Chaotic systems create feedback loops that tend to randomize the elements of the system, displace them, shake them around so they're next to elements they've never come in contact with before. Chaotic systems tend to increase in chaos, but not always. Sometimes they restabilize into a new level of order."

"Archimedes," Shirl said.

"And Poincaré. And Roentgen. All of their ideas came out of chaotic situations, not peace and quiet. And if a chaotic situation could be *induced* instead of us having to just wait for it to happen . . . It's just an idea, but it accounts for why dozens of scientists could experiment with electrically discharged gases and never discover X rays. It accounts for why so many discoveries are made by scientists outside their field. Which is why you specified 'circumstantially predisposed,' why you choose people working outside their field, because you knew how it worked, even if you didn't know why. Of course it's still just an idea. But it fits with Bennett's theory of the bellwether effect. I'll need a lot more data, and—"

Shirl was smiling a not-at-all-pinched smile at me. "And you still think I'm going about it all wrong?" she said. She leaned over to pull the copy out of the machine. "Interesting theory," she said, picking up a stack of papers. "If I ever run into whoever it is that gives the Niebnitz Grant, I'll be sure to pass it on." She started out the door.

"Goodbye," I said, and kissed her on her leathery cheek.

"What was that for?" she grumbled, rubbing at her cheek with her hand.

"Fixing the copy machine," I said. "Oh, by the way," I called after her. "Who's the Niebnitz Grant named after?"

"Alfred Taylor Niebnitz," she said without turning her head. "My high school physics teacher."

ouija board [1917–18]

Psychic game fad that purports to tell the future. Players push a planchette around a board with letters and numbers, spelling out answers to questions. Originated either in Maryland in the 1880s with C. W. Kennard or William and Isaac Fuld or in Europe in the 1850s, but did not become a fad until America entered World War I. Recurs every time there's a war. Popular during World War II and the Korean conflict. Hit its highest number of sales in 1966–67, during the Vietnam War.

A theory is only as good as its ability to predict behavior. Mendeleev predicted that the blanks in his periodic table would be filled with elements of certain atomic weights and properties. The subsequent discoveries of gallium, scandium, and germanium bore out his predictions. Einstein's special theory of relativity correctly predicted the deflection of light by the sun, tested out by the 1919 eclipse. Wegener's theory of continental drift was corroborated by fossils and satellite photographs. And Fleming's penicillin saved Winston Churchill's life during World War II.

The bellwether theory of chaotic systems is just that, and Ben and I are still in the early stages of our research. But I'm willing to hazard a few predictions:

HiTek will switch acronyms at least twice in the next year, establish a dress code, and make the staff hold hands and nurture their inner children.

Dr. Turnbull will spend all of next year attempting to handicap the Niebnitz Grant, to no avail. Science doesn't work like that.

I predict a number of new fads out of Prescott, Arizona, or Albuquerque or Fort Worth. Boulder, Seattle, and L.A. will fade out as trendsetters. Forehead brands will be big, and dental floss, and bobbed hair, particularly the marcel wave, will make a comeback.

As to the spiritual, angels are out and fairies will be in, particularly fairy godmothers, which, after all, do exist. Merchandisers will make a killing on them and then lose their shirts trying to anticipate the next craze.

I predict a sharp decline in sheep-raising, an increase in weddings, and no change at all in the personals. The hot dessert this fall will be pineapple upside-down cake.

And in some company or research institute or college, an overqualified mail clerk who is overweight or wears fur or carries a Bible will be hired, and the scientists therein would do well to remember their childhood fairy tales.

There will be a sharp upswing in significant scientific breakthroughs, and chaos, as usual, will reign. I predict great things.

This morning, I met Flip's replacement. I'd gone up to Stats to collect my hair-bobbing data, and she was coming out of the copy room, trailing someone's memos behind her.

She had lavender hair, arranged in a fountain effect, with several strands of barbed wire wrapped around it. She was wearing a bowling shirt, pedal pushers, black patent tap shoes, and orange lipstick.

"Are you the new mail clerk?"

She pursed her orange lips in disdain. "It's *workplace message facilitation director,*" she said, emphasizing every syllable. "And what business is it of yours, anyway?"

"Welcome to HiTek," I said, and would have shaken her hand except that she was wearing a barbed-wire ring.

Great things.